Billy's Boy

PATRICIA NELL WARREN

WILDCAT PRESS
http://www.wildcatcom.com

Jacket design:
Barbara Brown, Jay Fraley, Tyler St. Mark and Patricia Nell Warren

Jacket art, photographs and half-tone illustrations:
Jay Fraley

Book design:
Barbara Brown Desktop Publishing and Patricia Nell Warren

Typesetting:
Barbara Brown Desktop Publishing, La Crescenta, CA

Printed by Banta Book Group, La Costa, CA

First printing: October 1997

10 9 8 7 6 5 4 3 2 1

PRINTED IN THE UNITED STATES OF AMERICA

Library of Congress Catalog Card Number: 97-090281

ISBN: 0-9641099-4-8

Dedicated to all the young people who have been
part of my life since I began this book in earnest —
and to youth everywhere in the world
who are struggling to gain their human rights

Other Titles by Patricia Nell Warren

Fiction

Harlan's Race — Wildcat Press, 1994
One Is the Sun — Ballantine, 1991
The Beauty Queen — William Morrow, 1978
The Fancy Dancer — William Morrow, 1976
The Front Runner — William Morrow, 1974
The Last Centennial — Dial Press, 1971

Nonfiction

Ukrainian Dumy, co-translated with George Tarnawsky — Canadian Institute of Ukrainian Studies and Harvard Ukrainian Research Institute, 1979

Poetry

Horse With a Green Vinyl Mane — Novi Poezii, 1970
Rose-Hued Cities — Novi Poezii, 1966
Legends and Dreams — Novi Poezii, 1962
A Tragedy of Bees — Novi Poezii, 1959

About the Author

Patricia Nell Warren was born in 1936. She grew up on a Montana cattle ranch, and worked as a *Reader's Digest* editor for 22 years. Three of her novels were bestsellers. She has won numerous awards, including the 1978 Walt Whitman Award for Gay Literature and a 1982 Western Heritage Award from the National Cowboy Hall of Fame. In recent years she has also become a noted commentator, with editorials published widely in the mainstream and gay press. She lives in California today.

Author's Foreword

Billy's Boy is the third novel in my series that began with *The Front Runner* in 1974. There has never been a saga about gay family life, or gay generations passing. As a young book reader and writer-to-be, I was nurtured on classic dynasty literature like *The Forsythe Saga*. Today I want to be the one to write the first saga focusing on gay, lesbian, bisexual and transgendered family.

This novel can be read and appreciated as a self-contained unit. It is not necessary to have read the previous novels. Hopefully, the reader who is new to my work will want to do so.

However, for those who have read the previous works, be prepared for a paradigm shift! *The Front Runner*, a story of the 1970s, was written from the point of view of a 40-year-old track coach named Harlan Brown. *Harlan's Race*, the second book, hewed to the maturing observations of an older Brown through the 1980s. But *Billy's Boy* is a story of the 1990s, so it shifts to the viewpoint of a young boy named John William. He made his first appearance as a baby towards the end of *The Front Runner*. This book, a chronicle of youth in our time, must necessarily be his intensely personal story.

Stories of youth have been on my mind for almost 50 years.

I was born in 1936, and grew up on a big ranch near Deer Lodge, Montana. At the age of ten, writing captured my imagination for life. I completed my first novel while in high school in the 1950s. Titled *Whitey and Faith*, it was a saga about the dating-and-sex heartbreaks of a group of typical '50s students. Since one of its story-tracks was a dawning same-sex attraction between Whitey and another boy, Rob, under the watchful eyes of Whitey's girl-buddy Faith, this novel never saw the light of day, least of all my parents' awareness. Years later, when I searched for it in an attic box piled full of my childhood writings, the manuscript had vanished. *Whitey and Faith* was the seed from which a many-branched tree of all my later works about same-sex love, and my concern for youth, has grown.

At the age of 17, my first year in college, I began publishing professionally with a prizewinning short story in *The Atlantic Monthly*.

But not till age 38, in 1974, while working as a *Reader's Digest* editor in New York, did I finally go public with that same-sex personal vision and subject matter. *The Front Runner*, published by

William Morrow, became my first bestseller. It not only has stayed continuously in print since then, but has also achieved a life of its own for many readers all over the world. Despite its narrative voice of a 40-year-old gay man, *The Front Runner* has a strong focus on youth, with its story line of three Olympics-bound college athletes.

In 1994, the year I published *Harlan's Race*, I was living in Los Angeles, and opened the *Los Angeles Times* one day to read about a "gay high school" called EAGLES Center.

New policy by the Los Angeles Board of Education allowed for the creation of this continuation program for gay, lesbian, bisexual and transgendered dropouts, who had been driven out of their home schools by intolerance. Curious, I visited the school one morning... and wound up staying for six months of volunteer teaching. I taught history and creative writing, attended staff meetings, learned how to grade papers, and served as a chaperone at L.A.'s first Gay Prom. My days varied from advising on the EAGLES Yearbook, to helping staff find a shelter for a new student who had just been thrown out by his intolerant mom and had spent a rainy night on the street with no money or jacket.

There is no better way than being in the classroom every day with a bunch of gay, lesbian, bisexual and transgendered dropouts to realize that American youth and American education is in crisis! Some schools are increasingly intolerant of any and all students who are "different" — racially, ethnically, philosophically or sexually. It is apparent that there is a wide gap between what many people believe about gay kids, and what their lives are really like.

My 42 students, ages 14 to 22, were faced with sexual feelings surging within themselves that are deemed "immoral" by many in education. They were mostly Latinos and Blacks, with Whites and Asians in the minority — butch boys in shirts and ties, boys wearing makeup, gothic girls, Latino drag queens, Klub Kids, sex workers, several refugees from gangs, and a couple who had already done some time in juvenile detention for assorted minor crimes. They came from Catholic, Protestant, Mormon, Buddhist and liberal humanist families. A few had tolerant or loving parents who actually enrolled them at EAGLES because they feared for their kids' lives. But most of these students were living on the edge of family life, or independently, or in the system. They faced daily violence from parents or other students, as well as the lure of drugs, alcohol, clubbing, the street, the constant threat of being flung out of their homes into homelessness — and a legal system where minors have little say over their own destinies. One student had logged two dozen suicide attempts, in and out of various institutions. Many were extremely bright and gifted; despite their problems, they dreamed of doing great things with their lives.

This deeply unsettling yet inspiring experience made me realize that the high schools of America have become a bloody battleground. Religious extremists battle more moderate viewpoints, as both sides seek to capture the loyalties of our nation's young people, and the power to define what their future and well-being might be.

Today I serve on the Gay and Lesbian Education Commission in the Los Angeles Unified School District. LAUSD is a pioneer among U.S. school districts for its enlightened policy on non-straight students, and for its 1996 daring in electing Jeff Horton its first openly gay schoolboard president. In 1995 I helped found an online literary publication, *YouthArts*, which can be found at http://www. gaywired.com/yap. *YouthArts* publishes young (under 25) poets, artists, political writers, fashion illustrators, and cartoonists. Nationally, I am involved with the ACLU and other organizations in fighting the trend toward censorship in the United States. I recognize the need for young people to have access to all kinds of positive information that might be denied them by Americans who believe that youth must be tightly controlled.

In 1994, the time came to write this third book in the *Front Runner* series. In my first draft, the narrative focused on the awakening of a young teen — not just the physical awakening, but the spiritual, emotional and mental awakening, which is just as powerful and dizzying. The moment came when I realized that the real story had to be John William's questions about his vanished father.

Did I now dare to create a narrative in the voice of a young teenage boy? Yes, I did... as eagerly as I dared to write in the voice of a track coach in *The Front Runner*, or of a 65-year-old native woman chief in *One Is the Sun*, or of a 27-year-old Catholic priest in *The Fancy Dancer*. Part of my personal challenge as a writer is to create a universe of different viewpoints for the reader.

Several young consultants — all of them writers or artists — have read this manuscript and offered insightful comments — including Armond Anderson-Bell, Joshua Chaney, Ruben "Sick Pig" Gomez,

Bruce Heller, Christina Martinez, Christine Soto, and Massiell
Tiferino. I am deeply indebted for their help, for the frankness with
which they shared their own views, and for the never-ending question,
"When is *Billy's Boy* going to get done?"

I also benefitted from adult comments — those of my partner
Tyler St. Mark, as well as the Wildcat team, including sales manager
Jacqueline Londé, publicist Ross De Castro, controller Karen Connell,
copy editors Kim Krause and Alan Taylor, and typesetter/book
designer Barbara Brown. Barbara once told me she dreamed of doing
books instead of newletters; *Billy's Boy* is her eighth book with me.

My brother, inventor/writer Conrad Warren, an amateur astronomer, was very helpful in technical details; our shared love of the stars
goes back to childhood starings through binoculars in this or that
field on the ranch.

Fifty years later, my stillborn high school novel can now be
reincarnated into print. Times have changed, but the heartbreaks
have not.

        — Patricia Nell Warren
         Los Angeles
         June 21, 1997

Billy's Boy

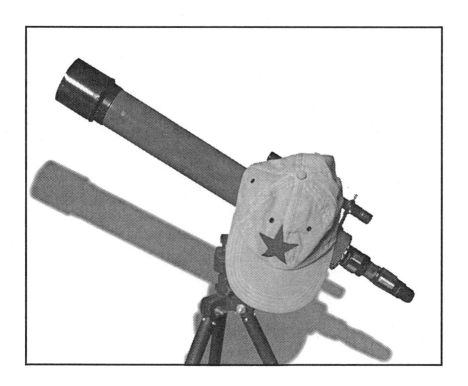

— 1 —

DARK SKY

The *USS Memo* was special, because they built her out of the rarest, safest metal in the universe. Xyzium didn't rust, or get metal fatigue, and it could go close to the stars without melting. So the *Memo* was the only ship in the fleet made mostly of xyzium, because she needed to be safe...they used her to train the best of the kids. We cadets didn't know what planetary system all that xyzium came from, because it was a state secret.

The *Memo* was on this routine training mission, when a freaky gravity thing interfered with our instruments, and we got lost. We were flying through dust lit up spookily by our running lights. Now and then a dwarf star zipped by, and the ship would jolt from the star's gravity pull. Our neutrino clock was messed up, and coordinates seemed to be changing every minute, so our star charts were useless. Commander was doing a great job of not looking scared, like Captain Kirk in *Star Trek*...only this was real, not TV.

The bored lady computer kept saying:

"Warning! You have just entered the Ancient Realms of the Dead. All time must now default. On my mark. Ten, nine..."

Most of the crew were cadets wearing black ninja suits and black baseball caps with a star patch. I was the navigator's mate, so I was sitting at the navigation console, checking the coordinates. Commander's face popped up on the video-com screen beside me.

"Mr. Heden, check the coordinates one more time," he ordered.

"Check coordinates, aye sir," I said. *Clackety-clackety-clacket*...went the keyboard as my shaky fingers tried to be superfast. Like everybody else, I was trying to be brave.

"Coordinates read default 20 degrees NC458 and default 41 degrees FC128, *sir*," I said.

The commander's face looked pissed.

"What is this default we're in? It doesn't make sense!" he said.

"I...uh...don't know, sir," I said.

The video-com screen went dark as he keyed off.

When we broke into the clear, the time was 23:09:30/7/25/1989/default by the crazy neutrino clock, which measured in nanoseconds. I could see through the window, which was right in front of me so I could get visual fixes. The ship stopped jolting. Suddenly it was *bright* out there — I could have studied my manual during a spacewalk. Ahead was a dark nebula, with one giant white star beside it, so hot white that I had to pull down my eyeshields to look at it. My scanner told me the nebula was 1.1 light-years wide, uncharted. The star was incredibly beautiful — and suddenly it started fading right before my eyes. It faded down three magnitudes, then pumped up bright again. So it was a variable star with an incredibly short period.

All around me the crew was exhausted, nodding off.

I was the only one awake, wildly excited about logging this important new star onto the star charts...except I didn't have a clue what its coordinates were. That nebula was so black that it looked like a hole we could fly through. The scanner locked on it, computed its configuration from every angle, and ran the message: "Dark nebula — uncharted." We all knew the Horsehead, the Ring, the Pillars and other nebulas from different angles. Commander had made me memorize their shapes. If your instruments get screwed up, he said, you go back to primitive skills — navigate by the spacemarks. Best of all, you can navigate by the variable stars because each one has a time period that is unique. Variables work the same way that beacons do for navigators on Earth, he said.

Suddenly the intercom crackled again.

A strange man's image downlinked onto the video-com screen. He was tall, with wide shoulders in a blue jacket. Through slits in his black eye-shield, his eyes stared at me. Right away I knew he wasn't on the ship. He was standing in some kind of docking space. It was empty except for a huge crane, and a few ore dumps standing around. Wherever he was located, they must ship ore out of there — maybe xyzium. How did he get onto my screen?

"Hello, Finder," he said quietly.

My heart almost stopped — this guy knew my secret name. Nobody on the ship, even Commander, knew my secret name.

I looked around. Everybody was asleep. Then I looked back at the man. "Who...uh, who are you?" My voice was quivery.

"I'm your father."

Now my heart was racing crazily. "My father's dead."

"No, Finder...I'm alive."

"You died before I was born. How do you know my name?"

"I'm going to zip you a window of my location. Fix it in your memory. I'm operating under extreme emergency conditions here, so I can only give you the information once."

On the screen, a window popped up, with a visual zoom on the dark spot. Now the nebula was close up, black, shaped like a big cat laying down, with a head and a long body. I could see dim stars inside the body — they looked like spots on the cat. The giant star was fading again. The scanner said this was a new star. Period: 60 seconds, said the display. This was a terrific find — we'd be able to reset our clocks, and have time again. Commander would be happy...I might get a promotion. Automatically my hand grabbed the mouse, and I pulled down the form for recording a new find. I was making astronomy history, naming a new spacemark. CAT NEBULA, I typed. Then I hit "save," recording the computer's measurements on the nebula and the pulsing star into the *Memo's* database. Now our time corrector, which had been stuck on search, locked onto the variable star too. All of a sudden we had time again. The ship's clocks came back up. Digital displays flashed red all over the place.

The zoom had blinked off. The man was back on the screen.

"I don't believe you're my Dad," I said. "Take off your eye-shield and show me your face."

"Trust me, son. I'm in the photo in your secret box," he said.

Emotion crashed through me, like a meteorite punching through a solar panel — happiness and pain and terror and excitement, all at once. Nobody knew about the box but me — I had smuggled it aboard the *Memo*. The man had to be my Dad. How he knew about the box, I didn't know. Tears filled my eyes — his image got runny. I dashed them away. Cadets weren't supposed to cry on duty.

I put my hand on the computer screen, trying to touch him.

"Dad...Dad, why did you leave me?" I said.

"If you find me," he said, "we can be together again. Come back as commander of your own ship, and get me out of here."

"Where are you?" I wasn't quite believing. "Are you a prisoner?"

"No time to explain. Listen carefully. To find me, locate the variable and reset time by it, then steer 23...to...of your..."

My fingers were racing again, typing down his information. But the transmission was glitching — radio interference from that powerful star out there.

"Say again? You're breaking up! Twenty-three what?"

Frantically I hit all the troubleshooting keys, one after the other, trying to clear the interference.

Below his eye-shield, his chin was moving, like he was still talking, but I couldn't hear him any more. He held out his arms, like he wanted to hug me. I could almost feel him, his smell of aftershave, his body heat. His nearness and realness roared inside me, like a newborn star going into the burn stage. All kinds of feelings were pouring out of that hole punched through me. "Daaaad, I can't hear you!" I yelled.

Memo's crew was waking up. Everybody was staring at me. I was screaming — I'd gone crazy.

His picture broke up on the screen, like a virus was eating it. My throat was tearing itself apart. "DAAAAD...."

I woke up with a jerk. I was back in 1989, thrashing around in a pile of my clothes in the back seat of Mom's car. My backpack slid to the floor, on top of the box with my telescope mirror packed in it. My baseball cap had fallen off. What happened was...I'd dozed off and had this incredibly real dream about my Dad and a rocket ship. The magic of actually seeing my Dad was still around me. I could still feel the glass of the computer screen under my hand as I was trying to touch him. What was the ship's name? *Mimo? Memo? Mumbo?*

Auntie Marian was in the front seat, driving our dusty old blue

Nash Rambler. Ahead of us was the dusty boring back-end of our U-Haul van, which my Mom was driving. A freeway sign went zipping by — LOS ANGELES 120 MILES. The dream was real as that sign.

Rescue my Dad? Go out there in my own ship and find him?

"What's with you?" asked Auntie Marian. She stared at me in the rearview mirror.

"Nothing," I mumbled, putting my cap back on.

My mind was trying to hold onto the dream before it slid away. I was actually still half asleep. Shapes like pure geometry flowed in front of my eyes. Xyzium. What the excuse-me was xyzium?

"You were yelling *dad...dad....*yelling your head off," said Auntie.

Her beauty-parlor hairdo rotated as she gave me a quick look. Auntie always looked like a hairspray ad. Usually she wore fussy suits and heels, but today she wore pants because she was helping us move. Auntie was too much like my least favorite teacher at Marysville Junior High to be trusted. "So you were dreaming?" she asked.

Suddenly the dream shapes stopped flowing.

"Nah. I just fell off the seat," I lied.

My blue backpack had a NASA patch on it, which I'd found at a yard sale. Getting the patch was a big concession on Mom's part, because she didn't approve of anything military. But I argued on the side of peaceful exploration of deep space, so she paid a buck for it. Touching the backpack full of my secret things helped me hold onto the dream. That feeling wrapped around me like a warm blanket — how alive he was. His eyes, behind the eye-shield — what color were they? Did default mean dead?

Goosebumps came up all over me.

Unzipping the backpack, I felt around for my treasures. Astronomy books, notebook for observations, my *Star Wars* video collection. The secret tin box with snapshots of my Dad in it. The framed photo of him. I hadn't been able to see his eyelashes through the eye-shield. Were they short, or long? The photo was small, so I couldn't tell. My Mom said he was five foot ten, but he'd looked taller in the dream. I had always imagined Dad as a combination of Ancient Sage and Barbarian Warrior, who would know way more than me.

Quickly, before I forgot, I grabbed the notebook and dug a pen out of the sidepocket, and wrote: "Cat Nebula, 1.8 light years. Pulsing variable white giant, 60 seconds. Set time by variable, steer 23...what?" I made a sketch of the nebula. It was important not to forget anything.

What variable star had such a short period? The only variables I knew about were Cepheid variables. They usually go from 1 to 70 days. But 60 seconds? And what was 23?

"Worried about moving?" Auntie asked.

"No, just kinda...tired," I said, swallowing the lump in my throat. "When do we get there?"

"What did you dream about?"

If I talked about the dream, Auntie would tell my Mom, and my Mom would drag me to the therapist again. Mom drove me nuts wondering why I had bad dreams that I couldn't remember. This dream was the first one that I did remember.

"Nothing," I said.

"It must have been something."

"Excuse-*me*."

Auntie didn't know I was cussing. The Marysville principal didn't allow potty mouth on campus, so the students said Excuse-me instead. It was the big school joke. I was going to miss that dumb school, even though I never had a friend there and was hassled all the time for being short and getting A's. I was the science geek from hell. My only best friend was my Mom.

"Auntie, did you really know my Dad?" I asked.

"Of course I did, dear."

"Tell me some stories about him."

"Well, I can't tell you any more than your mother has, I'm sure."

Always the mystery. "Did he do something bad?"

"Why do you think that?"

"Mom doesn't talk about him much. Did he go to jail?"

"William, your Dad was a good man. The best. But losing him was devastating for your mom...for all of us."

For the family? Other than Aunt Marian, I didn't have any family. I wished I had a grandma! Sometimes I wondered if I was adopted. I had already sneaked a look through some of Mom's papers, trying to find out.

My Mom and I were moving to southern California, to the Realm of the Pinheads. She was going to coach girl's sports at Orange College in Costa Mesa. Aunt Marian had come from Malibu to help.

Pinheads pissed Mom off because they worship a male God and

don't respect females. Mom was a liberal, and she talked about the stupidity of our Earth civilization — how the Pinheads disrespect women and wreck the planet and underpay teachers. In *Star Wars*, the Pinheads would have been an alien people with tiny brains and squeaky voices. My Mom was short, like me, so she'd learned to defend herself, like I did. She became an aikido master, because aikido is non-violent, and she lived to fight non-violently for the Great Shoe Goddess Nike. She said there were lots of Pinheads in Orange County, where we were going. I was ready to diss the Pinheads.

Behind us was the Sacramento Valley where I'd been a little kid. It was all orchards and rice fields, and Ricelands Community College where my Mom taught sports. Now and then, racing my bike along the country roads, I could see the Stealth aircraft fly over from Beale AFB — it was the only high-tech thing around. Marysville wasn't exactly a Pinhead zone. It was more of a Barbarian sector, where people drove pickups and tractors and were technologically backward. Barbarians were higher on the evolutionary scale than Pinheads — very intelligent beings, but they didn't have high technology. I felt honored to call myself a Barbarian, because it meant that I was ultimately smart and could invent a lot.

Since my Dad was dead, I was the man of the house. Mom knocked herself out to get home from school and spend time with me. After school, most kids I knew got in their house with a key, and nobody was there, so they watched TV shows about happy families with moms and dads. Even the Addams family had a mom and dad. But the Heden family was me and my Mom against the world.

Other kids called me mama's boy because I was short and helped my Mom. They said my long eyelashes looked girly. I was always getting in fights, and losing. Let's face it — nobody who is five foot three with long eyelashes ever conquered the Universe. Mom knew it was me against the world, so she taught me aikido, though she nixed karate. She made me promise I wouldn't be bloodthirsty. After that, I won the fights, but didn't win any friends. So I had these fantasies about being somewhere else in the cosmos, with highly civilized people in space battlecruisers. We were discovering new galaxies, and founding colonies where cyber slaves dug rare metals and did everybody's dishes for them. And somewhere out there was an Ancient Sage, a wise old guy like Yoda in *Star Wars*, who would help me figure things out.

The dream feeling was gone now. But I kept hearing my Dad's voice in my head. "Come back and find me...get me out of here..."

A lump bulged in my throat.

Up ahead, Mom's U-Haul was turning off Interstate 5 freeway. After we parked, I zoomed into the restaurant ahead of them because I was starved. The two ladies went to the bathroom, and then we ate burgers and fries. Mom hardly owned any rare metals, so Auntie Marian paid for lunch.

When Auntie Marian went to find a copy of *USA Today*, Mom asked me, "You had a dream?"

Auntie Marian had snitched — probably in the bathroom.

"Do you remember the dream?" Mom asked.

"No." I played with my fries.

Her blue warrioress eyes with their long girly eyelashes bored into mine for a nanosecond. "I think you do remember it. But I won't pry. You can tell me when you're ready."

"Why do kids look like their parents?" I asked.

"Genes."

"Jeans?"

"DNA. Remember? In Miss Haskell's class?"

"You mean that squiggly stuff in our cells."

"You know astronomy, but you don't know much about yourself, kid. DNA is a basic protein that grows into what you are. You get some from your father, and some from your mother."

Her face tightened up as she realized she'd said the dad word. She got up and emptied our trays into the trash.

"William, the move is going to be good for us," she said as we went back to the parking lot. "Someday soon, you're gonna remember your dreams. Ride with me in the truck?"

Later that day, we went past L.A. First, as we hit the top of the Grapevine, there was a mass of light way off in the smog dust — it seemed like a light year wide, like a galaxy. But when we got close, L.A. didn't look like a future city, just bigger and nastier than Sacramento. We passed by the L.A. airport, and instead of xyzium ore freighters, there were primitive passenger planes flying over us.

Major disappointment! The smog was so bad, I'd be lucky to see the Moon. When we finally got to the Realm of Orange County, we turned off the 405 freeway.

"Well, here it is...Pinhead country," my mother sniffed.

"I'll take care of the Pinheads." I aimed an invisible proton weapon. "Pow-pow."

She shook her head, turning the U-Haul onto Newport Boulevard. "It doesn't work to kill Pinheads. You have to educate them."

"Nah. You have to default them and start over."

"Goddess...how did I raise such a bloodthirsty kid?" She ground the gears like a trucker.

Now that I was 12, it sometimes embarrassed me that my Mom was such a jock. She was short and fast with her feet, like me. Her mother's side of the family, which was Lebanese, gave her the coffee skin. The Norwegian side didn't show, except her big blue eyes, with those super-long eyelashes that she'd cursed my DNA with. Her black wavy hair was whacked shorter than mine. She was a faster runner than most of the girls on her track team. Even for moving, she wore her varsity jacket with "Coach Betsy Heden" stitched on it.

Costa Mesa was definitely low-tech, made of concrete instead of the xyzium I'd dreamed about. There were more malls and parking lots than Marysville, way more palm trees and buildings, with neon brown smog pressing down on them like bad dreams.

Mom was still talking. "Women coaches get paid way less than men. And we're going to have a house payment..."

"We could rent again."

"And throw away money every month? No."

As I stared out the window, I was wondering if I might find one friend here. Not a Pinhead...maybe a Barbarian like me. I didn't like being lonely, though Mom seemed to like it. The faculty women at Ricelands were always pushing her to date guys and get married again. But she didn't seem interested. She loved my Dad, so maybe she didn't want anybody else. I liked her loyalty.

I was the only kid in the universe who didn't have a dad.

"You gonna date guys?" I asked casually.

"Are you kidding? I'll be working like a dog, and I'll need you to help out a little more." She didn't take her eyes off the road.

"Yeah, I'll have time to help. So much smog, I won't be able to use my telescope."

"I'll make it up to you. We'll go up to the desert for star parties...I'll take you to the Jet Propulsion Laboratory...or Griffith Observatory. Okay?"

I didn't answer even though it was my dream to visit JPL/NASA. She looked at me. "Something on your mind?"

I shrugged.

"You must have meant something by your little dating comment."

"New place, new dad."

"That," she said, almost running over a homeless person who was pushing a shopping cart, "is none of your business."

"Why don't you tell me more about my Dad?"

"You know that's a painful subject."

"But why don't you have more pictures of him? Why don't I have grandparents?"

"You do have grandparents. I just don't get along with them. Don't start in. I mean it, William."

The mystery about my Dad had always been there, like the bad dreams, like the stars. Staring out the window as we stopped at a Costa Mesa motel, I was remembering how Mom got me interested in astronomy. When I was really little, it started with seeing an eclipse of the Moon with her. Then when I was ten, she took me camping in the desert to see another eclipse. She had binoculars and a book she'd borrowed from Mr. Yamamoto, the Ricelands science professor. She had actually read the book. The minute I looked through the binoculars and saw the Moon so close and alive, with stars disappearing behind her rim, I was hooked. All night, Mom and I sat freezing, wrapped in sleeping bags. We didn't make a fire so we could see good. The farther out into space I looked, the more excited I got. She checked the book, and told me where to look. I found the moons of Jupiter with the binocs, then the double star in Orion's sword.

"The clouds are galaxies," she said. "They're right outside our own galaxy."

"Wow. How far away are they?"

"The book says 180,000 light years. A light year is the distance that photons can travel in a year. Photons...they're particles of light, they travel like bullets, and they go...well, forever. If they don't hit anything, that is."

"How far is a light year?" I asked my Mom.

"It says here that...5.878 trillion miles. So you multiply 180,000 times 5.878 trillion, and..."

"Rad." I did the math in my head, and ran out of zeros.

Mom wasn't a Sage, but she was the Warrior Priestess who knows some important stuff, so she talked about how everything is spirit...everything moves in cycles. "Galaxies," she said, "I think they're really the spirits of lost and mysterious civilizations."

"Yeah?" My skin prickled a little.

"Rome," she said dreamily, "Babylon, ancient China..."

I had my head on her shoulder, listening, still staring at those distant luminous things so far away — so alive, she said. Her arm was around me, the only warm thing around.

"We can here sit on Earth," she said, "and look way out there at the souls of all those ruins that archeologists are digging up some-where...in Turkey, Mexico." Her eyes woke up, and she wasn't sad like she usually was. She was different than the mom who blew her whistle and yelled at her track team to get those knees up.

"What happened to the people in those civilizations?" I asked.

"Oh...maybe the individual stars in galaxies are spirits of people. When a star blows up into a nova, and becomes a black hole, it isn't the end, because that spirit is coming back to Earth to be born. And when somebody dies, that isn't the end either, because she or he is a new star being born out there."

As I stared at all that awesome distance, with my mouth open, it seemed like a good place for my Dad to be.

"Is one of those stars really him?" I wanted to know.

"I think so," she said. "I've always felt it."

"What about double stars?"

"Maybe," she said, "those are people who love each other."

I snuggled closer to her, and she pulled the sleeping bag around us. Which star was my Dad? It was neat to know she'd loved him so much. She was looking at the sky, and her eyes filled up with tears. "And you were a star who came to be born with me," she said.

Back in Marysville, I hadn't stopped thinking about stars. Mom couldn't afford an amateur telescope. But Mr. Yamamoto sent me to the army-navy store, and for $10 I got a pair of World War II binoculars used for spotting submarines — they were great for star gazing. For my next birthday, Mom gave me this terrific book...it had a star-chart wheel in it. When you turned the wheel, you could look at the rim, and tell by the month what constellations were going to be crossing the meridian at any time. The book made it really easy to learn the whole sky, and use the constellations to find stars and nebulas.

With two bucks from lawn mowing, I found an old book called *Amateur Telescope Making*. For 5th grade science class, Mr. Yamamoto helped me turn the binoculars into a little telescope. But it couldn't see far enough for me. So Mr. Yamamoto helped me make a real telescope, with a 4-inch reflector mirror. When we plated the mirror with silver fulminate, we almost blew ourselves up — the stuff is very unstable. The silver mirror went bad with tarnish after only a year.

So for the 6th grade science project, I made a 6-inch telescope with a bigger reflector mirror. You take two pyrex blanks and grind them together with water and carborundum till one of them gets concave, spherical, and polished — not a scratch. The concave side is the mirror where you catch the reflections of stars. I sent it out to be aluminized. The telescope cost me $150 to build, and I paid for it with a paper route. Other kids made fun of me — their idea of high tech was four-wheeling. But I ignored the crude minions of attitude — nothing could ruin the fierce thrill when I adjusted the focus and actually saw the Horsehead Nebula for the first time. Every time I identified a new star, I wondered if it was my Dad.

Last year, Mom started talking about getting a better job and moving to a more urban sector, so I could go to a magnet high school and get accelerated into my career.

Now I wanted to tell Mom about the dream I'd just had. But she couldn't be trusted — she didn't want me to go near the father mystery. Maybe it wasn't a dream. Maybe he was out there somewhere, and I could actually find him by locating that flashing star. My skin got chilly. My Dad must still love me a lot if he tried to get in touch with me through a dream. Maybe he was a gazillion light years away.

Why did Dad hide his face behind the eye-shield? In my photos, he had the best-looking face in the world.

— 2 —

FUTURE CITY

Auntie Marian wanted to loan us money for the new house. But Mom said she could handle it. They let me have a motel room to myself. When they were out house-hunting, I couch-potatoed on the bed, watched science TV, and thought about my Dad in the Realms of the Dead.

After hours of bored channel-surfing, I found a special about the space program. My blurry eyes watched as the primitive spacecraft lifted off. The astronauts were going two inches into deep space. The Moon was old stuff...now they were orbiting the Earth. It'd take 227 days to Mars. Fourteen years just to get to Pluto...not to mention coming back. The nearest star outside our solar system, Proxima Centauri, is 4.3 light years away. By the year 2000, Arthur C. Clarke thought we could get there in 100,000 years. He said the best we could do would be 1/10 the speed of light.

I was scribbling wild calculations in my notebook. By the time I qualified as an astronaut, maybe the United States would know how to do the time-warp thing, or maybe the cryogenics thing, with the crew frozen solid, so we could explore outside the solar system without getting old. Or the scientists and the steely-eyed missilemen would discover some new kind of propulsion, like a photon accelerator or something, so we could go even faster than light. Booooom-*rroooarrr!* Or thought travel. You'd think about your destination, and be there! I could already do that in my dreams, because that was how my Dad found me. But it had to work in real time. So I didn't buy the cryogenics thing, and I wasn't thrilled about being frozen like a popsicle.

Maybe the dream was trying to tell me something. Maybe I could do the real Mission Impossible — go out there and find my Dad. NASA would have to accept me, or my Mom would do terrible things to them. I'd be a killer astronaut...with my astronomy and martial arts experience, and the highest scores ever posted in video games at Fergy's Arcade in Marysville.

When my Dad came home, people would look at me and say, "That's Billy's boy." Up to now, they called me "Betsy's kid".

What was the minimum height requirement for NASA?

And what kind of flashing star had a 60-second period? I knew about Cepheid variables, but they were never shorter than a day.

I looked at my *Memo* notes. The picture of the Cat Nebula and its variable star, winking like a beacon, was so clear in my brain. It could be billions of light years out...or it could be right in our own galaxy. We humans can't see the bright center of our own galaxy because of all the lanes of heavy dust in the way. Maybe that was the dust where the *Memo* got lost in my dream. Maybe powerful energies coming from the center were what disoriented the *Memo's* instruments. It made sense! That nebula might already be charted and numbered, and its photo was stuck away in some observatory's file.

If the Cat Nebula was close enough, I could find it with my own telescope! But I'd need a bigger, better mirror — a 10-inch.

What was the default? Was it death?

When the two ladies came back, they had cherry-pink smiles. Mom had held her Barbarian sword to a Pinhead banker's throat and got us a house. The payments would cost tons of rare metals, and Mom was still on my case about helping more.

"I will if you send me to astronaut school," I said.

She stared at me. "I thought you wanted to be a astronomer."

"Astronauts have to be astronomers," I reminded her.

She was too tired to give me a lecture about the military being violent and bad. "One step at a time. First you gotta finish 12th grade," she said. "But you're going to have an excellent science teacher here, Mr. Miller. I've checked him out. Deal?"

"Do I get a bigger room?"

"Of course. Deal?"

"And part of the garage for my workbench? I want to make a 10-inch mirror."

"Ambitious boy. Just don't let the silver explode. Okay?"

If you're rich, you have a house that is radically different. Our house looked like the other houses on Lemon Street. It was number 248, with earthquake cracks in the chimney, picket fence in front, and a dusty backyard with a hoop over the garage door. Auntie Marian teased Mom about selling out for the white picket fence. Mom didn't think this was funny.

The house next door was number 250, and had its earthquake crack under the bay window. In back, their patio had a teeny swimming pool, a chain-link dog fence around it, and no dog. But a boy's bike leaned against the garage. Probably this Pinhead kid was taller than me. Auntie Marian and Mom told me I could play later if I helped unpack. So I attacked kitchen boxes for two hours — then grabbed my basketball and went slamming outdoors.

With the hot breeze, I worked up a sweat. My Barbarian curls stuck to my forehead. Basketball was something to do with my energy, even though Magic Johnson's waistband was higher than me. I was fast with my feet, always pushing the envelope, so I slipped on rocks and dust as I played, fell a couple of times, and had blood running down my knee. Finally I invented a new move, trampolining myself off the chain-link so I could go higher and slam-dunk. Maybe the boy next door was watching through his window.

All of a sudden, he was there, staring through that chain link fence between our two yards.

He was skinny, so his blue Speedo and tight T-shirt made him look skinnier. He was the same height as me. He had a long neck, and long legs with dirty-blonde fur on them, and little hands and feet. His golden dirty-blond hair was lifting and waving in the wind. We looked at each other, with our hair waving to the same bursts of wind. His eyes did a missile lock on mine.

A spooky hot feeling flooded all over me. This was a Pinhead kid. Could he be trusted? His parents were Pinheads too. This was dangerous stuff. I had to be careful.

"Hi," he said.

Those two slanty brown eyes stared through two holes in the wire, and those little hands were clenched on the fence. He looked like an elf in a prison camp. He had short eyelashes, so at least he wasn't a longlash mutant like me. His eyes were hungry. Maybe he wanted a friend too. His arms and legs had lots of bruises, so I knew he was the daring type like me.

I had to flight-test him. "Wanna shoot hoops?" I said.

The gate between our yards was rusted shut. First he tried to climb the fence, but his foot slipped, and he fell off. The wire scratched his leg, and he bled. Finally he kicked the excuse-me out of the gate, and it flew open. He ran toward me with drops of blood jolting down his leg from the scratch. His silky dirty-blond hair was lifting up and down like crazy as he ran. I liked the happy way his hair lifted. His slanty eyes did a navigational fix on me, as if the only thing he wanted was to get to my sector of the Universe.

"I'm Shawn Heaster," he said. "What's your name?"

I didn't want to tell him my legal name, because it was dorky, but I couldn't trust him with my secret name.

"William."

"That's a dorky name." He did a hook shot that missed.

I snagged his rebound, and did a hook. It went straight in. "No dorkier than Shawn. And I've got another name. A cool one."

"Oh yeah?"

"Yeah. A *weird* cool name."

"How weird is weird?" He was scornful.

"I'm a Barbarian invader of your kingdom," I said. "So you wouldn't understand my name, because it's in an alien language."

We were matching each other hook shot for hook shot, with streaks of drying blood on our legs.

"Oh yeah?" He was starting to look impressed.

"Yeah. Barbarians get to be totally weird."

"Well, I've got a weird name too," he said with quiet pride, dribbling past me, faking me out, and shooting. He missed.

I grabbed the rebound and put it in. "So what is it?"

"Listen, stupid. I don't tell my weird name to just anybody." He jumped in the air, and sank another basket.

Suddenly a tall man towered over the fence. He had hard blue eyes, dirty-blonde hair that didn't lift, and looked like Chuck Norris.

"Hey, Shawn! Are you pestering the new family?" he roared.

Envy squinched inside me. I wouldn't mind a dad yelling at me.

Shawn's dad looked at me and his eyes got kinder. "My wife is all excited," he said. "She's been wanting neighbors. Your house was on the market three years. *Marilyyyyn!*" he yelled.

Marilyn had brown hair, a frilly apron, and smelled like fresh cookies. She yelled through the window at my Mom, and said hi and welcome, and could I come to her house and eat pie. In another nanosecond, I was in the Heasters' kitchen, sitting beside Shawn and chowing on ambrosia of the Goddesses and Gods, namely fresh apple pie. Marilyn took part of the pie to my Mom and Auntie Marian. My Mom actually smiled, and said she didn't know that people still did the pie thing for a new family. Finally I was in Shawn's room and we were looking at his sci-fi comics and playing his Nintendo games. He was bored and ready for something better. It was destiny that we met. The sages in the sci-fi stories are always talking about destiny.

That night, we were too pooped to cook, so the Heasters invited us to a cookout and a splash in their pool. Later my Mom said, "They may be Pinheads, but Marilyn bakes a mean pie."

Next day, my new buddy visited my new room, which had a balcony destined to be my observatory. We attacked my boxes of stuff. He helped me put up my posters, and said they were cool — especially the one of Darth Vader and Luke fighting with light sabers. But when my fiberglass tube with the 6-inch mirror came out of the box, Shawn was impressed. He helped me screw it back on the heavy stand, which was made of galvanized plumbing parts from a junkyard.

"It comes apart to go in a car," I said proudly.

"You *built* this?"

"Took me thirty-five hours to polish the mirror."

"Wow. That's a cool thing to do."

That night, we actually could see Polaris in the glary sky, above all the trees, and he helped me adjust the telescope. "Wooooow," he said after he looked through it. "Unbelievable." After more wowing, it felt like we'd grown up together. So we took a break, and I let him look at my secret box.

"You have such cool stuff," he said.

The top photo showed my Dad in a goofy retro suit, with long curly hair. He was grinning at the camera. I liked my Dad's grin — you could tell he was a neat guy. He looked disciplined too — my Mom always said how disciplined he was. His eyes were brave, but there was fun in them. Shawn looked at the other oldie pics — college runners, wearing clothes and shoes that were oldie looking. In one picture my Dad posed with his coach, wearing a varsity jacket saying PRESCOTT, holding a silver trophy. On the back, Mom had written "Van Cortlandt Cross-Country '76." Mom had trimmed the picture so Billy was in the center and all of Coach's face was gone. You could only see his shoulder and his coach jacket. In another snapshot, Dad and my Mom rode an oldie bike, sticking out their tongues at the camera.

"My parents were best friends in college," I said.

"Your mom is cool. My mom would never do that."

"My Dad was this national champion college runner."

"Where is he now?"

"He was killed. An accident with a gun." I turned away.

"Jeez, I'm sorry," he said behind me.

"Yeah...me too."

"My folks thought your mom was divorced."

"She hates guns."

"My dad loves guns. He takes me target shooting."

I drew a deep breath. "I had this wild dream about my Dad living in another galaxy. Weird, huh? But I have this feeling that...I don't know, that it's a *real* place I dreamed about. If I keep doing observations, maybe I'll...see it."

This was the big test. Would he buy it?

Shawn's eyes got round. "Really?"

I tried to explain what Mr. Yamamoto and Arthur C. Clarke said about relativity of time and space. The faster you go, the slower time goes. If you go at the speed of light, there is no time. If we could travel faster than light, maybe I could go backwards in time and find my Dad still alive. The light that comes from other galaxies is from the past. Not just in the sci-fi movies, but for real.

"I want to be an astronaut, and go out there and see," I said.

Slowly, Shawn closed the secret box, and handed it back to me. Could he really understand about my dream? To me, the details were still as clear as a photograph taken by a 100-inch telescope and published in *Scientific American* by some astronomer dude with a big name.

"That's awesome," he said with respect.

Suddenly he stared straight into my eyes. "I guess you need to know *my* magic name," he said.

"Yeah?" I was dizzy with relief.

"My name is Orik of the Sun."

"Orik," I said, standing up and putting out my hand. "Welcome to Mission Control of the *U.S.S. Memo*. My name is Commander Finder."

He stood up too. We shook hands.

"I guess I'm lucky. My dad's alive," he said.

"Yeah. Is your dad cool?"

"He's strict, but...he's never around...always working."

I was putting the tin box away.

"Hey...I'll volunteer to help you look for your dad," he said. "It's a fantastic mission. I'll go with you, and..."

"You mean it?" For a moment I wondered if this was a dream come true, the dream about having a friend. But I didn't want to wake up and be the lonely geek again.

"I'll be your senior officer, or whatever...."

"Till death?" I said.

"Till death. I thought you had to die anyway, to go out there."

"Nah...they'll just freeze you, or something, then resuscitate you when you get there. They're working on it."

We went back to the telescope, and I showed him something important. "See that triangle of three stars? Really bright ones?"

"Kind of. Yeah."

"That's the Summer Triangle. The stars are Deneb, Vega and Altair. Left of the center of the triangle, that dust cloud there?"

"Yeah?"

"Past that cloud is the center of our own galaxy. It'd be really bright, zillions of stars all jammed together. But you can't see it, because of the dust. I have this feeling that my Dad is out there."

"Why?" Orik was staring at me, open-mouthed.

"Because if he was zillions of light years outside our galaxy, I couldn't find him. By the time I got to the area I saw in the telescope, the Cat Nebula would be gone. What we see is light from…like, millions of years ago. He wouldn't ask me to find him if he wasn't somewhere that I could get to. Know what I mean?"

"I always thought that going out there was just…you know…something in the movies," he said.

When Orik went home, I carefully put the framed picture of my Dad on my dresser.

Downstairs, Mom was still slamming boxes around. She had already put the candle on the fireplace ledge, and lit it. It was one of those tall glass things that burned for a whole week. My Mom always said she burned the candle as a prayer for everybody she loved who had died, especially my Dad. I wondered who she cared about besides my Dad. She never talked about her own parents.

After that, Orik and I were hardly ever apart. We spent the summer in Speedos, running wild and having fun. Once the Heasters and Mom took us to Disneyland, and we ran wild on the rides and Tom Sawyer's Island. Mom kidded us about being Tom Sawyer and Huck Finn, which was one book I'd avoided reading in school because I was too busy with science.

Sometimes the Heasters took Orik to San Diego to visit his grandmother, and I went crazy missing him. When he got home, he came flying through the gate, hair lifting. My Mom put an extra bed in my room, and the Heasters put an extra bed in Orik's room, so on weekends we could stay up to star gaze and then sleep over.

Pretty soon I couldn't remember when Orik hadn't been part of my life.

Pretty soon I was practically living at the Heaster house. Marilyn didn't work, because Jerry said it was her duty to be home. She'd wanted tons of kids but stopped after Orik, because of a problem with her female tubing. When Marilyn wasn't shopping, she gave me hugs and Bandaids and fresh cookies, and sewed on new buttons. I was a good boy and helped her with stuff. Orik's house was where we studied. In a month, he knew all the constellations and could use my starbook wheel to find all kinds of things in the sky.

At my house, we did the telescope work. In August we used up the word "wow" watching for meteors during the Perseids.

When school started, Mom was away from home a lot — going to track meets, trying to win regional championships, making her career happen for $30,000 a year. One weekend when she was gone, the candle went out, so I lit a new one and moved it to my dresser, by my Dad's picture. She said that was okay, I could be the Keeper of the Flame now.

More and more I asked her about my Dad. We had fights.

One day I got really mad at her. So I took the bus over to the Orange campus library, saying I wanted to look up astronomy stuff. What I really did, was look up Prescott College in a big book of all the universities and colleges in the U.S. But it wasn't there. So now I knew for sure that she was hiding something. An attitude started to grow in me, dark and distant, but with a shape, like a nebula. I was profoundly pissed off with her. Maybe the teenage rebel stuff was kicking in, like with kids you see on TV.

Jerry Heaster was maybe going to be a substitute dad, even though he was away from 6 in the morning to 8 in the evening, slaving for rare metals to pay the bank, like my Mom.

Jerry had been in the Army quartermaster corps, so he was into rules and organization. He was good-looking, liked sports, knew how to do things...just like those TV soldiers and traders who go off on dangerous missions to other sectors, fighting the Klingons and the intergalactic drug cartels. Jerry still reminded me of Chuck Norris, in the movies where Norris plays a dad. The dads I liked were all TV dads, because real-life dads weren't around much. I especially liked *The Brady Bunch* and *Welcome Back, Kotter*, even the different alien dads in *Star Trek*, though none of them were as awesome as Luke's dad in *Star Wars*. Jerry gave me slaps on the back, and took me target shooting with Shawn. He only did it once though, because my Mom almost killed him for letting me touch a gun.

When the neighbors talked about Orik, they called him "Jerry's boy." I envied Orik for that.

But sometimes Jerry was kind of scary, the way he talked about war, and duty, and no compromises. Now and then he told us stories that he'd heard in Vietnam. His job was in the warehouses, so he never got into combat. But Jerry didn't like people of color too much. He told us stories that other guys told him, about what our men did to men prisoners from the other side, taking off their clothes and torturing them...which made our hair stand on end. What would an advanced civilization do to us space kids if we got caught?

My Mom didn't like to hear Jerry talk about war. She was a mercenary for peace, she said.

Orik was the same age as me — his birthday was September 9, two days after mine. So we had a terrific birthday party together. The gate was open between our houses, with cakes and candles and presents on both sides. It was like his star followed mine back to Earth so we could be born together.

When school started, we went off to 7th grade together. Every day was a new mission — an op that was part of the main mission. We got a little taller, but not much. It was obvious that we weren't going to be Magic Johnson — in fact, Jerry was always saying that Orik was taking after his mom, and she was as short as my Mom. We talked about the Curse of the Short Moms.

So we were two good boys going wild, with our parents shopping or slaving in the xyzium mines. We learned how to microwave TV dinners and clean house and take out the trash. We even knew how to take our parents' money to the ATM on Newport Boulevard, and make deposits for them. We were so terrifically good that they trusted us and didn't pay much attention to us. So we got to live on auto-pilot.

When we slept over, Orik and I always got dressed together, or took showers together, so we got to check out each other's bodies. Mom had never been ouchy about bodies, so we had no problems here. Shawn wanted to know why I had extra skin on my laser-gun. I already knew, because Mom once told me that there was this ancient rite where people cut off the piece of skin and sacrificed it to their Male God. Some parents still did it, she had said. I told Mom that I was glad she never sacrificed a piece of me, and she said she hadn't done it because I was born special.

"Yuck," Orik said when I told him about the ancient rite. He was fascinated with my extra skin. He couldn't leave it alone, and of course it liked being touched. He was pissed that his parents had cut his extra skin off.

From there we went to secret war games, finding each other being held prisoner, tied up and naked, and rescuing each other and being the hero. This was so fun that we got all goosefleshy, and couldn't wait for our parents to leave so we could get naked. Watching each other's hardware going into lock-and-load was as normal as watching *The Brady Bunch*.

One time, he was cold, because it's way below freezing in space, so I got the idea to get him warm after I rescued him. But he grunted and groaned, even when we used some of my Mom's vaseline, so I didn't really get in. But a lot of strange scary feelings came rushing over me like a fierce solar wind from a star, clearing the cosmic dust cloud around it, so it could shine fierce and clear. I moved back and forth against him, rubbing him to bring him back to life. He closed his eyes and said ohhh ooooh. Then he rescued me like that. It was a cool way to be space brothers.

There was this excitement and mystery about being alone together. We were always careful about people not finding out what we did. When we finally had enough hero stuff, we lay around reading *Astronomy Magazine* and looked through my telescope. Or we just watched movies about space, like *The Right Stuff*.

Sometimes we caught other boys doing the right kind of secret stuff. From what we knew, most boys did it. We wondered if girls did it too. Guys have different names for it — initiation rites, or fooling around. They always do it when they talk about being real men and having girls, so this makes it okay. The real-man code says that you never talk about the secret things. The bad thing is to be a sissyfag, not interested in girls. Orik and I were real men, and we'd have girls someday.

One day at school, there was this new Mexican kid named Alberto that everybody called a sissyfag. The 8th graders cornered him in the boys' bathroom, and pulled down his pants, and spread him. Then they all pissed on him and humped him. They even stuck pencils in him. "You want it, don't you...you want it, na na na-na na," they kept telling him. Orik and I watched. It was pretty exciting, but we felt weird about it, and didn't help. This was like what we did with each other, except it was done in a mean way, to hurt. Alberto was crying and obviously not having fun. We got a good look at the older boys' military secrets, and knew that our own were going to get that big, thought mine weren't quite as big as Orik's.

"You better not tell the teachers," the boys told Alberto, "or we'll do you worse next time."

Once I caught a look at Jerry on a camping trip, when he was naked in the camp shower. I was blown away by the size of Jerry's military secrets. I could hardly wait to look like that.

Sometimes I wondered if my Mom knew about our secret stuff. She was pretty smart. But our parents didn't pay much attention to us. They were slaving in the xyzium mines to earn enough to pay the space-trading banker for our houses. Jerry slaved in an insurance office, and Marilyn wanted to slave too — she went to college and studied business. But Jerry got mad and yelled about her duty to be home with her kid. Sometimes they argued about it.

Early every morning, my Mom went voyaging off to the college. A little later, Orik's mom dropped us at school. Orik and I took the school bus home at 4, and let ourselves in with our keys. Marilyn was always out shopping and doing errands by then. We always had an hour or two to play rescue for a little while. We always did it fast, because we didn't want to get caught. Weekends, we sometimes got more time when they went off to buy groceries and run errands all day. By the time we heard cars rolling into the driveway, we were showered, and helping each other with homework, or flopped on the couch like two good boys, watching TV.

A couple of times, we almost got caught, and had a thousand heart attacks as we jumped into clothes and got busy with homework.

But Mom only said, "Orik's cool, huh?"

"Yeah," I admitted.

"We don't get many real friends in life."

"Auntie Marian is *your* real friend, huh?" I asked. Suddenly I wondered if my Mom and Auntie Marian did secret stuff when they were alone.

"Oh, she's more like a mother," Mom grinned. "She tells me what to do."

Orik and I had so much energy, feeling driven by our secret Mission, that some teachers complained. Our science teacher, Mr. Miller, didn't complain, because our energy went into homework and he was totally impressed that I had built my own telescope. But the school counselor was a Ruler of the Empire type — she met with our parents, and wanted their permission to give us Ritalin to calm us down. Drugs are serious stuff. In the intergalactic empires, there are always drugs to control entire peoples. All the civilizations fight their space wars over rare drugs. Rulers drug the kids, so they will do your bidding. Orik and I talked about it, and we knew that Ritalin was one of those evil drugs. My Mom hated drugs. She told me that she smoked pot when she was young, and it melted some of her brain cells.

"You're going to need all your brain cells to be an astronomer," she warned me.

"You mean astronaut," I said.

The Heasters pushed Ritalin on Orik, but it made him sick and he puked it up. He begged them not to make him take it. Then he started ditching his pill. The school nurse made him swallow it in front of her, but he learned how to catch it in the side of his mouth, and later he'd spit it up. Finally our parents had a big fight with the school and called a lawyer. So we didn't have to take the stuff.

When the kid who sold drugs at school came around us, we kicked the excuse-me out of him and told him he was an agent of the Evil Empire.

At school, we were "William and Shawn." He was the one whose grin lit up the school...he was elected class president. I was the supergeek who got A's. People saw him as the leader of the two of us. They never knew that I was the secret operations leader. That was okay with me — I was a natural undercover. Now and then I took some fire from a few kids who didn't like my eyelashes. But I was so reckless in a fight that they were afraid of me, and I always won. "Crazy William," they called me.

At an army-navy store, Orik and I found a couple of star patches and sewed them on our baseball caps, like in my dream. I kept the bill of my baseball cap frontwards so people were clear that I wasn't cool. Cool kids wore their hats backwards because they did drugs or belonged to gangs, or whatever. I didn't have time for that kind of stuff.

Somehow we were so busy having fun together that the 10-inch telescope wasn't getting made.

— 3 —

FLASHING STARS

One day a science assignment got me feeling a step closer to my Dad.

Mr. Miller was talking about Mendel and his experiment with the pea genes. Miller was a good teacher, even though he couldn't control the class, so spitballs were always flying like meteor showers. I was one of the few kids who listened, because my Mom had mentioned DNA that time. Miller was at the blackboard, making an X that was the tall father pea, and he connected it to another X that was the short mother pea. As the students wrote notes and spitballs whizzed, Miller was talking about how each parent gives the baby some of its genetic DNA stuff. So Mendel's baby pea turned out to be tall but it still had the gene for short inside itself, as a secret.

Most of us didn't have a clue what a pea plant was, and thought it sounded funny. So Mr. Miller showed us a real plant that he grew. The light bulb went on in my head. This genetic stuff was about me.

"Any questions?" asked Miller.

I was never shy about raising my hand, especially in science class.

"Yes, William?" asked Mr. Miller.

"Yes, William?" said one of my enemies in a weird voice. A couple of kids laughed. I ignored the minions of attitude, because I knew I was going to do great things someday, and they weren't.

"Is it the same with people?" I asked Miller.

"It's the same with all living things," said Miller. "People, trees, elephants, butterflies. Both parents contribute the genetic material that is part of you for life. It determines how you look — what diseases you might get — even how long you will live."

I listened with that strange warm excited feeling of the Cat Nebula dream surging up again. There was actually something inside me, something alive, something secret, a coded message that came from my Dad. I couldn't see it, but it was there. Maybe that's why he came to me in the dream, so I'd really know what the message was. Maybe the coordinates for the Cat Nebula were hidden in the gene code. But a big question still bothered me.

So after class one day, Orik and I went up to Mr. Miller's desk with the question. It was hard to talk about something so embarrassing, so I um'ed and uh'ed, and finally said, "My Dad was tall. So how come I'm...uh, not as tall as he was?"

"Maybe your dad was carrying the gene for shorter," Mr. Miller said, "and the two short genes paired up...his and your mother's. Maybe your dad's mom was short! Or your dad's dad. The hidden recessive gene can go back for generations."

"Cool," said Orik. "Must be the same for me."

Over the next few weeks, I kept going up to Miller's desk. When he told me how all the elements of the body are out there in space too...carbon and calcium and hydrogen and all of them...I felt like I was high. I filled my notebook with family trees of X's, daydreaming. My science textbook had pictures of chromosomes. Those squiggly things have the DNA genetic codes on them. The genes actually come in an order, like letters in a word. Every cell in my body, which was billions of them, had my Dad's and my Mom's genetic stuff in them — except that each cell carried special orders that made it grow into what it was, like a brain cell or a blood cell. The DNA connected me to Dad, and to the stars, for real.

"Could I actually see my chromosomes?" I asked.

"Sure," said Mr. Miller. He had me take a scraping from the

inside of my mouth, with an ice-cream stick. Then he put it on a slide. We looked at it under the school's one microscope. There were my cells! Each one had a mess of twisted spaghetti things in the middle. The spaghetti was the DNA. I got cold shivers looking at it — almost hearing my Dad's voice.

"And there's a new process called electrophoresis," Mr. Miller said, "where you run an electric current through the cells, so you can actually scan the DNA sequence and see it on a chart, in the form of bandings. That's how they do paternity tests."

"What do you mean, paternity?"

"Paternity means father. Sometimes there's a question about who the father of a child is," said Mr. Miller. "The court orders up a paternity test to find out, and they look at the DNA."

At home, I daydreamed and doodled — drew an X which was my Dad, and an X that was Mom, and linked them together with an X that was me, trying to figure it out. Dad didn't look much like me — he was tall and skinny, with dirty-blonde hair and freckles. I didn't know how long his eyelashes were. I was short and dark, with my Mom's wide shoulders and excuse-me blue eyes and disgusting long eyelashes. My mama's-boy eyes, other kids still called them. Girlie eyes. So Mom was to blame for that too. I hated my eyes and my eyelashes. But I did have my Dad's curls.

Mr. Miller and Mr. Yamamoto knew stuff, but were they wise? I searched my archive of TV images for those pictures of ancient wisdom. Sci-fi said that there were Ancient Sages out in space somewhere. There was Guinan in *Star Trek*. In *Star Wars*, there was Yoda. But there didn't seem to be any real-life sages on Earth...not old ones, anyway. The old Earthlings that I saw on TV were mostly pathetic, worried about their dentures and arthritis, wearing diapers just in case. Even my Dad didn't strike me as the Sage type, though he was supposedly very smart and brave.

So the Sage was missing in my world.

The search for my Dad finally led Orik and me to the school librarian to ask where Prescott College was. She didn't know, so she sent us to the big library at UC Irvine, and a nice Mormon lady librarian named Mrs. Danich. When I showed Mrs. Danich the photos and pointed at my Dad's varsity jacket and asked her about Prescott, she went straight to the big fat book I remembered, that listed colleges and universities. Prescott wasn't in it. But then Mrs. Danich went in the back room, and found an older book. She never threw out the older books, she said. And there it was...in Sayville, New York. President Joseph A. Prescott, 2500 students. The phone and mailing address was there.

"Either the school doesn't exist now," she said, "or it changed its name...or it's part of a bigger school now."

"Maybe somebody still has my Dad's records?"

But the phone number was no good. Information didn't have a new listing. Mrs. Danich wrote a letter to the school, and the post office sent it back to her saying ADDRESSEE UNKNOWN.

"That college is gone," said Mrs. Danich. "But Van Cortlandt — your mom wrote that on your dad's photo. It's a big park in New York City, I think."

Mrs. Danich really got into helping us. For some reason I didn't understand, Mormons are into family history and genealogy. How could she resist two good boys who were looking for a dad? I did this as a deep black operation because my Mom would get weird if she knew. I just told Mrs. Danich I was doing science homework. She told me she was glad I was at the library instead of buying pot from the dealers at school.

Mrs. Danich helped us look at the photos in my secret box with a magnifying glass, and we made a list of clues. One official's jacket had AAU on it. The trophy had writing on it — RRC NATIONAL CROS was all we could see. My Mom had mentioned the NCAA.

"AAU is the Amateur Athletic Association. NCAA is the National Collegiate Athletic Association," Mrs. Danich said, and sat down at her computer. She got onto this new thing called the Internet, that my Mom talked about, where a college computer modems into the phone system, and colleges can message each other. Mrs. Danich could call up people and download printed information from all over the Earth, especially other universities, even the government, by typing on her keyboard. The information came up like magic on her screen. Orik and I hung over Mrs. Danich's shoulder, fascinated, learning the different code words, like gov and edu and org.

Mrs. Danich's quick little fingers tapped out messages, and

messages came back. The AAU was gone too — there was now a new athletes' org called TAC. The NCAA was still around, but when Mrs. Danich had somebody at another university search their records for a national cross-country champion in the 1970s named Billy Heden, they didn't find anything. RRC turned out to be the Road Runners Club of America. They had an office in New York, but when we called, somebody went down their old list and didn't find any Hedens. In the library basement Mrs. Danich even located boxes of oldie mags like *Track & Field News* and *Runner's World*. Orik and I sneezed at the dust, flipping through them, looking for runners around 1976. But the boxes didn't go earlier than 1980.

In fact, nobody seemed to have a lot of records going that far back. "Our country is gagging on information," Mrs. Danich said. "People run out of room, and they dump their files. Did you know the government dumped records on men who served in World War II? I found that out when I tried to trace my uncle Jim. It makes you wonder how the historians know so much about the Roman Empire!"

I was looking at the coach's shoulder in the picture. He was a total mystery. If only the name on his jacket wasn't cut off!

Mrs. Danich noticed my sad face. She said:

"I'm feeling uncomfortable about going this far without your mother's written permission."

"She doesn't want me to know."

"Why?"

"Dad was killed in an accident," I choked. "She doesn't like to talk about it."

"There must be other reasons. Every family has its secrets."

"I've already thought about that." A tear was rolling down my cheek. "You've got to help me, Mrs. Danich."

Mrs. Danich sighed. The tear did it. "There's another possibility," she said.

"What?" I blew my nose.

"Maybe Heden wasn't his last name. These days some liberated women use their own names. Have you seen your birth certificate?"

"No."

"That will give your father's real name. Without the right name, it's hard to find out any other information."

She didn't tell me to look in my Mom's drawers, but I knew what to do. Mrs. Danich was a true outlaw, like me.

Mrs. Danich also helped me grab more knowledge about flashing stars off the Internet. "I shouldn't do this, but...Maybe you're the next Edward Hubble."

So she let me sit at her computer, when she wasn't using it, and showed me how to use a search engine. All I had to do was type in "variable star" and *pow!* the modem would downlink thousands of listings. The Internet was getting a lot of astronomy resources. There was even a Variable Star Observers Society for amateurs. Using her "ucirvine.edu" account, I went wild at the keyboard and learned about R Coronae Borealis variables. They are rare, and do strange things with their hydrogen and carbon, so they fade and brighten on weird intervals. Mira variables are giant red stars, 80 to 1000 days, with emissions that put them in their own class. RV Tauri variables are yellow supergiants, 30 to 150 days.

But were there any short-period variables? There *had* to be...my Dad said so in the dream.

Things were good for a year, till 8th grade. Orik and I were 13, when things started to change between our two families.

One day Orik came over with a bruise on his face. He said it was no big deal — his dad had smacked him for saying an excuse-me word, starting with f. These days Jerry yelled more often. He'd tell us we were watching too much TV, and turn off our movie so he could watch CNN News. The news always made Jerry get pissed off at liberals, Mexicans, commies and fags. He said they were ruining the country. He said that fags were spreading that disease called AIDS. He said AIDS could leap through the air at you from a homosexual. "AIDS kills fags dead," he said. This was pretty scary. He also got pissed about pregnant girls in school...even liberal women like my Mom. My Mom got into hot political arguments with him. Both Jerry and Marilyn started ragging on my Mom about getting married again, so I could have a dad. They said it was morally wrong for me to grow up without a father.

"No thanks. Once was enough," said my Mom.

"You're my friend," said Marilyn, "but I have to say, that you're a truly godless woman."

"Ah, but I have the Goddess," my Mom shot back.

One weekend, Jerry and Marilyn dragged Orik off to something called a crusade. All weekend I moped around alone, missing him, helping Mom paint the kitchen. When they came back, Orik was depressed. All Jerry and Marilyn could talk about was the Rev. Edwin Dwight and his sermon, and how they had been born again. Jesus was going to save America from all the evil people in it.

"Did you get born again?" I asked Orik.

"My Dad said I had to."

After that, Jerry and Marilyn were always talking about how the family is the most important thing on Earth.

Jerry started coming home earlier, and pulled Orik away, into things that he wanted to do with him. "Quality dad time," he called it. All of a sudden they were dragging Orik to church. At first Orik argued, because church was boring and it meant that we couldn't spend half of Sunday playing Rescue. But he didn't get to have any say about it. So he went, looking scared in the dorky new grey suit they dragged him to the mall to get. His dad held him by the elbow, like cops do with prisoners on the TV news. His hair didn't lift up and down happily — it lay flat on top of his head.

These days Jerry was always trying to find out if Orik and I were doing sinful things with girls. Girls still seemed pretty dorky to me, though I was keeping an open mind. Jerry interrogated Orik for real, and gave him all the big no-nos about girls. But so far Orik didn't snitch to Jerry or Marilyn about our Rescue operations.

Sometimes I went to church with the Heasters, just to be with Orik. I was ready to do anything to stay with my best friend. Mom wasn't too thrilled with the idea of me going to church, but she was the big liberal and told me that I could decide what I believed in. I knew she had stopped going to church when my Dad died. But she never told me church was bad or good.

"You have to find your own way," she said.

"Okay, I will," I said.

Now and then Jerry and Marilyn tried to drag my Mom to church with them. My Mom said she didn't like their church because it didn't recognize the Goddess. Jerry and Marilyn said Goddesses are evil. They argued with Mom about it.

Sometimes I caught Orik hanging with girls. He confessed that his dad wanted him to do this, even though he was supposed to be careful about sex. At the 8th grade dance, the Heasters made Orik invite a girl. I went stag, and stood around frowning because I wasn't going to dance with some dumb female. So I just stood at the punch bowl and glowered at Orik who looked very cool in his blue jacket, dancing with his date, a girl named Donnala. The Heasters had met her family at church.

Now and then, the Heasters complained about my "pagan ancestor worship," and wanted me to stop doing it in front of Orik. "They mean your candles and your Dad's picture," my Mom growled. "You just do your thing, and don't listen to them." So they got around this by making Orik give me a picture of Jesus. Orik wanted me to tape it on the wall by my Dad's picture. So I did, just to make him happy.

The birth certificate investigation was still on. But now I did it alone. Sometimes, when Mom wasn't around, I snooped through her drawers, trying to find my certificate. Mrs. Danich told me that if I got Dad's right name, I could get the marriage certificate, his death certificate too, his voting records, his military record if he'd been in the military, even his criminal record if he had one. They were all public records, Mrs. Danich said.

I did find my Mom's birth certificate, which was stuck with some unpaid bills like she didn't care about it. Elizabeth Carey Heden, born November 2, 1955 in Lansing, Michigan. Father: Sven Heden, born in Menominee, Wisconsin. Mother: Sada LaTouf, born in Damascus, Syria. She was 22 when she had me. Like a spy, I had to leave everything exactly the way it was.

My birth certificate wasn't anywhere in the house.

"She probably keeps some papers in a safe deposit box," said Mrs. Danich. "That's where I keep mine. Or she lost it. Never mind — people lose birth certificates all the time. They're public records, so it's easy to get copies. Where and when were you born?"

"September 7, 1977. New York City...I think."

Mrs. Danich handed me the address of the Division of Vital Records office in New York City, and told me exactly what to say in the letter. I had to pay $15, so I saved my lunch money for a couple of weeks and got a postal money order because I couldn't write a check. We used Mrs. Danich's home address, since the answer letter couldn't come to my house.

Mrs. Danich had lots to say about birth certificates. "They don't always tell the truth," she said. "I have Native American blood in my family. Some Mormons married Indian people, because they are the descendants of the lost tribe of Israel. You wouldn't believe the white-washing on birth certificates that some Americans did, to hide the native blood in their families..."

It took almost a month. Finally, one day when I called Mrs. Danich from school, she said excitedly, "It's here."

"Open it and tell me," I said.

"This is your private business. Get over here, young man."

I had huge dramas getting to the Irvine library that day — missing a bus, getting stuck behind a car accident. The library clock was five minutes to closing when I ran in. Mrs. Danich had worry in her eyes as I ripped the envelope open. Inside was a Xerox copy. My hands were shaking as I unfolded that piece of paper where my destiny was going to be written in the stars.

It said I was born at Lenox Hill Hospital at 7:36 P.M. Under full name of child, it said: John William Heden. Mother's maiden name: Elizabeth Carey Heden. Mother's age: 22. Mother's birthplace: Michigan. Mother's trade or profession: Assistant coach.

Under Father, it said: Unknown. Under Legitimate, it was blank.

That fact on the paper crushed me like collapsing gravity...turned me inside out like an old star going into a black hole. My Mom had been one of those unmarried mothers that Jerry raved against. Maybe she had slept around, and didn't even know who my father was. Maybe the guy she called my dad just gave her some pictures so she could lie to me later.

I slumped in a chair beside my backpack.

Mrs. Danich guessed what I'd found out.

She cleared her throat. "Well, this may not mean what you think," she said gently.

"What?" I said in a voice from the black hole.

"Sometimes a mother has to hide the father's identity...if the parents are hostile. Adoption agencies sometimes change birth records too, especially the church agencies."

Or, sometimes the mother is a slut and doesn't know who the father is. Or the kid is adopted. I didn't want to be adopted.

As I trudged out of the library, Mrs. Danich said behind me, "Don't you give up now, young man."

The birth certificate almost went into the first trashcan I passed. But Mrs. Danich's words pulsed in my ears. So I carefully stuck the paper in a secret pocket in my backpack.

The next week, back at Mrs. Danich's keyboard on astronomy search, Orik was with me for the first time in a while. We finally found the secret wisdom that we had been searching the Universe for. The newsletter of the Variable Star Society had a little story about RR Lyrae stars…giant white stars that pulse on a short period. RR Lyrae was the first short-period star to be discovered.

"Wow. Look!" Orik said. "The period goes down to half a day."

A roaring sound filled my ears. I almost felt dizzy.

We shook hands. Then I hit "print" and when the download came out, I stuck it in the secret pocket of my backpack.

An Internet account at home would be cool. But Mom said I'd have to pay for it myself. Orik couldn't have one, because his dad said he already spent too much time at that evil computer in his room. Jerry didn't want a sissy computer wonk for a kid, he said. He wanted Orik to do sports, get out more. I could visit Mom's office at school and use her orange.edu account to browse the Net for free, but…she might see what I was doing.

That night we turned the telescope towards the constellation Lyra. Straining our eyes against light pollution and planes from John Wayne Airport, we tried to see RR Lyrae with the little 6-inch mirror. No luck. Finally Jerry made time and took us on a weekend stargazing trip in the desert. We had a perfect night, clear with low humidity. Around 10 P.M. we found the star, glowing white and steady. All night we watched, freezing, while Jerry snored in the campground. Our eyes ached with strain. Shivering with excitement, we watched RR Lyrae fade. By 4 A.M. we could hardly see it.

"There's got to be a variable at 60 seconds," I said.

It was a terrific night, and we traded 8th-grade graduation pictures, and swore to each other, "Till death," all over again.

This trip, it turned out, was the last time that Orik's dad did anything neat for us.

— 4 —

FEELINGS

Right after 8th-grade graduation, things got worse. It was June 1991 now.

The Heasters and my Mom and I went camping in the Sierras. We drove north for hours and boring hours, to a place called Tahoe, way in the mountains on a dirt road. Finally we came to a little lake. It was a weekday, so nobody else was there. The forest was awesomely beautiful, like the one in *Return of the Jedi*. I had never seen such huge trees — they had to be thousands and thousands of years old. There was a waterfall, coming down the mountain over lots of rocks — you could hear it from our camp. Right away I was sure that some planet somewhere looked like this, and wanted to explore with Orik. But his dad had him by the elbow all the time.

When we set up camp, Orik's dad and my Mom had a fight about whether Orik and I could have our own tent. Mom stood up for us. But Jerry said Orik wasn't a baby any more, so he should have his own tent. Orik didn't get any say about it. So the two of us felt depressed, and put up two tents. Then Orik came out of his tent wearing stupid-looking new plaid boxers, instead of his

36

rad black Speedo. His dad had made him cut his long, silky hair. He looked so dorky and humiliated that I had to laugh.

Orik turned red.

Jerry dragged the two of us in the water and we had to play water polo, while the two ladies put on lots of sun block and lay around in lawn chairs talking. My Mom's red bikini showed off her oily muscles — she looked like a bodybuilder. I had to admit she looked great compared to Marilyn, who was flabby and white in this one-piece suit with a skirt, like old ladies wear. On the picnic table was Marilyn's new Bible. It looked like the Heasters planned to do some preaching.

Jerry was pushing me and Orik to compete with each other.

"Hit hard," he yelled. "Hit fast."

"Harder! Faster!"

Orik was pissed at me, so we had an edge going with each other, and we churned the water to a frenzy. We were banging and scraping ourselves against the boat dock. I sprang a bloody nose, and ignored it as I leaped from the water to make a shot. Finally I missed a ball, and hit Orik by accident. I guess it really hurt him. Orik bit back the tears, and slugged me. I slugged him back. Jerry stopped the fight and directed our piss-off from each other to the game.

"You guys gotta be tough for Jesus," he urged. "Hit for Jesus."

"Jesuuuus!" Orik yelled. The ball exploded from his fist.

"Goddesssss!" I shouted because I knew it would piss Jerry, batting the ball back.

"Cut the pagan stuff," said Jerry.

"There's something called the First Amendment," called my Mom, "which gives my kid the right to call on any Deity he pleases while he's playing water polo."

Jerry muttered something about blasphemous liberals while we took a break, panting. My ears swiveled like radar dishes and started picking up the talk about me that the two women were having. Marilyn was passing my Mom the brownies she'd made, and saying, "...And Betsy, you've got to realize it's a problem."

"I don't have a problem right now," said my Mom, stretching in the sun, with cotton pads over her eyes. "I'm on vacation."

"Your son is looking more...er...grownup every day." Marilyn said "your son" now instead of "your kid." It was hard to believe that this was the neato Marilyn who made pies and took in a lonely latch-key kid from next door.

"This is a problem?" my Mom drawled, wiggling her toes.

"Girls are starting to...er...notice him."

What girls were talking about me behind my back?

"No problem, Marilyn," said Mom. "I'll hire him out as a model, and make $5000 a week. He can support me for a change."

My Mom liked to say stuff like this, to get Marilyn going. Marilyn took the bait, and scowled. "Seriously, Betsy..." She lowered her voice, but I could still hear it. "...You can't have him running around in skimpy briefs like that. He'll have every pedophile in Orange County running after him. If you don't have time to go shopping, I can pick up a pair of nice modest swim trunks at the mall, and you can pay us back. Jerry's really concerned."

"Okay, okay," Mom said, waving a hand like she was brushing away a fly. "Nothing over $10, though."

I was secretly feeling myself in the water. No kidding. The old red Speedo, that I had spent two summers in, was really tight now, and it showed whatever I had at 13. My Mom had told me about pedophiles. These are guys who get children into cars and take them away and do nasty sex things to them against their will. No pedophile was going to get me. I'd default him first.

A few minutes later, we took another break and I heard Marilyn going after more blood.

"...And we think you should be dating some good men. You've been carrying the burden alone for years. It's not godly for a woman to be alone. It's not godly for William to be without a father."

Now the two ladies had their own edge going — *ching, clang,* swords hitting together.

"Once was enough. William and I made it this far," my Mom said. "In a few years, he'll be flying the coop."

Marilyn reached for her Bible, opened it, and started reading. "Amen, said Jesus, a man shall leave his father and mother, and cleave unto his wife, and they shall be..."

Mom reached for her Pepsi. "Honey," she said over her shoulder, "there aren't a lot of good men to cleave to. I've met every wuss and wifebeater there is."

"Well, no wonder...if you go to those awful singles bars."

Mom cut across her like the last of the Barbarians, with her back to the wall. "I *never* go to singles bars," she said icily. "I work too hard, and I'm too deep in debt, to waste money on that kind of crap."

Now Marilyn was trying to smooth things over.

"I admit I'm lucky," she said, trying to glow as she gave Jerry the proud-of-my-husband look.

"Well," drawled my Mom, "if you want to keep him, don't encourage your single friends to go on the hunt."

Usually I liked the way Mom crushed Marilyn's religious stuff like a giant xyzium mining dredge. But this time, for some reason, Mom was pissing me off. Maybe it was the blank on the birth certificate, still haunting me. I made a big leap out of the water and stood there glaring at her, dripping wet. I wiped my bloody nose casually on my arm, like warning her that it could be her blood.

D inner was tense, especially with Jerry dropping a plate of hamburgers in the campfire.

Later on, the sky was dark and clear, and there were no city lights anywhere — perfect for a star party. But when I asked Orik to help me put the telescope together, he shrugged. "Not tonight," he said. "My dad wants me to read something." Later, I happened to see into his tent, and he was laying there looking at the Bible.

I tried to stargaze, but the old 6-inch mirror was really getting me frustrated. There was humidity in the air from the lake, and my optics kept dewing up. Back in my tent, I lay there feeling depressed.

N ext day started out even worse. Jerry took Orik away on a long hike. I spent the whole day roaming along the lake, bored and lonely. Maybe there was no other way to get to my Dad except die myself...I mean, really die. Maybe the default was death. Maybe I should drown myself in the lake. Forget astronaut school — just go to the stars the easy way, instead of putting myself through all this torture. On TV, *Unsolved Mysteries* said you get to be with the spirits of your loved ones...they are waiting for you when you get to the other side. My Dad would be as bright as the stars, and he would hug me.

I could make myself die and cross the default.

Breathing water and choking...would it be awful?

That night, while owls who-whooed in the forest, I dragged my telescope to a clearing above the lake. Conditions were drier, and perfect. It was the first time since Orik and I became friends that I did it alone. No serious observations...I just sat and stared at old friends, like the variable stars I already knew. At 10 P.M. La Superba was flashing red in the western sky. Near the North Star, I brooded over the first of the Cepheid variables to be discovered. Photographs were never as exciting as feeling the stars look at me with their fiery eyes, like they were trying to tell me something.

But none of them was that 60-second star.

The blinking lights of an airplane crossed my field, with shapes of passengers in the windows. Humans were boring. Finally I dragged the telescope back to camp, struggling with the flashlight and excuse-me'ing the day I was born.

Next morning, I woke up in my tent all alone again, with the new sadness and aloneness. I would have to drown myself all alone, with Orik not there.

On the shore outside, waves were sloshing on rocks. No familiar sounds of Lemon Street — no cars, kids' voices, rumble of skateboard wheels on the sidewalk. At Lemon Street, I had always woken up early, in the same room with Orik on weekends. I would get in his bed, or he got in mine, and we snuggled and played Rescue under the covers. It was always more high-tech at my Mom's house because we could steal her vaseline or hand lotion. We always jumped back in our own beds the minute we heard the first sound.

Shivery in my sleeping bag, I hugged myself with my arms, staring up at the ceiling of the tent, where swaying trees made cold, spooky shadows. The powerful cold tree smell seared my nose like turpentine. Those old trees were alive when my own Dad was alive. Could trees remember things? What did they remember about my Dad? Why did Orik's dad have to change and get religion?

Orik was leaving me, like my Dad did. He was probably awake now. Was he missing me? Or thinking about girls' hooters? He always rolled over, so that his head was right by mine, his breath on my face. His dirty-blonde hair looked so soft, that I wanted to touch it. But guys don't touch other guys' hair, except the barber and maybe when dads muss up their kids' hair. Otherwise you don't touch a guy's head, unless you want to take his power, and no real man lets anybody do that. Under the covers, his body felt different to my fingers...more muscle under his tits, stomach flatter, with abs showing, instead of the little-kid pot belly. He actually had some hair around his laser gun, which was bigger than mine. His eyes asked me to do more rescue.

"William!" Outside the tent, my Mom's voice shattered the magic.

"*William...*" Jerry made his voice faggy. "Why don't you give the kid a man's name? Call him Bill or something?"

It was a boring morning. The adults went fishing. Mom pissed off Jerry because he taught her how to cast better, and then she caught a bigger trout than he did. Orik and I were too itchy to sit still in a boat. We got so obnoxious that a miracle happened — our parents told us to get out of their hair and go somewhere together.

"But not far," Jerry frowned. "Be back in an hour."

"Watch out for poison oak!" Marilyn called as we walked away.

When we were into the first trees, Orik said quietly, "I'm sorry I was an excuse-me yesterday. My dad...uh...makes me do things that I don't want to do."

He actually caught my hand and squeezed it.

My heart went into supernova mode with happiness.

We raced through the woods, along a hiking trail through the great big trees. It was hard to get into the old magic, but we tried. We tried to make it like the church stuff had never happened. I talked to Orik about this being another planet. Pretty soon that old nervous, delicious, scary feeling was a buzzing blue sphere of energy around us. It was a while since we'd done any secret things, and we were starved for it.

Finally we skidded to a stop where the waterfall made white noise. The lake was Koolaid green, with deer drinking — they crashed into the brush when they saw us.

Here we found evidence that living beings had landed on this strange planet. There was a deserted camp, with interesting junk to look at. Deer horns with part of a bloody skull attached. Whisky bottles, bullet shells, a jar of vaseline, and a lot of empty condom packages plastered to the ground. Three magazines with pics of naked girls in weird positions, and some parachute cord, were also glued to the ground by rain. Nearby was a rotting boat dock, with a cattail swamp beyond it. I remembered cattails from Marysville, because they grow along the highways there where water runs off the rice fields.

"Jesus," I said, picking up the magazines. "It's creepy here."

"Don't blaspheme." He picked up the cords.

"You think they sacrificed a maiden and buried her in the woods?"

He pushed at the condom packages with his toe. I flipped through a magazine, staring at cosmic breasts. Was I destined for them?

"If they did, they had a slammin' good time with her first," he said.

"Hooters are boring," I said, giving him a manly shove. He picked up the vaseline. It stirred memories of deep black Saturday afternoons at my Mom's house, with parents away at the mall.

"Your Mom would kill you if she heard you say that."

"Let her try. I'm the Finder!"

He bent over to get another magazine, and I jumped him.

"Gotcha," I said. "Rescue time."

"No fair. We're on R & R."

"Fair. You let your guard down."

With that electric buzz of excitement around us, louder than ever, we looked for a safe place. Finally I tied his wrists behind his back with the cord, and marched him into the cattails, along a trail. I made him walk on his knees, enjoying the sight of those silly boxers slipping half down his butt, till we found a secret place where maybe deer slept at night, with cattails making a green wall around us. Dead leaves flattened into a nice bed. No trash here...everything nice and clean. A strong smell of water and plants drenched us.

I looked down at him. He lay on his side, awaiting my heroism.

He closed his eyes. "Uhh, maybe we shouldn't. They might come looking for us."

"We'll hear them coming," I said, pulling his boxers down, then tickling the bottoms of his feet. Naked and helpless, he started laughing and kicking at me, his eyes shut tight, his hair full of leaves. Even with his hair cut short, he looked so great. His laser gun was battle ready, full clip. That feeling was exploding inside of me, like a star going supernova, blowing shock waves of fiery hydrogen out into space.

"You like being tortured," I said as I kneeled between his knees and tickled him more, behind his knees, where I knew he couldn't stand it. "You want it. You want it bad."

"You can't intimidate me, Earthling." But he was choking with laughter.

"Tell me what your dad talked to you about."

"Never."

"The truth, you miserable asteroid eater."

Orik stopped laughing, even though I was now tickling the most sensitive spot in his groin. "He gave me a big talk about girls."

"Liar." I stopped tickling.

"How it's time for me to date...how most women are ho's and satan worshippers, so I've got to be careful."

"You've never done a girl," I said scornfully.

"Maybe I did Donnala after the graduation party."

Even with his hands tied, he suddenly wrapped his legs around me, and twisted me down, then rolled over on me. My heart melted like when I felt his naked weight on top of me.

"Now you're *my* prisoner," he growled.

But he didn't sound very convincing, and suddenly the space fantasy went away. He lay there half on top of me. The hot sun poured down on us. We wiggled our bodies around and I pulled my Speedo down so that we were spooned together. My arms were around him, and my classifieds were socked against his cheeks, where I liked having them most. Reaching into my jeans for my Swiss Army knife, I cut his wrists loose. Just one piece of cord trailed from his wrist. We closed our eyes in this magical comfort and closeness, with cattails hissing together in the breeze all around us. Far over the lake, some kind of bird made a loud whistling cry.

"Are you okay? Did the enemy hurt you?" I asked.

"No."

"I better examine you to make sure."

My hand was just going there when Orik suddenly said over his shoulder, "My dad says he's going to send me away to military school."

My stomach took a plunge. I twisted us over, so I was on top. I held him between my knees. "I won't let you go," I blurted.

"Oh Jesus." He closed his eyes. "Do you think I want to go?"

With parachute cord trailing from one wrist, he did something he'd never done before, which was actually put his arms around me and pull me down on top of him, so we were face to face. The feeling of my best friend's naked legs cradling me, and his arms sliding across my naked back, holding me so tightly, made an incredible rush of shivers go twisting over me. Our sweaty hair was plastered on our foreheads. Our lips were almost touching, warm breath puffing against each other's faces. This was getting close to the edge, a violation of the code. You aren't supposed to have feelings. You are supposed to be casual and nasty.

Eyes closed, he talked against my face. "If my parents send me somewhere, I swear I'll run away and come back."

"You swear?"

"I swear. We'll go to high school together, astronaut training, everything."

"You won't forget about our Mission?" Our cheeks were brushing together. For the first time I noticed the golden hairs on his upper lip and chin.

"I swore my oath to the Finder."

"Best friends forever?" I said, touching his hairy chin with shaky fingers.

"Forever," he whispered back. Our lips were barely touching.

"Till default?"

His legs were shivering. My legs were shivering. Our teeth were chattering. We hadn't done this for a month. "Till default," he whispered. His lips were trembling. "Ohhh," he breathed, as my hand did the prisoner inspection. His was bigger than mine now. We lay in each other's arms, faces together, working each other. Suddenly our lips were touching, wanting to crush together. Deep gulping breaths of relief and frustration. Lips almost touching again, mouths open. A kiss was going to happen. Guys only kiss girls, so I couldn't do that. What I could do, though, was give him all my body warmth, like I'd almost done before, but all the way this time, if I could figure out how. Maybe we would never see each other again.

My hand was just reaching for the jar of vaseline when we heard voices on the other side of the camp. They were Jerry's voice, our moms' voices.

An explosion of terror and hot sweat blew us apart. I dropped the jar. We were paralyzed.

Jerry was yelling, "Where in the heck are those darn boys?" My hands were fumbling at the parachute cord around his wrist.

"Jesus," said Orik. His eyes looked like an animal's just before it gets run over by a car. "Hurry! Jeez..."

I fumbled and tore at the knot. Where was my Swiss army knife? The voices were closer. I fumbled in the leaves, found my knife. The blade sliced his wrist and he bled.

"Jump in the water," I said past chattering teeth. The jar and cord went sailing into the cattails.

"Wh-why?" He was hauling his boxers back on.

"So it looks like we're playing, stupid. And we can wash off."

So we both took a deep breath, let out a kai-yai, and plunged through the cattails, and into the water with a huge splash. Diving to the bottom, I got sand and rubbed all the traces of anything off my hands. Orik was doing the same. We dived deep again and adjusted our clothes under water. When the adults came, we were splashing around by the dock, looking like what we hoped was normal, with wild battle yells.

"You were gone for two hours," Jerry barked from the dock.

"Sorry, dad...this place is cool," Orik called back.

"You disobeyed me. What were you doing?"

"Playing..."

"Out of the water! *On the double!*" Jerry screamed.

My hair stood on end. I had never seen Jerry Heaster scream like that. Veins bulged in his forehead. Shivering, Orik crawled out dripping. I could see how scared he was.

"How did you cut yourself?" Jerry growled.

"Dunno. Something sharp on the bottom."

Head bowed, Orik put on his shoes and let his dad march him dripping down the trail. From a distance, we could hear Jerry yelling about how obeying parents was the same as obeying the Lord. "When you forget about me, you forget about Jesus. I am the voice of Jesus in your world!"

My teeth were chattering. My heart thudded in my whole body.

Mom's hand squeezed my shoulder silently, letting me know she wasn't that pissed.

That night, alone in my tent, I listened to Jerry and Marilyn in their tent. Jerry was still interrogating Orik about what we were doing. Now and then, there was a smacking sound — Jerry hit him.

Now and then Marilyn mumbled something. So far, Orik had kept our secret. But maybe my buddy would crack under interrogation, and Jerry would go back up to the falls, and find the parachute cord and vaseline. In other words, the trip was ruined, and the Heasters said Orik had to be punished. They told my Mom that I was getting to be a satanic influence, and she needed to do something about me, or else.

Next morning Orik had a black eye. They packed up and went home.

Mom and I stayed for a few hours. She and I sat on a big rock by the lake, and she smoked a cigarette, which she seldom did. Ripples swished on the rocks. She tried to talk to me.

"What were you and Orik up to?"

"Nothing. Jeez, Mom. We were playing. Playing's a crime?"

"You don't have to lie to me." Her voice was quiet. "I was your age once. You were fooling around."

Hot sweat exploded over me again. She even knew the secret code words. "Mom, I swear..."

"Fooling around is normal. But Jerry is getting kind of crazy and controlling. So you have to be careful, okay?"

"Fooling around? Yuk!"

This was not about fooling around. It was about being a snitch.

"Have it your way." She stared across the lake.

Suddenly she said: "Where did you and I get off the track, huh? It started when we moved to Orange County. Are you mad at me about something?"

— 5 —

SECRETS BLOWN

That next week, there was a black hole between our houses. I wondered if the Heasters were going to let me and Orik even talk on the phone again. Pressures about Dad built up too. On Wednesday, which was Mrs. Danich's next full day at the library, I dragged myself to her office.

"You mustn't ever give up," she told me. "Fathers are the ones that most people search for. Did you know that? More than mothers, more than siblings, more than adopted parents. Mothers get to have custody...and fathers get left behind."

In her office, I sat and cried like an idiot. She thought my problems were totally due to my Dad, and gave me some Kleenex.

"Some new databases are coming online," she said. "It's getting easier to search for public records...births, deaths, divorces. We don't have the right last name, so that's a problem. But do you know where your dad was born...his birth date? And you're sure about his first name?"

"San Francisco...I think."

Mrs. Danich was a terror at the computer. Her tiny fingers, with wedding ring and diamond engagement ring, made the keyboard click like mine in the dream. She logged into vital records for San Francisco, and searched for Williams born in September 1953, because I wasn't sure about the day. As the printer spat paper, I thought how a search engine is like a telescope, because it looks into the past for data.

William Harry Bettleston
William Copley
William Marion Draves
William Harcourt Fallon III
William Bradford Gore
William Norwalk
William Bayley O'Brien
William O'Malley
William Harry Peterson
William Darrell Powers
William Sive
William Sorenson
William Tuttle Williams
William Yancey Zane II

"So any of these guys could be my Dad," I said.

"*If* you're right about San Francisco. We can search better if you know his mother's maiden name. Do you?"

I shook my head.

"Do you know where he died? Date of death? Death records are public too."

"He died before I was born." I was thinking how vague my Mom had kept things. And I hadn't asked enough questions.

"Then he must have died within nine months before your birth date. Just out of curiosity..." She tried death records for San Francisco, for the county in New York where Prescott had been — even Butte County, where Marysville was. Nothing.

"We need more information," she said.

Thursday, Orik called me. He was pissed at his parents. They had dragged him to the doctor for some dumb physical. I asked if he was okay. He said yeah, sure...offhand. Something to do with military school. No details. I got the feeling that the doctor visit had scared him and stressed him out. It was the first time he hid something from me.

Saturday, nothing was said about me coming over. That night, from my balcony, pretending to re-adjust my telescope, I saw Orik through his window, slumped at his Nintendo all alone, playing *Mortal Kombat*. My heart broke like a basketball hoop when a guy hangs on it too hard. I tried to stargaze, but there was too much smog. Saturday evening, I got brave and desperate, and asked the Heasters if I could go to church with them next day.

Jerry looked at me through the screen door like nothing had happened.

"Sure," he said. "If you behave."

"I'm a good kid," I said recklessly.

"No such thing as a good kid."

"We're going to the Irvine Bowl Crusade," Marilyn smiled.

When I told Mom, she shrugged. "So go. I know you miss your friend. And check out the religious thing...see what you think."

She drove off to the campus to do some file cleanup.

So I dragged out my own hated suit and tie. After a shower, I took a long look in the bathroom mirror. He-man enough? No. Stealing my Mom's leg-shaver, I worked my hair over till it was a radical buzz cut. Still not good enough. Those girlie eyes with the long lashes were still staring at me. Finding Mom's manicure scissors, I carefully cut my eyelashes back to virtual zero. In the mirror, the perfect cadet from the Realms of Death stared at me.

It was late, so I left the hair laying on the bathroom floor.

At the Irvine Crusade, I looked around — perfect cadet with laser rifle ready, deep in Pinhead Country. The stadium was crammed with 25,000 people who were saved, or wanted to be saved. Everybody was buzzing because the famous Dr. Dwight was preaching today. Palms and flowers made the stage look like it was Easter and Jesus was coming.

Next to me was Orik, in his grey suit and tie, looking stiff as an adult. Lately Orik looked so cool in a jacket. His eyelashes were just the right length, not girly. His skin was so clear that he looked like an ad for zit medicine. Today those slanty brown eyes were cold with a strange new defiance, almost cocky. I hoped it meant that he was holding his own under interrogation.

Next to Orik was Jerry, standing at attention. Then Marilyn in her white Sunday suit, all nicey-nice. But the family feeling was not around us anymore. Why did things have to change?

Suddenly the organ and choir blew the roof off. People were singing like crazy, holding their hands in the air. Marilyn leaned over and whispered that this meant they were receiving the Holy Spirit. Orik was pretending to sing but his eyes had done a missile lock on Donnala one row over. My heart sank. Was it possible that one more dad talk had cheated me of my best friend? Orik was giving her the look and she gave him the look back. So I reached under his jacket, where his parents couldn't see, and pinched his cheek.

"I will cleave to the old rugged — OW!" came out of Orik.

"Hey," Jerry hissed. "Eyes right, boys."

Then Dr. Dwight came marching to the podium.

This preacher's show fascinated me. He was weirder than an alien...jumped up and down, did funny dance steps, sweated like a basketball player, and yelled till his eyes bugged out. Today he was doing the teen sex thing. He got weepy over poor kids who were being corrupted by the Devil. He said the only sex that the Lord allowed was after marriage, with your opposite-sex partner. Dr. Dwight got in his chops at permissive parents like my Mom, and sex education, and filthy homosexual satanists who recruited kids and gave them AIDS. Teen sex was out of hand, he said. Especially here in our great godgiven state of California.

My mind drifted back to the lake. Nothing we'd ever done together stuck in my mind like that. Water on his face, shadows of cattails across his body, his smell, his whispers, his warm breath on my skin, were burned into my brain like new star photos on film at some big observatory. We'd left it unfinished somehow...I wasn't sure how. Now it would never be finished. Orik was discovering girls. Maybe soon he wouldn't be my friend.

Dr. Dwight was raving, leaping around the podium and punching the air.

"So I say! in the name of Jesus! that it's tiiiiime to take our children back from the Devil! In the name of Jesus! it's tiiiime to clean up California! Yes Lord! Hallelujiah! Our beautiful state needs a deeeeeeep religious *cleansing* in the fiiiiiire of the Holy Ghost!"

"Amen!" "Yes, Lord!" people yelled. Jerry and Marilyn and Orik had their hands in the air.

But some kids in the auditorium weren't yes-lording. Endless kid eyes stared at Dr. Dwight. About half of us, right down to the 10-year-olds, had already done some of the things he was screaming about. Or we'd tried them, anyway. All of a sudden I wondered if he was talking about the things that Orik and I did. That wasn't sex, was it? It wasn't supposed to be. Other Christian kids that we knew did them...at least the ones whose parents hadn't scared them too much.

I had figured out the way the whole secret system works. It was pretty simple. Every kid has his best friend or cousin or somebody else that he does guy stuff with. All you're doing is helping other guys out when they're horny, and girls aren't around. You keep it nasty, like the hazing and initiation stuff. You keep it fun, with lots of hee haws. If people get the idea that you *really* like doing it, if they catch you kissing a guy or something, then you're a fruit.

The fags that Rev. Dwight hated so much — they tell everybody in the world how much they like each other. People hate fags because they snitch on the secret stuff. They break the code of silence. But if you keep your mouth shut, and make like it's no big deal, you're not a fag. Obviously Orik and I were not fags. But right now, it seemed like I could feel every other boy's shivering in my own knees.

Orik wasn't eyeing Donnala now — just staring straight ahead. His eyes said that he had gone inside himself and was worrying.

When the preacher called people to come forward and accept the Lord Jesus, Jerry nudged me.

I desperately wanted to get myself back on track with the Heasters. But I couldn't do this. I shook my head.

"Come on, William," Jerry said. "Go for it."

"Time for you to give your heart to Jesus," said Marilyn.

"My Mom would kill me if I did it without asking her."

"Then ask her," said Jerry. "You can do it next Sunday."

After the crusade, we drove back to Costa Mesa. Orik and I sat silent in the back seat, each of us staring out our own window. If Jerry had cooled out, maybe I'd get to sleep over tonight. I wondered if I'd dare to get in Orik's bed. We were in real danger. If Jerry ever caught us, he definitely wouldn't understand. This was why I couldn't accept Jesus, even to please the Heasters. Some Pinhead preacher would get me to confess, and this would be snitching. Would my Dad snitch about anything? I didn't think so.

My Mom yelled out the kitchen window.

"William," she called, "come home for brunch."

"Spend more time with your mom," said Marilyn. "Maybe *you* can get her to come to church."

Jerry slapped my shoulder, and pushed me towards my house.

At his touch, my heart exploded with need. I was always so hungry for that dad to hug me and take me stargazing and throw me balls. There was that black hole in my world where a dad should have been. If a dad wasn't around, I knew from gossip at school that it meant divorce and the kids being pulled both ways by the divorce court. It meant a deadbeat dad who didn't pay child support. My Mom had tried hard to be a dad...I had to give her credit for that. But it wasn't the same thing. Women aren't men. Jerry had told me that God took my Dad for a reason. If God did that, then excuse-me God.

"Come back over later," Marilyn told me. "You can go to the mall with us."

My knees shivered again. The question about sleeping over was still in the air. I trudged home.

Mom was clinking in the kitchen. I trudged to my room to change. The sign had been on the door for a year now.

MISSION CONTROL — U.S.S. MEMO
AUTHORIZED PERSONNEL ONLY

Inside, my desk was a mess — old school papers, with my backpack on top. Posters and star charts and news pictures of astronauts plastered on all four walls. A bookshelf bulged with my video collection...just about every space movie that was ever made. I was hungry to be a war hero like Luke Skywalker...rescue my Dad, save democracy, save the Universe, whatever. Nobody cares if a war hero has zits or girly eyelashes. Movie heroes are always saving women's lives too, but I wouldn't go that far. Probably I'd throw the woman to the enemy, to distract them, and save my buddy's life instead. Except my Mom — I'd save her, I guess. In four more years, I'd be 17 and I could enlist.

Elite forces, definitely — Air Force or SEALs. From there, I could get myself into the astronaut program. That was years from now. I counted them up. Ten years, maybe. Forever. But by then, they'd have the photon accelerator so we could go into deep space. Maybe I'd have to save Orik too — save him from his dad and the dork military school.

In the bathroom, my blood ran cold. A new toothbrush sat on the counter. Mom had found the hair mess.

I threw my church clothes on the bathroom floor too, and jumped into jeans and T-shirt and Nikes. Pulling on my baseball cap, I stopped at the dresser and looked at my Dad's framed picture. Billy looked like a dressed-up jock too — blazer and tie. Did he hate those clothes as much as me? I leaned my elbows on the dresser.

"Why didn't you wait around for me?" I asked the picture. "You know...you were dumb to be in an accident with a gun. Everybody knows you have to be careful with guns."

My Dad just kept grinning. Beside him was the Jesus picture. The fact was, Jesus looked faggy, especially compared to those tired astronauts in the news pictures. Even the lady astronauts looked more jock. This Jesus wasn't a tough guy who could last three hours on the cross. I couldn't see giving my heart to a pansy.

Mom was in the kitchen, putting out some low-fat bakery stuff.

"Hi, Mom," I said.

"Hi, William," she said, all fakey and cheerful.

We sat down, and fished goodies right out of the bakery box, and tried to have one of those friendly family brunches you see on TV...the kind Mom and I used to have. She was in a good mood, so I thought I'd try to interrogate her.

"Hey...William is dorky. Didn't I ever have a he-man nickname?"

"William was your dad's name."

"I know, I know. But people don't..."

"William's a good name. William the Conqueror. William Tell."

I didn't have a clue who those people were. "Come on...didn't anybody ever call me Bill...Will...Chuck...whatever?"

Her back was turned, as she poured herself a mug of coffee. "Somebody used to call you Falcon."

"Who?" I asked.

"A friend of your dad's," she said, not looking at me. Instantly she was weird. Mom always got weird when I brought up the past.

"Why?" I asked, feeling a chill of excitement.

"Oh...when you learned to walk, you swooped around and grabbed things. He said that's how falcons hunt."

Suddenly I was seeing through a dark nebula, into a new vista of our galaxy's center, bright with massed stars. "Who was this guy? A biologist or something?"

"No."

"You dated him?"

She laughed, and headed for the refrigerator. "No. He was just a friend."

"What was his name?"

"Don't interrogate me." She took skim milk out of the fridge.

"I just want to know. What's the big deal?"

"His name was Harlan." She poured milk in her coffee mug.

"Harlan *what?*" It was really torture, dragging it out of her.

"Don't start in." She put the milk back in the refrigerator.

My stomach started feeling like an ulcer. "Why don't you ever talk about Dad? Tell me stuff about him?"

As she got the pot from the coffeemaker and poured more coffee, her hand shook. "Lookit, William. You have to understand — that whole thing was terrible." Her voice filled up.

"But you don't have a right not to tell me! I can handle it! I want to handle it!"

She stomped back to the cupboard with the glass coffee pot. Suddenly she spun around, and yelled:

"I do have a right not to tell you! I'm not your slave! And while we're on the subject, if you leave a mess in the bathroom again, I'm going to kick the excuse-me out of you."

For some reason, this pressed my nuclear-strike button. Everything hidden inside me went off like a star going nova. I got up and shoved her, forgetting that she had the glass coffee pot in her hand. It was the first time I'd ever done anything like that to my Mom. It took her by surprise. But she recovered fast and flung away the pot so neither of us got splashed by hot coffee. The pot crashed in a corner and broke. Right away she was in fighting stance, hands up. I thought aikido made me her equal, considering that I was a guy and she was only a woman. So we faced off, like Frank Dux and the big Asian bad guy in *Bloodsport*. For some stupid reason, I thought that she'd back off...be a bleeding-heart liberal mom and go non-violent.

So I made a movie-type karate move. She gave me a little push with one finger that flung me back. I charged her like a Klingon. Mom made two little moves that slammed me down on the kitchen floor. It was incredible how fast it happened — how hard that floor was.

"Come on," she yelled. "You wanna beat up your mother? Give it a try. What'sa matter? Afraid of your little old Mom?"

When I finally crawled to my feet, she'd gone upstairs. All shaky, I left the kitchen with brown puddles and broken glass all over the floor. Grabbing my backpack, I was out the door.

Next door, the Heasters piled us into their car, and we took off for the mall. I sat in my corner of the back seat with my butt stinging and my elbow throbbing. I wasn't going to tell them what happened. The nickname was ringing in my head. *Falcon, Falcon.* It was a neat name.

"What were you and your mom fighting about?" Jerry asked.

"The whole neighborhood could hear you yelling," Marilyn added.

"I was...uh...on her case about telling me more about my Dad," I whispered.

"You didn't ask her about Jesus, huh," Jerry probed.

"Didn't have time."

"Your mother should get married again. We've said it a thousand times," said Marilyn.

She gave Jerry the look. He grinned and give her the look back. She and Jerry didn't make any secret about having a good sex life. Sometimes, when I had slept over with Orik, we could hear through the wall how the two of them were going at it.

As we pulled into the mall parking lot, Jerry said, "Look at that! There's a homosexual kid."

"You can see the Devil in his eyes." Marilyn shivered, like the Devil made her feel cold.

It was Alberto, the faggy Mexican kid from Costa Mesa High, walking with an older boy. He wore thick glasses now, but I would know the long curls and girly face anywhere. To me, his eyes looked more like a sad puppy's than Satan's eyes. But maybe the Heasters could see the Devil better than me.

"His parents ought to knock the Devil out of him," Marilyn said.

"Oh, I'm sure other boys are doing that," Jerry said. "Real boys."

He looked at us like he was giving us a hint.

While Jerry and Marilyn went shopping, they let us go off to do our thing. They said to meet them in the ice cream shop.

It was getting dark. Orik and I reconned the parking lot, up and down the rows of parked cars. We were silent and wary in our star caps, which we wore bill front because we didn't want to send the message that we were cool. The floodlights came on, so we walked with our shadows going every which way. Our parents knew a little about the stuff that went on here, so they'd always told us never to talk to strangers or accept rides. But they didn't know the half of it. While the white kids were shoplifting, the black and Mexican kids were hanging around a lowrider car with a boom box, drinking and toking.

Orik and I stayed away from them all. Anyway, we had our own mission to carry out. Good soldiers don't drink or do drugs.

Sweeping the dark alley behind the stores, we finally located the swishy kid. He and his buddy were climbing out of a dumpster.

"They've probably been doing it doggy in there," I said.

Orik always thought about things. "How do you know? Maybe they were just dumpster diving."

I was always the action guy. "Come on. Let's get 'em."

We charged the two boys. The older one ran off down the alley, ditching his friend.

Then Orik and I cornered Alberto against the back wall of Thrifty's and got ready to kick him around pretty good. All the rage and edginess rolled up in me. No dad. A mom I was on the outs with. My life endangered. The Devil inside me. I grabbed a broken broomstick out of a dumpster, and was going to whack Alberto with it. Alberto knew what was coming, because he remembered us from the boys' bathroom at school. All of a sudden he just went down on his knees.

"Prepare to die, sissyfag Earthling," I said.

"Please," he said. "Please don't."

A puddle grew around his knees. He was so scared of us that he peed his pants.

Suddenly I had this strange feeling that my Dad was watching me. His eyes were on me, and he wasn't happy with what we were going to do.

"Jesus," Orik said with disgust.

Our victim was crying and blubbering. It made us want to puke. "Come on," I said to Orik, "let's get out of here."

I threw away the broomstick. As we walked back, Orik and I didn't look at each other.

At the ice cream shop, Jerry and Marilyn were looking at menus. "Did you run into that fag?" Jerry asked.

"Yeah, we chased him out of the mall," I lied.

"Yeah, he won't be sissyfagging around here," Orik added.

"Good for you," said Jerry. "Banana splits all around."

The Heasters feasted us warriors. But halfway through the whipped cream and chocolate sauce, came the real reason why Orik's parents took me to the mall. "We want you to talk to your mom about things," said Marilyn. "Sometimes a child can soften a mother's heart. If it comes from you, she'll listen."

"Your mother needs to come to the Lord," Jerry said. "She needs to find a good man, and get married again. She needs to stop working, and let her man take care of her, so she can devote herself to you and the Lord."

The spooky thing was, Jerry had vibed how much I wanted my Dad. But he had the wrong idea about it. Ice cream was sticking in my throat.

"Mom *is* devoted to me."

"The Bible says when a man died in the old days, his brother married his wife..."

"*Wives,*" added Marilyn.

"Keep out of this, woman. I'm the one who teaches." He glared at her, then looked back at me. "A brother took over the deceased man's family, so that the children would have a father of the family blood. This is what God wants. Your mom is acting like a man, and she's trying to do it all herself. It's not right."

People talking, dishes clattering, was suddenly deafening me. Tears surged up, blurring them all — even Orik, who was looking uncomfortable. "I don't want another dad," I said. "I just want the one who died."

"Well, your dad is with Jesus, or he's in hell if he was a wicked man, so you might as well..."

"My Dad wasn't wicked." I almost got up.

"What I mean is," Jerry said hurriedly, "that you can't bring him back. You have to accept God's will. You have to stop this ancestor worship of yours, and move on."

My sundae was melting. I didn't eat another bite. Orik didn't either. The Heasters argued with me, but I didn't give in. Finally the ice cream parlor was closing, so we had to leave.

On the way home, I finally blurted, "It's going to be late...can I sleep over?"

Jerry didn't even turn his head. The lights were streaming past us on Newport Boulevard. "Sleeping over is for little kids. Both of you are men now."

The universe was collapsing me into a black hole.

When I got home, I was panicked, and called Orik from our house. "What's your dad's problem? Did you tell him stuff about...us?"

"No. I swear..."

Suddenly the phone was disconnected. I raced out to my balcony, where my telescope was covered in plastic. Lurking there in the dark, I could hear Jerry talking to Orik in a loud voice. Orik was saying, "No...I didn't..." A cracking sound — Jerry had hit him. Crack, crack! Thud...something fell. A horrible feeling came over me, that Jerry was still asking what happened at the lake.

Mom was at my door, in her bedtime sweats. Her bedroom light was on. Now there was slamming and banging coming from Orik's room, through the open window. Orik was really getting it this time. "No, dad...please...noooo..."

"You'd better tell me what's going on..." *Crash, crash.* "The Bible says that a disobedient son shall be taken out and stoned by the priests..." *Bang, thud...*

"Oh, Goddess..." Mom said, listening.

I leaned against my desk, trembling all over. Through the open window, Orik was still screaming. Marilyn was yelling at Jerry. More thuds and crashes. "...Call the police...have that little son of Satan up on some kind of charges..." Jerry was raving.

"Are you crazy?" Marilyn screamed. "The doctor didn't find anything. The whole neighborhood is going to hear..."

"Screw the neighbors!" Jerry roared. "God is on my side! I'm taking control of my family again!"

Mom stared at me. "What happened with Jerry now?"

My lips were shivering so much, I could hardly talk.

"We were at the mall, and Jerry gave me this big lecture about how I was supposed to talk to you about Jesus, and getting married again, and I wouldn't. And then I asked if I could sleep over...Jerry said no...then I called Shawn up..."

"I told you Jerry is nuts," she said. "How come you don't cool it for a while, huh?"

"He's hurting Shawn."

Suddenly there were flashing red lights outside — a black-and-white police car through the trees.

"Oh no," Mom mumbled, "a neighbor must have called the police. Oh Goddess, now the big drama."

"You beat me yesterday," I said to her.

"Not like Jerry. You went for me," she said on her way out of the room. "And I didn't hurt you, did I?"

Two officers were standing at Orik's front door. Not high-tech and ominous looking cops, like on TV. One was fat, one was old. Jerry pissed them off by telling them they had no right to meddle in his family business. So they handcuffed him and made him sit in the patrol car. Then the old one went into Orik's house, leaving the fat one with Jerry. After a while, they came over and knocked on our door. Mom was the Barbarian warrioress in a fight — always cool, not your typical hysterical female that you see in the movies. She'd gotten dressed, pulled herself together, and she was polite.

"What kind of charges?" she asked.

They explained. I felt a sick hollow terror. It would be all over the school now.

My Mom was outraged, but she kept her voice quiet.

"If my kid was 20, sure...But 13? They're the same age, for chrissake. The boys have been friends for years...with the knowledge and consent of the Heasters, I might add. Shawn's two inches taller and a green belt in karate. If my kid made unwelcome advances, and Shawn had a problem with it, he could break my kid's neck. I'm more worried about what Heaster did to *his* kid. He was beating him bad. Is Shawn okay?"

The officers asked to talk to me, with my Mom present.

I looked in their eyes, like you're supposed to do.

"I didn't do anything like that to him," I said. "Yuck!"

The cops talked to neighbors, who told them Jerry beat his son. Then they went back to Orik's house. Their vibe said how bored they were, being dragged out in the middle of the night because two little kids might be fooling around, or one kid might be getting thumped. They had more important stuff to do, like bust people for pot and prostitution and so forth. This was just family stuff, punish-your-kid stuff, no broken bones or anything. You could see they didn't care. Marilyn was shivering on the front walk in her bathrobe, while the cops took the handcuffs off Jerry. All of them were lit up in the searchlight from the patrol car. Neighbors were watching across the street, while I listened out the window.

Finally, the sergeant looked in our door.

"The kid's a little bruised up. But he says he fell. He and the wife won't make any allegations against Heaster. Have a nice day."

The cops left.

At midnight, Mom was on the phone with some lawyer that she knew well enough to drag him out of bed. "John," I heard her say, "I'm really sorry I've been out of touch, but...I've got big problems here...." While she talked, I watched Orik's bedroom window with my old submarine binoculars, and finally saw Orik. He had bruises on his arm and face, and another black eye coming.

At one in the morning, Marilyn came through the gate with T-shirts and the star-wheel book that I'd left in Orik's room. She knocked on the door, and gave them to my Mom. Her voice was quivery.

"We want Shawn to have his own life from now on," she said.

Jerry yelled at Marilyn through the window. "Tell her to keep her evil spawn away from our son, or we'll see her in court."

"Go right ahead," my Mom yelled back. "You stay away from *my* kid. And if you keep beating *your* kid, somebody, maybe even me, is going to call Children's Services."

"Will you people kindly shut up?" a neighbor lady screamed. "Tomorrow's Monday and we need to get some sleep!"

"Yeah," the neighbor's husband roared, "or we'll call the National Guard!"

Marilyn ran back in her own yard, and slammed the gate shut.

— 6 —

OPERATION EXTRACTION

Next morning, I woke up around ten, feeling like I'd had the worst bad dream of my life — only I could remember it. The whole neighborhood probably knew. Through the open window, I thought I saw Orik inside his house. Later on, his parents got in the car and left. I dialed their number, and it took 20 rings for him to answer. His voice was shaky...he'd been crying.

"There's a lock on the phone now, so I can't call you any more," he said. "I'm not supposed to talk to you."

"Are you okay?" I asked.

"Dad's really mad," he whispered. "I'm not supposed to leave the house. You and me gotta go undercover for a while."

"Hang in there, bro. Remember what you swore."

"I remember."

"If things get bad, give me a signal. Like, put your cap in your window. If I see it, my Mom will have your dad arrested."

"Finder, please don't do that."

"He's being mean."

"Yeah, but he's my dad," Orik said.

"Hey, listen...he doesn't have the right to beat you up..."

"Oh-oh, I think I hear our car." Orik hung up on me.

In the kitchen, Mom was drinking a bottle of carrot juice, with her papers everywhere. She was getting her fall track program ready. Always the papers from school, even with drama going on. I ate a peanut butter sandwich at the counter, still wanting to piss her off because she'd hit me the day before. So I bragged about what Orik and I did to Alberto at the mall.

She put her pencil down. "Goddess, William...did you hurt him?"

"Nah. We were careful."

"I like how you define careful. His parents could have you arrested!"

"Whoa...everybody does boys' bathroom stuff to him."

Mom looked shocked. "When?"

I told her about what happened at school.

"You and Shawn helped them?" she asked.

"Not really. We...uh...watched."

"Do Jerry and Marilyn know about this?"

"Jerry...like...kind of told us to."

Mom stared at me. It was hard to know what she was thinking. Finally she put her face in her hands. "Sacred Goddess...."

"Fags aren't people," I yelled. "Jerry said they...they're filthy animals and they throw AIDS through the air."

"What the hell does he know about fags?"

"Why are you sticking up for fags?"

We got in a yelling match. I threw her papers everywhere. "If you do karate on me again," I yelled at her, "I'll get you for it. You'll never know when it's coming. And you lied to me."

"What...?"

"You never went to Prescott College. You never married my Dad. I looked it all up. You lied!"

The incriminating Xeroxes and printouts came out of my backpack, and flew all over her. Then I threw some dishes and coffee mugs at the wall. Mom picked up my investigation papers and stared at them. Finally she just left her own papers laying around, and went in her home office, and locked the door. Probably so I couldn't get to her. After that, I felt totally retarded, and did the good boy thing, cleaning up the mess. My shaky fingers smoothed her papers, and put my own papers back in the backpack.

Later on, Mom talked behind the door, on the phone again. I lurked at the keyhole. She was complaining to Auntie Marian about how the perfect neighbors had turned into Pinheads...what a fascist Pinhead monster I was turning into. Disgusted, I flung myself on the sofa and watched *Return of the Jedi* for the 2500th time, but lost interest after a while, and turned it off. For some reason, hot tears kept running down my face. Space war and ships going *ka-boom* didn't seem real, compared to Jerry's punches and slaps landing on my best friend. My substitute dad — a Pinhead after all. Marilyn too.

A few hours later, somebody in a grey Toyota 4 Runner dropped Auntie Marian off. She and my Mom got the Rambler and went somewhere for dinner, obviously to talk about me. I lay around my room, not knowing what to do. Make plans for the new mirror? Boring. After eleven, there were voices in our back yard. I lurked by the hall window to listen. Auntie and Mom were sitting down there in the dark on two lawn chairs, talking.

"...Carrying this thing alone for years," Auntie Marian's voice said. "Are you finally going to let the family help you carry it?"

What family?

My Mom cried. Probably Auntie Marian was patting her hand.

"So," my aunt was asking, "what *have* you told William?"

The sound of my Mom blowing her nose.

"As little as possible. But William's not buying it. Questions, questions. If I loved his dad, (sniff) why don't I have more photos around? Do I have his love letters? Where is he buried? Could he visit the grave? I told him Billy was cremated...the truth, of course. I also told him I don't want reminders around. But...(sniff) he's been looking for old records. He tried to get his dad's death certificate...I'm not sure where it's filed...Canada, I think."

Why Canada? Did my Dad go there to escape going in the Army? Jerry said some sissy guys did that — he hated them for it.

"If you keep the truth from him," said Auntie Marian, "it's going to blow up in your face. And he will hate you for it."

What was my Mom lying about? I felt faint.

"I do have a problem, don't I? But not the one Marilyn thinks

I've got. And the worst thing is — William is so worked up about it that he's gotten scary."

"What do you mean?"

"The other day he shoved me. Things escalated...I had to defend myself."

"When I was a kid, the idea of shoving your Mom..." Marian sounded shocked.

"Hey, God, are you listening? Why did You send me a boy?" Mom was probably glaring at the light-polluted sky. "I could kill You for this, God."

"A girl child would want the truth too. Children need to know about their parents. I don't understand why you won't tell him. Maybe you should see a therapist."

"Therapists...bah. I know damn well what the problem is. Seeing Billy killed, knowing it could happen again. Freaking out over Harlan. Losing Marla. The isolation I've lived in. Debt, burnout...."

Seeing my Dad *killed*? And who was Marla? Her sister?

"...Just excuses," my aunt said.

"I used to be able to talk to William — about life, even about his body. But now this wall is between us. It started with him spending so much time next door. And I know he needed a friend. But somehow...."

Mom sighed again.

"He's always been hyperactive...lately he's been depressed...and he's gotten really weird about this astronaut thing. Whenever he's not with Orik, he's alone in his room. He has accidents...I feel like he's kind of bordering on, well, suicidal..."

I didn't recognize my heroic self in the way she talked about me.

"...Maybe *he* needs the therapist," Auntie said.

"Ha! He already drove his school counselor and one cut-rate therapist crazy. He's not what you'd call cooperative."

"Do you think he's..."

"That's the *least* of my worries, right now."

Was I what?

"Betsy, will you let me tell Harlan what's going on?"

Even from the second-story window, I heard my Mom sigh.

"I give up. Okay. Just don't give him my phone number till I say it's all right. We have to handle this situation first."

"Let's go in, honey. You're shivering...."

"I've got the guest room all ready for you," Mom said.

In a leap, I was back in my room, going into shock. What had really happened to my Dad? Why all the cover-up? Harlan again, the old friend who called me Falcon. Who was he, that he was important enough to tell? As I lay trying to go to sleep, the other single bed was empty, with a bar of moonlight across it. Was Orik getting used to not seeing me — doing himself and thinking of girls?

Next morning, Mom was all nice and smiley. "Aunt Marian's inviting us to Malibu for a few weeks," she told me.

"Boring."

Mom oozed with niceness. "Look, William — we need to get away from the negative vibes next door. Spend some time together. I'm uptight...you're uptight. It doesn't have to be this way."

What if Orik made the signal, and I wasn't there to see it?

"There's no kids there. It'll be way boring," I said.

"Well, we're going," she said. "So pack. Take your telescope and everything. We'll leave around seven this evening."

"Kick it. I won't go."

"You're thirteen, and you'll do what I say."

"If you try to make me, I'll run away. I'll go to court and ask somebody else to adopt me."

"Anybody who adopts you will be sorry," she retorted.

That afternoon, I was alone in our front yard, kicking my basketball mindlessly against the picket fence, and watching for Orik's signal, when that shiny grey 4 Runner pulled into our drive again. A tough-looking old Mexican dude got out. Or maybe he was Asian. He strolled through the picket gate into our yard, looking around. Was this Harlan? He was not much taller than me, maybe five foot ten. His cold grey eyes checked out the Heaster house, then the neighborhood, then me. He must have spent the night at a motel. I stood under the old pepper tree, staring back at him. Something about the sun and shade playing over him, like live camouflage, made a chill go churning all over me, big as a storm on Jupiter.

Marian leaned out the door. "Hi, Chino."

"Hi," he said. He didn't smile, he just kept looking around.

So this wild-looking dude knew my aunt. She didn't fit with him, in her pink pantsuit and pearls. She looked like Rev. Dwight's wife.

"William," said Marian, all nice and smiley. "This is an old friend of mine...Chino Cabrera."

I stared at Chino, still feeling that chill. His face was an alien warlord's out of some sci-fi movie. He had the coldest, tiredest eyes I'd ever seen, and a long ponytail down his back. His face was light coffee color and clean-shaven — no Mexican mustache. He wasn't dressed funky or cholo — just jeans, plain T-shirt, old jungle boots, no belt. But the jeans actually had a crease.

"Hi, Chino," said my Mom, coming out. "Thanks for coming."

So my Mom knew Chino too. Maybe he had known my Dad.

Chino didn't say anything. He walked past me, and looked inside the door, scoping the house.

"William, are you packed?" she asked. "We need to go."

Suddenly I knew that Chino was there to help them make me go. Mom was afraid of me now. Through the living-room picture window, I could see into the Heasters' kitchen. They were eating dinner. Jerry and Marilyn were all nice and smiley and passing dishes of food around. The perfect TV family scene, except Orik had a Bandaid on his forehead, and he was only trying to smile. Donnala was there — they'd actually invited her. I wondered if Orik had put his hand up her skirt already.

Chino's hand clamped on my shoulder. Of course I tried to fight him with my junior high aikido. But there was not going to be a humonguous movie fight that wrecked the house, because this guy knew some black stuff. He put a little squeeze on my shoulder, and I wilted. Then he pushed me up to my room, glanced around at the astronaut posters and star charts.

"Pack," he said.

I decided to play for time and did what he said. I'd escape later, when his guard was down. Clothes, my Dad's pictures, a new candle, got jammed in my backpack. Chino helped me break down the telescope and pack it. Going downstairs, I could see Orik through the hall window and his bedroom window, and decided to fall down the stairs to delay things. If I broke a leg, they'd have to let me stay home. But just as I started to fall, Chino's hand grabbed my arm, clamping on it like he was a robot with no feelings. I banged my knee and shoulder, and that was all.

Outside, it was dark. Chino's merciless hand propelled me towards the 4 Runner

Jerry came out. "Where are you going?" he wanted to know, in a Rev. Dwight kind of voice.

"We need to be away from you guys for a while," said my Mom.

"You're running. You know he did something evil to my son."

"No, I don't know that. Neither do the police."

"You'll be hearing from our lawyer."

"Lawyer my ass!" she yelled. "I just heard about you teaching Assault and Battery 101 at the mall! Thanks for encouraging William to beat up other kids."

"You'd better come talk to our pastor. There are clinics where a boy like yours can get help. If you don't cooperate, we will definitely call the district attorney's office."

"Go right ahead," said my Mom. "You can explain to the district attorney how you battered your own child, and I'll be a witness against you."

Marian's arm shot at Jerry. "Here's my card. You know where to find us," she said.

"Sure, Councilwoman," said Jerry, "we'll charge you with aiding and abetting."

Still holding me, Chino slid between Mom and Jerry — they were yelling around him. If Chino and Jerry got into a fight, Chino would have to let me go, and I'd run for it. But Jerry looked into Chino's nasty grey alien eyes, and he decided not to mess with the alien warlord. Orik had slipped out the back door, and was staring through the wire fence at me. Each of his sad elf eyes was framed by a square in the wire. Now he was a prisoner for real.

Marian got behind the wheel, Mom on the passenger side. Chino pushed me in the back seat and got in beside me. My knee and shoulder throbbed. Marian snapped the power-locks on. I was a prisoner, too. The shiny 4 Runner screeched out of the driveway, leaving my Mom's dusty Rambler locked in the garage.

Suddenly Orik climbed over the fence and ran out in the street after us. His mouth moved like he was yelling "FINDERRRRR!" in some terrible screaming voice. He ran after us, hair lifting wildly. His dad ran after him, and grabbed at him. Orik dodged, fell down on the street, rolled and got up. He was limping now. He was getting smaller and smaller. His dad caught up with him, grabbed his arm, and smacked him across the face a few times.

Quicker than Chino, I hit Marian's head from behind. She lost control and the 4 Runner swerved and spun and almost hit another car. While Chino lunged forward to grab the wheel, I slammed against the rear window, to break through the glass and get to Orik's rescue. Then everything went dark.

When I opened my eyes again, Chino had a cloth against my forehead. The rear window was broken. My head throbbed and my face was sticky. A lighted freeway sign went by in the dark. Now we were going north towards L.A.

"You can't do anything for your buddy right now," the alien warlord said, lasering me with those grey eyes of his that looked like pure polished xyzium. "So pull yourself together and be a man."

Deepest fields of the universe were not as lonely for me as that ride up the 405 freeway. My head throbbed where I hit it. I was cold as nails, I'd tasted blood and death, lost my friend in combat, and been close to my Dad for a couple of minutes. My aunt was driving with one hand, and patting Mom's hand with the other hand. My Mom was crying. They were all talking about me like I was not there.

"He was going to fall down the stairs on purpose," said Chino.

"Solid gold jailbait. Thirteen, looks like eighteen. High IQ, and out of control. That's what I get for keeping him off Ritalin. And I've tried so hard."

Chino sat easy in his corner. Even in the dark cab, he looked so Asian. Why did he have grey eyes and look Asian? His hands, spread quietly on his strong thighs, had knife scars on them. His arms were scarred. Did he belong to the Mexican Mafia? No, he felt military, somehow. But he wasn't quite faster than me. He was old, and I'd almost gotten away from him.

"You always kidnap kids?" I said.

"Every day."

His voice was deep and hoarse, like a rock singer who strained his vocal cords. He didn't have any Mexican accent.

"I suppose you're some hot dog detective?" I wanted to know.

"Not even close," he said.

"You're a merc."

He didn't answer. My Mom was still crying in the front seat.

"William," she said, "when we get to Malibu, we're going to talk about your dad. It was…complicated."

"So…I was right, huh. Dad was a criminal or something?"

"Be patient with me, okay?"

"You start talking now!" I demanded.

Chino frowned. "Your disrespect for your mother makes me want to puke. Why are you dissing her?"

Something in his voice sent a chill down my back. So I shut up, and just stared out the window. The lights of Orange County and L.A. and Santa Monica streamed by in the dark, like fake stars in TV shows about space. In Malibu, at a sign that said "Caballo Canyon," we turned off the Pacific Coast Highway, and went winding up a dark canyon. This was really a primitive district — a deer jumped across the road in front of the 4 Runner.

Auntie Marian's house was a white mansion big as the excuse-me Pentagon. It stood alone on a high hill, in a loneliness of brush above the canyon. Auntie mentioned that the mansion farther up, with all its lights on, was Axl Rose's house. A quarter mile below was the Pacific — as we got out of the car, we could hear the surf. Auntie had mentioned how my uncle Joe bought that house. He had owned a computer company, which didn't exist any more. Two years ago, Uncle Joe had died of a heart attack. So my aunt had all kinds of money. She served on the Malibu city council, was bored with local politics and wanted to do bigger things. A Mexican lady, Nancy Perez, lived there with her as a housekeeper and office helper.

Marian put me in a room between Chino's room and Mom's room. Even after I stood my Dad's picture on the dresser, and lit the candle in front of it, I didn't like the room. Everything in it was fancy and breakable, nothing comfortable to slam around on. But there was a little balcony, where I set up my telescope. After everybody went to sleep, I sneaked to one of Marian's fancy phones and called Orik. Jerry answered, and I hung up. Next time I tried, Orik answered. His voice was shaky, and he really sounded strange.

"Did your dad hit you again?"

"No."

"I can tell he did." My fist was clenching on the phone.

"He didn't." His voice shook more.

"Get a pencil and write down my new number, and memorize it, then get rid of the paper."

"Okay."

I gave him the number.

"But I can't go on making my dad so mad. Anyway...what happened was all your fault," he said.

"My fault?"

"You were the one who wanted to do Rescue."

"You didn't say no."

"And now he won't get off my case because of you. Don't call me for a while."

And he hung up.

I was stunned. Maybe I should run away — hitchhike back to Costa Mesa. But if he was going to be pissed at me, and not be loyal, there wouldn't be a reason. Orik was part of my life almost from the beginning of the universe. I could look out in space for 20 billion years, and see his star somewhere. Now, just like that, he was going away, like light travelling away from me on the edges of the expanding universe.

When I turned around to sneak back to my room, the alien warlord was leaning against the wall in the dark, arms across his chest.

"You always spy on kids?" I hissed at him.

"Don't call him right now. It'll make things worse. Let the parents chill out."

I glared at Chino.

"Trust me," he said. "I'm on your side. Go to bed."

He walked away down the hall.

I found myself obeying him, and crawled into the fancy four-poster bed with the ocean view, feeling my head pulse — first major battle-scar. How did Chino know my Dad? Maybe I should adjust my telescope and do some observations. The Summer Triangle would be crossing the meridian at midnight. But I didn't have the energy. Finally I fell asleep, drifting into those swirling nebulas of geometric designs, and had a voyage dream again, except this time it wasn't the same. Chino was the commander and we were out there searching, only we couldn't find the Cat Nebula or the variable star anywhere.

— 7 —

MY COMMANDER

Next morning, I thought Mom was finally going to talk about my Dad. But she went back to Costa Mesa with Nancy Perez to get our car.

At breakfast, Auntie Marian and Chino were talking about the terrible state of the country. I sat bored and desperate, staring out the window at the ocean. It was a clear day, so you could actually see Catalina out there. I could probably see stars if I looked hard enough.

Times were changing, Marian said. Nine years to the Millennium. Religious fanatics taking over the country. Human rights violated all over the place, even by some Democrats, but especially by her own party. She was tired of bitching about it. She was tired of nasty local politics on the city council. So she was going to be a rebel Republican, and run for Assemblywoman from Malibu, 42nd district. She was already talking to Taylor somebody about being her campaign manager. Yada, yada, yada.

Chino agreed. Los Angeles was coming to a boil, he said. There was going to be trouble with racial hate.

"As bad as Watts?" she asked.

"Worse. More people. More anger. Higher-tech arson."

"Come on, William, " she said. "Join in. Where's your interest in current events?"

"It's boring here," I said, watching an oil tanker pass Catalina.

"We have the most beautiful beaches in the world. World-famous surfing, celebrities, movies at the Crosscreek Mall..." She was standing at the counter, buttering another bagel. "Seriously, there's the LaFonts, next house up the canyon — the blue house. Eileen's an old friend, and they have two children your age...."

One, I wasn't a child. Two, Orik was my only shot at a friend.

Chino was playing with his big folding knife, cleaning his nails with it. There was that darkness in the air around him, like he was thinking about thunderstorms on the other side of the planet.

"Well, you might as well get used to it," she said. "Your Mom has turned you over to Chino, so you're going to be here for a while."

"I'll run away."

Chino laughed. "Thanks for warning me." He snapped his knife shut.

"Chino will find you," Marian said.

Somehow, the way she said it gave me those creeping chills again.

Chino went outside, like he wanted to let us talk.

"Hey...is he a cop or something?" I demanded.

"Chino is..." Auntie Marian turned around, arms crossed against her chest. "...The kind of guy you call when you don't know what else to do. He was a SEAL lieutenant. He rescued prisoners of war. If he could find the Viet Cong, he can find you."

I was somewhat impressed. "He was in the Gulf War?"

"The Viet Cong were in Vietnam," said Marian. "Don't kids today learn any history?"

A SEAL officer? Jeez, guys like that got tapped for the Apollo program, and the Shuttle...and I had dissed him. He had to be Captain Kirk and Gordo Cooper rolled into one. Feeling weird, knowing I had just made a big tactical blunder, I got up and went outside too, to do some damage control.

Behind Marian's house, the fancy pool looked like it belonged in a movie about rich Hollywood people. But there was no basketball court, no footballs laying around, no sidewalks to skateboard on, no hot parking lots. On the edge of the canyon, Chino leaned against a rock, staring at the ocean, his pony tail lifting in the wind.

Near him, a gnarly apple tree grew, healthy and leafy, but looking like it was a big struggle to grow on that rocky ridge. The tree had a few wormy green apples that the birds were carving. It had a nice place in the branches, made for a kid to sit in. Feeling shy about approaching Chino, I climbed up and sat in the tree, and stared down the coast. If only I had my telescope out, I could almost see Orik's house. Was he all right? Was his dad hitting him again, right now?

Through a blur of tears, I studied the sky. It was wide — no trees or buildings hiding the view. When it was dark, I would be able to watch an evening star rise out of the L.A. glare, cross the meridian, then go down in the sea without a single house or tree getting in the way. In other words, it was an outstanding place for star watching, except this was the last thing I felt like doing. Tears would dew up my optics.

Suddenly, there was that chill again. I twisted around in the tree.

Chino was standing right behind me. His jungle boots had walked over that dry brush and grass without making a sound. My heart almost jumped out my mouth.

"Very good," he said. "Most people don't sense anything."

I looked back at the sky, rubbing my tears on my arm.

"I know you're worried about your buddy." His voice was even, quiet...not exactly friendly, just neutral and calm.

"We've got to rescue him."

"It's not so simple."

"You rescued POWs."

"This is not like going in and cutting throats. Shawn is thirteen — his parents own his ass for five more years. The law gives them the right to punish him...short of felony assault and battery. If Jerry keeps beating him, your Mom can file a complaint with Children's Services. But this is not necessarily the way to go."

"Why?"

"One phone call..." He snapped his fingers. "...Children's Services takes your buddy away. Then the system owns his ass for five years. I guarantee you won't be hanging out with him. And kids aren't safe in the system either."

My stomach trembled. "It's not fair."

"History is all about what's fair and what isn't. So...can you keep cool till we see which way Jerry is going to leap?"

"Sorry I called you a cop," I mumbled.

"No problem." He flipped his folded knife, caught it.

"Did you ever try out for the space program?" I asked.

"I'm not the rocket jockey type. Some of us have to stay on this planet and do...other stuff."

His quiet, even voice was calming me a little. "What do you do now? I mean...for a living and stuff?"

"Valhalla studio security...bodyguard...PI. Tired of it too. I'm like Marian...thinking of going into politics."

Okay, this conversation was going better.

"You're going to be a freshman this fall, right?" he asked.

"Yeah."

"Kids with weapons in your school?"

My mind was veering into the nightmare of a freshman year without Orik around. Everybody would want to know why we weren't friends any more. "Some of the guys carry knives. I do."

"Let's see your knife."

"Don't tell my Mom, okay? She doesn't know I carry." Shyly I pulled out my Swiss Army knife.

"Yours can kill...like those handmade shivs that guys carry in prison," he said, looking at it. "Don't let anyone see it...the principal will have the sheriff take you away in shackles." Then he handed it back to me. "See any guns at school?"

"A few bangers and skins are around. You never know what's in another guy's backpack."

"School's getting scary, huh."

"Mom won't let me carry anything, because a gun killed my Dad."

Fishing, to see what he'd say about my Dad.

"Guns aren't everything," he said. "Some puke points his daddy's .45 at you, you can disarm him."

"Whoa. He'd shoot me first."

"Not if you move fast. He doesn't know what you're going to do. He has to react to you. You *know* what you're going to do."

So he picked up a stick that was gun size, and showed me how to disarm somebody who was right in front of me, pointing a gun at me. He had me hold the stick. Chino swung his body to the right, brought his left arm down on my gun wrist, and made the gun point away from him. "Then," he said, "I grab the gun with my right — not by the muzzle though — and twist it up, like this —" We went over it a dozen times. Then he had me do it, touching me lightly now and then to correct my movements. His touches made my skin feel like wind was blowing inside it, star wind from another galaxy.

"That is pretty cool," I said, catching my breath.

We were more relaxed now. I was curious about his life.

"You...uh...you were talking Spanish with Nancy, but you look...Asian, or something."

"My papa was Mexican and Spanish. My mama was Japanese and Chumash and Chicano. But I'm not Mexican enough...or Asian enough...or white enough, that I belong anywhere."

My arm went out, beside his scarred arm. "I'm almost the same color as you."

"Coffee with milk."

"My Mom is half Norwegian, and half Lebanese. I don't know anything about my Dad's side of the family. She won't talk about it."

He hurled the stick out over the canyon. Suddenly something inside me pushed up with the old questions. "So...is Mom paying you to keep me here? Am I a prisoner, or what?"

"Your mom doesn't have that kind of money. Anyway, you're such a brat, that no amount of money would be enough."

In the movies, the great Warrior is always mean to the geeky Barbarian kid at first. "How long have you known my Mom?"

"Since 1976."

"Did you..." My heart was pounding fast. "...know my Dad?"

"Yeah, I did."

The heartbeat was almost blurring my vision. "How?"

"I was his bodyguard."

Those icy grey slant-eyes of his had actually seen my Dad alive. If I looked hard enough, like looking into the past with a telescope, fading traces of light from my Dad's image might actually be swimming somewhere in the depths of Chino's eyes, like the last wisps of shell from an exploded star.

"Why did he need a bodyguard?" I asked.

"It's your mom's right to tell you first."

The anger exploded in me, massive, like a giant star going off. "It's like...like nobody wants me to know!"

I lost it, forgetting the kind of guy he was. The rage swept me away, like the shockwaves I'd seen in photos, racing through galaxies at millions of miles a minute — photos taken by astronomers who could look out there farther than I could. I threw myself at Chino to attack him. Only he wasn't there. He was way better at aikido than me — faded to one side, and I fell past him and landed with a splat on the grass. He looked down at me, and laughed softly.

"That's no way to help your buddy out. You want to help your buddy?"

Chino turned and walked away, leaving me laying there with grass stains on my jacket.

I'd blown it. Blown it with this real warrior who had information about my Dad. Who could maybe help me get into astronaut school. I felt like a complete retard. I hated that easy way that grown-ups have, of making kids feel like retards. I wanted to jump off the edge of the canyon, clear into the ocean, and drown myself.

The next day, I was desperately depressed — slept late, didn't eat much. My Mom still wasn't back. Legal stuff, Marian said. Mom must be trying to quiet Jerry's threats. Chino went into L.A. to work. I didn't want any bloodthirsty SEAL tracking me down, so I stayed around. Out of somewhere, a handyman came with a basketball backboard, and bolted it to the garage. Marian, at least, had heard what I was trying to tell her. Bored to death, I practiced shooting fouls with the new ball.

Would Chino come back?

The awesomely big house echoed like a school after hours. My boredom drove me to explore it. There were tons of fancy old furniture with skinny legs, that Chino could destroy with one kick. There was a library full of books. I didn't read anything besides science, so I passed on those. But in the den, there was a 50-inch TV with a super-nice VCR, set in a whole wall of videos. I watched *Return of the Jedi* for the millionth time, and died with envy at Luke getting it together with his dad.

Next I checked out the gym room with an exercycle and weight machines. Empty guest rooms. An office in the east wing, where the housekeeper Nancy Perez had two bedrooms and a bathroom. Nancy had a married sister who lived in East L.A. She mentioned that her father had worked with Cesar Chavez, whoever that was. She and

Marian talked politics a lot. Nancy's English was good, but my aunt had actually learned some Spanish.

That night, when I asked my aunt if Chino was coming again, she handed me the phone.

Chino answered right away — he must have a cellular phone on his belt.

"Hey, dude," I said. My heart was pounding. "I was...uh...you know...I was a retard the other day."

"Apology accepted."

My head was pulsing where it still hurt. "Are you coming out again...sir?"

Chino appeared out of nowhere. When I got up next morning, he was in the gym room, working out in faded khaki shorts and boxing shoes and tank top. *Bop-ata, bop-ata* from the punching bag filled the house. Chino was not stiff and pumped, like Stallone. Instead he was flowing and limber, like one of those wild cougars you see flowing down rocks on *Discovery*. He had wide shoulders, a little waist, and abs that were really cut. Years of combat swimming powered his legs. But he had scars all over. You never see scars on movie heroes, except Tom Berenger in *Platoon* with his scarred face. But Chino had been hurt bad — burn scars on his legs, and an awful-looking chest scar that showed just above his tank top. I wondered if the Navy offered Chino his own ship, if he turned it down because he was sick of war. Better for me — he was my commander now, and he'd help me rescue Orik and put me on my way to the stars.

When he finished, I said, "Navy guys are supposed to have tattoos."

"Not me."

"Why?"

"Tattoos peg you." He was wiping his neck with a towel.

"What school of martial arts are you?"

"The Chino Cabrera School."

"Sure," I scoffed. All real warriors are modest. Probably he could get in the kick-boxing ring, and take on Frank Dux and the Asian bad guy in *Bloodsport*, and jump in the air and kick their heads off...one head with each foot.

Chino grinned — the first grin I'd seen. "My school is a mix, like me. SEAL stuff...street stuff...boxing...aikido. Whatever works."

From somewhere, I pulled my own grin.

"Show me some more moves?" I asked.

Chino pointed me over to the mat. But instead of showing me Frank Dux stuff, he started talking about movies, like he'd read my mind. A lot of movie stuff is fake, he said. Fight scenes are choreographed, like dance scenes. It isn't what you use in combat or on the street. Roundhouse kicks, for example. All you have to do is kick the base leg from under the other guy while he has his foot in the air. Chino said he liked low-line kicks better.

"I break the other guy's knee before he breaks my knee. Not arty. But effective. Especially for short guys."

He actually mentioned being short, so it didn't seem to bother him. I was amazed. The Navy had given some big responsibility to a short guy. It was something to think about.

Then he made me work on the disarming maneuver again.

That night, I disobeyed Chino and called Orik's private line. I couldn't help myself — thoughts of Orik were pestering me. I could smell blood and bruises. Orik actually answered the phone. Just hearing his voice made my skin shimmer all over with feeling.

But he didn't sound too friendly. "My dad knows you're calling and hanging up. He's going to change our number."

"Are you okay?"

"My dad is still asking me about what you did."

My stomach was shivering. Had Orik broken under interrogation? "What do you mean...what *I* did?"

"You know. Stuff you always did to me."

For a minute, I couldn't believe what he'd said. Then it pissed me off so much that I broke the code of secrecy. After all, he'd talked about it first.

"What *I* did? You did it to me too."

"I didn't know what was going on."

"Liar. Yes, you did." I couldn't believe I was hearing this.

"I was asleep." His voice was quivering, like he was totally stressed.

"If you didn't know, how could you tell your dad what I did?"

"I didn't squeal, if you're so worried. But it'll never happen again, 'cause I really gave my heart to Jesus this time. You better repent, Finder. You got to. I'm scared for you. You're a homo, and you're going to die of AIDS." A last quaver of friendly feeling was in his voice.

"You snitch," I said. "You told your dad everything."

"I did *not*. He guessed."

"You're a snitch. And I'm not queer."

Orik hung up on me.

I went to bed angry, and dreamed about my room at home. Chino was there. He was asleep on his back in the other twin bed. His naked body was half covered with a sheet. He was wearing his underwater SEAL watch — this detail made it real. It seemed to be a hot summer night, and his limbs were all sweaty. He was deep asleep. I stood there looking down at him, listening to his breathing. His black ponytail had come undone, and it was all tangled, sticking to his shoulders. He groaned, and stretched, then turned on his stomach, pulling the sheet off his butt, halfway down his strong slippery thighs. I'd never been able to inspect a grown guy's butt close up, and strained to see Chino's, but it was like trying to see the Horsehead Nebula with my tarnished old silver mirror.

Next day, when Mom came home with the car, she was all upset. She said Jerry yelled at her over the fence, that if I called his son again, he'd get a court order to keep me away. She asked: "Look, your thing with Shawn...is this some kind of...special thing? More than friends?"

"Are you crazy?" I exploded.

"I'm your mother...you can tell me."

"Excuse-*me*...he's my friend, and that's it. Can't I be worried about my friend?"

"Okay, okay." She shrugged. "Don't ever say I didn't ask."

"Can we talk about my Dad now?" I asked her.

"Tonight," she promised.

Then she and Marian and Chino went off into the office and shut the door, and talked about private stuff. One more time people were discussing me behind my back.

So I went to the den. A good action flick, one I hadn't seen before, would take my mind off the nastiness. So I snooped around in Marian's tape library to see what she had. There were fitness tapes, political speeches, and pirate copies of HBO movies that I'd already seen. Boring, boring. At the end of a shelf, in a corner, was this movie from a studio I'd never heard of — Valhalla Productions. The title was *Billy Sive*. This got me curious, since my Dad's name was Billy. Maybe it was a sequel to *Billy Jack*.

I shoved the tape in the VCR, then lay on the rug to watch. Oh Jesus, a documentary. Maybe it'd be boring.

Oldie TV news stuff, starting with this ancient talk show, hosted by a guy named Dick Cavett that I'd never heard of. This Cavett guy was interviewing six athletes who were going to some stone-age Olympic Games before I was born. Billy Sive was this good-looking blond guy, with curly hair and glasses, tall and skinny. He kept all the others laughing. You could see how everybody liked him. Sive was a distance runner, and he wanted the double gold in the 10,000 and 5000 meters.

And...Sive looked like my Dad in the photos. At the Olympic trials, he was wearing a Prescott College jersey. My stomach fell 20 stories and splatted on the sidewalk.

I stopped the tape, ran to my room, got the framed picture. As I held it beside the TV image, my legs were turning to Jello. Yeah, this guy had to be my Dad. Only his last name was not Heden, just like Mrs. Danich said. The name was familiar too — I raced upstairs again, and got my backpack. Out came the Internet downloads that Mrs. Danich had made. The name was there on the San Francisco list — William Sive. He'd been there all along. And he was queer. He was "out." He didn't care who knew, or what people said. He looked proud — the way he held himself. I couldn't believe it. And his coach, a guy named Harlan Brown, was his *boyfriend*. The coach's jacket matched up with the jacket in the photo in my secret box. So it was Brown's image that my Mom cut out of the picture — the guy who called me Falcon. My Mom and Marian had talked about "letting Harlan know," so this boyfriend dude was still around.

I wasn't a jock, but I'd watched TV sports and heard all the talk at school...there wasn't one famous athlete or coach who was known to be totally, awesomely queer by the whole country. People said things about some men figure skaters, but who cared?

So the tape rolled. My Dad was a celeb. He was ultimately controversial. People hated him. People loved him. People wanted him off the Olympic team. Demonstrations. Police holding back crowds. Interviews with his boyfriend. Interviews with his best friend, Vince Matti, who was a big fag activist. Interviews with his father, John Sive, a lawyer who was also queer. I had a fag *grandfather*, for chrissake. Did I have a grandmother too?

I was going into shock.

There was ABC news footage of Billy Sive running in the 10,000 meter. And he *won* the thing. He stood on the victory stand, proud like anything, with the gold medal hanging on his queer chest. How could my Mom not tell me about this? The whole stadium was going crazy — people who liked him were screaming and throwing flowers, people who hated him were jumping down on the track to try to beat him up. His bodyguards kept people away. A close-up on the bodyguards showed a young Mexican-Asian guy fighting the crowd off Sive. Was that Chino? When Sive left the track, this Brown guy was there, and they threw their arms around each other right in front of the TV cameras.

When I saw this, I slid down into the sofa, so embarrassed that I almost cried. Football players and soccer players throw their arms around each other after a goal, and wrap their legs around each other, and it gets pretty physical, but it's just guy stuff. This was different. The whole world must have been thinking how my Dad had sex with Brown. My good-looking Dad, in bed with this Brown guy. Yuck!

My body was shaking all over.

The tape rolled on. Next thing, Sive was running in the 5000 meter. Neck and neck with this Finnish guy. Then he was pulling away. Holy Jesus, he was going to win the 5000 too. *Two* gold medals for a fag. Every jock in the country must have died. How could my Mom keep the secret?

Sive was a few yards from the finish line. And then...he fell down on the track. Stumbled, probably.

My Dad just lay there. The Finnish guy won. Brown and Matti and everybody ran on the track to check Sive. They piled up around him. An ambulance came. And then...the announcer was talking about a gun. Matti, the best friend, was holding my Dad's feet, crying. Somebody in the stands had shot my Dad in the head.

"Momm!" I was standing at the top of the stairs, yelling. Hot tears were all over my face. My legs crumpled, and I sat down on the top step. She came charging up, with Marian and Chino after her. Her face was absolutely white. She probably thought I had hurt myself and was dying. In a way, I was.

"William...what is it?"

"Why didn't you tell me?"

The sound of the TV filled the second floor. The roar of the crowd, the voices of the news anchors.

"Oh god," said Marian. "He found the tape."

Mom was trying to hug me. "Baby...please," she said. "Please listen. I didn't want you to find out this way."

I twisted away, and belted her in the face. She wasn't thinking about self defense right then, and I caught her with her hands down.

"You lied to me! You lied!"

Chino tried to pull me off Mom. To divert him, I gave Nancy a kick in the shins, the one that Chino taught me to do. When Chino went to help Nancy, I faked my way around him, ran to my room, and locked the door. I also locked the window, so they couldn't get in. Next, I hurled my Dad's picture against the wall, and glass flew everywhere. After that, I proceeded to wreck the room.

The last thing I did was throw my telescope off the balcony, into the driveway. It hit the concrete with a terrifying clank. Some of the galvanized pipe actually broke. Glass from the optics exploded everywhere.

Then I really cried, shocked at what I'd done. It was devastating — what I'd done. Why had I done it? My telescope was destroyed. My dream was dead. In a way, I'd killed my Dad myself.

— 8 —

FINDING OUT

There was a knock at my door. "William."

That was Chino's voice. Hours must have gone by. The room was dark and quiet. It must be night.

"Hey, William. Open up."

His voice was that quiet, steady tone. I was in the huge bed, under the covers, curled up like a baby.

"I can kick the door in," he said. "Or pick the lock. Or take the hinges off. Or...you can let me in."

His tone didn't threaten. But he was the commander who expected to be obeyed. So I unlocked the door, then crawled back in bed.

The hall light glared in — showed that the bathroom mirror was broken, glass and broken stuff everywhere, drawers emptied, chairs turned over, the rug half pulled up. Chino shut the door, and everything went dark again. I was laying on my back, covers pulled to my chin, head turned away, arm over my face. The bed sagged — he sat down by me. I could smell him — sweaty clothes, gun oil. He'd probably come from bodyguarding somewhere.

Then his warm hand took my clenched fist, and held it. Finally my fist opened all by itself, like a flower opening to the sun, and his fingers rubbed my palm. It seemed like I had hungered for male affection ever since I was a baby — wanted to suck it from my bottle, wanted to pedal my bike after it as fast as I could...wanted it from Orik in a way that we were both afraid to give. That was the first time I had ever felt it from anyone...Chino rubbing my hand.

My chest heaved. Tears were locked inside my ribs, but they wouldn't come out.

"Listen to me now," he said.

"Y-y-yeah." My chest jerked with sobs.

"Do you know how many men I've seen in combat? Seen their hearts and their spirits? Nothing left hidden? My own men...enemy men? Do you know how many men that is?"

"A l-l-lot."

"I saw your Dad in combat. Not Vietnam. Another kind of war. He was the best. He deserves that you be proud of him."

"Excuse-*me*, he was a queer."

"What do you know about queers? Are you the big expert?"

I was silent.

"Your intelligence on queers is wacko, my friend. If I had run my ops that way, with hearsay instead of hard intell, my men and I would have died."

My fingers curled around his.

"So you were there?" I whispered.

"Your grandfather hired me to be one of your Dad's bodyguards. Yeah, I was right there. I came close to putting a bullet through my own head because I couldn't stop what happened."

"I didn't even know I had a g-g-grandfather."

"Come on...sit up."

I obeyed.

"Have some dinner with us. A kid needs to eat. *I* need to eat. Then you'd better see the rest of the tape."

"I don't want to see my Mom. She's a liar."

"Your mom doesn't deserve this from you either. She's another one of the best. You don't have any right to judge her. You don't have a clue what really happened. So you'd better find out. You'd better apologize to her. And Nancy, whose leg you just about broke."

Again no menace — just the commander voice. A commander who said my Mom was one of the best.

Slowly I crawled off the bed. He went on: "If you ever hit your mother again, or *any* woman, you'd better be ready to face me. I'm not nice when I'm mad."

The house felt like we were all sick and trying to get well. In the dining room, Chino and Marian and Nancy and my Mom and I sat around the table. It was definitely not a family Thanksgiving. Nancy was limping a little — I'd really nailed her. My mom was holding a towel and ice to her black eye.

I stared at my plate. Dishes were clinking.

We ate some burgers and Japanese take-out food that Marian had called down to the Crosscreek Mall to have delivered. Chino liked Asian food. There were slabs of raw tuna that he chowed down without soy sauce or anything. Mom was always riding him about what he ate, calling him Tuna Breath. But tonight there was no kidding around. I ate half a burger, drank a little milk, and didn't want to look at anybody.

Then we went back to the TV room.

Our faces glowed in the light from the screen. Nancy had never seen the tape, and she put her hands over her face, weeping furiously and talking to Chino in Spanish. She seemed to be pretty sympathetic to queers. Little did I know that I would soon find out why. My mom's face looked like it was carved out of rock. Marian kept fingering her pearls and blowing her nose. Only Chino was not crying. But the feeling in the room was all three of them remembering things that they could hardly stand to remember. Even Chino, who must be maxed out on blood and killing.

"Hey Chino, is that you in front of Brown?" I asked.

He rewound the tape, then put it on freeze frame.

"Here I am," he said. "And here." He pointed to that blurred brown guy pushing spectators off boyfriend Brown. "Here's Marian, right near me. Here's your mom. Your grandfather, over here..."

The sound track poured over us. Marian and my mom and Harlan were trapped against the stadium wall by reporters. Marian was trying to push the reporters back. Voices, voices. Suddenly Aunt Marian was lunging forward, past Chino — charging like a lion. Her hand with a bloody handerchief was coming at the camera.

She yelled, "I have a statement! Sniper, hell! Everyone who hated Billy fired that round! You can quote me directly!"

The camera tilted, and the screen went brown-red and blurred with something on the lens. Jesus, it must be my Dad's blood.

Now a jump cut to the funeral at a queer church in New York, and my Dad in the open casket, wearing a brown suit, with a bunch of Easter lilies on his chest. An interview with boyfriend Brown, who was not crying, but really sad. I had to admit he was an impressive guy, dark hair, athletic-looking. But he gave me the willies. My Dad had been in his power — evil power. He was a Darth Vader type. An ex-Marine, they said. Jesus, the military must be crawling with fags. And there was another interview with Vince, who was as goodlooking as a movie star. Vince was so choked up that he could hardly talk. There was an interview with Marian's husband Joe, who was the president of Prescott College. Mrs. Danich would be happy to know the mystery of Prescott was solved. The college was where my Dad trained for the Olympics.

The tape skipped through a few more years. The trial of Richard Mech, one of the two gunman dudes who shot my Dad. Controversy about Brown, because he was still coaching track at Prescott, and the religious nuts calling him a pedophile and wanting him away from kids. Brown finally quitting. Stuff about the other shooter, who was stalking Brown and Matti for years, till the police finally got him. In the last interview, Harlan had his arm around Vince, who was his new boyfriend. I was disgusted at this.

Finally the screen went dark, and the tape rewound.

"So Brown was...really into runners, huh," I said.

Nobody said anything.

I pushed it. "He forgot about my Dad pretty fast."

"You don't have a right to judge that either," Chino said, getting up and leaving, like he couldn't stand to be around me.

It was around 2 in the morning. Nancy limped off to bed. Marian went into the kitchen to make some cocoa. My mom and I were alone. She had cried herself out, and just sat staring at the dark screen. "Why didn't you put Dad's name on my birth certificate?" I asked.

"Because," she said violently, "straight people don't like queer people having children. They go to court and take the children away."

I stared into her eyes. "So...*you're* queer."

She stared back. "The word is lesbian."

How did I not know this before? My feelings started fading, going dark, like a variable star.

She went on: "Billy's mother Leda was crazy with hate...she tried to get between Harlan and Billy, even though Billy was an adult already...he was 22. Leda would have taken you away from me if she'd known! Legally she could have done that. Grandparents can and do sue for custody. How would you like that?"

"I guess not," I mumbled.

"And there were other things to worry about," she said, sounding like she had a cold. "That second shooter was stalking Harlan for years. He belonged to this right-wing paramilitary group who hate homosexuals. Chino lived with Harlan, to be his bodyguard all the time. Things got so dangerous that it was no place for a baby, William. I just left. I bailed. Cut the ties. Didn't see them any more. Went clear to the other side of the country, and tried to start a new life. I didn't want anything to happen to you. The only people I stayed in touch with were Joe and Marian...she's my best friend. It would have broken my heart to lose Marian."

"But you didn't have to lie...."

"It's hard to get a teaching job if you don't have a certain profile. I wasn't a good enough athlete to make it in competition. I could teach. But...an unmarried mother with a baby? I didn't have a lover then. Harlan wanted to help, but...he and I don't always get along. So Marian and Joe helped me put together a paper trail, young graduate, married, husband dead...and I landed the position at Ricelands. The school didn't do a background check to find out if I'd really married...they were so thrilled to get someone from a big-name college with a gold-medal graduate. Once I got a rep there, I jumped to something better at Orange—"

My emotions flashed hot again, like a variable star.

I interrupted her. "If my Dad was queer, and he was into this Brown guy, how did you and my Dad have a kid? Did the two of you, like, share him, or what?"

She sat up straight and glared at me. "You've got a lot to learn about gay people."

"Excuse-*me*. I looked at the paper trail too. My Dad died in August 1976, and I was born a year later. Babies only take nine months. I don't even *look* like Billy Sive."

"You do look like him, in little ways. And you look like me. Like your grandpa Sive."

"You better explain that year!"

She stood up and glared down at me. "Don't you dare talk to me like you're the goddam Gestapo!"

I stood up too, threatening. But Chino's voice sounded the warning in my mind.

Tears rolled down her face. I had never seen her cry, except once when I broke one of her trophies, and that was about it. It made me feel really bad.

"I'd planned to tell you...someday. But somehow, it got harder and harder to talk about — I kept putting it off. William, forgive me. If I made a mistake, I admit it. But I never meant to hurt you."

I shrugged furiously.

"Forgive me?" she asked.

"Just...tell me everything now. Okay?"

She drew a deep sigh. "Okay. Artificial insemination. You know what that is?"

"Teacher told us in sex ed. Why?"

Adults talk about "long nights." It was the first time I'd ever lived through one.

Outside, in the apple tree, I crouched with my jacket collar turned up. It was dawn and cold — a few stars still glowed in the deep green sky. Summer solstice had gone, the days were getting shorter. I'd watched Ursa Major go down behind Axl Rose's house, and the Summer Triangle swing towards the meridian without any sad feelings about my broken telescope laying smashed by the driveway. There was a weird emptiness inside me. Now what? Why would my rocket ship go racing through the Summer Triangle to find something that was a lie?

Over Los Angeles, a hot orange glow showed the pollution in the air. Purple smog lay on the ocean. The whole world looked sick and poisoned. My muscles were still trembling all over with the violence that I'd been feeling.

Chino was squatting Asian-style, leaning against the trunk of the tree. I was looking down on his head, with the wet hair pulled so slick. He smelled like the shower.

"You haven't apologized to your mother yet," he said.

"My Mom is a lezzie."

"The word is lesbian."

"Sounds the same to me."

"Lezzie is what people say if they hate women like your mom. Do you hate her?"

I was supposed to be having this big emotional reaction to the news that my mother was queer. Instead, I just felt dead.

"She was living with a woman named Marla when you were a baby. You were only three. Marla died in a car accident. Your mom lost heart about relationships. So much death. This family is haunted by death. So many ghosts. Funny how the people who killed your Dad robbed every one of us of something family. Your mom's hard on men, but Billy got behind that hardness. To this day, he's the only guy who was ever close to her. Just the other day, she told me how she still misses him. Some losses, it's hard to talk about —"

I sat there thinking about how he'd included himself in the "family". What a weird family — full of queers. How could queers have a real family?

On the horizon, the first burning blob of sun was showing over L.A. The tree, and Chino and I, were suddenly spotlighted with fiery orange light.

"It's funny...about this tree," he said.

"Why?"

"You always go to it. Know where the tree came from?"

"No."

"The campus at Prescott, behind Marian's house. It was a favorite tree of hers — she planted it when her daughter Sara was born. All kinds of family things happened under this tree. Your Dad and Harlan were married under it."

"*Married?*"

"They wanted it to be a sacred thing."

"Two guys...married," I scoffed.

He ignored me. "When Marian and Joe moved west, she had the tree dug up and shipped out here."

"Where's Sara?"

"A lot you don't know about your family, huh? Sara lives in Mexico, practicing herbal medicine. Want to hear more?"

"Who cares?" I said with bored exhaustion.

"Marian's not your blood aunt. Your mom has you call her 'auntie' because she's like a sister to your mom. Your mom lost her own family, her own sister, when she came out. They still live in Michigan, and they haven't spoken to her since 1975."

"Lonely, huh?" I didn't know what else to say.

"Marian's close with Harlan too, like a brother. Harlan's parents cut the ties too. Your grandfather lives in San Francisco. He's an excellent lawyer. Harlan lives with Vince in West Hollywood, half an hour from here. Harlan's son Michael lives in L.A. too, and Michael's wife. Harlan's other son doesn't speak to him. Your mom and I sometimes fight like cats and dogs, but that's okay...she's like the little sister I never got to have. So we've all kind of adopted each other...we make our own *familia*."

Little by little, he had laid it out for me — a star chart with strange new constellations that were too scary to look at. The sun was up now — a glaring red ball resting on the smog.

"*La familia*," he said softly. "You don't know how important it is till you don't have it."

"So you see this Brown guy?" I asked.

"All the time. Vince too...the kid brother I never got to have."

"I suppose they're gonna die of AIDS?" I said sarcastically.

Chino stood up, and dusted off his clothes carefully.

"You don't know any more about AIDS than you know about queers," he said, looking at me sideways out of those warlord eyes.

I couldn't hold back the sarcasm. "So you and Marian are the only ones in the whole...family...who aren't queer."

"The word is gay."

Why were these people so touchy about words?

"Whatever," I said.

"What makes you think I'm not gay?" he said softly.

There was a sudden sick caving in of my whole insides. Could it be true? My trusted commander was a pedophile? Jerry said all queer men are pedophiles. But Jerry was crazy, wasn't he?

"Harlan and Billy hired me because they wanted security men who'd be loyal," he went on. "I was fresh from Vietnam, trying to adjust...still in the Naval Reserve. After your Dad was killed, all the publicity brought me to the Navy brass's attention. I'd been careful in the SEALs. I never did anything with mates, though I think a couple of them knew. Whatever I did, was somewhere else. But the Navy chaptered me out of the Reserve."

"After everything you did in the war?"

He laughed. "Oh, there's plenty of us in the military. The brass know damn well that we are there. They always have. The brass never cared much, as long as you kept it quiet. After all, some of the brass are gay too. But if you come out, or your cover is blown, they do the lip service thing, and they get rid of you."

While he was talking, my fantasy about the perfect starship commander was collapsing. I hardly heard what Chino was saying.

"So all these people who loved your Dad," he said quietly, "are still around. Your Mom is back in touch with them. You're Billy's boy — they'd like to see you."

"I don't want to see any queers."

"Harlan's your second father."

"He's not. He's nothing."

Those warlord eyes bored through me. "You're only thirteen," he said evenly, "but you're a grownup kind of mean."

Maybe it wasn't smart to shoot off my mouth. But I'd already said the words. So I just pressed my face into the rough bark.

There was a long silence. Then Chino turned away.

"Nobody says you have to like queers," he said over his shoulder. "But you have to clean up your room. And you have to apologize to the women. If you don't, you're out of my program."

Chino walked away. I felt like all my blood and guts and brains were being torn out of me and dragged after him. In a little while, his 4 Runner was gunning down the canyon.

My room stayed torn up. I got my sleeping bag and slept in a corner where there wasn't broken glass. Outside, everybody had kicked my broken telescope off the driveway, into the ice plant on the side, because they weren't going to clean it up. Chino didn't come around. So I worked up the kind of courage that only a truly desperate and lonely kid can have, and packed a few things in my blue NASA backpack. I noticed it was getting worn-looking.

Next day I walked up the canyon, to check out the LaFont kids.

— 9 —

MEETING ANA

The LaFont house was where Marian said it was. It was blue, on a steep hillside. The Force was with me — a kid was skateboarding in the driveway. I watched him jump his board onto a railing and grind down it. A reckless spirit like me.

"Yeah, my mom mentioned you. Come on in," he said.

Ziggy was 15. For a while I hung out with him, and listened to his favorite heavy metal on his terrific stereo. Somehow it didn't feel like the chemistry was right for a friendship. But we talked. His mom was in the hospital, and his stepdad was visiting her. They owned the restaurant called The Cove, down on the PCH. The restaurant was killer successful, so the parents worked all the time — more slaves for the xyzium mines.

Lured by the music, his sister Ana came downstairs, and hung with us. Jailbait like me...she was 13 and looked like she was 20. She showed me the condoms in her pocket, and didn't seem to give an excuse-me what boys thought of her. In other words, Ana was not the usual dork girl. If Orik was going to mess around with girls, then I would mess around with girls too. Besides, with a whole family full

of queers, it was up to me to continue the heterosexual tradition.
I called home.

"This is the required phone call from your son," I told Mom. "I'm at the LaFonts, so I'd appreciate it if you don't send Chino looking for me."

"Right now, I doubt Chino would strain himself for you," said my Mom coldly. "Come back when you're ready to clean your room."

Ziggy and Ana called their mom at the hospital, and told her I was there. So it was cool all around.

"You're just in time for a party," Ziggy said.

He, Ana and I visited the next house up the canyon. It was a pink mansion bigger than Marian's. Ace and his girlfriend Mia let us hang with them and plan the next party for 15 or 20 other "housers," who were into big house parties. They were 17, looked and acted way older — also into heavy metal. Ace's parents were rich — they had their own communications company. They made sure the refrigerator was full, then went off to Burbank Airport and took a plane somewhere on business, leaving us alone. The ultimately permissive parents. Jerry would have a fit if he knew. I had a feeling that the LaFonts would have a fit too, if they knew we were going to party.

Just out of curiosity, I called Orik's house. The old number had been disconnected. The new number was unlisted. Orik was probably out with Donnala, or whoever.

The two-day party started at Ace's house. Twenty kids smoked outside by the pool, because Ace's mom got torqued if the smell was in the house. I had my first cigarettes and my first joint of Mendocino Express on the same day, and couldn't believe how tweaked I got. The older people gave me a lot of grief about being a baby, so I had to show them. That night, we got into Ace's parents' liquor, and Ziggy and I drank about 25 pre-mixed kiwi daiquiris each. I got so sick that Ziggy dragged me out in the bushes so I didn't puke all over the living room. I passed out, and woke up to a dawn sky — Aldebaran just ascending over L.A., bright as an airplane light in the orange glare. I was covered with dew and ticks, with my head throbbing again where I'd hit it the other day.

Eight of us spent the second day at Zuma Beach. I got sunburned and had hungover intentions of losing the last shreds of my virginity with Ana, since I seemed to be the only guy in Malibu that she hadn't rolled a condom onto. While we were in the water, I got her in my arms and made a serious attempt at my first kiss, but she slithered away.

Malibu girls were more stylin' than the little misses in Costa Mesa. Ana was the most stylin' of all — the Queen of Malibu. She liked to party, but she also worked out and swam and did gymnastics and karate. She was a fanatic about fitness, very buff and tensed up, like those Olympic girl gymnasts you see on TV, all muscles and no tits. Her hair was incredible — this mass of red frizz, clear to her waist. The first time I saw it, I thought it was a wig. She wore a little silver coat hanger in one ear, and informed me that she was pro-choice. I expected her to wear a thong bikini, and flaunt herself all over the beach, but she surprised me by wearing a one-piece thing that covered her totally. She pushed her way into the guys' surfing party — even when we told her she was supposed to stay on the beach and be decorative. She even helped us beat up some visiting surfers and chase them off our beach.

And she laughed at me when I wiped out. I had spent so much time with my nose in the stars that I didn't know excuse-me about normal things like surfing.

"Your little sister talks big," I said to Ziggy.

"Aw...she thinks she's...like, ugly, and stuff," said Ziggy.

"*Ugly?* Her?"

"She actually turned down a couple of modeling jobs. Can you believe? She's interested in *birds*."

If Miss Frizz was ugly, then Mr. Short ought to be good enough for her.

That night, Ace and Mia had fifteen tickets for the Guns 'N' Roses concert in town. Ace used his dad's credit card, and a stretch limo took us to the concert grounds in L.A. Everybody else was old, eighteen or twenty, and I was getting older by the minute. On the way in, everybody else swallowed some new drug called Ecstasy, so I did too. Then we threw ourselves into the yelling, swaying mass of bodies. Fireworks and smoke and lights dizzied us, as the musicians crossed back and forth, jerking off their guitars, spreading their thighs and flaunting their packages at us. I was lost in the glare, flying my spacecraft into a dangerous new galaxy. Suddenly I loved everybody, including all movie mutants and monsters. I even loved heavy metal. Simultaneously, I loved Ana. Any minute now, that body of hers, which was supposed to be so attractive, was going to light me up like the sky at night.

"Don't want to lose you in the crowd, honey," I said, getting my arm around her waist.

Somehow we fought our way to the front. Ziggy dared me to dive. He and Ace boosted me onto the stage. I spread my arms. I, the Finder, unique among humans, had given up a stellar destiny so I could build my empire on Earth. The slave masses cheered me on. Axl and the lead guitarist were on the other side of the stage, doing a big riff together, so the coast was clear. A thousand pairs of hands went up, waiting to catch me. They were going to float me around on their hands, like a river. I loved them all. I wanted to lose my virgin with them all. Oh-oh, here came Axl Rose, maybe to kick my butt. So I made a terrific launch, up and out over the crowd, out, out...with my arms doing the wing thing. I was the pilot in *The Right Stuff*, trying to put his test plane into space. Down, down, and...

...And they fumbled me, and dropped me.

I hit the ground hard. Even in my cosmos-loving state, I could feel one butt muscle making a bruise. Three hundred people stepped on me, including one guy's boot gave me a bloody nose. I lost my star cap. When I fought my way back to the Caballo Canyon gang, I hoped that Ana was impressed with a good try.

"God, what a loser," she said, and turned her back.

B ack at Ziggy's and Ana's house, their stepdad, Glenn, was waiting. He could tell we'd been partying, and he was very pissed. The prison menace in Glenn's eyes made us good kids, like, instantly.

Glenn had been a bad guy. (Ziggy had told me the story.) Glenn did 15 years for different drug and weapons stuff, and was off probation now, trying to do his own mission impossible and learn to be a good guy. Mrs. LaFont had kept her own name when she married Glenn, and the two of them co-owned the restaurant. I wondered how a lady like Ana's mom had hooked up with this desperado. But Ana and Ziggy said he really cared about their mom. He was about Chino's height, leathery and quick as an alligator on *Discovery*, covered with prison tattoos — even the backs of his hands. Guess he didn't mind being pegged.

"Your mom still isn't feeling good," Glenn said to Ana and Ziggy. "She wants to see you. And she wants to see *you*," he said to me.

My Mom was given the required call, and it was cool.

So away we went, in the LaFonts' van.

On the freeway, another one of those informative talks happened…showing me how I was still walking across galactic mine fields full of black holes that were really the family past, and I was trying pitifully not to get myself blown up.

"You know what my mom's got, right?" asked Ana.

"No," I said.

"Something called CFS," she said.

Ziggy added in, "She may have gotten something from Ana's dad. He died of AIDS. But her HIV test is negative, so the doctors can't figure it out. Most of the time, she's mostly okay. Now and then, she gets really tired and we put her in for a few days."

Fear flashed through me. "I thought only queers get AIDS."

Glenn laughed, shifting gears. "I'm not gay and I'm not sick, but I'm HIV positive, whatever that means. I got it in prison. I met my wife at a clinic when I was on probation."

My mouth almost fell open.

"Hey, Glenn, how many guys did you do in prison?" Ziggy asked.

"Oh…" said Glenn cheerfully. "I don't even know who gave it to me. Maybe my cellie. My wife knew your dad," he told me over his shoulder. "Eileen's first marriage was to Jacques LaFont…and Jacques was a friend of your dad's."

I was trapped by gravity curves of the dark past again. Pulled inexorably towards mysterious dark planets of destiny. Jacques LaFont? The name was familiar. My mind did a search back over the video footage I'd watched. Jacques was Vince's boyfriend for a while. He was one of the three runners at Prescott who wanted to make the Olympic team.

Ana added in, "My dad was bisexual, you know."

"Sounds like it," I said.

"He ran track and cross-country with your dad in college. He went to Prescott with your dad and Vince after Oregon State threw them out. But he couldn't handle all the publicity and hate and stuff. So he quit running and married my Mom."

I was shocked by the easy way that this family talked about secret things. These kids knew way too much about my family past.

"Kids don't always get it, though," Ana said. "I'm HIV negative and I don't have CFS either. But my baby brother died of something weird."

"Our mom wanted a boy, so she adopted me," said Ziggy.

Ana smiled, looking proud that she had so much to tell. "Then my grandparents tried to take us away from our mom because she was sick. They really hated my Dad because he was bi."

"My Mom told me that," I said. "So you went to court?"

"Yeah," said Ziggy. "Your grandfather is a killer lawyer...he represented our mom."

My grandfather? Did they mean Billy Sive's dad, the lawyer?

"Ziggy and I got to testify, and we told the judge we wanted to stay with Mom. We won, and Mom got to keep us," Ana said.

"Drama," I said.

"Wanna know the best part of the story?"

"Does it get better?" I asked wearily.

She gave me a big grin. "It does, it does! You and I met when we were babies. We were all living in New York then. I guess you and me got into some wild-ass baby fights."

Ziggy was giggling like a retard. "Sister dear, we'll have to show William the incriminating pictures in the family album..."

Mrs. LaFont's private hospital room was full of flowers, which Glenn had bought to cheer her up, and she was all comfortable in a fancy robe. She looked like a skinny person who'd put on weight, with skinny hands and a puffy face. Glenn gave her a kiss on the cheek. It was nice to see this ex-bad guy love his wife.

"How's my girl?" Glenn asked her.

"Get me out of here. I hate being sick."

"The new antibiotic working? What's it called?"

"Doxycycline. The doctor said it'll take a while."

"And this is Billy's boy?" She inspected me with those intense blue eyes of hers — another pair of eyes that had seen my dad alive. His living image was parked somewhere on the hard drive of her brain where I could never access it. "It's about time your mom brought you around."

I stood there with my hands in my pockets, not wanting to shake the skinny hand that she put out. She seemed like a hard person — all rules, no heart. I wasn't sure I liked her. "Hi," I said from where I was.

She looked at Glenn. "I guess he didn't inherit Billy's manners. Billy was such a thoughtful person."

For the first time, I felt that having my dad in my world might be a problem. People were going to compare me to him.

Back at the LaFont house, Ana and Ziggy could hardly wait to show me the old pictures. There I was at my first birthday, on the rug with another baby. We were beating each other up. One picture was blurred, with Ana's fist slamming my nose. In the next picture, I was crying and Ana was crawling away with her diaper half off. In the background, I recognized the same faces as always — Mom, Marian, Chino, Vince...and Harlan. And a little dark-haired guy who had to be my grandfather, John Sive.

Ana was giggling and screeching, rubbing it in.

And there was a pic of Ana's dad, skinny and sick, at his research camp in Hawaii, where he'd been studying endangered birds. Jacques' long frizzy red hair looked just like Ana's—but it had mostly fallen out, and his eyes were sad.

Glenn dropped me at my house. Then the van raced on down the hill, leaving me standing alone by the side of the road.

There I was. Backpack over shoulder. No hat, shoelaces untied. I smelled like cigarettes and barf, and had a draining sugar thirst from all the pot I smoked. So I jumped in the pool and swam 20 furious laps, and gargled with pool water, hoping that chlorine would kill the smell. In the dining room, Marian and my Mom and Nancy were sitting with coffee cups and brownies, talking about Marian's political career. The phone was ringing off the hook, and Nancy was taking calls. They stared at my bruises and torn clothes.

My Mom followed me into the den. Her nose wrinkled — as a non-smoker, she could smell a cigarette miles away.

"They should put a leash on you," I said, "and have you sniff airport baggage for drugs."

"Don't you dare talk to me like that! I suppose you got laid, and polluted with multiple diseases."

"If only," I mumbled, getting out the Valhalla video again.

"Keep up the good work. You might live till you're old enough to vote."

"Why didn't you tell me about the LaFonts?"

"Too busy telling you other stuff."

I watched the tape again. Ancient history, from the beginning of the universe. The big bang was my dad and Vince Matti and Jacques LaFont, three gay college students and Olympic hopefuls, getting kicked off the Oregon track team because they were queer. They went to Prescott College, where Harlan Brown became their coach.

My Mom came in and sat beside me, watching too.

When the video ended, I took a deep breath and said, "Okay...Mom, I apologize."

"We'll see if you mean it," she said coldly. "Because next time, you won't catch me with my guard down."

"I do mean it."

She jumped up, and paced back and forth like she always did when she was giving a pep talk to her own team.

"Look," she said. "Let's get something clear. If you think I want you to be gay, then spare us all the drama. I would actually be *relieved* if you turn out straight. Okay? I know it's not politically correct to say this. But now and then, I'd think to myself, well, I'm not telling him everything, but this way, if he turns out gay, he'll find it out from scratch, the way the rest of us did. So you don't *have* to fling yourself into bed with girls. You don't *have* to beat up every fag in sight. Just try to be a normally destructive teenager, okay?"

I listened to this speech in amazement.

"*Okay?*" she yelled.

"Sure," I said, feeling confused.

Upstairs, the destroyed room was still there. In the middle of all the mess, the unlit candle still stood in its place on the dresser. It was the only thing in the room that I hadn't destroyed.

Billy's picture lay in the corner. The frame was bent. My Dad grinned up at me behind a nova of cracked glass.

Funny...every time I looked at him now, he looked different. It was like orbiting a nebula, seeing it from different coordinates. I'd been hanging out with housers. All they did was party. When my Dad was that same age, he dreamed about Olympic gold. Did he ever party? He must have loved life. Maybe he partied sometimes. Maybe he got tired of discipline every minute of the day, and had to cut loose. Maybe he even smoked a doobie or two. What did it feel like — that awesome rush when he knew he'd won a second gold medal, just before the bullet hit him? Did he ever want to do other things besides run? A career, maybe? I couldn't see him slaving in the xyzium mines somewhere. Did he wonder about girls? Did he have any feelings for my Mom besides friendly and brotherly?

Creaking sobs tore through me. I actually held the picture to my chest. Finally I searched in the backpack for my new lighter, and relit the candle.

"I'm sorry," I whispered to it. "Don't be mad at me. I'm trying to understand...."

After a long shower, I went to the kitchen and swallowed the rest of the brownies. Taylor was there, with a clipboard and his spin-doctor talk. They were planning Marian's campaign — fundraising, where they'd locate her office, how they'd get her on the ballot. Ignoring them, I got the vacuum cleaner and some garbage bags, and cleaned my room. Outside, the wreckage of my telescope got dumped in the trash bin. The tears came again. I must have been temporarily insane to break it. As I was sweeping up glass from the broken mirror, Nancy came limping down the drive with her briefcase.

"Nancy, I'm sorry I kicked you," I said.

She stopped. "Too bad," she said, looking at the glass.

I shrugged. "I was going to build a bigger one, anyway."

As we all sat down to dinner, I swallowed and said, "Marian, I'm sorry I broke your stuff. I'll pay for it."

"You'll have to work five hundred years to pay for the Chinese porcelains."

"I'll mow the lawn...anything. Okay?"

"You can help with my campaign," she said.

"Is Chino coming to dinner?" I asked.

Wordlessly, my Mom held out the phone. I punched his beeper number. In ten minutes, our phone rang back. I pulled the long cord into the pantry and shut the door, so I could talk privately.

"Hi, Chino."

"Hi," he said shortly. "I hear you met the LaFonts."

"Yeah." Emotion surged up in me. "Hey, Chino, you know...uh...you were right, man. About everything."

"You think you can get back in my program just like that?"

"I apologize." My knees were quivering. My eyes burned.

"Not good enough. I hear you came home smelling like pot."

"I won't touch it again, I promise."

"You're not even getting warm." He sounded bored and disgusted.

Desperation was clawing me. "I'll...hey, I'll even see that Brown guy."

"Oh," he said. "You mean your other father?"

Later that night, when Chino got to Malibu, I trailed after him to his room, and asked him, "You were on a job, huh."

"Yeah." He was taking off his shoulder holster.

"Bodyguarding Madonna?"

"A job for your mom."

"Yeah?" Suddenly I knew what he was hinting at. "Are the Heasters going to sue Mom, or something?"

"I doubt it. Jerry is chilling...he knows it wouldn't be smart to draw fire from Children's Services. The district attorney's office didn't give him any support on his allegations. You and Shawn are the same age, so they don't consider what Jerry is alleging to be a crime. Anyway, he and Marilyn have their hands full with Shawn."

I was blushing and wishing everybody would stop talking about the allegations. "How do you know?"

"Don't ask," he said, opening the closet door.

"Are they still going to send him to military school?"

"Hard to say what they're going to do."

What would happen to Orik now? His parents would be really pissed if he wasn't obeying them. For a minute I fantasized about Orik running away and finding us in Malibu. But the fantasy faded...Jerry and Marilyn would have the police look for him, and the first place they'd look would be my house.

A few days later, the big historic family meeting was going to happen at a beach house on Matador Beach. My Mom wanted it to be a low-key fun thing, so things wouldn't get too freaky for me. But I was freaked anyway.

My Mom briefed me, so I could keep everybody straight. Harlan would be coming with the Valhalla people, who owned the beach house. His career as a track coach got wrecked by the Sive thing, so he became a writer. He did scripts for Valhalla Productions, who made the *Billy Sive* video. Valhalla started out in TV commercials. Now they were doing feature films, trying to get a few good gay movies into the theaters, she said. Vince Matti, my dad's best friend, was their associate producer. Vince was still Harlan's boyfriend...and people said he had AIDS. I was still revolted that Brown wasn't faithful to my dad.

"So Brown must have AIDS too," I wanted to know.

"No, he doesn't," my Mom said. "Some people never get it."

A letter from Orik actually came, to Marian's address. The handwriting was his, but the ideas weren't. I'd helped him with a lot of homework, so I knew the way he said things. His parents wrote this, and made him copy it. The letter went on and on about how I was going to go to hell — how I needed to come to Jesus. Mom said she needed it for the legal file, so I gave it to her.

"How can Shawn let them do this?" I asked Chino.

"Don't be judgmental. It's easy for parents to terrorize a kid."

I moped, and wrote him a letter back:

Dear Orik,

Hi...how are you? Fine, I hope. I got your letter. I know your parents make you say all that stuff. As for me I am trying to get my life together, but I am not doing so good. Orik, you are a great guy and that is why I miss you so much. When you are with me I am so happy and when you are not with me I am sad because I miss you so much. It is no fun without you. I hope your dad isn't hurting you. Don't let him get to you, okay? I hope he doesn't send you away so I won't see you again. Well I got to go. See you whenever. I miss you. Don't forget that.

Your friend, Finder

Then I tore the letter into tiny pieces and flushed it down the toilet. No star cadet would write that kind of thing to another cadet. Besides, if Orik's parents found out, we'd be in court over my letter.

— 10 —

MEETING HARLAN

The beach house was on some rocks right at the end of Matador. We got there early, and waited in the driveway, watching the breeze raise some surf. My stomach was wobbling like a space probe with a mechanical problem. Finally the Valhalla people drove up in a dusty Jeep Cherokee. My stomach tightened even more.

"Incoming, incoming," I said. "Here's the queers."

My Mom scowled at me.

Two black ladies and two white guys dragged a volleyball net and stands out of the Jeep. The third white guy was Brown — I recognized him from all the pictures. He was tall — the way I wished I was — a Clint Eastwood type with metal-grey hair. He had a quietness and a sadness around him. His terry beach robe blew around his long runner's legs full of tendons. The robe had red dragons on it, which made him look more like a sci-fi sorcerer than a coach. His hair was longer than a Marine buzz cut.

Brown and Mom stood and looked at each other for a minute. I guessed they hadn't seen each other in years. Mom had her arms crossed on her chest. Finally he put his hand out. She took it, but I could see she was not feeling all that friendly towards him.

Chino made the introductions. "William, this is Harlan Brown...Paul Eckhardt...Darryl Fals...they are the co-owners of Valhalla. And Rose Bass, CFO of Valhalla. And Vivian Whitmore, who is Valhalla's office manager."

I glanced at Brown. He squinted back at me, sharp clear eyes that were sea-green, looking right into me. Most old people's eyes look at you through personal smog. I closed myself up, locking my vibro-magnetic shields in place. Brown's hand was held out to me. Strong hand, long fingers with metal-grey hairs. He had touched my Dad's body with that hand. The thought weirded me out. So I turned my back on him and walked away.

"Hi, everybody," I said over my shoulder.

If Brown's feelings were hurt, he didn't show it. We all dragged our gear onto the beach.

"Where's Vince?" Marian asked.

"Tired," Brown said. "He just got back from Mexico. William can meet him next time."

The great lame beach party got started. Queer guys were into rules as bad as Jerry Heaster. Everything had to be organized, and go like clockwork. They set up the volleyball net like it was a space launch, and chose teams — without me. Brown, Rose, my Mom and Paul were Blue Team. Chino, Vivian, Darryl and Marian were Red Team. There were yells and wild shots and people diving onto the sand to make saves. Chino shot straight in the air like a dolphin, with his muscles rippling, and punched deadly angle shots over the net. Red Team was ahead.

"Hey William," called Mom, "we're over-faced. Help us, will you?"

Chino scored another point.

"William, we're being *murdered*," called Rose.

"Looks like William is a natural benchwarmer," Brown said casually. This made me mad, but I wouldn't show it.

After two wins by Red Team, we went to the beach house for lunch. Paul was this ranch boy from Texas, but now and then he got faggy. He and his boyfriend, Darryl, had a friendly argument over the only beef sandwich with avocado.

"Okay, honey, you take it," said Paul. "But I get the only bag of barbecue nachos. So there."

And he did this girlie thing in the air with his hand and snapped his fingers.

Now and then, I watched Brown out of the corners of my eyes. The old Marine didn't say much, and he ignored me now. When the dragon robe came off, his shoulder had a tattoo on it — a lion. So he didn't mind being pegged. My eyes followed him around. This guy had loved my Dad with a movie passion, and almost went crazy when he died. But I couldn't think of a thing to say to him.

My Mom was laughing with Rose and Vivian. I wondered if she had the hots for either of them. Jesus, all this queer sex going on around me. Me and Marian were the only normal ones. Everybody was talking movie-making. Pitching ideas to Warner's...getting a script to Robert Redford...yada yada yada. Boring.

After lunch, the waves were pumping pretty good. So Paul and Darryl dragged this ancient longboard from under the deck, with the paint peeling off it. "Chino, do the honors?" they asked.

"I haven't surfed since SEAL basic at Coronado," said Chino. "So we'll keep this real simple."

Chino gave longboard lessons to everybody. Ducking under, I watched him swim, his brown body streaming silver bubbles, with that long hair floating loose over his shoulders and his wet Speedo hinting at what he owned. His strong legs made those frogman scissor-kicks that thrust him along like a shark. When he helped me get control of the board, I got to hold his waist for just a sec, and his bare chest brushed mine. I was wishing that, just by accident, a wave would pull down his Speedo. Then he swam off to help my Mom, who was disgustingly good on the board, screaming a kai-yai when she rode her first wave. Brown was pretty good too. Marian wiped out every time. Next wave, I stood the board easy, my arms held out like wings.

Toward the end of the afternoon, we all watched Chino catch a big one. As he angled down the wave, he backed deep into the tube. His coffee shape was visible through water wrapping down over him. He slowed to the wave's speed by dragging his hand along the wall of water. My chest tightened — I could hardly breathe.

The afternoon wasn't over too soon for me. As we left, Paul and Darryl said to me, "Come see us. We'll give you a tour of Valhalla."

Heading back to Caballo in Chino's 4 Runner, everybody was quiet, waiting to hear my reaction.

"*Honey*," I said. "Chino *honey*. Darryl *baby*."

Chino was driving. He laughed. "Do they scare you that much?"

"Paul and Darryl seem kinda okay to me. Rose is stylin'. Too bad she's a lesbian. I'd go out with her in a minute...if I had a car."

"Listen to *Señor* Jailbait," my Mom said. "Rose is twenty years older, and he wants to date her."

"That faggy stuff that Paul was doing with his hands," I said.

"Snapping," said Marian.

"What?"

"It's called snapping. It's a thing some of the guys do."

"Why do queers act like..."

"Gay men," said my Mom. "Not queers."

"Why do they act like...like girls?"

"Do I act like a girl?" Chino asked.

"Uh...no."

"Different kinds of people have different shades of sexuality," said Marian.

I shrugged. "Your point is?"

"Would you like to chase Darryl around the mall?" my Mom asked me. "Throw Paul in a dumpster?"

"Me and Shawn never hurt anybody," I said.

"How about Rose?" Marian added in. "Oh, I forgot...you don't beat up girls yet. Except your mom."

My cheeks burned.

"Tell you what," said Chino. "I'll teach you how to break knees. Nobody does that better than me. Then you can break Rose's knees. One, or both. Your choice."

A shudder went through me. My mind fought against getting the point.

"The guys who dusted your dad," said Chino, "they probably started out young...chasing some queeny little kid...stealing his lunch money. Is this the kind of person you want to be?"

Later that night, my Mom nailed me alone in the kitchen. "You'll break Harlan's heart," she said.

"Why should I care? He's not my biological Dad."

"You owe it to him that you got born," she reminded me.

I was feeling frantic. "No way."

"It's true. Billy was okay with just the two of them. Harlan wanted a family. Billy loved kids, so he went along with it. I came in later, when I heard they were looking for a surrogate mother."

This sounded so bizarre.

Mom controlled herself, but her eyes blazed.

"Thousands of kids get born every minute," she said, "and most of them just happen. But...people *wanted* you. Harlan *wanted* you to be born. After Billy was killed, all Harlan could think about was your safety. He even wanted to marry me, so he could be around you all the time and protect you."

Now she was crying. I turned my back on her.

"Jesus christ," she exploded. "Kids. You're all the same. Heartless. You don't care about your own lives...or other people's lives."

"I get tired of life sometimes," I said.

"I don't know what the hell to do with you."

Chino's voice came from the next room. "Take him back to the store," he said. "Exchange him for a pet."

I trudged upstairs.

In my room, in the dark, I leaned on the dresser and looked at my Dad's picture for a long time. There was still no candle burning there. All I could see was the green wave curling over Chino's naked back. Suddenly all the feelings of the last few weeks came over me. Was I queer too? With a queer Mom and a queer Dad, I *had* to be queer, right? So why did I think Ana was cool?

Lurking on my balcony, I tried to hear more talk. Marian and my Mom were sitting outside in the dark, talking alone together like they always did.

"...And I've tried to look into his world, and know what he needs," said my Mom's voice. "But something major has gone wrong."

"Don't blame yourself. I don't think your being a lesbian is the problem."

"I've tried to give him a balanced example. I mean, I don't *hate* men...do I? Admittedly I don't get along with a few of them! But...I never had any of the big dramatic reasons to hate men that some women have. I was never abused by family males. Never date-raped. Never bashed around. I just...love women. Always did, from eight years old. Loved my Mom, loved my girlfriends, loved my women teachers, loved beautiful actresses, loved ladies I saw on the street, loved Goddesses. I love you too...and I don't have to jump in bed with you, I just appreciate you wildly. And I love the loyalty that you've had for me, which I haven't always deserved. But somehow, with all my trying, I've messed up my kid."

Did this mean Marian was queer too? Was I really the only normal person here?

"William lives in some kind of world of his own," Marian said.

"He's been asking me questions about genes. I think he must be freaking out. With a gay dad and a lesbian mom, he's probably thinking he's queer for sure...freaked to death. No wonder he didn't want to see Harlan."

"Do you think it's genetic?" Marian's voice asked.

"I've known other lesbians and gay men who had kids together, and the kids turned out certifiably straight. If it's genetic, it sure isn't predictable. I don't know the technical terms."

"Michael would."

"Yeah. Too bad he's missing this. Michael just loves family drama."

Michael was Harlan's son? I remembered Chino telling me this.

"He and Astarte are wrapping up the gene research — they'll be back in August. I got a letter last week," Marian was saying.

"Now there's an interesting example of genes. Harlan's other kid seems to be relentlessly straight...though who knows? But Michael is...who knows what Michael is?"

So Brown had two kids of his own.

"Vince was definitely bi when he was young," said Marian. "Joe and I watched him sleep his way across campus. But Vince was an only child, so we don't have any siblings to compare him with."

Now the two ladies were going inside. "When Michael gets back," said my Mom, "we'll get him and William together, so William can ask..."

Their voices died.

No way was I going to ask "Brown's boy" about my genes, even if he was the last scientist left on Earth.

July came. Mom gave me the phone numbers for Brown and Valhalla, but I never called. Now and then, I still got to spend a couple hours with Chino. Whenever Chino left, I watched the 4 Runner go to a dot down the canyon with my heart bleeding everywhere.

Chino was not a kid, so it was hard to work into fooling-around ops with him. No sleep-overs, no drunken blasts, no showers for two. It seemed like he avoided this kind of situation with me. One time, I was sure I had him. It was a windy night — a summer storm happening, lightning and rain. When we got back to Marian's from a quick Thai dinner on the PCH, nobody else was there. Upstairs in the hallway, I mumbled, "Hey, Chino...I'm scared of lightning...tuck me in?" I tried to sound like a helpless and needy little kid. Without a word, he walked me into my bedroom, turned on the bedside light. My heart was pounding wildly. I was too shy to strip down to my Jockeys, so I just crawled in bed with my clothes on.

He looked down at me coldly, tense and graceful, like he was made of jungle shadows. A flicker of lightning lit him from behind. Please, please, Chino, get in bed with me and stay all night, so I can feel your arm over me, and your dreams, maybe your military secrets against my leg, just by accident.

I grinned, teeth chattering.

"I wouldn't mind a bedtime story," I said.

"Harlan can tell you one," the heartless commander replied, and snapped off the light.

His footsteps went away down the hall, leaving me alone.

When no one was home, I sometimes sneaked into his room and snooped around. Like the jungle he'd slid through, he didn't leave many traces here. A few shirts hung in the closet. I stroked them. Behind them was a metal gun cabinet with a big padlock on it — I wondered what kind of guns. Probably primitive weapons like shotguns and full-auto rifles. A couple changes of underwear in the dresser drawer. He wore Jockeys too, and I buried my nose in them, hoping for a whiff. But Marian's relentless washing machine had done its job, so they smelled like fabric softener. His pure nature was missing — who he was, pure and alive and dangerous as the stars. I buried my face in them, and blissfully fooled with myself.

Since Chino was queer, he had to be (1) a pedophile, and (2) an authority on the wild thing.

I was fascinated by the wild thing...the abomination. The preachers had screamed about it so much, that they had gotten me curious about it. Why weren't they smart enough to keep their big mouths shut? The Bible said that the wild thing is a major deal. Jerry had read us the verses about guys doing guys like they were women. Chino was probably excellent at this, like he was excellent at tactics and Barbarian firearms. I would have to let him do me. That was the rule. The younger one always gives it up. Kids know that when they fool around. The idea of Chino trying that with me scared me to death, and also thrilled me beyond thrills...and it also made me remember fooling around with Orik, and how it hurt when we tried it, and how much I missed Orik and wanted him back.

I almost had electrifying fantasies about a kiss. But when the kissing scene with Chino came up on the big monitor screen in my mind, I switched fast to imagining a kiss with Ana. A normal guy can mess with a friend out of friendship or horniness, but he doesn't let a friend kiss him.

Fourth of July came. We sat on Marian's lawn and watched amazing fireworks. Some rich dude had a whole barge of fireworks towed over from Santa Monica, and anchored it in front of his beach house.

To the Caballo kid tribe, I bragged about getting tons of girls. Ace and Mia didn't believe it, and kept calling me the "baby." After I started saying no to Ecstasy and pot, they suddenly weren't available for concerts or mall-crawling. But Ziggy and Ana kept in touch. So we shuttled back and forth between our two houses.

Malibu was a sector of the planet that was cooler, and foggier, and wilder than anywhere I'd been. Up on the hills where Marian lived, it was actually quiet. You couldn't hear children's voices, or people's TVs, or domestic quarrels, or bells of the ice-cream truck. The hills were covered with bushes called chaparral, and full of wild animals. Deer were as alien to me as men from Mars, but here, you practically fell over the deer when you went outdoors in the morning. Maybe I could like Malibu...if only Orik were here.

Ana LaFont was my chance to do scientific exploration of girls.

So we started hanging together — biking down to the mall and the beach. She taught me how to do a kick flip on her skateboard. She taught me the different buses into Santa Monica and L.A. She told me about every bird on Earth. I watched her putting up bird feeders and studying deer through her own binoculars. She even picked up a baby rattlesnake that got in the house, and it let her dump it outside. She let me read a school essay, about her worries about the Earth. She wanted to lead the Green Party, she said.

Maybe it was a good thing that Orik wasn't around, so I could focus on girls. He'd understand, because he was doing the same thing. I was supposed to try women, and all the secret guy stuff would suddenly go away, like the movie goes away from the TV screen when the video tape breaks. The guy stuff was just part of your training, like learning about weightlessness for being an astronaut. But every time I thought about it, my stomach felt like a weightless chamber.

A week after the Fourth, Ana and I took a private walk down in the canyon. I had invited her to go bird watching because I was too nervous about trying to kiss her in my house, or her parents' house. I was still culturally deprived, without a car to take her somewhere in, and I wasn't going to kiss her on the excuse-me bus. For some strange reason I didn't want Chino to catch me in the middle of my scientific experiment, which might blow up on me like the silver fulminate did. We were walking along the horse trail in the hot sun, with chaparral smelling good all around us, and also the yucky smell of some horse turds nearby. She wore an old Sierra Club cap. I had a new cap, no star.

"Look," she said, "there's an Anna's hummingbird."

"Named after you, huh."

"No. My name is Ah-na. It's Hawaiian."

"Miss your dad?"

"Yeah, he was cool. I was pretty little when he died. But I remember how we'd sit really still in the forest and he'd show me animals...including all the exotics invading Hawaii...rats and stuff." She sniffed.

"I'm sorry." After hesitating, I grabbed her fingers.

This time she didn't pull away. We were two dadless kids. We could take care of each other. I was truly feeling a care for her. But I was having the usual problems with saying what I wanted. So, when we got out of range of the horse turds, I swung around to face her. She bumped into me, and my lips were waiting in ambush. No SEAL could have ambushed her better — except the bills of our baseball hats collided. Her lips were small, and very warm.

"Mmmm," she said. She turned her bill sideways without taking her mouth away.

Then this hot 13-year-old wound her arms around my neck, and pressed her 18-year-old breasts into my rib cage, and kissed me good. All the while, I was focusing on the sector below my belt. It was really happening. Inside my pants, and all over my body, it felt terrific. She slid her hands under my T-shirt and caressed my back, and I went wild with shivers. It was different from what I felt with Orik — maybe less electric — but I got busy making all the right moves with my lips.

Then we had to jump apart — three dorks on horses almost ran over us. As we coughed in the dust, Ana grinned at me. I guess my persistence had given her self-esteem a push.

"You're pretty good," she said. Out of her pocket came one of those famous condoms. She wiggled it at me.

"We...uh...better be getting back," I said.

"I don't believe this. A guy who actually doesn't want to."

My cheeks burned. "Not on such...uh...short notice."

We started walking back. The birds were in a frenzy of singing in the chaparral.

"You've got another option," she said.

"What?"

"You can be my guy friend."

"I thought you...uh...had lots of boyfriends and stuff."

"A *guy* friend, dummy. *Friend.*"

"Why not?" I said, trying to be casual.

I caught her hand again, and she didn't pull it away. Her hand was smaller than Orik's. Ana wasn't exactly delicate, she could even slamdunk better than me, but somehow she gave me this tender feeling. I wanted to protect her.

She met my eyes and grinned. I grinned back.

"Buddy," I said.

"Whatever," she said.

On the 11th, we watched the partial eclipse of the sun together.

On the days when Chino came, we worked out together, and he started teaching me more defensive moves. Mom got mad about this and told him not to make me more bloodthirsty.

"If you're going to be seriously out, he's going to run into problems at school," Chino said.

"I don't want him getting into fights on my behalf," she said. "He can walk away from fights."

"You can't always walk away and be safe."

So I learned about moves with a guy who has a knife. If Chino touched me a little to guide my movements, I shivered all over.

Chino was always caring...and always distant. One time I was in the tree, and had an impulse to jump out at him, to make him catch me like dads do to kids. He caught me, and laughed...then did a surprise move that spun me around in the air, then landed me on the grass without hurting me. It was amazing how strong he was — he twirled me like I was a baton. He was the star you can never touch.

Who was Chino's boyfriend? He was always alone. When he was horny, did he just go out and have some guy in an alley?

I was hungry for touch...girl touch, guy touch. Worse than anything I'd felt with Orik. And I felt sneaky too...betraying Orik.

One day Ana and I were standing on the road when Ace came thundering down the hill on his skateboard. He looked very warrior in his kneepads and helmet. He buzzed us, and almost rammed me. Then he braked with lots of drama, and picked up his board.

"Hey, what's *your* problem today?" I asked.

"I hear your mom is a lezzzz-bo," he said.

"Your mom is a drunk."

"Drunk is better than deviate." He looked at Ana. "I don't know what that makes *you*, little girl, but..."

I lunged for Ace, but he jumped on his board and rocketed down the hill, screaming with laughter like some satanic rock star.

"I told you," Chino said to my Mom.

Mom sighed. "Ten years I've braced myself for this. Okay, go ahead and teach him some serious self-defense."

Two weeks after the Fourth, my commander and I looked at the stars together, for the first time. Since I didn't have a telescope now, I was using my old submarine spotters and Chino was using his old Navy B&L binoculars that he'd carried in Vietnam. We sat on some rocks overlooking the canyon. It was a perfect night — no Moon, no smog, the air very clear and dry. I was shivering because of sitting close to my commander.

"Chino, your binocs are so old."

"Don't kid yourself. The old optics are better than some of the new stuff."

"You use those in your PI work, huh? And you haven't been working because of me."

"Don't worry about it. A few years ago, a friend of ours died and left me well fixed. He was an old veteran, another spec/war guy. I have my little portfolio, and I can draw on it when I have to."

"He was your...uh...sugar daddy?"

Chino was in a quiet, almost sad mood.

"If you learn to look beyond the obvious," he said, "like those stars out there, you can start seeing what's real in your family. I did PI work for Russell, and he knew my situation. Yeah, I was in a bad way, for a while. Russell didn't want me to need again, ever. He was wealthy, and when he finally came out, he took care of us — gave it to us before he died, so his family couldn't sue us for it. He helped Harry and me with our security business. Helped Harlan and Vince buy the house. Eileen and Glenn with the restaurant. Money to your Grandpa Sive for human-rights litigation. Money to Michael's research. Venture capital to Valhalla. His scholarship fund is still putting kids through school. Russell was one rich gay man who decided to spend his money on real things instead of glitz."

Suddenly he chuckled. "The only one who wouldn't take his money was your mom."

Chino broke off, like he'd said too much, and polished his lenses with a special cloth.

"Let's get to work here," he said. His shoulder managed not to brush mine.

It was after 9 P.M., with Cassiopeia and Andromeda still low in the glow of L.A. to the east, and Ursa Major descending in the west. The meridian was dark and clear overhead, with bright scratches of meteors through it. Lights of planes taking off from LAX moved across the sky like fast planets. I said hello to all my oldest star-friends. Polaris stood right over Axl Rose's roof. We had fun resolving all the double stars in Draco.

The stars made my confusion look so huge! They were so totally clear on what they wanted to be, churning and burning themselves into stars, more stars, living out their millions of light years without the threat of therapists or courtrooms or the smell of tears around them. I had to get going on my Mission again. My gay Dad had come to me in a dream, or God and Goddess sent me a dream about him, and asked me to find him. There had to be a reason. Did his spirit know what a mess I was? Did he know how I hadn't shaken hands with Brown? He was probably saying, *You've forgotten me.*

Chino knew the sky. As a sailor, he had to, for navigation. But I felt proud to be able to tell him some new things, and he let me teach him.

"And those three stars...that's the Summer Triangle. Look through it, into that dark place...that's the center of our galaxy. Only you can't see it, because of dust."

Chino studied the Triangle silently.

I looked through the Triangle till my arms got tired. Somewhere out there was the Cat Nebula. My brain could still see its shape in every detail. But I could only look one inch into the millions of miles, unless the Cat was close enough to our solar system for my planned 10" mirror to catch its faint light. Big observatories already had tons of photographs of nebulas. So did NASA. Maybe I should forget about building a new telescope, and go check out other people's work, which was done with bigger telescopes than mine.

"Some special reason you're interested in astronomy?" he asked.

It was spooky how Chino could read minds.

"Oh, my Mom got me interested."

"When are you starting the new mirror?"

"Maybe after vacation. I've gotta get the pyrex blanks."

"How long will it take you?"

"Thirty, forty hours, maybe."

For the first time I considered telling an adult about my Mission. Should I tell Chino? Could I trust him? Maybe he could help.

"Would you like to help me on the mirror?" I asked.

Chino looked at me. I thought he might move and get closer to me, so our arms could touch or something. There was this intense buzz of energy between us. Why did I feel this thing for him? I was supposed to be loyal to Orik.

But he didn't move. "I won't be around as much," he said. "I'm moving across a meridian myself...giving up the security business, working more for Marian on strategies and campaign security. And your mom's talking about moving."

My heart went down. A cold ocean breath came up the canyon.

"I guess she won't want us to live next door to the Heasters any more," I said.

"Hey, listen...tomorrow's an anniversary of mine. Want to spend it with me?"

"Sure," I said. My heart went up again like a bright star ascending. But I tried to sound cool.

A whole day alone with him. Tomorrow, something was going to happen. Maybe my commander was going to make a move on me — try the wild thing on me. I was totally terrified — and trembling with hope and curiosity as to what it would be like, and worried about him seeing my size. He wouldn't be impressed.

"And tomorrow night," he went on, "you're spending in West Hollywood. Your mom wants you to meet Vince."

My heart sank again. "Yuck."

"He was your dad's best friend, so I think you can have some respect."

As a star, Chino was close and hot and bright, a first magnitude star. Brown was too far away to see — some black hole about twenty billion light years out. I didn't even want to gaze that far. But Chino was proposing a deal, and I knew he meant it when he talked about respect, so I said, "Yeah, maybe I can."

— 11 —

CHINO'S MOVE

The next morning I had a zit on my nose, and wanted to throw myself out the window. While I was covering the thing with a dab of my Mom's extra-cover makeup, Chino braked his 4 Runner in the drive with a screech of tires. Did my Mom know that he was maybe going to try something today? Did she approve? Did she even care?

Chino was in a bad mood for an anniversary — showered, creased jeans, but hollow-eyed, like he hadn't slept good. I tried to force a change in his vibe. Going across the lawn, I jumped him from behind, riding him with arms around his neck, legs wrapped around his waist. Bored, patient, surly, he carried me towards the 4 Runner. Chino was amazingly strong for a short guy.

"You're not going to give up on me, are you?" I demanded.

At the truck, he dumped me on the driveway. "You've been nothing but worry and flurry, ever since you were born."

"What do you mean?" We got in the 4 Runner.

"Long story." As he started the ignition, his hand was trembling.

"Why are you...like...shaking?" I asked.

"The old malaria flared up. Got it in Nam," Chino said.

As we drove down the PCH, I kept on digging at my commander, trying to get him reacting. "Marian told me that you turned guys in Vietnam. What does that mean?"

"There were good fighters in the Viet Cong," he said. "I was running a program that needed native fighters. This was during Vietnamization. I suppose you don't know what Vietnamization was. They don't teach you kids any history now."

Why did adults always complain about history?

"When the U.S. finally decided to get out of Vietnam," he went on, "we handed the fighting over to the South Vietnamese. I got promoted and reassigned to train an indigenous team — a provincial reconaissance unit. PRUs, we called them. They were mercenaries...Hmongs, Montagnards, Nungs, whoever."

"Hmongs?"

"Tribes who live in the mountains."

Wow...alien peoples, like the Wookies in *Star Wars*.

"I paid them by the ear. We were going to do..."

"Whoa. Ears? Human ears?"

"If they brought me an ear as proof of a kill, I paid them in green. We did Bright Light operations — rescued POWs. As many as we could before the U.S. pulled out...and a few more after that."

The hair on my head and body prickled all over.

"So...tell me about being gay. What's it like?" I asked.

He shrugged. "I wouldn't know. I'm bi."

"You've been with *women?*"

"Yes."

"But you must have a...a boyfriend."

"No.. I don't."

"It must be weird, having people hate you and stuff."

"I try not to let the hate run my life."

"People hate you because you do kids, right?"

"That, and other reasons."

"So you do kids."

"Not personally, no."

"Come on. Queers do kids."

My commander veered into the fast lane to pass a white stretch limo. "If you know so much about queers, why are you asking me?"

"Uh...everybody knows that queers do that."

Chino laughed a little. He didn't even take his eyes off the highway, watching a car approach us that was close to the center line. He edged the 4 Runner over to the shoulder.

"You want to be a scientist? You won't get far if you believe everything you're told."

At the Sunset junction, a grey-bearded homeless man with a torn khaki jacket came up to us at the red light. His sign said VIET VET NEEDS WORK. Chino reached out the window and stuffed twenty dollars and a bunch of supermarket coupons into the guy's pocket. "Oh God bless you," said the vet, breaking down and crying. He threw his arm around Chino's neck, while people behind us got pissed and leaned on their horns.

Then we drove east across L.A. along Sunset Boulevard.

"This is Silverlake," he said, gunning the 4 Runner across Western. "My old barrio."

"You grew up here?"

"I was born here. I grew up in Vietnam."

Silverlake was Whites, Latinos, Mexicans and Asians living mixed, he said. There was a nice neighborhood, where professional people lived. The rest of the sector was poor. He showed me the alley where his stepdad, Eulogio, beat him up. His stepdad had caught him fooling with another 12-year-old. Chino showed me the working-class gay bar where he used to hang outside when he was fourteen and have heartbreaks over a car mechanic named Jorge who was inside. There was one of those gloomy city schools that look like a jail, where other kids knew about him, and beat him up so much that he dropped out. There was the little wooden house with paint peeling and a half-dead palm, where he'd hated his stepfather's guts.

"I was an obvious *joto* then," he said.

"Hoto," I repeated, trying to wrap my mouth around the Spanish word. It was hard to imagine him being anything but a movie macho. "D'ja play with dolls?"

"My *jefita*, my mama tried to give me to the social workers. She was afraid I'd get killed. Gang *vatos* were picking on me and I was carrying a knife and learning how to fight with them. My uncle was in the Navy, and he gave me tips on knife fighting. But nobody wanted to adopt a crazy little queen. Finally my uncle took me to the Navy recruiter. I was seventeen and too numb to care. It didn't take the Navy long to figure out that the *loca* from Silverlake could be a world-class bad guy. For the next seven years, the Navy was my home."

He leaned out to some lady's rose hedge with his big folding knife, and stole two perfect roses. Was he saying that he was a little sissy, like Alberto? But sissies don't do knife fighting.

Next thing, we were parking by a Catholic cemetery. He locked the 4 Runner, and we went through the iron gate. The sun was hot. There were rows and rows of hot shiny new gravestones in the grass. A realm of the dead for Earthlings.

W e walked to the other side of the cemetery, getting sweaty. Right here, a huge tree was dripping red blossoms like blood all over the grass. All the time I was thinking that this was a weird way for Chino to work into the wild thing. Was he going to do me right in the cemetery...in a corner behind some bushes?

Chino stopped by a black headstone with a photograph set in it, under some glass. MARIA CONCEPCION CABRERA 1932-1977, it said. He put one rose on it. "My *jefita* always stood up for me. She lived long enough to see the President hang a medal on me."

"What medal?"

"Navy Cross."

"Hey...can I see it sometime?"

"I burned it."

"*Burned* it?" My hair prickled again. Medals were holy, weren't they? Astronauts got medals. "Whoa. You...like, put the Navy Cross in a fire and burned it up?"

"I did it when I got out of the hospital in '75. There was a trash barrel in Harry's back yard. He was a buddy of mine. I burned most of my stuff. Uniforms, decorations, dress sword...trying to get rid of my ghosts."

"Jesus," I whispered in awe. "Were you..." My lips would hardly make the words. "Were you...uh...boyfriends with Harry?"

"No. He tried to help me get my head together after Nam. He and Harlan."

We kept walking. On the next headstone, the letters said EULOGIO MORILLO 1927-1972, with a photo of a Mexican dude with a big mustache. Chino put his jungle boot down right on the photo, and walked on. That time, my hair prickled hard to see his hate for his stepdad. Beyond, Chino stopped at a plain black stone with an Asian name. The little glass slot for a photo was empty.

YUKIO SHUGAWARA
Dai Uy
July 13, 1974

Chino squatted Asian style. Feeling awkward, I kneeled on the other side of the headstone. Carefully he placed the second rose there. His ponytail's loose ends stirred in the breeze.

"What's dai...dai...?" I asked.

"Vietnamese for lieutenant," he said, sounding like he had a sore throat.

Today was July 13. Lieutenant Shugawara, whoever he was, died seventeen years ago today. So this was the anniversary. Now chills were racing over me wildly. When I looked up at Chino again, a tear was trickling down his cheek. Then he bowed his head. The only thing that moved was the tear. It fell off his jaw, and made a spot on the hot stone, and dried up right away. A feeling came up in me — so big and strong that I forgot about the wild thing. Lieutenant Shugawara was Chino's secret. He'd lost Shugawara, like Brown had lost my Dad, like I'd lost Orik. I wanted to take his pain, and put it in my backpack, and carry it for him forever. But first I looked around, to see if anybody was watching.

The cemetery was almost empty.

So I awkwardly stuck my fingers out and touched his hair. My knees were shivering.

Then both my hands were holding his head. He leaned across the grave, and put his face against my chest. I stroked his head, feeling like I was petting some wounded animal that crawled out of the jungle and was laying at my feet. It was the first time in my life I ever actually comforted an adult person. Now and then I'd tried to make Orik feel better about something, but this was different. His face was against my shirt, and I could feel his hot breath on my chest, as his body shivered with the sobs held inside. Nobody noticed us. People cried in the cemetery all the time.

After a while, it got hot in the sun, so we moved into the shade of the tree. He lay on his back in the splash of red flowers, and stared up at the sky. I sat by him, and smoothed his hair back from his damp forehead, feeling like my hand was very awkward. Our shadows stretched longer, across Shugawara's grave. His eyes were dry now.

He drew a shuddery breath, and swallowed.

"One day my PRUs brought in some VC officers to question. He was one of them. Half-naked, blindfold on, his arms tied to a bamboo pole. He held himself real quiet. The PRUs were going to torture him. I could see he wasn't going to tell us anything. They'd do him and do him...and finally they'd cut his throat...and officially I wouldn't be there, but I'd have to watch."

The picture sent a dark, creepy shock along my nerves. Pictures from ancient times, a war on a primitive planet with primitive weapons, that happened a long time before I was born. Chino took my hand, and held it against his chest, rubbing his heart with it. His palm was hot, almost feverish.

"Something came over me. The carnage was starting to wake me out of being numb. And I had a feeling I could *chu hoi* him...turn him. I sensed I could trust him.So I ordered them to release him, and I gave him clothes. He was surprised — he'd expected to die. We got a little drunk on rice wine. He was a mercenary, didn't care about the politics of the war. Halfbreed like me, Vietnamese citizen, but half Japanese and half French. Educated — school in Europe. The VC had paid him a lot. I said I'd pay him more. Beaucoup green, I told him...guns, women, whatever he wanted. He said he'd do it for the green, no women."

I rubbed Chino's hand the way he had rubbed mine, that time. The sun was going down. Our two shadows were twenty feet long.

Chino's eyes were closed.

"Shuga, I called him. His English was good, so he knew it sounded like Sugar. This cracked him up. The PRUs liked him, but our thing took a while to happen. Now and then, we went to Saigon on business. We'd have dinner. Afterwards, we'd go into the part of the city where Americans and Europeans didn't go...to his family's house. It finally happened there. For six months we pulled it off. He was put in command of a PRU, and I was his SEAL liaison. He was 37, I was 21. If we'd been caught, I would have been flown out in shackles, and Shuga..."

Chino stopped talking.

I felt myself go strangely quiet inside. Distorted pictures of sex acts flipped through my mind. Did they do the wild thing? Which of them did the other? Chino was the young one, so the rules said that he gave it up to Shuga. A SEAL officer giving it up to a Viet Cong officer? The Navy would have shot him if they knew. But Chino stayed silent. He wasn't going to talk about how Shuga made love, or how he died. His hand lay inert in mine, unresponding. There was none of the electricity that always happened between Orik's hand and mine. Chino wasn't going to make a move.

It was getting dark, and a traffic chopper flew over. Chino's eyes opened, and followed the chopper's lights across the sky. He was listening to the *thud, thud, thud* of the rotors.

"You...tortured people?" I whispered.

His eyes stared up at the faint stars coming out. Corona Borealis and Serpens Caput would be right at the meridian.

"William...let's say somebody kidnapped you, and was going to kill you. I could find out where you were by torturing somebody. Don't you think I might tear the guy apart with my bare hands?"

Now it was so quiet inside me that I was standing on that default line across the universe in my dream, the place where there were no more galaxies or dust clouds, just black space. Maybe he'd told me the story to let me know that his heart was buried there under that black stone, so he wouldn't be loving anybody else, least of all some weeny teenager. There was no way he would feel anything for me, beyond doing his duty as family and bodyguard.

He must have known what I was thinking, because he suddenly said in a quiet voice:

"A man...a real man, an officer, learns to take care of his people, because otherwise they get hurt. The Navy didn't want me, but I'm still an officer in my own world. Understand?"

I nodded numbly.

"That's why it's a matter of personal honor with me to look after kids...including girl kids, who are just as wonderful as boy kids. Like Ana. I knew her dad too. She has so much promise. I hold my breath for her, like I do for you."

I flushed and sat there staring at Shuga's grave, arms hugging my knees. The hurt was like a meteor slice across my brain. Somehow he'd known what was on my mind, and his answer was basically no. Yet he was saying he cared about me in a different way.

"How did you get his body home?" I whispered.

"His body isn't here. I buried him where he died, in the jungle.

He's probably still there. My uncle went back to Mexico, so there was this empty plot here and I used it. It was the best I could do."

Chino drew a deep breath. "Too many ghosts around," he said. "The whole family has them. You, your mom, Harlan, all of us. We've lost so much. Time to deal with our ghosts."

He sat up, and brushed the grass off his shirt.

They'd closed the gates, and locked us in the cemetery. So we climbed over the iron fence in the dark. In the 4 Runner, he didn't start the engine right away, just sat with his eyes closed. The empty street was half lit by a street light. "Thanks for being there for me," he said.

"Am I back in your program?"

"You've been in my program all your life."

"So you were...like, around when I was born?"

"In the hospital."

"No kidding."

The feeling inside me changed, like when your foot goes numb and then suddenly you feel the blood surging back into it, the pins and needles — a scary feeling, but wonderful, because you know it's coming back to life.

His eyes met mine, and suddenly he smiled.

"There was a power blackout while your mom was in labor," he said. "The staff were running around dealing with patient emergencies, and they forgot about your mom in the labor room. Harlan was trying to find a doctor, a goddam nurse, anybody. Marian was helping your mother stay calm and do the breathing. All of a sudden you were there. Like you were in a big hurry to get born. And me...well, I'm a trained medic, so..."

I had to laugh, glowing all over. Once again I was having this feeling of seeing past a huge nebula, into the bright and beautiful center of a new galaxy — my own past, which had been lost like the spirit of some great vanished civilization out there in space.

"You slapped my butt and everything?"

"You were the loudest, slipperiest baby I ever saw." Suddenly he actually grinned. "I cleared your airways. I put you on top of your mom...and the first thing you did was punch her in the nose."

Chino's hand jammed the key into the ignition. I noticed it wasn't trembling any more. He gunned the engine, and we shot down the street with a screech of tires. "But I didn't know you were Billy's kid then," he said. "Your mom and Harlan didn't tell me the big secret till later."

The 4 Runner wove in and out of traffic, went left on Western, right on Hollywood Boulevard, staying just under the speed limit. I sat tensed in the opposite corner, a knot of tears in my throat, watching the lights of theaters and porn shops and cheap clothing stores stream past, the shapes of hookers and homeless people — left on La Brea, back into West Hollywood.

I felt strangely brave, curiously courageous, violently emotional. Chino would never fool around with me, but he would die for me. He might even command my ship to the Cat Nebula...except he didn't know that I wanted this from him. He didn't know anything about my war. Suddenly the sobs racked me.

"What a day," he said. "First I cry, then you cry. What's going on?"

"Chino, I want to tell you something, okay? It's really important, okay?"

He pulled over into a shady place on Rosewood, away from streetlights, and shut off the engine, and looked at me warily. We sat there in the dark, and I told him the whole thing — the Cat Nebula dream, the variable star, the Mission. He relaxed, and listened.

"So...let me get this straight," he said. "You're not telling me some story that you were abducted by aliens."

"No way. It was a dream."

"Everybody has dreams. I've had a few that would pucker your ass in your sleep."

"This was a *real* kind of dream. It was like I went there in my sleep. It was real, Chino!"

"So?"

"So I'm having problems doing what my Dad asked. Like, the nearest star is four light-years from here. Ten years to Pluto, two years to Mars and back...and we haven't even been there yet. So far, I can't even find the Cat Nebula...but even if it's nearby, there's no way I'll get there alive, unless they hurry up with technology. I feel like I'm letting my Dad down."

For a while Chino sat silent. Finally he said, half dreamily:

"Do you ever talk to your dad?"

My hair started prickling again. "You mean...like, pray?"

"The spirits can hear us."

"You mean...like a seance or something?" My hair was standing on end. My body prickled all over.

"No. I don't need some dipdunk psychic to talk to people that I talked to every day when they were alive. Understand?"

"Do you, uh, do you talk to Shuga?"

"Never had the guts. Because I know he'd tell me to let go, and I never wanted to let go."

Finally I said, "If he wants you to let go, why don't you?"

His eyes got misty. "Now and then there's a place I go to think about it...a place my Indian grandma took me when I was little. Whites call it Point Reyes. It sticks out in the Pacific. My ancestors thought it was something like the Launch Pad to the Spirit World...where you went to have a ceremony with death. People spent the last years of their lives walking to get there. They talked to their family spirits, or they just went there to die. I always think about going to Point Reyes to deal with my ghosts, but when I get there..."

"So you never did it."

"Not yet. Like I said, I don't have the guts."

He started the vehicle and drove on to Brown's house, and stopped. I felt let down, and opened the door. Was this all he was going to say? I was almost sorry I'd told him. I was just grabbing my backpack and climbing out, with my heart half broken, when he said behind me:

"I'll pick you up tomorrow around 1800 hours. We'll talk about your Mission then. I want some time to think. So relax...okay?"

"Okay."

"See that yellow house next door? That's Paul and Darryl's house. Remember Paul and Darryl? I live there. My window is by the palm there. If you need me. And Rose and Vivian live in the brown house six doors down."

"What are you doing tomorrow?"

"Checking up on Shawn," he said.

"How do you do that?"

"None of your business."

— 12 —

MOVING AGAIN

All movie people are supposed to live in mansions in Beverly Hills. But Harlan and Vince lived in this plain white house on Rosewood Avenue, about six blocks from Santa Monica Boulevard. It was hidden in palms and banana trees, behind this killer wall with iron spikes on top — they buzzed you through a security gate with an intercom. As the door opened, I shuddered at the idea of two guys being hubby and wifey. But my Dad had been Brown's wifey too.

"Got some dinner for you," Brown said. "Vince is tired and he's already asleep — you'll see him tomorrow. Your room is the guest room, last door on the right."

Brown's cooking didn't appeal, so I just picked. Brown tried to make small talk, but my head was so full of ghosts that he finally went to his computer to write, with his old dog sleeping by his feet. I watched TV on his couch. Everything was boring, even a Nova program about the size of the universe. I couldn't stop thinking about blown-apart bodies, and the smell of tears, and Chino's deathless love. Finally I went into the guest room, and shut the door.

Being in a strange room bothered me. Brown had already turned the bed down — he'd tried to make the room nice. There was a note on the bedside table, OUR FRIDGE IS YOUR FRIDGE, IF YOU GET HUNGRY IN THE MIDDLE OF THE NIGHT.

I stared at the bed. How many men had sex there? Did any of them have deathless love for each other? I couldn't stop thinking about it — the kind of feelings that went down in history, like Romeo and Juliet. Shuga and Chino, enemies in war, discovering the love. How did they show feelings? Did they ever kiss each other, or hold hands, maybe? How did his buddy die? How did Chino react? How did he hide his feelings from his superiors? My Dad must have felt those actual deathless feelings for Brown. It was hard to imagine, because I had never seen it in the movies.

Finally I got Orik's 8th grade picture out of my backpack, and put it on the bedside table, and looked at it, really missing him.

It was easy to fantasize that Orik had run away, and found this house in the Realm of L.A. with his astronaut wrist scanner. You input the compressed file for a person's voice signature, and it scans a light-year radius to find those vibrations. He crawled through the banana trees, the window. The strange bed creaked as he got in beside me. He was shaking violently as I cuddled him against me — he had lost all his clothes, so he was naked and freezing, on the run from the parents and police, and I needed to get him warm. The thought of kissing him crossed my mind. That couldn't happen, because it was queer. But we wrapped our arms and legs around each other, and got our hands in all the usual places, and I had a colossal spunk. I was really a man now.

Tomorrow I was going to meet the man who was my Dad's best friend in high school. Did they fool around too?

The next morning I woke up late. A marine layer covered Los Angeles — the sky was grey, mist drifting over the palm tops. Chino's 4 Runner was gone — he was in Orange County already. Vince and Brown had gone for a bike ride, and now Vince was working on the patio. As I fixed breakfast, Brown was around the house, but he didn't talk much. He didn't act like he had a lot of feelings. How did this quiet old sorcerer with dragons on his bathrobe ever have a passionate public love thing with my Dad that drove the whole country crazy and made a lot of people want to kill them both?

"Before you meet Vince," he said, "I want to go over some AIDS questions with you…"

Why did adults talk about AIDS so much?

"…Your buddy's parents told you that AIDS jumps through the air at people," Brown was saying. "But that's just not true."

At this point I was ready to mistrust anything that Orik's parents said. But why would I want to touch Vince anyway? Was Brown going to pester me about whether I thought I was queer? He must be dying to know.

T he patio was private with that high spikey wall around it. There was a little iron gate that led into a back alley. You could follow the alley to Paul's and Darryl's house, or Rose's and Vivian's house. In the shade of tangled banana trees and bamboos, with beautiful tropical flowers all around him, Vince was working at a glass table. Piles of paper, a cordless phone, a pitcher of water. As he opened his laptop, he didn't even look at me.

In the *Billy Sive* video, Vince was 20 something and movie-star good-looking, with long eyelashes. Mom said a whole generation of queer guys fell crazy in love with Vince. Now he was old, almost 40, with grey-black hair and a lined face. Even the long eyelashes were shorter. The long legs that rocketed him to a world record mile were skinny, making his feet look big in his athletic shoes. But he didn't look very sick. The good-looking eyes — strange golden eyes — were alert, like Chino's eyes. I knew the story from Chino…that after my Dad was killed, Vince became a mercenary for a while because he wanted to fight and get revenge on the kind of people who killed my Dad. I prayed that Vince wasn't going to get all weepy and smarmy about seeing "Billy's boy" for the first time.

"He's all yours," Brown said.

Then Brown went back in the house to work, leaving me alone with the notorious queer who had the disease.

Vince was clicking keys on his laptop. Suddenly he held the phone out to me. His voice was strong as his eyes.

"I hear you're into movies. Wanna help me get a movie made?" he asked.

"Uh…okay." Why not? "Don't you work indoors?"

"Being sick taught me to appreciate the fleeting beauty of every flower. You are line producer's assistant today. Get me the first number on this list."

So I punched up phone numbers.

Vince grabbed the phone away from me in his shaky hand, to talk below-the-line costs with Lennie, Darryl, Gary, Philip, Paul, Richard, Margaret, Derek. Most of the paper, I found out, was rewrites of the script for Valhalla's new documentary *Left Handed*. It was about how queers have this different perspective on everything. They were hoping to get it on PBS or *Discovery*. But the script wasn't happening. Between calls, Vince read a rewrite that Harlan was doctoring. I took a diskette inside to Harlan, with notes that Vince had typed on it.

Brown was in his office, with the *Left Handed* script downloaded on his Mac screen. He'd jam the disk into his machine. Now and then he faxed a page over to the Valhalla office. Vince would fax things right off his laptop. Paul would call, and they'd discuss. Somehow I'd expected to be the center of attention, so I felt lost.

Standing by Brown's computer, I noticed photographs of me on the wall by his desk...from my 8th grade picture to that snapshot at my first birthday party, fighting with Ana. Seeing them made me feel very emotional and upset, like my privacy had been invaded.

"How did you get those?" I asked.

"Your mom sent me one every year."

"How come you were never around?" I blurted.

Brown leaned back in his chair and swung around to face me. "Your mom wanted to be away from everything...everybody. I couldn't fight it."

"If my Dad was alive, he would have been around."

"Yes. Everything would have been different."

"So...my Mom doesn't like you?"

"We don't always see eye to eye on things."

"How come you didn't sue her for custody, or something?" I demanded.

Brown crossed his arms over his chest, looking into my eyes. He was trying to be patient, but I could feel dragons fighting inside of him.

"To be honest with you, I thought about it...talked to your grandfather about going to court for visitation rights. But he told me I had no standing whatsoever. A lawsuit might have antagonized your mother for good. So he advised me to wait...that someday your mom would come around."

Brown's eyes said more — about how sad he'd been, how much he'd missed being around me. If my Mom had been willing, he would have been there...teaching me stuff. He was a coach. He would have been throwing balls to me, maybe even helping me grow taller. The more I could see this, the more freaked I felt.

Outside, I accidentally knocked over one of Vince's paper piles.

"Excuse-*me*," I said, pissed at my own Pinhead stupidity.

"Ooooo, temper, temper," Vince said. "Your dad had a temper."

"Yeah?" I was picking up the papers.

"You remind me of him that way."

It was nice to know that I inherited some attitude problems from my Dad. At least I got *something* from him. So I sat cautiously on an iron chair, looking at Vince's skinny bare feet, which he put on the table as he studied his budget.

"But Dad was this nice guy," I said.

"He was a fab human being, but no angel. One day...this was right after Billy and I made the Prescott team. He and Harlan were starting to fall in love. This was in early 1976. Your Dad was 22 then...Harlan was 39. Neither of them had ever been in love before, and they couldn't handle it. One afternoon they had this *huge* bitch-fight about Billy's training. Billy was being the stubborn juvenile...Harlan was being the creepy Republican hard-ass. So he finally hauled off and belted Billy. I mean...it was the good old military slap on the face. And Billy went cross-eyed, and he belted Harlan right back."

Vince did the slap in the air, with his skinny arm.

"Whoa!" I had to laugh.

Vince laughed too. Then he started coughing. I got scared, and poured him a glass of water. He hacked and argghed, lungs sounding terrible. I wound up thumping his skinny back. Touching him broke the ice — the sky didn't fall. So we ditched his work for a while. So there I was in West Hollywood, having fun with this sick notorious queer who was telling me cool stories about my Dad.

Finally he looked at his watch. "Back to work."

"You're...um...really organized."

"Honey, if I wasn't organized, I wouldn't have lived this long."

"Are you...like, going to get sicker, or something?"

He leaned back in his chair, looking around at all his flowers.

"A few years ago," he said, "I thought I was gone. But it was the drugs...they were making me sicker. I quit them and...surprise, I'm better. So all the people who are so sure that God is punishing me are going to get the surprise of their lives. And you know what...I planted all these flowers myself."

Suddenly Vince lay back in the lounge. "I need to close my eyes for a minute, okay?"

I sat there watching the bamboo shadows moving on his thin face. Maybe it was okay to be friends with a sick notorious queer if he was my Dad's high school friend. Carefully I put the phone where he could reach it. Just as I was tiptoeing away, he mumbled, "William?"

"Yeah?"

"I've got some great old pictures of your dad too. You can look at them next time."

Inside, I turned on the TV. "Where's my next page?" Brown yelled.

"He's asleep."

"Oh. Okay...*you* start reading."

"I don't know anything about scripts."

"Doesn't matter. Most filmmakers don't ever ask kids what they think. So I want your comments, okay? We'll list you in the thank you's."

Eyes narrowed, I looked at Brown. An adult wanted my opinion? Why? Was bait being pulled in front of me?

Brown didn't look back at me — he was busy faxing something. It would be cool to have my opinion in a movie. So I tiptoed out and got Vince's pile of pages.

"Okay, Scene 3 here," Harlan said. "We need a payoff, but the one we've got has been done to death."

He explained about payoffs being needed every two minutes, to keep tweaking the audience. I went to work.

When Chino came back, he and Brown traded looks, and I wondered if they had talked about me behind my back. Then Chino said to me: "Time to go home."

"You're not a bad helper," Brown told me. "We could use you."

He put out his hand. I almost put my hands in my pockets again — but decided not to. Harlan Brown and I finally shook hands.

Outside, in the cab, Chino threw an envelope of photographs at me. The envelope spilled photos of Orik. He was helping his parents load the car. They'd made him cut his hair in a buzz cut. His face looked sad, under the bill of his baseball cap. The star was gone off his cap — they'd made him rip it off.

"Vacation?" I asked.

"I don't think so."

"They talked about sending him to military school."

Chino didn't answer. He was driving fiercely. Jesus, when would I get to drive like that? Three more years till I could get my license.

The 4 Runner raced back up the PCH. A fog bank on the ocean swallowed the sun, and everything went gloomy grey. Inside my jacket I was shivering, and my knees were vibrating like some little electronic device was hidden in them. My mind was going crazy about the pictures of Orik.

At the Sunset junction, the homeless vet was working the other side of the PCH now.

Chino said quietly: "You and I need to talk."

My stomach took a plunge. Were we finally going to a private place together?

Past the Malibu mall, he suddenly made a U-turn at Corral Canyon, and parked on the shoulder by the beach. The wind was cold and damp, so he grabbed an army blanket off the back seat, and we ran down the bank onto the sand. Shivering people were grabbing their dogs and coolers of food, and going to their cars. The tide was way out. We walked along, watching gulls pick at people's thrown-away sandwiches. Chino had the blanket wrapped around him like a poncho. My shameless body was shivering more than ever, half from the cold. I wished Chino would pull me into his blanket, and get me warm. My blood pounded in my ears. A real warrior knew what he wanted and wasn't afraid to take it.

But he hunkered down on the sand six feet away from me, Asian style, and said quietly:

"I've been thinking about your Mission."

My body became a pulse of terror and joy. There was this long awful silence, with the waves rushing at us. I was shaking almost out of control. Chino was looking at me, with that warlord face that showed everything life had done to him.

But he didn't say what I thought he would.

"In the Nam I had an 11-year-old who ran missions for me...carried messages, grenades, did sapper stuff. Nyen was a real officer...a noncom. The VC killed him. You want to guess how many ears my platoon took because of Nyen?"

"A lot."

"You think you're in Nyen's class?"

My cheeks started burning.

"Are you man enough for a mission on Earth? Some officers' training at 13?" he asked.

"Who cares?" I said in a smothered voice.

"Did you ever think you have a better chance of finding your dad by finding people who knew him?"

I stared at him. This was my *Memo* commander talking. A glimmer of interest showed in the black hole inside me.

"Okay...what's my mission?"

"Work on yourself. Get some command of yourself."

"That sounds totally thrilling."

"I'm serious. Phase 1 — you need to get tighter with other kids. You don't want to spend all your time with an old snake-eater like me. Spend time with Ana and Ziggy. Get tighter with your mom...you owe her big time, and she needs you. And get tight with Harlan and Vince."

"Vince is cool, for a qu...uh...gay guy. But I don't like Brown."

"Call him by his name, or I will be pissed."

I sighed. "Harlan."

He went on. "Phase 2 of your mission is Harlan. An officer needs to know people. He takes care of his people. Discover Harlan, and you'll learn a lot of things about your dad."

"What about Shawn?"

"That's Phase 3. Your buddy is going to need your support."

"Where are they taking him?"

"I don't know yet. But his parents are putting a lot of pressure on him, and he's not doing well. And he's still holding out...he won't admit that it was bad to be friends with you."

"Why hasn't he run away?" I wanted to know.

"When you're abused at home, it's complicated. Having a family means a lot. You tend to hang in there past time to bug out. Shawn loves his mom, and I think he still hopes she will stand up for him."

"Were you...abused?"

"Don't change the subject."

"Did you sit there on the street and take these pictures?"

"I have my professional resources. You don't need to know."

"He told me if they sent him somewhere, he would run away and find me."

"Yeah, he might do that. But you can't help him if you're a mess. Right?"

"Right," I had to admit.

Suddenly Chino was shivering violently.

"You okay?" I asked.

"I have the kind of malaria that you can never get rid of."

There wasn't a lot of choice about what to say next. So I said it to him.

"Chino, please help me with my Mission."

"I'll help," he said. "But you'll have to take responsibility. No different than Nyen. Lives depended on him. He couldn't screw up. He was a man, totally a man, at 11."

"Deal," I said, putting out my hand.

We shook on it.

Then he got up, and we started back up the empty beach. The only person left was an old guy throwing a frisbee to his dog.

We climbed into the truck. The whole strategy was very obvious to me. Chino was going to stay away from me, be fatherly, and keep me busy, so I would forget him. I should have been heartbroken. But I wasn't. A SEAL officer, somebody who was good enough to command real ops in combat, maybe command a space flight, had just sent me on a mission. The thought ran through my mind that if I had refused to shake Harlan's hand, I wouldn't have gotten this assignment from Chino.

B ack at Malibu, I wasn't hungry for dinner, and locked myself in my room. After dinner, I heard Mom and Chino talking quietly together out on the terrace. She was sitting on the balustrade, and he was leaning on it — two short people having a summit meeting. I watched them through the window, my toes curling with anxiety. Were they talking about me? I strained to hear voices.

Finally the 4 Runner was gunning out the drive. From my window, I watched the red taillights disappear down the canyon.

Probably Chino was going off on a trip and he'd coldly sleep with somebody over 18 to get relief. It was dawning on me that I could be monstrously jealous. Adults come trampling through your world with all their past stuff that they've done, and whole crowds of people they still sort of like, and they expect you to understand their adult thing, when you've just given them your bleeding virgin heart that you cut out of your chest with your own Scout knife.

About 10, there was a knock on my door. "Permission to enter Mission Control," my Mom called.

Why do adults always want to invade your room right when your heart is cut out? I opened the door, then threw myself into the bed again. She came in without turning on the light, and sat on the foot of the bed. The feeling in the air around her said that Chino had talked to her about something. I prayed that he hadn't snitched on the mission. What kind of officer didn't keep secrets?

"Chino and I had a talk about Shawn's situation," she said. "I'm really worried for him."

Suddenly those tears were choking me half to death.

"Feel like crying, sweetie?" she said.

The next thing I knew, I was in my mother's arms, crying like my ribs were going to come unsprung. She stroked my head, and held me against those little breasts of hers, that had fed me a long time ago. She rocked me. Her quiet voice seemed to fill me, and calm me, the way it did on that night in the desert 5 billion years ago when she talked to me about the stars.

"Honey, listen. Maybe you're going to be into guys…maybe not. I've never wanted to push you either way. I think it's one of the reasons why I stayed away from everybody…to give you your space. Whatever your feelings for Shawn are…I respect that, okay?"

I sniffled into her shoulder. It was almost a relief that the awful subject was brought up by somebody else. Was I that obvious? What's a secret if everybody can see it in the air around you?

"Can we trust you to have some self-control? You've got to learn not to crash through windows and try to kill yourself. Chino and I are wondering if you can make one more step, maybe?"

My tears had stopped, and my face was buried in her sweatshirt. I could smell the sportsy perfume she always wore. Drawing a shaky breath, I sat up. She smoothed the hair back from my hot forehead. For some reason I thought of the Vietnamese kid that Chino knew. I guessed that I could have that much self-control.

My Mom smiled a little. I hadn't seen her smile for weeks.

"You've got a lot ahead of you. New family to get to know. School starts in a month. Hopefully be a guy who can say more than *cool* and *uh*. Be the astronomer who discovers the 10th planet, or something."

"Yeah...I guess."

"Look. How would you like to move up here for good? Marian is inviting us to share the house. Malibu Hills High is a good school. I've checked it out."

I shrugged. With Orik gone, Costa Mesa meant nothing to me.

"We'll be closer to the Griffith Observatory...JPL/NASA...any astronomy-related thing in L.A. that you want. I'll take you there myself."

"What about your job?" I asked.

"Oh," she smiled, "I've taught school for 11 years. Maybe it's time to do something else. Like politics. Marian is putting together a staff."

I wiped my eyes on my sleeve.

"You decide, Mom."

"Nuh-uh. If you're old enough to make decisions about sex," she said, "then you're old enough to help me decide where to live."

Right. Be a commander.

"Okay," I said. "Let's move."

Our moving van stood on Lemon Street. Jerry and Marilyn tried to come in our yard and talk to my Mom about how I needed therapy and my Mom needed therapy too. But Chino kept them away. So Jerry yelled over the wire fence, how my Mom was dragging me away from my neighborhood, my friends, my school, and the only decent influence in my life, which was Jerry and Marilyn.

We ignored him, and kept packing. As I dragged my *Memo* Mission Control boxes out, I kept looking through the window to see Orik. He wasn't anywhere around, so maybe it was true that they had taken him somewhere. I folded the faggy Jesus picture into a paper airplane, wrote "Have a nice day" on it, and sailed it into their yard, right against the dining room window. His dad went and picked it up and yelled at me that I was blasphemous. Next, the pastor of the Heasters' church showed up, supposedly on a drop-in visit. But my Mom wouldn't talk to him. Jerry was yelling about how it was all my Mom's fault, because she was one of those permissive liberal satanic parents.

Finally another neighbor yelled that they were glad the Hedens were moving, because maybe the yelling would stop.

The gate between our two yards had a padlock on it.

On the way out of town, we stopped at New Century Optics and I got two 10-inch pyrex blanks. I decided to use diamond dust for polishing this time. Mom and Marian paid for it.

"Your birthday present, early," they said.

Looking at the skies would be lonely now, without Orik.

Next day, we unpacked in Malibu. Mom put our Costa Mesa house on the market. Houses weren't selling very well, so she didn't hope for much. But at least we had a place to go.

"I'm starting a campaign staff," Aunt Marian said to me. "Your mom is going to work with me, for a salary. Nothing wrong with a little healthy nepotism. Maybe you could stuff envelopes."

"Good idea," said Mom. "He can pay for the stuff he broke."

My room upstairs was now Mission Control. I set up a table for polishing, with a plastic tent around it. Nobody would dare come in and clean, and make dust, because I had to be so careful not to scratch the mirror. The balcony outside would be my new observatory. When everything was all set up, I put my Dad's picture and Orik's graduation picture on the dresser. I took a deep breath, and lit the candle again. It had been out for six weeks. The flame was soft and tender in the dark, making the room dance.

Then I slid into bed. The river of geometry washed over me and my Dad's image downlinked onto the screen.

"I have to know for sure," I said. "Take off your eye-shield."

"The photo...the one in your box," he kept repeating.

"Where are you?" I wasn't quite believing. "Are you a prisoner?"

"No time to explain. Listen carefully. When you come back, set time by the variable, then steer 23...steer 23..."

My fingers were racing again, typing down his information. But the transmission was glitching.

"Twenty-three," he kept repeating. "Twenty-three."

His picture was breaking up on the screen, like a virus was eating it. My throat was tearing itself apart.

"DAAAAD...What's 23?"

I woke up with a jerk. Hot sweat was washing over me. The room swayed sickeningly with shadows. I jumped out of bed. In a total frenzy, I tore my backpack open. The secret box dropped, and snapshots flew everywhere. I grabbed for the important one, and stared at it. What was I missing? What was 23?

— 13 —

A KID NAMED VINCE

Mom and I started our new life in Malibu. By midnight the Summer Triangle was west of the meridian. But one thing was the same. Every day I worried about Orik.

On some old homework, I found Donnala's phone number. After we talked a little, I asked her casually, "Have you seen Shawn around?"

She was nosy. "Why don't *you* know where he is?

"I moved. I live in L.A. now."

"Oh. Well, his parents sent him to summer camp. I haven't heard from him either."

With Orik not around, the new telescope was hard to do.

Harlan said he'd help. I had to be a good boy, and let him. He took me around town in his Jeep Cherokee, and we found the parts. Darryl told us where the good optics places were. We found plumbing parts for the base in a junkyard that Chino knew about. For the tube, I got six feet of fiberglass. If I could save enough money for a used camera, and a clock drive so the telescope could track the moving stars, I could start doing the long exposures to catch better details.

Mom was working in Marian's office, learning politics. She seemed totally ready to dump me on the men for a while. "You guys owe me light-years of kid-sitting," she told them.

Now and then I heard her and Nancy talking about Nancy's nephew Teak, that I ought to meet. Teak was another science geek.

So my Dad's ex-hubby and I tried to talk. It was more like interviews, holding a mike up to each other's faces on the evening news. I never felt comfortable.

Harlan let me keep the construction mess in a corner of his patio. The telescope base was tippy, so one day he got an idea how to make it stand level. We were sitting on the patio bricks. Harlan was working one corner of the base with a rasp. Vince was in his flowery corner, talking on the cellular phone. So I tried to interview Harlan.

"You know how to do lots of different stuff, huh?" I said. "You coached...now you do movies...you can build stuff..."

Harlan was so serious — never smiled much.

"You learn what you have to," he said. "I spent a few years in a Fire Island beach house that needed major repair."

"So you totally quit sports, huh."

"It started with heartbreak anyway...I missed my own shot at Olympic gold, in the 1500 meter. So I coached as a way of getting in. But I was a writer all along...just didn't know it. Sportswriting, autobiography, now screenwriting..."

He leaned over to his tool box for a smaller rasp, making a face, like his hip hurt. Probably he couldn't run because he was old now.

"How did you get into movies? People wanting to film my Dad's life?"

"Through writing, actually. Inheriting the rights to some books written by a guy who was my best friend...Steve Goodnight. Valhalla wanted the film rights to one of them, and..."

I had noticed the row of Goodnight books on his office shelf.

"Steve didn't leave rights to his kids?"

"He didn't have kids."

Right. I kept forgetting that the rules were different here...people didn't have regular families.

"...And a lot of gay people look after each other," he was saying, "when it comes to money. No one else gives a hell. Most of the time, the courts go along with us. Sometimes not...that's when the straight relatives take it all. Like Vince's mother...lurking, hoping he'll die. She thinks she'll get the house and turn me out. That's why Vince's name isn't on the deed. Vince is lucky he can trust me that much."

I was kind of shocked. "But that's not fair."

Vince's voice came from his orchidy corner. "She says she'll grab my body too, so she can have a Catholic funeral...she knows I want to be cremated."

"Can she legally do that?"

"Legally, Harlan is nothing...even though he and I have lived together for over 10 years. In some states, that would make us common-law married...if we were straight."

"Jeez. That's really not fair."

The phone rang, and Vince was off and talking. Harlan kept rasping on the base. "So your grandfather has tried to build legal walls around us," he said.

"I guess I have to meet him, huh?" I wasn't going to call him Grandpa yet.

"You don't sound too thrilled."

"No."

"Well, John's in court right now, so you won't see him till this case is over."

Time to change the subject. "Ever get an Oscar?"

Harlan wiggled the telescope base. It still wasn't quite level. He actually laughed, a little. "A nomination," he said. "Along with four other guys who chewed on the rewrite."

"Did you ever want Valhalla to make a feature film about my Dad?"

Suddenly a dark shape of cosmic space dust was between us. Harlan didn't look at me. His hands gripped the galvanized pipe — strong, not too big, with silky dark hair on the backs. They worked the rasp like crazy. He said, "I am very controlling about the story and how it's done. But certain details, well..."

"Like what?"

Bits of metal were sticking to his jeans legs.

"Like special effects. Darryl wanted to do something pretty graphic...rubbing people's noses in how a person's life is destroyed by hate. He wanted to get the uncommitted viewer to commit and feel outraged. I, uh, appreciated his idea, but...I wasn't thrilled about getting that close to the industry magic. So he even offered to tone it down. But that wouldn't have been real. So..."

I felt sick. He was talking about the bullet hitting my Dad's head.

"Nobody else wanted to do the movie?" I asked.

"Most people in this town are afraid of your dad's story," he said bitterly. "It presses too many buttons."

Suddenly Harlan broke off and picked up the padded box with the new mirror blanks in it. They threw a flash of sun at his face.

"So what are you looking for, with this thing? Do you have a goal? How far can astronomers see, anyway?" he asked.

If I told him about the Mission, he'd think I was a retard. Or he'd want to control it.

"Really far," I said. "It's measured in light years. You know...the distance that photons can travel in a year, which is 5 trillion 880 billion miles. The nearest star is Proxima Centauri...4.3 light-years away. So 4.3 times 5 trillion..."

He whistled. "My imagination stubs its toe on that one."

"Actually, I'm more interested in our own galaxy...not the way-out stuff."

"You're excellent at math. I thought schools did a lousy job teaching math these days..."

"Mom helped me a little. But I never had much trouble with it."

He was shaking his head.

"I struggled with school," he said. "Everything I've learned was hard. With you, it seems to come naturally." Suddenly he was shy again, pulling back behind his cloud. "Billy would be proud. Maybe you'll be the one to reel in a Nobel Prize."

Harlan handed me the box. It was time to start polishing.

Staring at my own face in the glass, I suddenly got this brilliant idea. It stood out clear and bright like a giant new star. Why hadn't I thought of it before?

"Chino, listen to my cool idea. My Dad died 15 years ago, right? What I've gotta do is...examine the, like, belt of space that is 15 light-years away. Whatever I see right in that area is light that goes back to when he died. The Cat Nebula *has* to be there."

"Great idea. But it's still looking for a needle in a haystack. A PI doesn't like the haystack odds."

"But the haystack is a lot smaller."

"With your equipment, it will take you the rest of your life to do the photography, you know that? A 75-minute exposure — let's say two a weekend? Because your equipment, and your lifestyle, and school, can't handle more than that. Across 365 degrees of arc? And supposing it's not visible from the northern hemisphere? You're looking at moving to Australia."

I was crushed. "What would *you* do?"

"When I was in combat, I wasn't expected to do the air strikes myself...just call the fighter jocks in. I had resources and support. You could have that too."

"Like what?"

"Talk to your mother. I think she already mentioned the local resources to you."

"Chino, do you think I'm a retard for doing this?"

He was quiet for a minute.

"No," he said finally. "For some reason, I think something real is going on here."

"Chino, don't tell anybody else about this. Don't tell Harlan."

"I wouldn't think of it. You'll tell him...when it's time."

"Anything new on Shawn?"

"Not a thing."

It was a go for hanging at Valhalla, and I was trying to have fun with three notorious queers. Vince and I were in the editing room, helping Paul and Darryl lay in the last 8 minutes of voice-over that Harlan had written for *Left Handed*.

Paul was at the EPIX console — Hawaiian shirt, bare feet, his fingers flying on the keyboard — with the external hard drive towering over him. Darryl kept his eyes on the big overhead monitor, watching the scenes. They'd given me the classroom talk about the space-age laser-disk system. How it was to movie-making what the new space-platform telescopes would be to astronomy. Only nine or ten other studios in town had an EPIX. The primitive system of cutting and splicing real physical film was going away. It was all digital now. *Left Handed* had wrapped in spring, and Valhalla finally found one more investor who covered the cost of editing and posting.

We'd done an all-nighter. The investor wanted to see the final cut at 4, and Valhalla was almost missing their deadline for some dorky-sounding film festival. Blue nebulas of cigarette smoke floated. Paul and Darryl smoked like chimneys. Finally, I lit one.

Vince took the cigarette right out of my mouth.

"Your mom will kill you," he said.

"She already tried," I said, grabbing it again. "I'm the out-of-control adolescent, so she can't stop me."

Vince went to grab it back. I did an aikido move, and took another drag. I wasn't sure I wanted him dragging on it.

"Hey, dude," I said, "you have tons of energy for a guy who's supposed to be dying."

Vince laughed and ruffled my hair. "Harlan made me quit. But now and then I get the urge. You can leave the butt for me."

Paul and Darryl screeched with laughter, but never missed a beat on the EPIX. They loved wild fag jokes, and Vince had stepped right into that one. He actually blushed a little bit. There was a youngness about Vince that I liked — sometimes you forgot that you were talking to an adult.

If only Orik was here — he liked to giggle and be silly. Probably he wasn't doing any giggling right now.

Valhalla wasn't colossally macro, like Paramount a few blocks away. This studio was micro, crammed into the top floor of an old sound stage. The editing room was cluttered with EPIX equipment, sagging leather couches, messy ashtrays and yesterday's pizza boxes. On the walls were dozens of awards. Outside our window, BMWs and movie sets on trucks and homeless people with shopping carts went by, along with old newspapers and paper cups blowing in the wind.

Rose and Vivian were down the hall, working up a budget for a new commercial. Downstairs, a shoot was happening — Valhalla made extra money by renting the sound stage.

Darryl: "This two minutes is a teeny bit too cutty."

Paul: "What do you think?" (to me)

Me: "It's slow, actually. Boring. I told Harlan already."

Darryl: "Go easy on the politics, kid. Adults see this thing too."

Vince: "I agree with William. Go more cutty."

Paul: "More cutty, it'll be the Keystone cops in fast forward."

Vince: "Kids like action."

Me: "Bam bam, pow pow."

Darryl: "Kid, what the hell do you see in astronomy? Don't you get *bored?* I mean, there's no action out there."

Me: "There's action *everywhere* in space. Variables, supernovas, comets, galaxies colliding, bam bam...." (waving my hands)

Paul: "Whatever blows your skirt up, honey. (Fingers rattling on the keys, cutting and pasting like crazy). We'll shave ten seconds here, four seconds there."

When Paul played it again, we all agreed that more cutty was great.

The receptionist put his head in the door.

Receptionist: "Paul, it's twenty to four."

Paul: "Rats. One more tweak, then I'll put on my shoes."

At 5 after 4, the investor and Harlan were sitting on the couch with us. Everybody was watching *Left Handed* for the millionth time.

The warm smoky room put me into z's. Weird yellow glows spread around me. Was I dreaming? That rainbow geometry was swimming around me again, like after the Cat Nebula dream. I had never forgotten that feeling. It always meant my Dad was near, somehow. Voices were around me. The investor was saying that it was fab...better than he'd hoped. A door shut. Phones rang down the hall. I had slumped against Vince's shoulder. He felt skinny, but hard and strong. I was starting to feel safe and protected with him, like I did with Chino. Maybe my Dad was glad I was here.

Why did I feel safe with all these queers?

Vince's voice, right next to me: "...Can't believe Billy's kid is finally with us. I get to be an uncle in my old age."

Paul's voice: "...Sleeping like an angel."

Harlan's voice (with a growl in it): "More like a demon."

Vince's voice: "Aw, he reminds me of me when I was his age...and look how terrific I turned out."

Harlan's voice: "Look how long it took you. I'll be in my dotage by the time this one grows into a human being."

Vince's voice: "Honey, if you don't want this child, I'll take him. I never had the luck to knock up a girl when I was bi-ing around. His mom and I get along too."

Harlan's voice (suddenly angry): "With you, below the belt isn't always sex." Vince got up and I fell over. They left the room, and argued in the office next door.

My eyes opened. Bags of sandwiches and coffee sat everywhere. The remaining queers were being lovey-dovey. Paul was rubbing Darryl's migraine. Vivian was sitting behind Rose on the sofa arm, with her chin resting on Rose's nappy hair. Harlan and Vince weren't there. The rest smiled at me. I was up to my stripped-down eyelashes in happy queer couples. On the monitor, credits were still rolling. Suddenly I saw my name in "special thanks to."

"Hey," I said, "you put me in the credits."

"You're taken seriously here. Get used to it," Rose grinned.

Harlan and Vince came back, quiet now. I could tell they were still mad at each other.

Paul clinked a fork against a mug, to get attention.

"So...it's a burn?" he asked everybody.

"Burn it," Darryl said.

With a snap, Paul hit the command to burn the whole film onto a laser disk. Lights flashed on the EPIX hard drive — it did everything but chirp and whistle like R2D2. Everybody cheered. Paul dragged two bottles of champagne out of the fridge in the kitchenette, and cans of Pepsi for me and Harlan. There I was, celebrating with the fags and having a great time. A messenger took the disk down the street to Paragon Post. More people came in — my Mom, Ana's mom Eileen, Marian and Chino. My stomach still did a slight burn on Chino.

Mom looked at all the pairs sitting around.

"Well, aren't we poster couples for the PTA," she said.

More champagne, except for Chino — I got him a Pepsi. Everybody talked about old times and people who were dead, till I got bored and closed my eyes again. Suddenly this feeling came out of nowhere, of missing Orik so much that I wanted to curl up in a ball somewhere, and just feel miserable. And I'd been putting off polishing the new mirror. For some reason I couldn't focus on it.

Going back to Malibu that night, Chino was the designated driver. Vince rode with us. He wanted to get away from Harlan for a few days — be with my Mom and talk about old times. And he said he had something special to tell us. Mom and Marian nodded off, sleepy from champagne. Chino felt like he was thinking about thunderstorms on Jupiter. In the back seat, Vince pulled a photo album out of his briefcase and gave it to me. My stomach went weightless — it was the one he'd promised. I was almost afraid to look at it, and jammed it in my backpack.

When we got home, Chino handed me a manila envelope. Manila

envelopes meant PI stuff. Inside was an envelope addressed to the Heasters. It was from the Sunny Valley Youth Center, in Willits, CA.

"What's this?" I asked Chino.

"A bill for Shawn's first month of care."

"Where'd you get this?"

"Never mind."

"So he's not at summer camp. He's not at military school."

"No."

"This is a *hospital*. Is he sick?"

"This is a private clinic in northern California. Run by people who believe like Shawn's parents. Their ads say they offer therapy on teenage drug and alcohol abuse. But they come down hard on pre-marital sex, disobedience to parents...and homosexuals."

He handed me a copy of a bill. It listed charges for drugs. They were drugging him. They might as well be torturing him. I was panicking. "But Shawn isn't gay," I said.

"Well, they believe he's been contaminated, so they're trying to fry it out of him. Shawn's dad says that he'll do whatever it takes."

"Did you tap their phone, or something?"

"The Navy didn't spend millions training me for nothing."

"Do you think he can run away from there?"

"He's in the locked part of the facility. Depends on how good their security is."

"Locked. Like a jail?"

Chino shoved the papers back in the envelope. "It's important to stay calm."

Upstairs, I locked myself in the new Mission Control, and threw myself on the bed. The candle made nebulas dance on the walls.

To keep from thinking about Orik being tortured by the Empire Rulers, I looked at the photo album. It opened like an ancient Book of Wisdom that I had found in some sci-fi fable. Prom pictures...Vince in a tux at El Monte High, dancing with a girl. Snapshots from a track meet. Vince standing with another young guy with light-colored curly hair. It was my Dad. I'd know that grin anywhere. There were lots of running pictures. The Bay to Breakers in San Francisco. The Culver City Marathon. My Dad and Vince always together. They must have been close, maybe even boyfriends for a while. Bet Harlan was jealous.

Getting my magnifying glass, I studied the photos, like I was looking for that variable star in my Dad's face.

On Sunday Vince told Ana's mom he had an important thing to tell her. So she invited him and my Mom and me to her house for brunch. Glenn was down at the restaurant. Ana was up in her room. I knocked but she was in a bad mood and wouldn't open up, so I went back downstairs. Ziggy wasn't around...I wondered where he was.

We ate on the patio, looking down the hill at another tile roof. Between two brushy hills was a blue triangle of ocean. Squinting at the sun, I missed the night. What was I doing in the sun so much? I was a night person — my girlfriend was the dark sky. The new mirror was my way to be with her, and I hadn't even started it yet.

Eileen was a terrific cook, but I didn't feel like pigging out on her pancakes and fresh fruit salsa, because Shawn was locked up somewhere. Ana came downstairs for a minute, said hi over her shoulder, got a little dish of salsa and left.

Eileen sighed, staring after her.

"She still doesn't eat, huh?" Vince said, handing her an envelope.

"I worry about her. Maybe we ought to get her into therapy."

Oh please, please, I thought. Don't do that.

Ana's mom was opening the envelope. Her eyes got big. She looked at Vince. "Oh..." Tears started in her eyes. "That's amazing." She hugged him...a big long brother-sister kind of hug.

Mom smiled, and handed me the paper. It was a lab report, with different test results. At the bottom it read *HIV — INCONCLUSIVE.*

I stared at Vince. "What does this mean?" I asked.

"It means the herbal treatments have boosted my immune system. It means there's hope," said Vince.

"Like...I thought guys automatically died if they got AIDS."

Everything that I'd seen on TV was pouring through my head, along with Marilyn and Jerry's voices. *AIDS KILLS FAGS...AIDS KILLS FAGS...AIDS KILLS FAGS...*

"They lie a lot about AIDS," said Vince.

"Why would they do that?" I was bewildered. Telling the truth is what scientists are supposed to do.

"Ooooh, AIDS is big money. Replace that S with a dollar sign, baby. The medical system is bankrupt, and AIDS is going to bail it out. Millions of sick people locked into years of expensive drugs. How can they lose?"

"Who?" I asked.

"Some researchers, the government, some drug companies...They don't really study women either. And wait till we have mandatory testing...'cause it's coming," said Ana's mom darkly.

I couldn't believe how cynical they were.

Vince added:

"And poor Harlan...he was ready to nurse me through the final days. AZT, 3TC, they made me sicker. Finally I quit them. I talked to Marian's daughter about herbal treatment. Sara's an herbalist, studied tropical plants in Africa, then Brazil...got a clinic down in Mexico City now. I go down there, and smuggle the pills home."

As usual, my brain was spinning, as new incoming information collided with old information...like two galaxies slowly crossing through each other, ripping at each other's gravitational fields, sucking away each other's stars.

Ana's mom was looking at me.

"Whatever I got from Ana's dad," she told me, "it didn't develop the same way that it did for Jacques. We didn't know much in the early '80s. Jacques felt so guilty, especially after the baby died. I think he wanted to be punished. And he did suffer — his brain degenerated..." She shivered. "But my first HIV test must have been a false positive, because all the others were negative."

Her voice choked up. Somehow the sunlight felt hotter with her tears in it. Vince took both her hands and held them, still explaining to me.

"So here we are...the same profile," he said. "We both have traces of this and that...hepatitis B, CMV, Epstein Barr and HHV6. But our brains are okay — so far. And we think they haven't found the key virus yet...the one that really attacks the immune system."

"What about your parents?" I asked Eileen.

"Jacques' parents accepted him. We still visit. Mine were the parents from hell. My own mother tried to take Ana and Ziggy. In her eyes, my having AIDS made me a bad mother. And if it weren't for the negative test, the judge might have given her my children."

Eileen was drying her eyes with her free hand.

I wasn't sure what I could contribute to this Earth-shaking

conversation. Finally I said to them: "Mom got me vaccinated for hepatitis B."

"When we were young, there was *no* hepatitis vaccine," Eileen said.

Suddenly Vince laughed strangely. "Those were the days, huh? When we thought herpes II was the only thing to worry about? Remember when you and I hated each other so much that we couldn't be in the same room together?"

She bit her lips. "One door shuts, another opens."

Eileen looked at me. "William, we're so glad you're here. You are...the missing piece of the puzzle. And maybe you can help us get Ana to eat. She thinks a lot of you, you know." She slapped one pancake on a plate. "Take this up to her."

I was about to say no, I wasn't a babysitter, when suddenly I remembered Chino's voice talking about being a commander, taking care of my people.

Upstairs, Ana was sitting on her windowsill, hugging her knees, staring at the ocean. That amazing hair was all around her, like a magic cloak. The dish of salsa had a fly sitting on it.

"Hey," I said, sitting by her, feeling nervous. "I have got the ultimate pancake. It fell from the sky, like a meteorite."

She wasn't having my fantasy. "I gained two ounces, so I have to lose them by tonight," she barked in my face. Then, "There! I actually confessed my secret to a guy! How majorly liberating!"

I tried flattery. "My fair maiden has to eat." Then competition, which usually worked with her. "O Princess of All Planets, you won't be able to keep up with me if you don't eat."

"Your fair maiden? Really?" she said, sounding more cynical than Vince.

"Yeah. Really."

"If a guy knew what I went through, he wouldn't want me for his girl."

"You eat a bite...I eat a bite. We'll get fat together."

"Guys don't worry about their weight," she scoffed.

"Oh yes they do. I have been hanging with queer guys. All you have to do is *listen* to them, and you'll know all the mysteries of men. I sit around listening to Vince and Paul, and I can't believe the stuff

I hear. I swear that's why straight guys hate fags so much. It's because they *talk*."

"Seriously?"

"Gay guys *die* about how they look. Worse than women."

Her eyebrows wrinkled...she didn't believe me. "One bite, and that's it."

"No going back?"

"One bite."

"No sticking your finger down your throat when I leave."

She frowned. "How'd you know about that?"

"Just a wild guess." I put a piece of pancake between my lips.

Suddenly she grinned. "Oh, I get it. Jesus, men are such perverts. They will do anything for touch."

I didn't say anything, just waited..

She leaned toward me. Piece by piece, she ate the whole pancake from between my lips, and licked them clean with her tongue. We had a hot kiss that tasted of fruit salsa and lasted a long time. She took my hand and put it gently on the front of her slippery silk blouse, over her breast. My fingers rubbed the silk on her nipple, which exploded with hardness. Layered under this was Orik's chest, with more muscles here and there, skin all goosebumps, and his nipple hard like that. The front of my jeans was glued against her thigh, and I was getting that wild feeling of wanting to get between the legs of anything alive. But her legs stayed together. She was scared.

Later on, Vince, Ana and I took a walk in Solstice Canyon Park. For a while she and I exploded with energy, chasing each other along a higher trail, while Vince walked the road below. It seemed like he was stronger and healthier than when I first met him. A bunch of quail flew up under our feet and scared me to death. Finally I got bored with bird-watching, and let her go ahead with the binoculars, while I went back down to Vince. His eyes followed her. He was totally the big-time uncle about the daughter of his ex-best friend. A hummingbird poked its beak in some wild fuschia by the road, then zoomed past our faces, heading for Ana. Birds always seemed to go for her, like they knew she wanted to see them.

"We're becoming a dynasty," he said. "Look at her."

"So you're really not going to die."

"I'm going to live to be 95, and break my neck slipping in the shower. And outlive my mother. Did you like the pictures?"

"They were cool. But..." I kicked a rock.

"But what?"

"I keep wondering how I'm like Billy. I don't look like him much. Even in the pictures where he's my age."

"You're kidding. Your hair is the same kind of curly...you have his hands, I think. Though I have to admit, your mom came out pretty heavy on the genetic side. Which she must like. I didn't look much like my dad either."

This reassured me a little.

"How did you and Harlan...uh...um...I don't know how to say this."

"You think Harlan was unfaithful to your dad, huh? By being with me?"

My face got red. "Kind of. Yeah."

"I'll tell you a secret. About a month before they smoked him, your dad made me promise that if anything happened to him, I'd take care of Harlan."

My scalp prickled. "He, like, knew? So my Dad kind of, like, gave Harlan to you?"

"Yeah. And Harlan and I had a hard time getting our scene together. If that makes you feel any better. What we have, we work at."

His eyes drilled mine, from a foot higher. He was so tall! I couldn't meet his eyes. His voice hit the top of my head.

"And I did my bad-boy thing when I was young. If it wasn't for Harlan, I wouldn't even be alive today. He saved my ass a few times."

His eyelashes were long. A little grey, but long. Killer eyelashes, the kind that only girls were supposed to have.

Vince was still talking.

"...Might seem a little strange to you, kind of incestuous, maybe. But I was never close with my biological Dad. Harlan did all the things for me that my own Dad never did. Not the — you know, the classic daddy stuff — giving me a car in trade for sex. He never pulled that stuff with me. Although I expected it from him, for a while. I was a big user, ya know?"

We started walking again. A hiker passed us, going the other way.

I said: "It always feels awkward, talking with him. And sometimes he's an asshole."

"Yeah. Never a jerk...just an asshole. There's a difference."

"So...you're gonna make up with him?"

"I was the one who started the fight...over nothing. So I have to go home tomorrow and eat crow."

"It was over me, right?"

"Over old stuff not worth fighting for."

A breeze was shaking the sycamore leaves all around us — Vince's eyes were on the trees as they shimmered and quivered. Men loving and having fights and making up...the idea was hard to imagine. I looked back at him, getting this feeling of dumb amazement again, about feelings that weren't supposed to be admirable.

Ana was running toward us, waving her arms with excitement. Puffs of dust went up from her feet. Her loose hair was a streaming comet of red frizz.

"What a girl," Vince said quietly.

"Yeah," I said.

"She's so much like her dad. A free spirit in chains." He seemed sad, remembering.

"Her dad was your second choice, huh?"

"Yeah...Billy was first with me, always. But he'd never let me." Suddenly he grinned. "You're dating her...kind of?"

"Something like that." Was he going to ask me if I'd been with a girl yet?

But he didn't.

"I saw a peregrine!" Ana panted. "The first one I ever saw. And two bush wrens. And tons of hummingbirds."

Vince threw a fatherly arm around each of us, and we walked on. Very cautiously I settled my arm in place around Vince's waist, against Ana's bare arm. Her hand squeezed my arm. She blew me a kiss behind his back, and stuck out her sexy tongue at me. Did I feel okay about this? It felt really good...comforting and safe, the two of us with Uncle Vince. Then I remembered how lonely Orik must feel...how much Orik might want a comforting arm thrown around him. A pain went streaming through me like a meteor.

— 14 —

ANOTHER GEEK

It was the end of July. Mission Phase 1: get tight with Mom.

She and I still hadn't made up 100 percent. She was busy with her life, and I was busy with mine. Some things we'd said to each other still hurt. And I still was pissed over how she lied to me. But the men said I had to deal with her. So I tried. Next time I was in Malibu, I reminded her about the promise to visit JPL and the Griffith Observatory. The next visitor day at JPL wasn't for two weeks. So she took me to Griffith. As we were driving out of Malibu through the canyon, I asked her:

"How do people get to be...like...who they are?"

"What do you mean?"

"How do...I mean, how can I be straight if you're gay?"

"I'm a lesbian, remember?"

"Whatever. Do people teach kids to be gay?"

Mom sighed. "Who told you that?"

"Shawn's dad. Miss Bircher, in sex-ed class..."

"So you think I taught you to be gay?" She frowned.

I frowned too. Was this what I really thought?

"Not only did I *not* teach you about gay and lesbian stuff, but I hid it from you," she reminded me.

"Right."

"Spare me the sarcasm, okay? It's not my job to tell you who you are. Mother Life says you get to figure that out yourself."

"I guess so."

"Ever since you were old enough to remember, I didn't have a partner. I didn't force you to be around lesbian lovemaking. Besides, living in a houseful of queer women wouldn't exactly turn you on to men, would it?"

"I guess not."

"I'd have a hard time teaching you that men are sexually attractive. Their women would be better off with *me*. And why would anybody with half a heart teach a kid to be gay? Jesus, the misery we go through..." She gave a quick stare into my eyes, then looked back at the road.

I stared back. "But you've been dumping me with queer guys."

"Have any of them molested you?"

"Uh...no."

"If any of them lay a hand on you, you tell me, okay? It's grounds to prosecute for statutory rape. Understand?"

"You'd...put Chino in jail?"

"In a minute, if he messes with you. Has he?"

Had she sensed my feelings? There was a glow of terror around me, like a nebula glowing red with hydrogen particles all agitated by some shockwave coming through. "No way."

"I didn't think so," she said. "I know Chino pretty well. He'd let himself be torn to pieces for you. And he'd never cross me on this."

My muscles were trembling. "But some queer guys mess with kids."

"What they call pedophiles are mostly straight men who have a sick power thing about little kids. You're way too old for that. But there are men in their 20s, 30s, 40s, who like teenage boyfriends. You're prime for this, so watch out."

"Yuck. Any guy touches me, I'll kill him."

We left the canyon, passed the Hindu temple, then the Soka University campus. More of the scary questions kept welling up.

"Jerry said that single moms and lesbian moms raise boy kids who aren't masculine. They're...feminine and sissy. They don't like sports and stuff."

My Mom howled with laughter.

"Well, guess what? This single lesbian mom raised the John Wayne of teenagers. In fact, you're the only kid I know who cuts his eyelashes to look more macho. That has gotta be a *first* in history."

Heat went up my neck. She knew about this? Other people had noticed?

"And Shawn," she went on without any pity, "didn't have a single mom, *or* a lesbian mom, *plus* he had a macho Pinhead for a dad, *and* his eyelashes are very butch...but he had his hands in your pants, huh?"

"No *way* is Shawn queer," I burst out. "He's just..."

The movie scene at the lake, the weight of his body on top of me, me on top of him, fingers in deep, the warmth and the pungent smells, came over me. My throat filled up.

My Mom went relentlessly right on.

"So Miss Bircher was teaching you what some Pinhead preacher taught her. But saying it's so doesn't make it so. For hundreds of years, the churches said the Earth was flat. But they were wrong, weren't they? *You* were the one who told me about Ptolemy, right? Come on...what did Ptolemy say about the Earth?"

"Uh...Ptolemy noticed that if you went farther north, the North Star was higher in the sky. Also, he noticed that eclipses were recorded at different times in different places. So he thought the Earth had to be round."

"And this was when?"

"He said that in the *Almagest,* which was 140 B.C."

"And how many centuries after that did the churches go on saying that the Earth was flat?"

It was a relief to hear Mom talk like this — almost like the fierce warrioress of old.

"Uh — around seventeen hundred years," I said.

"So if some people have a mind-set about something geographical that everybody can see, then I guess they'll have a massive mind-set about things that are less obvious. Like sexuality. Right?"

Mom stopped at a gas station by the 101 freeway, and I pumped gas into the old Rambler while she paid. She came walking back with her usual bounce. She knew she'd won. She always did. I had a big mouth, but hers was bigger. No doubt I got my big mouth from her. Or I learned it from her. Or both. Suddenly it made me feel good to hear her talk like that. It was like old times, when we were friends.

"Kewl," I admitted, as we got on the 101 freeway. "But what about genes? I was thinking about all the stuff that Mr. Miller told us."

She had the pedal to the floor, getting into the fast lane.

"That's a big question. You're asking if it's heredity or environment? Or both? Look, we'll work on this together. And when Michael comes home, you can pick his brains till you drop."

The Observatory sat on the Hollywood Hills, in the higher altitudes of smog. The telescope was gorgeous, and I wanted to get my hands on it, make love to it, shoot it at the skies. But the tour bored me to screaming desperation. We could get on their mailing list, belong to Friends of Griffith, maybe come back for a star party when a comet approached the Earth. I was one of a million kids with K-Mart telescopes bothering them. My Dad needed to get found *now*.

Mom was about to sign me up for Friends of Griffith when she noticed I was ready to explode.

Outside, she said, "JPL will be better. NASA has a vested interest in spotting young scientists. They have high school programs. Chino still has military connections. Maybe he can get you inside."

Next day we went to the Malibu library and looked at books on genetics. It was hard to remember what Chino said...how I might find my Dad on Earth.

More on Mission Phase 1: get tight with other kids.

After the second kiss, I was seeing Ana more. When Ana slept over at our house, Marian gave her one of the guest rooms. At Ana's house, there was a spare room where I could crash on a cot. When people weren't watching, we lurked around the edges of what the adults called "intimacy." Intimacy was a spooky word, not clear and scientific — like RR Lyrae, which meant just one star and no other.

Intimacy meant everything and anything, and nothing in particular.

She had a pretty bedroom with a TV and VCR, and a huge bed with lots of stuffed wild animals. When she and I and Ziggy weren't roaring down the canyon on skateboards, or making a sweep through the beach or the mall, we lay around on the bed watching movies till 3 in the morning. Nights when Glenn and Eileen worked late at the restaurant, sometimes the three of us fell asleep on top of the stuffed tigers and bears, with our clothes on. It was nice to wake up with my head on Ana's stomach. I was so hungry for touch.

If Ziggy wasn't around, she and I would do the sleepy kid thing and kiss like it happened by accident. She'd feel my butt through my jeans, and I'd feel her breasts through her shirt. Finally she opened her shirt one day. I had seen tons of women's breasts on TV, and a few more flashed at parties, but Ana's breasts left me feeling like I'd just had my first close-up look at Saturn, and if I touched the rings from 5 million miles away, they'd quiver and I actually could see them shimmer in the telescope, with ripples going through them. Her breasts were delicate and small, and when I touched them, they went all goosebumpy, and the nipples got hard, just like Orik's did. Right away I was kissing them all over. She'd hold my face between them, and she'd touch my nipples too. I'd close my eyes and sometimes I'd pretend she was Orik, but sometimes I didn't.

But she was ouchy about being touched farther down, and so was I. How many penises had she seen that were bigger than mine? (My mother had always taught me to say penis instead of dick.) So we'd get pissed at each other and stop messing around, and go take a shower. Ziggy and I would make ourselves a huge breakfast with eggs and sausage, while Ana told us we were meat-eating monsters and took tiny bites on an apple. Now and then I fed her a pancake, bite by bite.

"God, I *hate* my hair," she complained one night when we were laying around. That amazing frizz of hers, her dad's hair, was spread all over the pillow. I envied the clear proof of being her dad's kid.

"Why? It's really...impressive," I said, taking her hairbrush and smoothing the frizz. "You, uh, look like a Goddess or something."

Tears welled in her eyes. "I don't like myself, actually."

"Why?"

"Can I tell you something, William? I mean, you're my guy friend. I can tell you stuff, right?"

"Sure." I was working on a tangle by her neck.

"Kids are so mean, you can't tell them anything."

"This is a secret?"

"Yeah. You promise not to be mean?"

"Promise."

"Last year I dated this 21-year-old guy without my Mom knowing. I met him at the Crosscreek Mall, and I let him take me home. He did it for hours, and wouldn't stop, and hurt me. I could hardly walk."

Her eyes swept mine, runny with tears. Last year she had been 12.

What was it about me that people cried on my shoulder and confessed their secrets? Even adults, for chrissake. Chino in the cemetery...my Mom. I felt bad for Ana. The hurt had been done to me too, somehow. *Take care of your people*, Chino's voice came back to me. So I kissed her carefully. She kissed me back with salty wet kisses and shook in my arms with violent weeping.

"You're not ever going to hurt me, are you?" she sobbed.

"No way. Jesus, why did you act like such a slut when I first met you?"

"I felt like a slut! And the condom thing made guys stay away. They think condoms are a gay thing."

"Did your mom figure out what happened?"

"She had the guy arrested. His family was rich, and they got him off. So Glenn got a couple of his cheezy friends to beat him up."

"Has Glenn ever bothered you?"

"When they started dating, my Mom told him to never touch me, and he didn't. Please promise you won't ever try to..."

"I promise."

"So...you like me anyway?"

"You're my girl," I said, putting my arms around her.

She cried some more, hugging me with relief, saying she'd been so afraid to tell me, but she had to know how I felt, because some guys are such pigs. Tears drying, she let me play with her hair and tell her how different and unusual her hair was. I kissed her belly, which went all goosebumpy when I told her that it was the neatest belly in the world, though secretly I still had the opinion that Orik's belly was neater.

Was some adult doing things to Orik too? Some guy in that

hospital where he was, who thought he was cute, and wouldn't stop when Orik asked him?

I knew my buddy would ask him to stop.

When I got home, my Mom frowned. "*Another* night at the LaFonts?"

"Just get off my back, Mom. It's no big deal."

"Do you know how many boys get girls pregnant while they're deciding if they like girls or not?" she wanted to know.

"Give me a break. I like girls."

"You and Ana are going to think, Oh, I'll use a condom. Condoms break, baby. Especially when you're learning how to use them."

Something in me felt like throwing myself through a window. But I pulled myself together just in time.

The first week in August, another kid fell into my world like a meteorite. Nancy came bursting into the kitchen one evening. She was talking Spanish, waving her hands and crying. Chino frowned. He got Marian, and the three of them talked Spanish. Then Nancy and Chino jumped in his 4 Runner and left, like it was some emergency.

I was trying to get started polishing my new mirror and didn't pay much attention till the 4 Runner came back after midnight. Chino and Nancy were helping an injured kid between them. He had been beaten up pretty bad. He must have lost his jacket, because he was wearing the spare that Chino kept in the 4 Runner.

"This is Nancy's nephew, Teak," Chino said to my Mom.

Teak was two inches taller than me, with a bloody cut in his frizzy curls, and one eye all puffy. His girlie eyes were full of terror. His hair was dyed orange, and he was dressed faggy... tight satin pants. One gold earring was ripped out of his ear, and blood had dripped all over his dirty T-shirt that said NOBODY KNOWS I'M A LESBIAN. And he was fat. Not *fat* fat, just lurking on the edges of fat. The satin pants made his butt look a yard wide. What a mess! He didn't look like a science geek to me.

Nancy and Chino took him into the spare bedroom in Nancy's

part of the house. Marian went down to the supermarket on the PCH, which was open all night, to get him some clothes.

Finally, everybody slumped around the table, and had coffee. Chino said Teak was asleep.

"I knew this was coming," said Nancy. "Why didn't I try to help more?"

"Nothing you could have done," said Chino. "You got to let people have their leap."

"He...uh...going to be okay?" I asked.

"His family thumped him pretty good. His own brother kicked him in the nuts. He got out of the house and ran like hell before they could break any bones."

"What did he do?" I asked.

"He came out. He's thirteen."

A horrible feeling shot through me, about how I had almost beaten Alberto.

"His best friend Elena was the only one who knew," Nancy said. "And I wondered about both of them for years. This morning he and Elena just...went to school dressed like that. They'd changed clothes somewhere. A few of the boys shoved them around. The principal called my sister, and Consuela came and got him. She called his father and he came home from work. Then he...and Teak's older brother Louis..." Nancy pounded her strong brown fist on the table, with rage. "And his mother told him if God allowed abortion, she would have aborted him. Then they threw him out."

"No jacket, no money," said Chino.

I shuddered, seeing Orik running along the street, stumbling. Marian was shaking her head.

Chino looked at me, like he knew about Alberto.

"Most kids who get thrown away," he said, "in a week most of them are working the streets. A few get to the shelters. There's a few hundred shelter beds in L.A., for 20,000 runaways. The rest... And parents can find them in the shelters, so a lot of them don't want to be found."

"How did you know what happened?" I asked Nancy.

"Teak called me collect," Nancy said. "I was the only person he knew who might take him in. I told him to wait right there at the phone booth."

Would Orik call me collect? Did he still remember my number?

For a few days, Teak slept and ate and cried alone. I felt edgy. The way I saw it, Chino had moved fast to get a gay boy into my world. Were they trying to recruit me? I made sure everybody knew that things were pretty serious between Ana and me, and got a lecture from Ana's mom, who wanted to make sure I would respect Ana's boundaries. I blushed and felt really angry, and told her that I would.

Somehow I had thought that Teak was from barrio poor people, and ran with the Crips or Bloods, or whatever. It turned out that Teak didn't speak much Spanish, and he'd never been near a gang. Chino told me that his family, the Guajiras, were two generations away from Mexico — they lived on a nice street in Highland Park, owned a chain of Mexican supermarkets, and were Pentecostals. Teak was the baby of the family, their pride and joy, the math and computer nerd who was going to inherit the family business. His parents didn't have a clue why their straight-A son had gotten so moody, and started flunking all his classes.

Nancy and Chino drove over to the Guajiras' to see if they could get his clothes and books and computer. But all his stuff had gone in the trash. Mrs. Guajira told Nancy that she was no longer her sister.

Teak lay with his head buried in the pillow, sobbing. Nancy rubbed his head and called him *mi'jito*.

"All my computer games," he said. "My math books. I'll *never* get them together again."

I felt bad, looking at his fat back covered with bruises.

"*Jito*, be glad you're alive," said Nancy. "You can get another computer."

"*Tia*," he said to her, "*please* find out what happened to Elena."

He was freaked because a 15-year-old lesbian at his school had killed herself. During rush hour one day, this other girl jumped off a bridge onto the 5 freeway, and let a big truck run over her. This was after her Anglo parents tried to de-gay her by having men friends of the family come in and have sex with her. It turned out that Elena was okay. Her mother was a single mom who was actually trying to understand. Elena and Teak had long talks on the phone.

My grandfather came down from San Francisco to handle Teak's legal stuff. His spooky eyes stared into mine — so pale blue they almost weren't there, like two holes of sky in his face. John Sive had finally finished his big court case and I had to meet him.

"So you're Billy's boy."

Grandpa didn't look much different than the news photos I'd seen. He had silver hair that was my brunette color once, and a dark suit, and that knife-edge manner that famous lawyers have in the TV shows. And he was short, like me. Definitely, between my Mom and my grandpa Sive, I had gotten stuck with short genes.

A dorky law student, Mitch, came with Grandpa. His job was to drive Grandpa, carry his briefcase, do research, and be a gofer.

I stared back at Grandpa. "I hope I get taller than you," I said.

"Sorry, John," my Mom drawled. "This may be Billy's kid, but he didn't inherit Billy's winning personality. Lately he's about as charming as a mad rhino."

Grandpa just snorted, and turned away.

"How tall do you want to be, young man?" he asked me.

"My Dad was six feet," I said.

"Your dad was as tall as it took," Grandpa said. "He was tall in his heart."

I felt deflated.

"Your grandpa is five foot eight," Marian grinned. "A few six-foot judges look up to him."

"Nancy," said Grandpa, "where's that kid of yours?" His mind was already into business, and he had Mitch spreading legal papers on Marian's dining table.

"What's your fee?" Nancy asked Grandpa nervously.

"Family pro bono," Grandpa growled. He squinted at me, like an old movie pirate who was considering making me walk the plank. "If I billed my family for all the years of saving their gay asses, I'd be richer than Ross Perot. Mitch, some coffee, please. Let's get to work."

"Yessir," said Mitch, heading for the kitchen.

Teak came in, his eyes scared. He was wearing new size 40 jeans instead of the satin pants. Even in the jeans, his butt looked big.

"Teak," said Nancy, "this is John Sive. He's your lawyer."

Grandpa riveted Teak with those eyes of his. But when he talked, his deep voice was quiet and calm.

"Teak, I know you're worried about your family coming after you. But we're going to do some legal things, so you'll be safe. Understand?"

Teak nodded, swallowing hard.

That week, my grandpa's law office started some proceedings. Teak's parents may have thrown him out of the house, but they still had all the legal rights over him. They could change their minds and drag him home, or have him put in juvenile jail for being disobedient. But now they said they didn't want him at all. Teak was dead to them, they said. So Nancy asked them to give up their rights. They said no problem, send over the papers. She could adopt him, they said, or drown him in the L.A. River like a batch of puppies. But he had to give up the Guajira name. Open and shut case.

Meanwhile, Teak was going to live with his aunt, in our house. Meaning I had to deal with this fat fag on a daily basis. On the next visit to the doctor, to check his injuries, Nancy had his HIV test done. She was assuming he'd been around. My Mom dragged me in, and they ran my HIV test too. How did she know where Shawn had been? she said. Yada, yada, yada. I was extremely pissed off at this invasion of privacy.

Both our tests were neg.

"Teak is your buddy," Chino told me. "You're six months older than he is. So I'm making you responsible for him."

"I thought my Mission was about Orik, and my Dad."

"Your Mission is about becoming an officer in your own world. It takes two in life...whether it's war, or love," Chino said. "One to watch the other's back. And you never know who you might need to watch your back."

One hot afternoon, Ana and I were swimming laps in Marian's pool. I was showing off because Teak was hiding behind the bird of paradise plants, watching us. I wanted him to see what a real guy looked like. He was sitting cross-legged on a towel, spying on me. His scabs were peeling. Finally Ana and I lay on my towel. The sun poured down on us. Teak and I eyed each other suspiciously. He was wearing a weeny little red Speedo. Nancy had taken him for new clothes, and this was what he picked. It made his butt look wider than a yard. He peered down the front of it.

"Gurrrl, I'm getting soooo well," he said.

"Don't call me girl," I said.

Teak's hands did a snap. "Ooooo, I love mean men," he purred.

I was ready to puke.

Just then a black BMW came down the driveway. Teak's face looked like Alberto's when he thought Orik and I were going to thump him. He disappeared into the birds of paradise.

"Hey...it's just Taylor," Ana called. "Marian's PR guy."

Not a sound. Finally I got worried, because Chino would skin me if anything happened to Teak, so I walked over there. Hidden way in the shadows of some big leaves, Teak was sitting with his knees drawn up. He was shaking, and tears were brimming over his supershort supercurly eyelashes. I could see how violated he felt.

"My brother Louis drives a black BMW," he mumbled.

"Well, it's not your brother, dummy. It's Taylor."

Teak hugged his knees, sobbing. The smell of tears hung around him.

"Your folks aren't gonna come here," Ana said, trying to comfort him. "Chino will tear their heads off."

After my brave try at comforting Chino in the cemetery, I felt helpless to say anything. So I just sat there, holding my own knees, and thought about poor Orik getting slammed around. Teak stayed behind the bird of paradise plant. We eyed each other, shipwrecked on the same desert island, wondering how we'd put up with each other. When Ana went in, he said to me:

"Are you gay?"

"No effing way."

"Everybody's a *fruta* in this house."

"Well, I'm not, so watch your mouth."

"Sorr-eeee." A last tear rolled down his face.

Long silence. A hawk was drifting on the hot air over the canyon. Suddenly Teak laughed nervously, and rubbed the tear off on his endless brown arm. "Mondo Malibu. My parents will die, when they find out they kicked me upstairs socially...instead of down."

Silence.

"Chino says you're a science wonk," he said.

What else had Chino told him?

He got to his knees, and pulled his confidence together one more time. "Hey...my aunt got me a Macintosh SE, a used one. And a whole box of softwear. Wanna hang out while I load my programs?"

His eyes held mine, asking the big question. If I was straight, would I treat him like the studs who smacked him around at school? And if I did treat him that way, I'd have to face Chino.

Ana and I perched on the end of his bed, while he sprawled at the spare desk that Marian found in the garage. Expertly he shoved disks into his machine. He had borrowed Nancy's radio, and it was blasting Madonna singing "Vogue" — not my fave kind of music. Poor Nancy would have to wear earplugs now. I wondered if he'd try and fool with me. I couldn't stand the idea. He was too pitiful to kill, but I'd definitely have to smack him. But he was the computer wiz now, lost in his electronic world, while he created files and whipped icons around the screen with awesome speed. It probably made him feel better, like the dark sky made me feel better. I could see him on Channel 3...one of the white-collar honchos at a NASA computer, during some space mission. Maybe Teak would steer me to the stars someday, and watch my back on his screen.

"Where's the action in 'Bu?" Teak yelled over the music.

"The Crosscreek Mall," Ana yelled.

"*Action*, silly child. Clubs and stuff."

Clubs at thirteen? "We don't club in Malibu," I said.

"God," he said, rolling his eyes up. "You're not very (snap) user friendly, are you?"

Mission Phase 2: get tight with Harlan. "Hey, Harlan, did my Dad ever club?"

Harlan stopped typing and leaned back in his chair. "Oh — when Billy was sad, he'd go find the Life."

What this meant, Harlan told me, was that my Dad would go into New York and hang out on the queer streets alone. He was 22 when he did this. Sometimes he went to old movies alone. He loved drag queens. I almost died when I heard this. Harlan told me about a black drag queen, Delfeen somebody, who was a special friend of my Dad's. So I had to check the Life out. But it was too scary to investigate alone. Teak felt the same way. So Ana rode the bus into West Hollywood with us. Orik's dad would have told us that Jesus was coming on the next marine-layer of clouds to drag us to hell.

Teak met Harlan and Vince and Paul and Darryl and Rose and Vivian. The Valhalla gang liked having us three teenagers around. Rose had us gofer at shoots, so we were earning some change and had money to spend. The Rosewood Avenue gang were running out of guest rooms, so Paul and Darryl found two old pop-up tents, and let us camp in a private corner of their backyard, behind some trees near the wall. Rose and Vivian's house was half a block down, and we were up and down the alley to all the houses, and had keys.

From our home base on Rosewood, we nervously checked out the queer scene in West Hollywood, which everybody called WeHo. Ana was wildly curious. Teak was ready for what Chino called "shooting and looting." For me, this was scientific research. So how come my knees quivered? Did steely-eyed missilemen quiver all over when they pressed the launch button?

Late in the afternoon, Vince went with us. We walked the few blocks north to the Santa Monica strip. Between Robertson and La Brea, it was all queer-owned businesses...like restaurants, clubs, bars, junk food places, gyms, jewelry stores, galleries, clothes stores, and a video rental place where you could get the raddest sex films in the Universe. My Dad had walked those same kinds of streets. It was the family law, laid down by both the women and the men (even Rose and Vivian, who acted like strict lesbian moms), that we didn't talk to strange adult men, or hitchhike home. Did my Dad ever have any close calls?

I thought the Life was all about sex. But it wasn't. There were T-shirt stores and Hamburger Haven and Different Light Bookstore. In the Wells Fargo bank, Vince introduced us to a gay vice president. At the Six Gallery coffeehouse, other teens were hanging out, with caps backwards and cool. They were itching with guilt and curiosity like we were, and looked or acted older than they were. Teak already knew a few. We'd collapse on the half-destroyed sofas with our Cokes, and rap with them. Some had boyfriends. Some were desperate virgins, like Teak. A few were already HIV poz. One guy who was 16 told us he got HIV on his first time experience.

"I always knew I wouldn't live past 18 anyway," he said.

"Hey, Teak, this your boyfriend?" they asked, staring at me.

I was busy disappearing behind my star-less baseball cap, holding Ana's hand. The bill pointed frontwards like a battery of missiles.

"Nuh-uh." Teak said. "He's straight."

"Straight to bed," said one Mexican kid, staring into my eyes.

My arm tightened across Ana's shoulders.

Sometimes, with Vince and Chino, we cruised the Boulevard in the evening before curfew. No harm in getting a peek at the Life, Vince said. Chino knew frigging well (he said) that the night life fascinated us, because it had fascinated him when he was our age. No, he wasn't taking us to any leather bars or back rooms or sex clubs or circuit parties. When we were 18, we could go there and get laid — and get riddled with disease, if we were stupid. Right now, we would go where *he* said, and hopefully our little recons with him would de-glamorize the Life. Had he made himself clear?

"A real bodyguard," said Teak. "That is soooo rad. Chino, you body-guarded for Madonna once, right?"

Late at night, in Chino's 4 Runner, we drove the Santa Monica strip between Vine and Western. I stared out at the hookers leaning on park benches, getting into cars. They were all my age. I wondered how my Dad felt about homeless kids selling their sex to get food. The idea made me desperately sad. We hung outside the Arena Cafe, and watched hundreds of older kids going in to dance. West, towards Robertson, we checked out the leather daddies and Levi queens and other street stars in the glare of light from clubs — Micky's, Rage, Peanuts, Studio One. We saw the UCLA college boys leaving Revolver hand in hand, and the Street Cats doing their citizen's street patrol. A few gay vets that Chino knew were bouncers at clubs. Chino said that my Dad hung with all these different kinds of people.

Somewhere in the reflections of store windows, if only I looked hard enough, I might see some fading blur of my Dad, in a galaxy called New York that existed 5 million years ago.

One night we almost got bashed. Chino and Teak and I were walking a side street, to where Chino had left the 4 Runner, when three guys drove alongside in a red Corvette. They yelled some stuff at Chino for being with two boys. Chino told us quietly to stay back. So the Corvette guys pulled to the curb ahead of us, and got out. They weren't skinheads — just normal looking college guys. One carried a baseball bat. Another had a bicycle chain.

"You guys don't want to mess with me," Chino told them, sounding like he was telling them it might rain.

"You're dead, faggot," said Mr. Baseball Bat.

They closed on Chino.

He went into a blur. It was over in four nanoseconds. Nothing spectacular like the movies, with all the staged moves. Disappointing, in fact. Just dirty and effective. I wished I'd seen it in slo-mo. Anyway, two of them were laying on the sidewalk, groaning and gagging. Chino stood over them, with the bat in one hand and the chain in the other. The third guy was backed against the Corvette. His eyes were bulging like a frog's when you squeeze it.

"I left you in one piece," Chino said to him, "so you can be the designated driver."

I saw many different kinds of things, and Jesus didn't appear in the clouds and drag me away to hell. Now and then, through the glare and palm trees, in the purple neon night sky, I thought I could see a constellation crossing the meridian.

One night, outside Girl Bar, an embarrassing thing happened. We actually ran into my Mom. She was on a date, and hadn't told me. She was dressed to kill, with a flush in her cheeks and her eyes all bright. She and her lady were laughing and talking, and having a slammin' time. I don't know why I felt so embarrassed at seeing my Mom at a club, because everybody had been on her case to date for years. It was just weird...seeing her date a woman.

Mom waved at us, and we went over.

"Hi," she said. "Everybody...this is Joyce. Joyce, this is William, my son, and his friend Teak. You know Chino."

Joyce was a lady basketball player. She looked down at us boys from her six feet of black men's suit. You could tell she was one of those strict lesbian moms.

"What are these babies doing on the Strip at this hour?" Joyce wanted to know.

Next day I yelled at Mom: "You didn't tell me."

"I don't need your permission to date anybody," she yelled back.

Elena's mom hooked up with Nancy, and started letting Elena see us. That was how I met Teak's best friend. Elena was a tiny, dark Mexican girl, with a face like an Indian mask. She was shorter than me, two months younger than me. Elena had always been quiet, Nancy warned us, even when she came home from school with her hair full of spit. Now she was out and tired of being spit on, and thinking about joining a girl gang of bi's and baby dykes who were all mad about stuff. Her mom wanted her off the street. Being with Teak in Malibu was a way of getting her out of L.A.

But when Teak and Elena got together again, they weren't so quiet. She sat in Teak's lap, and got his morale going again, and they hugged, and giggled and kidded around about queer stuff that I didn't understand. Both of them were different people when they were with each other. Mom got the long-ago look in her eyes, and said they reminded her of long talks with Billy in the dormitory. Did Elena and Teak fool around like Ana and I did? If so, how were they queer? Jesus, it was really confusing.

Teak bothered me about it. "Come on, I gotta go club. I want to meet somebody nice. Go with me."

"How can you meet somebody if I'm with you? Take Elena."

"If I'm already with a guy, it's…like…I'm hard to get, so everybody will want me."

"I don't dance."

"I'll teach you. You'll love it. We'll do Arena…Circus…Dome… ."

"Arena? You gotta be eighteen."

"For ten dollars I can get you fake ID."

"My mom would throw ten fits."

Elena harassed me too. "Hey…at least we can go to baby night at Micky's. Bust a few dances. Maybe Shayla will be there."

"Yeah, Elena has been trying to meet Shayla. Come on, girl…"

"If you call me girl one more time, I'll break your neck."

Teak grinned at Elena. "It's soooo easy to get William going."

Ana was bored with Malibu surfers, and thought Teak and Elena were the coolest kids on the planet. "Let's do a foursome. You'll be totally safe, William. I'll protect you."

As casually as possible, I asked Harlan again about my Dad and clubbing. He leaned back in his chair, forgetting his script, and got this long-ago look in his eyes. He talked about clubs in New York like the Ice Palace and the Tubs, only he called them discotheques, which was one of those strange old words from a prehistoric language.

"Your dad," he said, "was a helluva dancer. He was one of those people that everybody stopped to watch on the dance floor. I used to watch him. Your dad wasn't a sexy dancer, exactly. Somehow when he did the moves, you could see all his dreams for himself…his joy in being alive…."

Joy in being alive?

"Okay, let's club," I told Teak.

I felt weird about clubbing because Orik was locked up and not having a good time. Mission Phase 3 wasn't happening. The new mirror wasn't happening. But I had to know more about my Dad.

— 15 —

WEHO NIGHTS

Orik was still writing me a letter every week. He copied more stuff from the Bible, and said he wished I'd repent. He said he was doing good in camp. His parents had him accepted at the Citadel in Virginia and he was supposed to go there in the fall. He sure sounded miserable.

I wrote back, saying I was having a terrific summer, hanging out with lots of kids. I told him I wasn't interested in the Bible, so he could be environmentally responsible and save paper. My Mom and Chino okayed the letter. But I didn't think the clinic would let Orik read it.

Micky's was this little video club on the Strip. Every Wednesday, they had baby night — $2 cover, no liquor, nobody over 18, house music, closing at 9, which gave you an hour to get home before curfew.

Teak told me about his adventures at Micky's. He never met anybody there, but he always went back because it was home. He'd tell his parents he and Elena were going to the movies. Elena would tell her parents the same lie. Then he and Elena would leave home in normal clothes, with voguey party rags in their backpacks. They'd ride the bus from Highland Park into West L.A. When they got off the bus, they'd find a dumpster or a hedge to hide behind, and jump in their vogues. Then they'd go to Micky's. Elena would hang with girls, and Teak would try to hang with boys. They took turns watching each other's backpacks. Elena found cool girls to dance with. Teak had to dance alone. Black and Mexican boys didn't like fat boys any more than white boys did. Teak's heart got broken every weekend. But he kept going back. You could catch a big crowd and a lot of high energy at Micky's at quarter to nine. By 10, Elena and Teak would be back in Highland Park. They made sure they could talk about the movie they'd "seen." Their parents bought the lie totally.

Now we told the all-controlling adults that we wanted to go to baby night at Micky's.

"Be home by curfew," the parents said.

Around 6, we got dressed in my guest room at Harlan's house.

Ana, the Queen of Malibu, turned her hair loose and wore her best designer jeans and her silver-hanger earring. Teak jumped into vogue — sparkly gold tank-top and patent-leather dance shoes. His velvet pants, that Nancy got him, made his butt look a light-year wide. Elena had a red satin shirt that she'd bought at a thrift store, and platform shoes. She sat in front of Teak and did his face. He kept his makeup in his own secret box. I had never seen a guy wear makeup except on a film set, so I was in shock. Teak glowed as Elena put the last swipe of mascara on his eyelashes. My homely fat buddy actually looked like a star.

"You are soooo glamorous," Elena told Teak. She kissed him on the cheek, then stuck her diamond bead in the side of her nose.

"I am the soul of *(snap, snap, snap, snap)* glama!" Teak said. He looked at me.

"I'm not your date, okay?" I said. "You're the *fruta* who wants to go to the *fruta* club. And we're your bodyguards, okay?"

"Yeah," said Ana, "we're doing this for you, stupid."

"Don't diss him now." Elena gave us a gangsta glare.

I dressed like I felt — Orange County straight boy going to a WeHo club to look for fading light from his gay father, and wanting to be invisible. That meant old jeans, *Star Wars* T-shirt, Nikes, and a new baseball cap that Mom gave me, that said "Clinton in '92". The bill was frontwards so ethnic dudes wouldn't think I was an enemy homeboy. With the bathroom door locked, I gave myself a cadet glare and trimmed my eyelashes super-short.

We had gofered for a Valhalla commercial shoot, so we had $50 to spend. Elena had a few secret tabs of Ecstasy in her jeans pocket.

"Oh my, we are gonna *jam*," Teak said as we headed for the Boulevard.

Elena and Teak popped an Ecstasy in their mouths before I could stop them. Ana looked at me, like asking for my permission. I shook my head "no" and set my watch for 9:45. I was in charge of this mission, so I had to keep myself together.

That five blocks to the Strip was longer and scarier than a 10-year trip to Proxima Centauri.

In front of Micky's, the sidewalk was crowded with high school and college students. They were smoking cigarettes and throwing attitude and staring at each other. We lit up our smokes, and stared back. It was the same stuff you see at school dances, except that guys were checking out guys' butts instead of girls' butts. My cheeks squeezed together nervously. Did guys stare at my Dad's butt like this? If Jerry could see me now, I thought. If Orik could see me! My stomach was shivering. A few guys were looking at me. A few girls stared at Ana and Elena. Nobody was looking at Teak.

As we headed for the door, this ancient leather troll in a Harley jacket leaned out at us from his sidewalk table, where he had flyers.

"Play safely, kids," he said, and plopped condoms into our hands.

We shoved the condoms in our pockets and forgot them, as we pushed past the security studs. They were turning back adult men who wanted to go in and pick up kids.

Inside, feeling jittery, Ana and I stayed behind Teak and Elena, the experts, as they pushed through the shoulders, biceps and elbows of white boys, black boys, Mexican boys, Filipino boys, Japanese boys. "Look at all these handsome honeys," Teak said in my ear. All of them were horny, and some of them were looking at me. Had my Dad enjoyed this crap? The air reeked with teenage overkill on cologne. I thanked the Goddesses and Gods that I'd trimmed my eyelashes. Teak talked quietly in my ear about gang colors...blue bandana, jacket hanging open to show orange. "Some bangers come over to WeHo for closet sex," he hissed in my ear, "but this is a neutral zone, so everybody's cool."

He grinned, and caught my fingers to pull me along.

"Don't hold my effing hand," I hissed back.

"Oh my god, there's Shayla," said Elena.

Her eyes did a missile lock on a tall black girl in a silver cowboy shirt. She left us. Even with those platform shoes, Elena was so short that we couldn't see her pushing through the crowd. All we could see was the ripple she made.

Teak pushed me and Ana past the bartenders serving pop and juice, toward the crowded smoky dance floor.

The whole wall behind the dance floor was video screens with the identical image. A thousand Madonnas danced and sang "Vogue." The air shuddered with the same machine music that Teak listened to in his room. Everybody was grinding and rump-shaking enough to send the Rev. Dwight into a coma.

I had literally never seen two guys dancing together, not even in the movies or TV. So a whole roomful of teenage studs pumping their packages at each other was sending me into shock. Then I was getting hard, and not needing Ecstasy to feel it. I was fighting my own heat. Guys are pure mindless heat with a brain loosely attached. Women, and other guys, and sheep and dogs, are not safe around us. In Costa Mesa, Orik and I knew a horny kid who was always looking for relief. Finally his parents caught him with his German Shepherd. He had smeared peanut butter on his penis, and the dog was licking it off. His parents threw him out. We never did hear what happened to him. The parents kept the dog.

"C'mon...let's vogue," said Teak, pulling me towards the dance floor.

"Bodyguards don't dance. Go find somebody."

Teak's cool was starting to melt down. He blurted, "You don't want to dance with me 'cause I'm colored, huh."

Teak stormed off and worked the crowd, asking this guy and that guy. He hung out at the bar for a while. Everybody ignored him. We watched his face get sadder and sadder. Elena was ignoring us, dancing with Shayla. Ana was outraged on Teak's behalf. She hissed in my ear, "You're being mean, and I won't speak to you if you're mean."

"Excuse-me *you*."

"Then the three of us can dance," diplomat Ana said.

My piss-off flamed out, and I felt bad. Chino's voice came, saying, *Be a commander...look after your people.* So I pulled myself together and went to where Teak was leaning, with his empty pop can. "Look," I said, "don't do the racist stuff with me. If I was racist, I wouldn't let you come in my room."

"Sorry," he said. A tear streaked down his cheek.

"And I don't know why these lame jerks aren't all over you. You look so rad tonight."

"Really!" Teak said sarcastically. "I was starting to think you don't appreciate (snap snap) a big *queena* like me."

He rubbed away the tear.

"Anyway, buddies are better than a date," I said. "A date might ditch you."

"Like Shayla just ditched Elena," said Ana, watching the black girl leaving alone.

Teak's eyes searched mine. Jesus, he did have nice eyes — so black they were purple. And his nice short eyelashes were to be envied, even with mascara on them. "Buddies?" he said. "Brothers?"

"Yeah." I put out my hand. We shook.

"You'll have to show me how to dance," I said.

"Just do what I do."

"Not where every big *queena* in the world can watch, though."

Elena came back with a disgusted shrug. So the four of us found a dark corner on the dance floor, with a speaker right in our ears. There Ana faced Elena, and I faced Teak, and Teak started going through the vogue moves like Madonna and her male dancers were doing. I guessed he had been practicing for months, alone in his room with his radio. Elena's dancing was stiff, like a robot, but Teak was fluid. His big butt moved like a movie star's.

"Catch the beat. Christ, it's so easy," he said.

I tried.

Teak got frustrated with me. "Stop (snap-snap) that!" Then he went macho again. "Here...let's shadow dance, so you can feel it." He spun me around, pressed behind me, and glommed his big arms around me. "Just relax. God, you're like a broom, or something."

So I leaned back on him stiffly, and Ana leaned on me, and Elena leaned on Ana, and we sandwiched into the beat as a foursome. Teak stood there in place, pumping his body under mine with that vogueing beat. I relaxed and closed my eyes, and the thump of the music filled me. I held his arms in place around my waist, and Ana held my arms around her. I let his hot sweaty cheek press against my cheek, and pressed my hot sweaty nose against the back of Ana's slippery neck, under her hair, which was getting hotter and wetter by the minute. Her silver-hanger earring almost put my eye out. The floor was packed now — the four of us lost in a mass of sweaty bodies. The whole crowd amped off into the flashing light show and the space-hammer beat.

Did my Dad move like this?

When we got thirsty, we fought our way back to the bar for Cokes, then found an inch of space where we could look cool and watch everybody.

Right next to me, a Filipino boy and a white boy were deep-kissing, eyes closed, with their tongues down each other's throats. I stared at them, remembering being at the lake with Orik. I leaned against the wall. I could feel their body heat and hear their lips sliding. Their arms were wrapped around each other, their bodies tight together — not humping, just tight. Their elbows brushed me. They were tasting each other's faces with their lips, and the Filipino boy was holding the other boy's face in his hand. "Oh baby," he whispered. Then they sank into another kiss, tongues driving deep. I actually watched their tongues sliding. A guy calling a guy baby...

I stared back at the dance floor. So that was what my Dad looked like when he kissed Harlan. He'd probably kissed other guys too. My hard-on was going crazy. Was this how my Dad felt? Were his feelings were right inside me, bursting into light and shockwaves like a supernova going off with incredible violence and beauty, and this time I wasn't staring at it through some telescope, I was in the middle of it. This was what I'd wanted to do with Orik...and now I'd never have the chance.

Teak nudged me with his elbow. Face on fire, I pulled my bill low over my eyes.

"Nobody in here is very worried about AIDS," I said.

"No, but the right guy could format my hard drive." Teak had a weird defensive look in his eyes.

"Oh yeah?" I punched his shoulder.

He blurted, "My drive's never been did."

I stared at him, full of questions, as we finished our Cokes. Suddenly my watch beeped. Jesus, it was 9:45.

"Fifteen minutes to curfew," I said. "Home...on the double."

O utside, Elena said, "I'm going to mom's," and disappeared. We knew she'd do another Ecstasy, and swing by more clubs, hoping to run into Shayla. We walked the eight blocks to Harlan's house because Teak was too fat to run, and burst in the front door. It was 5 minutes after 10.

My Mom looked at her watch, and frowned.

"You're five minutes late." She narrowed her eyes.

But tonight she wasn't in the mood for cruel and unusual punishment. The house was full of adults. In the TV room, Marian was pacing around with the long-cord phone, talking politics to Taylor. In the dining room, Paul, Darryl, Harlan, Rose, Vivian and Vince were having a story conference. Chino wasn't around. So Mom just waved us off.

Since we were starving, we grabbed some cold pizza out of the fridge and microwaved it. Then we ran to our camp in Paul's yard.

I t was a hot August night, with the purple sky full of the sound of choppers and cars on the streets. Teak and I went to our tent, and Ana went to hers. Teak fell down on the sleeping bags with a disgusted sigh.

"So, tell me something," I said.

"What?"

"You came out at school, and...went through all that drama, and got beat up, over something you didn't even do yet?"

"William, I want to have my first time, and I'm getting loco about it." He pushed his face in his pillow.

"Maybe you won't like it."

"I'll like it," he said into the pillow.

Long silence.

"*You* ever done it with a guy?" he asked me.

"Are you kidding?"

He rolled onto his back again, keeping his anxious short-eyelashed eyes fixed on mine. It dawned on me that my fat buddy was so desperate that he wanted me to fool around with him. My knees were shaking. It wasn't panic I was feeling. I was choking with feelings about Orik...missing him, wishing he was here. Totally heartless, I got up and left him, and went over to Ana's tent in my underwear. She was curled on her sleeping bag, wearing just a baggy T-shirt.

"What a cool club," she said sleepily.

"Too gay for me," I said, over her on hands and knees.

She trusted me by now, so she vibed back that it was a go. She sat up and pulled off her T-shirt, then leaned over to her radio, and found a station with some heavy metal, and the music filled us. "Just don't actually do anything," she whispered.

"I promise."

We cuddled together on her rumpled sleeping bag. She was turned on too. Her smell was so different from the guy smell, more like a funky kind of tropical flower. That was what my Mom always called it — the flower. I'd never seen my Mom's, but she'd talked about it when she taught me about sex, which was ever since I could remember, in hopes that I would respect women. Ana wouldn't let me touch her, but she got her hand in my Jockeys. My legs were quivering and I didn't even dare ask her if it was big enough. But she must have vibed my worry, because she whispered, "That guy, you know the one, was...way too big."

"You think so?" I was trembling all over.

"What's important is how you feel with the person," she whispered, taking a better hold on me.

With the fading light of two boys kissing all around us, we kissed and suddenly a meteoric itch went exploding out of me, and I went "Oooh!" We were both in shock, like we'd almost been hit by a bus, and we lay there for a while, listening to a chopper fly over. I was feeling this incredible relief, and sadness, all together. Finally we wiped up and unzipped the tent and lay on our backs with our heads out. I was pulling myself together by trying to see Deneb, the brightest star in the Summer Triangle, which would be crossing the meridian right now. But the sky was too polluted, and Paul's trees were in the way.

"You had sex before?" she whispered.

"Kind of."

"What do you mean?"

"Fooled around...." I was having a hard time meeting her eyes.

"Orange County girls, hmmm?"

I blushed. She looked at me for a long time. "Guys?"

"Guys always fool around."

"Your friend Shawn?"

I blushed worse. "Hey, he and I are...just buddies, okay?"

"Relax, William. I don't care." She was looking at me sideways through her tangled hair.

"Hey, let's get something straight," I said. "You're my first girl, and I can't imagine being with any other girl."

"A guy who doesn't lie about his first girl. How did I get lucky?"

Paul and Darryl's cat, Son-of-Nefertiti, was sharpening her claws on the tent. Then she came and curled between us. She liked our vibe, and the way we smelled.

Next morning, in my room, I checked the photos of my Dad and Orik. The candle had gone out. I felt guilty, and my hand shook as I got the lighter out of my backpack and lit it again. Then I stared at the photograph of my Dad and Orik's 8th-grade photo.

"You two guys are creeps," I said to them. "How could you put me through all this?"

In a few days, the Rosewood Avenue adult gang knew things were more serious with me and Ana. Teak wasn't speaking to me because (in his mind) I'd dumped him. I writhed with nervousness. The moms, of course, had to get together and talk about it. Back in Malibu, my Mom and I happened to be in the kitchen together, and she was eating yogurt, and I was eating a huge sandwich, and she steered the conversation around to sex. She must have been dying of curiosity. First it was Orik, now it was Ana. What was the deal?

"So...you and Ana are...?"

I tried to sound casual. "Not really."

"Come on."

"She doesn't let me. We just...fool around."

"That's how Harlan had his first kid...fooling around on a prom date."

"I'm not effing Harlan." I was getting ready to be a Klingon invasion, all over her sky, and she was going to be the loser going down in flames.

"I don't mind you two cuddling around home, but...it's risky. I know about Ana, okay? And her mom knows that you know, because Ana told her. So don't hurt her or get her pregnant, okay? Her mother is very concerned."

"I *won't*. She doesn't let me do *anything*."

"I *do* mind you sneaking around...in cars, or wherever...places where I don't know what's happening with you." She tossed the empty yogurt cup in the trash. "Most kids have their first time on the back seat of a car. I did. There isn't any dignity in it."

How could women even *talk* to us guys about what we did?

"Wouldn't you rather not sneak around?" she asked.

My mouth fell open. Was she giving me permission?

Mom's eyes were begging me not to go Klingon on her. Just in time, I remembered Chino's demand that I stay tight with her. She had brought me up alone with no dad, no family, all by herself. The only thing that scared my warrioress Mom were bankers and her kid not listening to her.

"You mean...I can officially sleep over with her?"

"Here...in your bedroom. Or at Rosewood. Eileen and I...and Marian too...want those places to be okay for you. We'll respect your privacy. But you have to respect some limits too."

Jesus, they'd *all* talked about this behind our backs. Like it was the Presidential election or something. I was speechless.

"Um...gee, Mom, that would be...uh...great."

"You see...Eileen and I have a choice."

"What?"

"We could lock the two of you up till you're 18. Chain you in the basement, or something. How would you like that?"

"Aw, man," I groaned.

"Yeah, I know it wouldn't work."

Mom had never been weird about sex. According to her, every part of my body was part of the Goddess Earth, therefore okay. For some reason I remembered when I had my first erection. I must have been eight. I thought something had gone extremely wrong with me, so I stood there screaming, with my weenie sticking out. She said, "This is a neat thing that happens to boys. So stop screaming and enjoy it." But right now, my mother acquired an awesome new power as she talked about sex in my face. A fierce blush ate me.

She went on. "You get the wake-up call from life when you get it. Not when you're 18. And all the laws and religious rules are like...trying to control the weather. Nobody controls the weather. When it rains, you don't try to cover Los Angeles with an umbrella. You enjoy the rain and drive safely."

I was amazed. When did my mother get to be so smart?

"So this is the deal," she went on. "The two of you drive safely. And be 100 percent responsible...take care of each other. That means if you are sloppy with somebody else, and you get a disease, and you give it to Ana, Eileen will kill you, and when she gets done, I will kill you. Understand?"

"Uh...yeah."

"And there's one more thing. Did you use protection?"

The condom that the troll gave me had already gone through the washer in my jeans pocket.

"There is something called splash conception. You might be old enough to get her pregnant with heavy petting. How would you like to be a father at 13? If you think Eileen and I are going to support you, think again. The two of you will have to work, forget school, forget careers...or give the kid up for adoption. One more kid without a father, and it would be your bleeping fault. How would you like that?"

The thought totally crushed me.

A kid without a father...my fault.

While Eileen was cutting the same deal with Ana, Chino and the other men stayed miles away from this discussion.

My 14th birthday was a month away. The box of mirror blanks was gathering dust on my desk.

— 16 —

NEWS OF ORIK

It was September now. In two weeks, we'd start school. The moms dragged us off on shopping voyages for clothes and books.

Teak's parents signed the adoption papers on September 2. He took Nancy's last name. Teak Perez was happy. That night we had a party for him...he said he wanted to celebrate his birthday on Sept. 2 from now on. The family who flushed him down the toilet was something he was trying to forget. Elena and her mom came to the party. They were moving to Malibu so they could be near us. Elena's mom had gotten a job in a store on the mall. This way, Elena could go to Malibu Hills High with us.

Orik had stopped writing to me.

Chino kept his promise to get me into JPL and look at photos.

"If you're going to look for a needle in a haystack, you better know what the needle looks like," he said.

I tortured myself with the question. The shape of the nebula was not the right needle. In the dream, I hadn't seen the Cat Nebula from Earth. From Earth telescopes, it might not look like a cat. No, I had to look for the variable star. The period of its luminosity change could be measured exactly...from any coordinate in the universe, no matter how many billions of light-years away. If we could find that 60-second variable star, we'd find the Cat Nebula.

Chino drove me to Pasadena, and we parked in the JPL visitor's lot. NASA, home of U.S. exploration of deep space. The real deal. My knees were shivering like for sex.

As we walked into the Visitor's Center to get our passes, Chino said: "The cover story is that you're doing a school science project. Dorie has a weird sense of humor, so watch out."

"Dorie?"

"Floradora Houghton. Astrophysicist. She's investigating the feasibility of using these stars as navigational aids. Remember Russell Houghton? I told you about him. She's his niece."

NASA was on the same wavelength as me.

We had to wait while the receptionist called Dorie to verify that we had an appointment. We spent a while in Building 180, looking at exhibits. But the model of Galileo made me depressed. Galileo was out there, plowing along at its slow Barbarian speed, like a covered wagon, compared to what I needed. Another six years would go by before Galileo even passed the moons of Jupiter and took pictures of them. By then I'd be an old troll — 20. Finally we went to another building, where astronomers had their offices.

"Dorie, this is William," Chino said.

The astrophysicist looked at my membership cards — Astronomy Club, ATM Society, Variable Star Club. She had a silver streak in her hair. My hyperwave vibrometer told me that she was maybe a lesbian and Chino had pulled some strings with her, through the network of queers in the military and government.

"So," she said to Chino without a smile, "we knock ourselves out on Galileo, and everybody is holding their breath for the close look at Jupiter...and this kid is not interested."

I stared at her.

"Just kidding," she said. "I'm not too focused on the planets either. Always wanted to see to the end of time myself. I got my first telescope in fifth grade, and it was a Christmas present from my rich uncle." She leaned back in her chair. "So...you built your own, huh?"

I cleared my throat. "My first was a 4-inch reflector mirror. I used silver fulminate."

"Silver? Holy moley, did you blow yourself up?"

I managed to grin. "Almost."

"What can I get you? The menu's great here. Comets? Quasars?"

"Uh...variables. Short-period variables."

"RR lyrae variables?"

"Right. The most up-to-date photos you have. See — the kids in my class think that nothing changes out there. I want to knock their socks off with some star action."

Dorie took me in her library room. She sat me at a light table and pulled up a rolling file labeled VARIABLES. "Five years of work," she said. My head swam...there was stuff here from observatories and amateur astronomers all over the world...Australia, Sweden, England. She told me not to take anything out of the sleeves and get fingerprints on them.

"And if you put anything back in the wrong folder, I'll check my menu of appropriate punishments."

Then she and Chino went back into her office. They had coffee and sat talking about old times.

My knees shivered, as I fingered through the sections — CEPHEIDS...R CORONAE...IRREGULARS...RR LYRAE. Wow! Everything was there...series of photos of each star blinking on and off, and graphs with light curves and time intervals, and all kinds of spectometry stuff that was way over my head. My hands were shaking as I put the first negative on the light table. Then the next. Slow at first, then faster and faster. There were hundreds, some associated with dark nebulas of different shapes. Intervals of 0.05 days to 1.2 days. I tried to clear my mind. Forget the Cat Nebula...look for the period. If it was in the 15-light-year range and had a 60-second cycle, that might be the one. I tried to scribble notes in my notebook.

A sleeve fell on the floor. I put it back in the right place. Chino sensed my pain, and came in. Dorie was talking on the phone.

"Problems?" he asked.

"There's so many," I whispered.

For a while, I kept shuffling, while Chino looked over my shoulder. But it was all a blur. The back of the file came. No 60-second star. Not in the 15-year band. Not anywhere.

When Dorie came back, she asked, "Well?"

"Do you have any that are...like...60 seconds?"

"Why 60 seconds?"

"Oh..." My mind searched for the appropriate lie. "It's a round number. What are you finding towards the center of our galaxy?"

"That's a tough one...piercing the veil of heavy nebulas."

"If a 60-second one comes in, would you...uh...please let me know?"

"I have Chino's number. Interested in working for NASA someday?" she asked.

"Yeah."

"We're going to have programs for high school students. And someday I might have an internship for a likely college student. America will be all right as long as she still has amateur telescope makers."

Dorie gave me her card. It was the first time ever that an adult gave me a card.

"Thanks a lot," I said.

O n the way home, I was even more depressed. Chino noticed it as he drove us south on the 2 freeway. The tall buildings of downtown L.A. stood jumbled in the smog ahead. "Your dream was really clear, huh," Chino said.

"I have the dream, like, every few months now. The computer display on the *Memo* always says the same thing...60 seconds. And there's another number that comes up — 23. I don't have a clue what 23 is." I looked at him. "You think I'm making it up. You're going to tell my Mom, and she'll drag me to some dork therapist."

"Relax. I still think you're on the trail of something. But dreams are funny. Maybe yours doesn't mean what you think. Maybe it's...a metaphor."

"What's a metaphor?"

"You should ask Harlan. He's always talking about metaphor in a film."

"But what is it?"

"A hidden message or meaning."

"Like a code?"

"Ask him. I'm not enough of an intellectual to explain."

"No way. I would *never* tell Harlan. Not even Vince."

Chino shrugged. "Suit yourself," he said.

"Looking at Galileo today, I felt just...kind of hopeless."

"Why?"

"Even the unmanned probes take, like, *forever* to get way out there. Even if they use fusion for power, Arthur C. Clarke says they can only get close to the speed of light. It's kind of incredible how people really believe they're going to go out there tomorrow. People believe in UFOs, but you never see any of those weird creatures with black eyes on the news. People can believe anything, I guess. Like Shawn's dad, believing that Jesus is going to come back."

"There's a difference between belief and knowing something. Some people have dreams about things that really happen...plane crashes, murders. Or they just have a strong feeling about something. Combat taught me to trust that kind of feeling."

Listening to him made me feel a little better.

"What do I do now?" I asked him.

"For the moment, keep on learning about Billy's life. And school opens in two weeks. Maybe something will break."

For the first time, I wasn't hot for school.

"Chino, did you ever go to Point Reyes, and do like you said?"

"No. I thought about it, though."

"Let's go there. Maybe I'll have another dream...with more details."

"We should all go...the whole family." Chino didn't want to discuss it more. "Now is not a good time, though."

He was quiet for a minute, driving. Then he said, "What about Shawn? Mission Phase 3, remember?"

"What about him?"

"I notice that you haven't mentioned him much all summer."

Panic flashed inside me. "I don't know what you mean."

His voice went hard. "Cut the crap, you little punk. This is your friend we're talking about. There was all this uproar about you two, and suddenly you're acting like you don't care."

"He doesn't write me any more."

"Don't be so quick to judge. He's scared. He's alone in that place. They probably don't let him write."

The hot tears welled. "I was sooo pissed off at him...afraid that he'd tell."

I turned my face away so my alien warlord wouldn't see me cry.

Feelings from the years that Orik and I were friends came bursting up. I hid my face against the window and wanted to strangle myself before I'd cry. There was a rustle, and he reached over and squeezed my shoulder while I choked and tried to keep from sobbing, and messed the window up with my breath.   .

"You be there for your friend," he said. "You light another candle and pray like a son of a bitch. Maybe he'll hold out because of you."

"Chino, we've got to help him more than that!"

"Not much we can do, legally. Maybe he'll run away."

"So he's there all alone?"

"His parents go up there once a week to see him."

That night, my candle-flame danced gently with its mysterious beauty, so alive, reflected in its pool of hot wax, making little shadows move on my Dad's and Orik's faces. I stared at them with my burning eyes.

"Orik, I'm sorry. I'm so sorry...Please God, Goddess, I want my Dad. I want my buddy back. I'm trying so hard...."

Suddenly another new idea came.

Maybe what I saw in my dream was not a place that a real spacecraft could take me to. There were powers in the universe that NASA couldn't discover. Maybe there was a special spirit spacecraft for dead people, that took them across the universe, to wherever the spirits of dead people went. Maybe it got launched at Point Reyes. Maybe each continent had its launch pads. The Sages of the Ancient Wisdom knew where they were, and people made journeys to Point Reyes. Maybe I could magically stow away on this craft. When it landed, the hatch would open, and I could climb through, and my Dad would be there.

In fact, when I died, I *would* go there somewhere. I *would* see my Dad, someday. It made the idea of dying less scary...kind of comforting. Orik could go there with me too, and we'd be safe.

Later, Teak came in and threw himself across my bed. It was the first time he'd talked to me since our "hot date" at Micky's.

"You okay?" he asked.

"Yeah."

"Hey, guess what. Marian is upgrading the office computer, and she's giving me her old Mac Performa 450 and modem. It's running 100 meg! And I get an Internet account with it."

"Cool," I said. "We can search the searchable universe."

He looked at my red eyes. "Hey...you can use it when I'm not here."

That night, the dream came again. The eye-shielded man was back on the screen. The voice roared in my ears. "Set time by the variable, then steer 23...to..."

My fingers were racing again, typing. Transmission was glitching.

"Say again? You're breaking up! What's twenty-three?"

"Set time by the variable..."

A virus was eating his picture on the screen.

"DAAAAD..." I woke up in the usual sweat.

Mom was at my door.

"What is it?" she asked.

She sat on my bed, tried to hold my head.

"Just dreams about my Dad," was all I'd say.

"What's going on with you? What kind of dreams?"

"He wants me to find him."

"Is that all? Well, you *are* finding him, honey. And I'm glad you're remembering your dreams."

The last free days of September, wild desperate sex energies drove the Malibu Four. We tore Malibu up. Chasing each other along Zuma Beach. Wild basketball, wild volleyball, wild leaps into the water, desperate downhills on Ana's board. Life had wound us tight, and we were coming unsprung. Now and then Teak got a gay sex mag on the Strip. He tried to show it to me, but I said to get those fag mags out of here. When he wasn't in his room, I went in to use his computer and snuck looks at the magazines. Elena was less interested in humpy sex — she got free copies of *Lesbian News*.

Teak had tons of new questions. Who to ask was a problem. All of a sudden, we had several potential "gay dads." But Harlan and Chino were too scary to ask. Paul and Darryl were always schmoozing with clients, or racing off to a shoot. So Uncle Vince was the one. Sometimes, he'd drive us to his favorite outdoor restaurant on Sunset

Boulevard, because his stomach couldn't handle the kind of fast-food stuff we ate. Sometimes Vince got bitter about the drug companies and politicians who lied about AIDS so sick people would buy expensive drugs that might not help them. Mostly he got us laughing about things that scared us or made us nervous. Teak asked all the Gay 101 questions. I was the straight boy who got to audit this terrific course, without even raising my hand.

Sometimes Vince pulled back from us, into his private world with Harlan. One evening, Teak and I went bursting into the house and found Harlan sitting on the sofa with Vince in his arms. They had a blanket thrown over them, and were laying there quiet and close. Harlan looked halfway human, all of a sudden — caring and protective, stroking Vince's hair. For the first time, I felt a flicker of something for the old man.

"Hey guys, there's something called a door, that you knock on first," Harlan said.

"Sorry," we said, tails between our legs.

From what we knew, Elena and Ana took their gay sex questions to my Mom.

Chino gave us more self-defense lessons. Now he was talking to all four of us, and he was worried. "You two planning on coming out at school?" he asked Teak and Elena.

"We're going to be cool," said Elena. "See how things go."

"I am sooo femmie," said Teak, "everybody will know my scene in a minute."

"You going to stick up for your friends?" Chino asked Ana.

"Of course," she said.

"You already know some students who are going to be problems."

"Yeah...Ace and Mia and a couple of other dudes," I said.

"If the four of you work together," Chino said, "you can hold some ground. The trouble with most gay kids at school, they get outnumbered."

The moms were worried too, and thought self-defense was a great idea. Even my own liberal anti-war Mom was coming around.

So Chino drilled us on tactics, everything from evading attack at the lockers, to evading a knife attack on the bus. We kept practicing, with a plastic handgun and a rubber knife. How we'd do it singly.

How we'd do it together. I was only 13...but I could remember the good old days when I was a little kid and nobody shot at you on the playground. Chino had been beaten up in school, so he knew all the bad situations. Teak was a wiz on the dance floor, and a retard when it came to martial arts. But he was scared of being hurt again, so he worked hard. His butt was actually getting smaller.

We tried hard to remember everything Chino said. As he talked, Ana frowned. Elena stared. Teak peeled some purple polish off his nails. I took notes.

"As a Vietnam vet, I hate telling you that you shouldn't shoot unless you're shot at. But you have to live with other kids' parents, and laws, and courts. Try not to maim anybody if you can. There will only be a few problem kids. All you have to do is intimidate the few into leaving you alone. The moment you let your guard down, is when they'll get you. That includes the morning you're tired from partying, or scared about a test. Or bored.

"Never brag about your skills, or show your weapons. It's to your advantage to be underestimated.

"You can't fight everybody who messes with you. Try and talk them out of it. Humor helps. If you can't talk them out of it, finish the fight fast. This is your best chance of not getting hurt. Nobody wins a long war.

"If the school calls the cops, and they arrest you, don't talk to them till you talk to us. Don't let them scare you into talking. Don't argue no matter how unfair they're being. You have the right to remain silent. Let us handle the legal stuff."

"Is it ever okay to run?" Teak whispered.

"It's always okay...if that's the best move," Chino said.

Still no word from Orik. One day I exploded at Chino: "Why isn't he writing?"

"Probably his therapist thinks it's a bad idea."

"He promised me he'd run away."

"If he wants to — if he can — he will."

"Look...why can't we get him out of there?"

"So you want to do the big movie rescue?"

"Yeah I do."

"That'll take a covert op. Then we'd have to hide him, so his parents can't find him. If we're caught, it's kidnapping. Plus charges of contributing to the delinquency of a minor because we're gay. Even if we get away with it, he couldn't have a normal life. He'd have to disappear till he was 18."

"Can you just...find out if he's okay? Please, Chino?"

So Chino did some more detective stuff. If this was the movies, we four would be helping — the little band of teenage geniuses helping the adult hero save the world. Teak and Elena and Ana knew now that there was someone in a hospital that I was kinda worried about. No big deal, just a friend from my old school. But Chino never let us see what kind of PI stuff he did. Probably it was illegal.

"No need for you to know," he said.

"Betcha Chino is hacking into the hospital computer," Teak told me.

"Hacking?"

"You break into their computer, look in Shawn's records."

"How do you do that?"

"Easy...through the phone system, the Net. All you have to do is figure out passwords, and stuff." Teak took me to his computer and showed me. Pretty soon he had Guajira files and money figures on the screen.

"What's this?" I asked.

"Bank of America. My parents' personal account."

"Jesus! Get out of there before we get caught!"

"Wanna break into NASA?"

"Christ, no." If Dorie found out, she would keep the 60-second variable to herself.

September 7, my birthday.

Everybody tried to make it terrific, but it was the unhappiest birthday of my life. Looking in the mirror, I saw a different guy, who was an inch taller now, but still short. The short eyelashes hadn't helped. But all of a sudden there were lots of dark hairs on my chin and upper lip. I had to shave every other day now.

Chino, Mom and Marian loaded me, Teak, Elena, Ziggy and Ana into two vehicles, and drove us to Universal City for video arcades. Later, the Rosewood clique and Billy's dad joined us for a movie, dinner and a magic show that Harlan arranged. When the waiters brought the cake and sang "Happy Birthday," I felt my heart ripping in two, wishing that Orik was there. His birthday was in two days, and he was locked up in some psycho ward for kids. My throat was so choked, I could hardly blow out the candles.

John Sive gave me a little bankbook of money that he'd put away for my college. It was amazing...all these strangers worrying about me all my life, and I didn't even know who they were.

"Gee, thanks," I said.

"You going to call him Grandpa one of these days?" Mom prodded.

"Thanks...uh...Grandpa," I said.

"Legally," said my grandfather with a grin, "you are now considered old enough to understand whether you've committed a crime or not. That's what the law says."

I allowed Uncle Vince to give me a birthday hug. "Wish my Dad was here."

"He's around, babe. He's watching over you. Your dad too, Ana. I can feel it."

"Guess I'm the only one who can't feel it," I said bitterly.

While Marian was paying the bill for the party, Chino, Vince, Harlan and Grandpa took me aside, into the video arcade. With all the flashing lights and sound effects exploding around us, Chino said, "Well, my birthday present is news."

Right away I knew. "Shawn ran away," I said.

"Helluva kid, to get out of *that* place," Grandpa growled.

I was wishing Harlan wasn't there. "When?"

"About the time we went to JPL," Chino said. "Funny how we were talking about it...like you sensed something."

"How did he do it?"

"His mother has her own problems with Jerry," Chino said. "She isn't as hard as he is. She visited Sunny Valley on her own and took Shawn on an overnight pass. They were staying at a motel. Shawn took all her cash, about $60, and bugged out during the night."

Joy exploded inside me. Orik had promised to come back. He was keeping his oath.

"His parents are going crazy. Police...flyers," Grandpa said. "His dad has been overheard saying that when they catch him, it's jail this time...teach him a lesson."

My hair stood on end. Out of Chino's jacket pocket came a missing-children flyer. I'd seen them all my life — other people's kids on milk cartons on the kitchen table. Now it was personal. I grabbed it. Shawn Heaster's 8th grade picture — his hair looking like it was lifting in the photographer's studio lights, and that grin I always liked. He probably didn't grin much now.

"Don't get your hopes up," Chino said. "Most kids who run away go home. It's too scary out there."

"He won't go home," I burst out. "He'll call me."

"Maybe. Maybe you can help your buddy out...before his parents get him, and put him away."

"How can they put him in jail? He didn't do anything wrong."

"It's a crime for a juvenile to run away from home. Didn't you know that?" Grandpa asked.

I stood there with my mouth open. In my own life, the question had never come up. Would my Mom put me in jail?

"But...but that's not fair. He's running away because they hurt him."

"Not fair, but legal," Vince said.

"Drinking, running away, truancy, violating curfew, disobeying parents, endangering yourself — these are status offenses for kids, not for adults." Grandpa was rubbing the silver stubble on his chin.

I looked from one serious adult face to the other. No galactic empire of the future, no future mind control and slaves working in xyzium mines, looked more spooky than the Barbarian laws of America that I was starting to see.

"How'd you find out about this?" I asked Chino.

"Never mind."

"Do you think we...can find him?"

"Sit tight and let him find you," Grandpa said. "That's the best option."

"Why?"

"Because it's not illegal to harbor a runaway," Grandpa said. "Not yet, anyway. With all the runaways in the country, some states are starting to talk about harboring as a felony. If he gets here, maybe we can do something for him. I have some ideas."

"This may seem heartless to you, but we have to be careful," Harlan said. "The legal trouble we'd be in if a parent like Jerry Heaster catches us tracking down his kid."

"Shawn is better off than most runaways...he has a little money, and he knows your address and phone number," Grandpa added. "Hopefully he will be all right."

Chino opened a road map of California, and pointed.

"Sunny Valley is not far from Ukiah...here in northern California. If he's smart enough to get a bus ticket to L.A. you'll probably hear from him in a few days. Greyhound is only $40." His finger followed the 5, straight down the state to L.A. The video lights were flashing on the map.

"Is it dangerous?" I asked.

"If he hitchhikes, and rides with the wrong people...yes."

"Could...like...something really bad happen to him?"

"Look," Vince said. "Thousands of kids run away every year...most of them survive it. I ran away when I was 17. Went from Anaheim to L.A. and had my first sex fling. John did. Chino did. The only one who didn't was Harlan...he was such a good boy."

They all laughed grimly.

"Hell, your dad ran away on me," Grandpa told me.

"He did?" I blinked.

"He was 16 and I was giving him a bad time about drugs. I died a thousand deaths. He came home after a month. He'd been staying with some friends in L.A."

"And there was the time," Harlan said, "he and Vince and Jacques hitchhiked from Oregon to Prescott. In the dead of winter yet. Of course, there were three of them, and they were 22..."

Feeling a little better, I looked from one man to the other. It was nice to know they cared.

"Everybody is being briefed," said Chino. "If Shawn calls collect, somebody will accept the call, and get the information on exactly where he is, the location of the phone, everything. He might call only once, and we can't blow that call. Then we go get him and we'll have to be very covert from that point on."

Grandpa was dropping a quarter in the nearest machine. "How the hell do these things work?" he asked.

"I'll show you, Grandpa," I said.

Next day, September 8, was pre-registration for school. Back to dealing with the dangers and pressures of other kids, and their parents' attitude. I raced to register, then home, sure that Orik would call. His dad had called, actually. He raved and screamed at my Mom, saying that he had found out all about her — that she was an evil homo and he was having her watched by a private investigator.

"If my son shows up at your door, and you don't turn him over to me immediately," Jerry told her, "I will have you arrested for contributing to the delinquency of a minor."

Mom had taped the phone call.

That night, I sat on the rock by the apple tree, with my binoculars. It was an autumn sky now, with Lyra west of the meridian by 9 P.M. My old submarine binocs weren't powerful enough to see that pulsating variable, RR Lyrae. I was just having a last smoke and resolving Lyra's double-double into its four stars when a marine layer started moving in. Suddenly it was cold, and damp.

A shape came out of the house. It was Chino, zipping his jacket.

"You okay?" he asked.

"Shawn didn't call."

"You'll hear from him. I know it." Chino leaned against one branch of the tree, right beside me. His shoulder was near my knee. I offered him the binocs, and he looked for a while.

"I'm not thrilled about school, somehow," I said.

"Some of my Navy chiefs were what you'd call boring. But they taught me things that saved my life."

"So?"

"Think of high school as practice. Do the military ever practice?"

"Yeah."

"Astronauts?"

"All the time." I had watched a zillion PBS and *Discovery* specials about the space program.

"Practice your skills. Practice being an officer. Take care of your people. Always help them learn. And listen to them…learn from them too. I learned more from Nyen and my PRUs than they ever learned from me. Okay?"

His words spread a vision in front of me, like that shining mist of the Milky Way across the zenith above us. It was a delicate, shaky vision. "Can I make a recommendation?" he added.

"Sure."

"You're on the ground floor of a major political thing, here. If they find the cops innocent in the Rodney King trial, I hate to think what will happen. If Marian gets elected, you can be as involved as school gives you time for. If you think laws are unfair, you can try to change them. Don't just complain, or be the victim. And I guarantee politics isn't boring."

Mist had turned the stars to bleary points. He was staring out over the ocean, and kept talking:

"After Vietnam I went through years of struggling with drugs, drinking, malaria, my own personal crap to get a degree in political science. Harlan helped me. Dark years...spooky years. I'm finally going to use all those skills...combat...everything, as Marian's tactical planner."

"Cool." Why had he told me this?

"I'm going to be away more. You have to hold up your end."

Heart pounding, I slid out of the tree and stood looking up at him. The old tension buzzed between us. Was it possible that he still wanted to be closer with me?

"What if Shawn calls, and you're in D.C.?" I said.

He stayed as remote as the Summer Triangle. "You page me, okay? Stay tight with Harlan and your grandpa. But you will have to take point on some things."

My whole body seemed to blur through the air at him, at his warmth and his strong arms, his scars and his strength.

"I'll do what you say, Chino," I said.

"Don't do it for me. Things happen to other people. They change, they go away...they die. In the long run, all you have is yourself."

He saw me shivering. "Off to bed now. Big day tomorrow."

We were walking in.

"By the way," he said, "I caught the Heasters' PI on Rosewood. He was sitting in his van doing a video of people going in and out of Harlan's house."

My heart almost stopped.

"What did you do?" I asked.

Chino laughed. "There's only one of him, and many of me. The Heasters can't afford more than one PI. I'm arranging a little diversion... a Shawn sighting in San Francisco."

— 17 —

HALLWAY COMBAT

Fall 1991

Math was the first class of the day. Teak sat slumped, staring at his notebook. Ana and I were slumped behind him. Elena was slumped in the corner seat, black beret pulled down to her eyes.

One week into the term, we freshmen already knew that math class was a problem. Mr. Foley was so ultimately boring that we sat there starving for basketball, dance grinds, moshing and stage-diving, cutting the curls off waves, sex with girls...and boys. I was even starved for enjoying math...a subject that I needed for space travel. Foley was a flatliner.

We four slid our eyes around the room. Jim, a metalhead friend of Ace's, was in the back row by the door. He'd be out the door ahead of us...could ambush us somewhere. He was writing a note, decorated with skulls. I sat there trying to remember Chino's rules of war, as applied to high school:

The moment you let your guard down, is the moment when they'll get you...

Our low profile was not working. Teak had left makeup and

snapping at home, but he was...obvious. Since our night at Micky's, he was starving himself (Ana gave him tips on how to do it.). He'd lost weight, especially in his butt. He was the only student with two earrings in each ear. "By New Year's, I'm going to be unbearably gorgeous," he told me. As he got skinnier, it seemed like he got more gay.

This school was nothing like Costa Mesa...or even the big schools in L.A. I'd heard about, where shootings and stabbings were pretty routine now. A few students carried knives, but nobody had seen a gun yet...out in the open, anyway. There weren't any gangbangers that we knew of. Most of the 400 students were from liberal families, but Malibu had its Pinhead hard core. Besides Teak and Elena, there were 20 other blacks and Mexicans and two Asians. We'd heard talk about "niggers and beaners and slant-eyes invading *our* beaches." Teak and Elena were "beaner trash", and so was I, because I was hanging with them and had a coffee skin color. The cowardly part of me wanted to tell everybody I'm part Lebanese, as if Lebanese was somehow more "white."

The school supposedly had its rules about hate speech and student safety. But the four metalheads...Ace and Mia, and Jim and his girlfriend Sheri...were on our case. In the hall, Jim had already let a glob of spit fall on Teak's voguey patent leather loafers. Every morning I got off the bus holding Ana's hand, but it didn't help...I was pegged as Teak's associate and therefore potentially queer. Ana was loyal, so she instantly lost her crown as queen of Malibu. Ziggy was a coward, and faded into the crowd, so Ana stopped speaking to him. If Teak decided to wear his NOBODY KNOWS I'M A LESBIAN shirt, life was going to be hell.

My dad had faced the same crap in school. Had he been as scared as me?

While Foley had his back turned at the board, Ace passed the note to Teak. Ana and I could see the skulls and the big black letters over Teak's shoulder:

DIE FAG

Teak tried to keep his face in casual mode, but I knew he was totally terrified. War had been declared.

The bell electrified us out of our coma. Everybody ran for the door.

The four of us left the room last, so nobody could attack from the rear. We'd put our books back in our packs, to keep our hands free for trouble. As we hurried down the hall toward English, Teak grabbed a drink from the fountain without telling me ahead of time. Ace was lurking there, standing behind somebody. He'd noticed that Teak always stopped to drink there. Now he jammed Teak's face in the fountain, bruising his lip.

We were being jostled by shoulders and backpacks. I spun at Ace. He telegraphed a left punch, but I faded and slammed his shin with a low-line kick before he got within punching reach. "Ow," he screamed. Jim was right on top of me, and I was trying to twist sideways and slam him with an elbow, when Teak recovered. Now all our weeks of drill with Chino kicked in. Teak caught Jim behind the knee with another dirty kick, making him fall backwards. Just then, Mia came flouncing along in her black leather jacket, being the little headbanger slut. She screamed, "Fag hag!" at Ana and went to shove her. Our dear Ana used Mia's momentum to do a Chinese train wreck, slamming her against the lockers. Ace went to slam Ana, and I kicked Ace behind the knee and he went down. Crazy William rides again! Just as Jim was trying to get up, little Elena tripped him. Books and papers were flying everywhere.

Teak made a victory fist at the ceiling. "Ooooh, yes!"

Covering each other's backs really worked.

The whole thing took about six seconds — just a ripple in the crowded hall. In another minute, we were all catching our breath in English class. The halls were back to coma quiet.

Later that day, Jim tried to bait me. "So your buddy Teak eats cock," he asked. "What do you eat?"

Try humor, Chino had said. But I couldn't think of a stand-up comedy one-liner. Panic blurred everything. Finally I said, "You...for breakfast."

They all were honking with Pinhead laughter.

The hallways buzzed with news bulletins of Teak kicking Ace. Fags aren't supposed to fight back. They are supposed to submit — be squealing little victims who pee their pants.

Elena was the next target. It didn't take long for the little "beaner" in her black beret to be pegged as a lezbo. We lived in non-stop anxiety. Every day was a new war — getting on the bus at the corner of PCH and Caballo Drive, riding to school, then riding the bus back to Caballo. Ace rode the bus too, and kept up the big talk about fags and their habits. We couldn't always go to the bathroom in pairs. One day Teak forgot about the buddy system and went to the bathroom alone, and three guys grabbed him and held him, while one guy peed on him. A few girls were nasty to Elena in the girls' room.

My first test grades came in B's and C's.

But everybody at home was supportive, and Chino answered pages to advise us on smart moves. Teak came to my bed non-sexually and cried on my shoulder, and talked about how bad it was for the girl who committed suicide in his old school. For the moment, our moms decided they wouldn't talk to the principal. We'd get bigger respect if we held our own without adult help.

Being publicly labeled as a fag made me so mad that the day came when I started finding the right one-liners.

"Hey, so you're a fag too, right?" Ace asked me casually. "Like your faggy friend? Come on...you can tell me."

"Why?" I asked. "You wanna go out with me?" I grabbed my crotch at him.

Ace flushed and hesitated. A few kids laughed at him.

The metalheads didn't go crying to the principal either. They couldn't admit that the little fag and dyke, and their two questionable friends, were winning most of the tactical victories. The teachers knew what was going on, but they didn't try to stop the harassment.

"Boys will be boys," said Coach Rodale.

We were now the "gay clique."

Ana's parents were upset about her involvement. Eileen was prepared to be gay-friendly, but she drew the line at having a homosexual kid. She didn't want Ana to go through what Jacques had gone through. Maybe she was wondering if Ana was a baby dyke monster crawling out of the egg, like in *Alien?*

"God," Ana screamed at them. "It doesn't mean I'm gay. It just means I'm sticking up for my friends. You wanna have a daughter who doesn't stick up for her friends?"

Teak and I decided to go out for track. Ana told him he could lose more weight this way. I thought I could honor my dad this way.

With my build, and maybe my dad's athletic genes, I could be a colossal sprinter. But Coach Rodale sent us to work out with the girls. We were disgusted and humiliated. We told Harlan and he suggested that we pretend like it wasn't punishment...like we loved it. Maybe we could manipulate Rodale to make things tougher on us and send us back to the boys' team. But it didn't work.

"We don't want you feeling us in the showers," Ace sneered.

"I wouldn't feel you with a ten-foot pole," I told Ace. "You've got bad breath."

"You've got a lezbo mom."

"At least my Mom's around. Yours is always drying out somewhere."

Ace jumped at me to tear me up. I faded, and he hit the lockers.

"Go ahead...make my day," I said.

By Thanksgiving weekend, Teak said to me: "Ace feels like he's getting ready to do something nasty."

"Why hasn't Shawn gotten here?" I asked Chino.

"Maybe he got arrested."

"That's bad, huh? The cops have to call his parents."

"If he gives them his real name, yes."

Chino was already jiggling his police sources to find out if a male minor named Shawn Heaster was presently being held in Sylmar, or wherever, by California Youth Authority.

"Looks like your buddy is still at large," Chino told me.

Surviving at school, and worrying about Orik, took so much energy that I didn't think about Chino much. He was traveling with Marian as her campaign advisor. While she made her speeches, he was the silent suit in the dark glasses, looking around for trouble. He had lost weight too, still wrestling with his own dragons. Now and then I felt jealous of the time he and Marian spent together.

One time Chino came home with his hair cut high and tight. I almost cried over his murdered ponytail. Where was my alien warlord? Now he looked like some FBI guy on TV.

"Taylor was on my case about image," he said.

Marian laughed. "I can even remember when you talked like a sailor," she told Chino.

Marian opened her campaign headquarters on Webb Avenue, near city hall. Sometimes on weekends Teak and I went there, stuffed envelopes and answered phones, like we'd promised. Teak got paid, I didn't. Marian's platform had some human-rights planks that Taylor hoped would make a moderate Republican platform look good to women, young voters, gays and lesbians, immigrants and ethnic groups. She didn't make the gay issue into a big thing right yet. But we knew she wouldn't back down later.

"My feet are in concrete on this one," she told Teak and me. She made sure we had hamburgers to eat.

The principal, Mr. Franco, was showing his colors about the gay clique. Some teachers had told him we were the ones who always started the trouble. We had saved the "die fag" notes, and showed him. But he didn't do anything about the harassment.

In the cafeteria, there were tables for the different cliques — jocks, surfers, headbangers, metalheads, geeks, nerds, dopers, boozers, and housers. Teak and I might have hung out with the science nerds if we'd been welcome. If the jocks had known that my dad won an Olympic gold medal, or the science nerds knew that astrophysicist Floradora Houghton of NASA gave me her card, it wouldn't have made any difference. Only a few kids ate with us — most of them had weird ideas about how AIDS is spread. Ziggy finally joined us, embarrassed at what a coward he'd been. We were called the Unstable Table.

Teak and Elena wanted to wear their queer T-shirts. Elena had one in Spanish, that said VIVA LA JOTERIA. But Chino advised against it, because parents had found out about the gay clique. The school fell over themselves to assure parents that we were unofficial. Two parents didn't want their children sitting next to us. Several wanted us expelled, because we were supposedly there to recruit other students to the gay thing. Lucky for us, Mr. Franco and the school board didn't like being pressured by either liberal or conservative parents. It was *their* school. So we got to stay.

Over Thanksgiving, we all went into town and ate turkey with Harlan and Vince and Paul and Darryl and Rose and Vivian. Harlan was in his glory, carving the turkey. It was kind of touching to see the old guy play head of the family.

I tried spending a little more time with Harlan. He never pushed into my world. But if I hinted that I wanted to see him, he always made time for me — even if it meant he had to drag me around L.A. with him on business. He kept updated on what was going on at school, and told me stories of my dad. Billy didn't dare come out at his high school. What Teak and Elena were doing was unheard of in the '70s, he said. So Billy had waited till college.

"Michael will be home in a few months," he said. "I've been telling him about you."

After Thanksgiving break, the first day of school started out quiet. In the afternoon, hundreds of us were crossing the lawn to the curb where the buses stood. I turned to say something to Ana. All of a sudden, some girls screamed, and I looked around. Ace was standing there, facing Teak, his eyes cold. Teak's eyes had that old terror in them.

Ace had pulled a great big handgun out of his backpack, and he was pointing it at Teak's brown face. It looked like a .357 Magnum. Chino had one in his gun closet.

Ace said, "Hey fag, suck *this!*"

For a second I froze, at the sight of that monstrous weapon.

Then adrenaline blasted through me. My buddy's head was about to be blown off. The months of practice were right there inside me. Ace had his back to me, so I moved in from behind, to grab his arm up. If he pulled the trigger, the gun would fire in the air.

"Behind you!" Jim yelled to warn Ace.

Startled, Ace whirled around.

That gun muzzle was swinging around at me. It yawned at me like a wormhole into hell. Students were running for cover. Ditzy girls were screaming everywhere.

"Gun! He's got a guuun!"

"Go tell Mr. Franco!"

"Get down, everybody!" Ana yelled. "Down!" She and Elena and a few other girls who were not ditzy had already hit the dirt.

By the time Ace turned, I was past the gun muzzle, with the disarming move. *Remember, his trigger finger has to react to your move. You can move quicker than his finger, because you already know what you're going to do.* I swung to the right, and slammed my left forearm against his pistol wrist, so the gun jerked past me and up. I grabbed the barrel with my right. Ace went to wrestle me, but I was ahead of his move, like Chino had taught me — pushing him off balance, twisting the gun up and back. He fought to hold on, but my twist was trapping his finger in the trigger guard.

Suddenly Ace screamed with pain — his finger was breaking.

He let go. The gun was in my hand now. Jesus, it was heavy.

Crazy with pain, Ace lunged at me. But Teak had pulled himself together. With the wrath of ancient warriors in his face, my fat dance-clubbing buddy snapped a hook kick into Ace's leg from behind, using his hip just like Chino had taught him. Ace's leg buckled, and he dropped flat on his back on the grass. The assistant principal, the school security guy and two bus drivers were running toward us...I guess they would have been smarter to hit the dirt too.

I was standing over Ace. My vocal cords almost shredded as I yelled:

"Now you're gonna eat *my* dick, you pathetic piece of shit!"

Half the school stood there frozen, hearing me scream the "d" word and the "s" word. The teachers stood frozen. I had the gun, probably with six great big armor-piercing rounds in it, and they didn't know what I was going to do next. I had seen the bullets in Chino's hand — huge things. Probably Mr. Franco was peeing his pants. I could feel their fear.

My hand was trembling. The gun was so heavy, it dragged me down.

Teak was back-to-back with me.

"Yeah, I'm a fag," he screamed at everybody. "G-A-Y. You wanna do something about it? C'mon, let's go, gurrrls!"

My hand was shaking so much I could hardly hold the gun now. Jesus, something could have gone wrong. Teak could have been killed...I could have been killed. Both of us shot dead. I had to unload the gun, before things got screwed up any further. So I fumbled around and finally popped the cylinder out, like I'd seen Chino do, to eject those six awful bullets.

Surprise. The cylinder was empty.

Ace was crawling to his feet, humiliated and shaken.

"Hey, look at this." I showed everybody. "No bullets. He's a fake."

"Nya nya nya-nya nya...." Teak got right in Ace's face. "Hope you're better prepared for shooting in bed, *honey.*"

Teak Perez now did his first on-camera snap at Malibu Hills High. It was a good one.

I handed the gun to the assistant principal. One security guy took hold of Ace. Another one grabbed me.

In a few minutes, the cops were there. To our surprise, the principal had them arrest me and Teak too. They actually handcuffed us — scary stuff. Later, at the Malibu station, we did like Chino said...stayed cool, said *nada*, demanded to make the phone call. Our moms were at the station in a flash. Mine almost had a heart attack that I could have been killed by a gun. We were released to our parents' custody.

M̲r. Franco was not happy. A gun had finally come to his school.

The story was splashed all over the Malibu *Times.* To the police and teachers and school board, he was snide about the "two little faggots and their fag-hag friends." He tried to blame the whole thing on us. But even the cops couldn't buy his story. The gun belonged to Ace's dad, Ace had brought it to school, he'd threatened us with it, we'd acted in self-defense, we'd disarmed him, and we'd turned in the piece right away. Dozens of witnesses said so. End of story. But instead of saying I was a hero, Mr. Franco complained to the cops that Teak and I had disturbed the peace at school, and I had said two bad words in public.

Chino didn't say much, but what he said was enough, as he debriefed with us. "Well done, all four of you," he said.

We glowed.

"You knew it was going to happen," I told Chino. "The first thing you ever did was drill me on that move."

Mom was recovering from her heart attack, and she actually thanked Chino.

"One of the boys could be dead," she said.

Ace, Teak and I had to go to juvenile court. Teak and I got off — first offense, and the judge agreed that we had acted in self-defense. But I had to do 25 hours of community service for using offensive language at school. Ace got off totally — the gun wasn't loaded, it was his first offense, and he hadn't used a nasty word. And probably the judge thought he was cool for baiting queers. But Ace didn't come back to school — he was embarrassed that two fags had beaten him. His parents transferred him to Santa Monica High. Mia switched schools to be with her boyfriend. Jim and Sheri stayed.

The worst thing that happened was, the first week in December, Ana's mom and Glenn pulled her out of school. The gun thing made Eileen LaFont forget that I fed her daughter pancakes and didn't get her pregnant. So Ana was being enrolled in Payton, which was some private girls' school in New York.

"Her education is being disrupted by you," Eileen told me. "I won't have it."

This time there was no drama, no me or Ana running down the street in tears. "They'll be sorry," she said. "And I'll be back, okay?" She gave me a huge kiss, and Glenn drove her to LAX and put her on the plane. I was in shock. Things chilled between the LaFonts and the rest of us.

"Maybe Shawn lost my phone number. Maybe he's afraid."

"Maybe," Chino said.

"If he got to L.A., where would he go?" I asked.

"Maybe a shelter. Shelters are required by law to notify the parents when a runaway comes in. But sometimes they don't."

Research was no big deal. All I had to do was look in the yellow pages. There were 26 shelters in L.A. I decided to be a bad boy for once and run my own investigation. We weren't supposed to be seen hunting for Shawn, but I had to. When Chino was away, I did it on weekdays, because most shelter staff weren't around on weekends. I didn't want Chino to know.

After school got out at 2, I'd ride the bus into town, along streets sparkling with fakey tinsel trees and crowded with people coming out of stores. The family didn't mind — I told them I was researching optics for my new telescope. I got blisters on the bottoms of my feet walking around. The shelters that didn't take minors, or were run by churches, got crossed off the list. So did the shelter at the Gay and Lesbian Community Center, which didn't take minors. Pretty soon the list was down to 13. Instead of calling them up, which got them nervous and weird, plus they might tell Orik's parents I was asking around, I just hung out in the shelter block, hoping I'd see him. Sometimes I dared to show kids the 8th grade pic in my wallet.

Homeless kids jostled me. It tore me up to look at them. Mostly the shelters had kids who hadn't been away from home long, who still had hope. I hung with a few, and heard them talk about getting jobs and GEDs. The ones who had been around, you could tell by their hard eyes and the way they smelled. Especially their bad teeth. They talked about sex — even the really young ones hooked, or had girlfriends or boyfriends who hooked. Every shelter had a street corner nearby where the drug dealer waited to sell them pot, crystal or rock.

Nobody had seen Orik.

By early evening I'd be at Harlan's, and mention some optics store where I'd been. At 5 in the morning, I'd be dozing on an early bus back to Malibu, dreaming of the day when I could have a car.

Two days before Christmas, there was my thing with a guy named Ethan.

That Saturday afternoon I was hanging at the Crosscreek Mall, burned out on worrying about Orik. I was playing games at the video arcade, and had racked up the highest score known to man, when this UCLA surfer type asked to play doubles with me. We talked. He was old, maybe 20. Six foot two, with the same blond slippery hair as Orik's, and a neat grin. Ethan was sure of himself, warm and sunny. The compulsion came over me, that I wanted to get close with him. I lied, and told him I was 18. He said his family had a beach house near Paradise Cove, and invited me to go surf. It seemed okay. He was a local guy from a local family, right?

So we drove up to Paradise Cove in his Acura. That familiar electric buzz was around us, that I knew from Orik.

In the house, we started changing for the beach, and he loaned me a Speedo. But once we got naked, he snapped my butt with a towel, and we exploded into rough play. I smacked his butt with my hand. We fell on the bed, and he bit my cheek. His body was great to feel and hug — it glowed with health and fitness. He started touching me, and I almost went crazy. He said how lonely he was for a solid guy friend, somebody he could really trust. How glad he was to meet me, how mature and masculine I was. He was tired of guys who were flakes. Yada yada, yada. Maybe Orik was hooked up with another best friend, and Ethan was going to be my buddy now.

But then he wanted the wild thing.

"That's gay," I said.

"So?"

He pressured me. I backed away. There was a loyalty thing here, that I couldn't explain. Nobody but Orik had ever touched me there. Ethan got pissed. I got pissed, and jumped off the bed. All of a sudden, his face went cold and hard, and he grabbed me from behind. It wasn't play now. Oh God and Goddess...it was like the movies, where all of a sudden you know you're in the clutches of the monster. My training kicked in. I spun and whammed him with an elbow. Before he could recover, I kicked his knee. Chino was right — being short gave you the perfect shot at a guy's knee.

While Ethan lay groaning on the rug, I spit on him.

"You lousy little bastard," he wept. "I'm calling the cops."

"Go ahead. I'm fourteen. You're gonna get arrested for statutory rape."

I grabbed my clothes and backpack, and ran out of the house naked. In front I hid in the bushes, and dragged on my clothes. Then I walked up to the PCH and a bus stop. I was shivering violently and praying that he wouldn't call the cops. The bus came and I rode it back to the Caballo exit, and walked home.

For days, my face burned with embarrassment every time I remembered what happened. Vince's fight to live, Chino's self-control — even Harlan's dignity! — looked pretty extraordinary. I felt cheesy next to them. Lucky I didn't get hacked in six pieces and scattered up some canyon for a hiker to find. The thought crossed my mind that he was the guy who did Ana. Same M.O.

My B's slid to C's. I'd sit in class and that picture would crowd into my mind. Something had almost happened to me that I thought happened only to girls. I almost lost everything precious, not only Orik's friendship but my Mission and my feeling that I was born to be special. I had questions...and I wasn't even sure what they were. But if my Dad was gay, and my Mom was lesbian, did that mean that instead of being born special, I was born out of control? Did my genes make me get in the car with Ethan?

To my candle, I prayed, "Chino and Mom, thanks...thanks... thanks for teaching me to take care of myself."

210

But I didn't dare thank them personally. This was one of those kid secrets destined to get buried forever in the backyard of the Universe.

I spent the next couple of weeks worrying if I caught some disease from Ethan. At school, kids tried to keep a low profile on STDs. Only one of our classmates had ever seen anybody die of AIDS. Ana had told me she knew one girl who got HIV from her boyfriend, but she wouldn't say who it was. Some students had a vague idea about other diseases. A few had herpes sores on their faces. My more wary peers kept track of who slept with who — if they could — and quietly avoided the herpes clique. If you got crabs, you dragged yourself to the drug store and tried to doctor yourself before your parents found out. Things were pretty slack.

Because it was in the news that gays use condoms for AIDS protection, most of the students believed that only queers use them. We all knew girls who got beaten by their Pinhead boyfriend because they asked him to glove it. If gay activists stood on our sidewalk and handed us condoms as we went to class, most of the things would be slam-dunked in the first trash can.

Christmas was boring and sad. Marian had a fancy sparkly tree, and everybody came to Malibu and tried hard to do the family thing. Mom even helped Paul and Darryl bake cookies. Harlan gave me $100 toward my new telescope, and asked why it wasn't getting done...my construction mess was abandoned on his patio, under a piece of plastic. On Christmas Eve I went outdoors with my old binocs, and realized I hadn't looked at the dark sky for weeks.

Orik was somewhere, crying because he was alone at Christmas.

In January, the rains came. The dark sky was blacked out with storms. Some days the PCH was blocked by mudslides. When I could get into town, I still trudged around to the shelters. They were full up — coughing kids trying to get out of the wet.

Los Angeles Youth Alliance was a shelter six blocks from Valhalla. Street kids told me that their social worker, Sylvette, was cool. She didn't snitch to parents. I went to LAYA three times before I found out anything.

Sylvette was a big black lady. Her office was a corner of "the system" — courts, custody, jail, hospitals, adoption centers, foster parents — anywhere that kids got controlled by government instead of parents. By now I knew that some social workers didn't care about kids, or they had seen so much misery that they'd gone numb. But Sylvette had escaped the curse. She always dressed nice, with lots of 14-carat jewelry, and gave off waves of perfume and power. She never smiled, and gave orders with quiet menace like Chino. But with me, she relaxed as she sorted folders containing lives of lost kids, her bracelets jingling on her big arms. Sylvette had raised five kids of her own. She looked at Orik's 8th-grade picture. Then she leaned back in her creaky chair.

"Honey, you impress me. I have *never* seen a kid look for his friend the way you do. I shouldn't tell you this. But the boy in that picture came through here a month ago," she said.

I was going hot and cold.

"I remember him because *he* said he was looking for a friend...probably you. He begged me not to notify his parents. I could see he was afraid of them. Finally they contacted us. When he found out they were coming to get him, he cleared out. They came anyway, and I listened to their story." She pulled out a file and looked in it. "I'm not putting them down, understand. There's parents out there with genuine broken hearts, looking for their children. This father...he has a broken heart, but he's *mean*. I am a church-going woman, and I believe in the blood of the Lamb. But my religion doesn't make me mean. Understand what I'm saying? So if I was your friend, I wouldn't want my dad to find me no *way*."

She fixed me with her sharp black eyes. Her amazing eyelashes curled up like she did them with curling irons.

"So you haven't seen him lately?" I asked.

"That was a month ago. He was with us five days."

"Did he still have my phone number and stuff?"

"Somebody steals your backpack, you lose your addresses. When you're on the street, it's hard to replace information if you lose it. Making one phone call is a big thing. Remember that."

I sat there feeling wild happiness. A month ago, Shawn had been alive, and okay, and looking for me.

"So let's say you find him," she demanded. "What's your plan?"

"Um, well, get him to a doctor, make sure he's all right. He's probably hungry and needs his clothes washed. Get him where he's safe. Back in school. Maybe he needs legal help. My grandpa is a lawyer, and he said he'll help."

"Sounds like a plan. But his parents have the law on their side."

"The law is wrong," I said.

She drummed her long red nails on her desk. "Last kid of mine that a parent put in jail to teach him a lesson was gang-raped the first night," she said. "That was in Juvie. Honey, a stray cat be safer in the pound on gas-chamber day than a kid in our jails. And if you tell anybody I said this, I'll deny it."

She looked at me, chin in her hand, bracelets silent.

"Will you call me if he shows up?" I asked her.

Recklessly I gave her my home phone. If Orik showed up, and I found him, and Mom found out I had lied, I'd be happy to take whatever punishment was coming.

One Friday afternoon in February, I rode down to the Malibu mall with Mom. I was going to take the bus into WeHo to check another shelter. In the car, Mom said, "Make sure you get to school Monday morning."

"Can you *try* not to supervise every detail of my life?" I burst out. "I'm a big boy, remember?"

"You're failing your classes, big boy."

"The teachers are boring. Classes are boring."

"Then let's transfer you to a magnet school in town. You can stay with Harlan. If he'll put up with such a sourpuss...."

She had the car radio on, and the news was talking about the Rodney King trial. I tried to change the subject. "Chino says there's going to be trouble if the cops get off," I said.

"The question is...do you get off the hook with me?"

At the mall, Mom walked off without a word. She had a million errands to do. I watched her go — always bustling off into some mysterious future with that small-person energy.

With an hour to kill before the bus, I hung out.

This mall made the one in Costa Mesa look cheesy. It had Malibu rich people walking around in their voguey clothes, walking their voguey dogs and eating Haagen-Daz cones. I was momentarily rich, as Mom had just laid $10 on me for the weekend, so I blew two bucks on a cone. I sat there on an expensive tile bench, legs sprawled, watching the BMWs pulling in.

I noticed two homeless guys shuffling along the storefronts. They were reflected in the windows, tangled into all the expensive clothes and shoes and chachkas. They were tired and hungry — an old guy in an army jacket, and a kid in tattered jeans, with a black bandana tied around his head gangster style. Their backs were stooped under big backpacks. More homeless people were drifting into Malibu, making secret camps up the canyons. The citizens of the Kingdom of 'Bu were paranoid that homeless campfires would start the next world-famous brushfire in their realm. Chino had drifted through every homeless camp he knew, showing Orik's picture. Nobody had seen him.

At the supermarket, the two guys stared through the windows at the expensive food. They panhandled a while, but nobody gave them a cent. A kid and his daddy, I thought. Chino told me there are pairs of gay and lesbian homeless. Some have AIDS — they went bankrupt from medical bills. I tried to imagine Vince dying in a homeless camp by the L.A. River, without a family to love him and take care of him. Chino told me that straight homeless men pair up too — if they don't have a woman, they pair up with a kid, and the kid gives sex for protection. I wondered if Orik had done that, and shuddered.

The two were about 50 feet from me, with their backs turned, when the kid turned his head a little and I got a hint of slanted eyes. A flash of recognition roared through me. I stood up and stared at him. Suddenly my heart was pounding so hard that the blood roared in my ears like traffic on the freeway at rush hour.

The kid must have felt something. He turned around, in that alert way that street people have, and stared at me.

It wasn't Orik.

The kid just stood there in his worn-out athletic shoes. He had probably shoplifted them, or dived into somebody's trash bin for them. "Hey, whatcha looking at, dude?" he yelled at me. "How about a dollar?"

But I was walking away, toward the bus stop. Embarrassed at eating spendy ice cream when Orik might be hungry, I dropped it in the next trash can.

In town I had another heart attack when I was lurking outside Children of the Night, wondering if Orik might be staying there. It was the last shelter on my list. I'd learned that homeless kids sometimes went through every shelter in town, and used up all their chances for a month's free living.

Suddenly Chino's 4 Runner pulled up by the curb. He was home early from a political trip and he had vibed what I was doing.

"Get in," he said in that cold voice.

I did, shaking all over.

"Leave the investigating to me," he said.

"I don't actually go in. The staff doesn't even know me!" I protested.

"Stop doing this. The Heasters might try to say you're stalking Shawn."

Desperate to get the mirror started, I finally jumped into the polishing that next weekend. It went along pretty well for 20 hours, till I got in too much of a hurry. All of a sudden the mirror had this colossal scratch on it. Maybe it was from lint off my clothes. Maybe I'd just been careless.

Feeling like a complete retard, I cried for a while. Then I left the mirror and the diamond-dust mess there on the table, and just closed the plastic curtain around it, and gave up.

— 18 —

TIGHT GENES

In spring semester, Teak, Elena and I started burning out on harassment in school. In deep space, there is always this background radiation everywhere. At school, there was this background of attitude every day — things said, laughter, notes stuck in my locker, shoves and pushes. I didn't have Ana's hand to hold now, and I didn't feel like holding some other chick's hand just for show. Our grades were down to D's.

After Valentine's Day, Teak and Elena said they were over it. They wanted to move into town with Elena's mom's sister Magda.

On the street, they'd heard about a dropout program called EAGLES in the L.A. school district. EAGLES was for gay kids. Nancy and Elena's mom checked it out, and it looked okay, so they enrolled Teak and Elena. They were afraid that Teak and Elena would run away if they didn't let them move into town. I knew I was expected to go on being the buddy, so I went to see them a few times. Magda had problems of her own, with a night job and a boyfriend she was trying to keep. So she wasn't keeping tabs. Teak and Elena were ditching school and clubbing — places like the Arena, the Temple, the Beverly Room, Afterhours — and coming home early in the morning while Magda was still at work. Teak's butt was getting smaller with time, wearing away like comets do. He hadn't even taken his computer into town with him.

"You can use it till I come back," he said. "I need to do my own programming for a while. Like, reboot. Ya know?"

"They're tweaking all day," I told Ana on the phone. "They won't tell me what they're doing, but it's gotta be crystal. I've tried talking to them, but...I can't be Teak's buddy if he doesn't want me to."

"It's really lonely and boring here," she said. "I miss you."

"I miss you too. Harlan tries to get through to me, but... I'm just not into him."

Michael and his wife Astarte came home in March. They made Harlan's house pulsate with talk and laughter and baggage, and boxes of research stuff. Michael looked so much like his dad that it put me off him totally. That first evening, Harlan and Vince and Paul and Darryl and Rose and Vivian were barbecuing chicken and fish on the patio for a big family dinner. Even Chino was so busy chopping stuff for homemade salsa that I felt lost and flopped down on the lounge chair under the banana trees. Finally Michael came over and sat on the end of the lounge.

"Dad talked about you nonstop in his letters," he said.

"Yeah?"

"He tells me you're into science big time."

"I'm failing my classes, actually." Talking with him felt awkward.

"Boring teachers?"

"Something like that."

Michael told me a story about a boring professor, that forced me to smile just a shade. I was a good boy and asked about his work.

"Simple," he said. "Life is blood."

He told me how he started out working on inherited blood diseases like hemophilia, went on to hemophiliacs who got HIV from transfusions. Finally he moved on to inherited immunity to viral disease. In Europe he learned a new research process called PRC.

Now he could use it to locate individual genes, and groups of genes, for the first time. He sounded just like Dorie and her file crammed with variables. I wondered if galaxies look as tiny to God and Goddess as genes look to us.

"...A new grant," he was saying, "so I'll be setting up a lab at UCLA."

"Disease can really be inherited?" My mind snapped back.

"I got interested in this because my dad has to be immune to HIV. There's evidently a DNA protein," Michael explained, "that makes it possible for the HIV virus to penetrate a cell. If he has a defective copy of this gene, it could make him immune to HIV. My dad has been with Vince ever since 1978, but he never seroconverted. I have to know why! I'm not the only one working on this, but... anyway I'm doing a complete DNA workup on my Dad."

Right away Michael was grabbing a paper plate from the table, drawing the tree on it, showing how one defective copy could come from each of Harlan's parents.

Suddenly I couldn't help myself...this was kind of interesting.

"Cool. Maybe you have the gene too?" I asked.

"I don't know what that would mean, in terms of HIV resistance. And I'm not about to expose myself to find out."

Beyond the smoke from the grill, Harlan was turning chicken legs with a pair of tongs. Vince had his arm around Harlan's waist, and Chino had one hand on Harlan's shoulder. The three of them were laughing with Paul and Astarte about some dumb thing. I envied Michael's ability to talk about which genes he got from his dad.

Michael shrugged. "To be sure about that, I'd have to check out my Mom's DNA. Anyway, she would have only a 50 percent chance of passing the immunity gene to me — if there is one." He laughed. "And Mother and I aren't speaking, so I won't be getting any blood samples from her real soon!"

"Why did you fight with her?"

"Because I wanted to be friends with my dad. She hates his guts."

My thoughts stretched painfully to my own Mom.

"...And HIV isn't necessarily what destroys people's immune systems, anyway."

"Huh?" I said, Jerry's statements still ringing in my ears.

"I said, the evidence is piling up that there's more to AIDS than we thought."

"You mean, what happened to Vince."

"Yeah, Vince is the interesting case here. His immune system is actually recovering. And I'm not sure we can attribute everything to heredity. I have to look at his herbal treatment...his incredible attitude. If Vince can recover, there's hope for everybody, not just people who might be genetically endowed. An immunity factor could help us develop an inexpensive vaccine or treatment. But we have to find out exactly what we're dealing with."

"Chow time, everybody," Harlan called. The old guy was actually smiling — he was so glad to have Michael back.

Michael got up, then looked down at me.

"Astronomy and genetics," he said. "Interesting combination, huh? The universe outside, and the universe inside."

I didn't like being reminded of the scratched mirror.

Moping about Ana, I watched the TV news one night. They did a special on the Jeffrey Dahmer murders. My skin was crawling as I watched the police opening the refrigerator where he kept the pieces of the dead boys.

Not even Harlan or Chino said what was on our minds — that Orik wasn't alive any more. Maybe he was hooking and they made him pose for nasty pictures. Maybe he was chained in a closet somewhere, being starved and treated bad by some crazy person. Maybe he got into drugs and died of an OD. Or he went home with the wrong person, and his body got cut in pieces and put in different dumpsters. Or he jumped off a freeway bridge like Elena's friend did. My mind went crazy imagining all the stuff I'd heard.

Chino told me that the L.A. morgue was full of unclaimed remains of kids. Their deaths never even made the news. I wondered why he told me all this scary stuff. I lay awake at night thinking about it.

Maybe Michael slipped so easily into my life, alongside Vince, because I was so worried about Orik that I didn't notice. He was not the secretive type, and told me things about himself. He and Astarte never had kids because there were enough kids on Earth, and they wanted to be into their work. She was a smart businesswoman, and did the grant-writing and handled all the business part of the work. He had a brother, Kevin, who had made Harlan a grandfather five times now. But Kevin hated his dad for being queer, and wouldn't let him see the grandkids.

"I'll bet," Michael said, "that my dad's homosexual DNA is drifting around in Kevin's kids. Kevin will get the shock of his life..."

This statement made me feel panicky.

"You think there's a gay gene?" I asked.

"Ooooh, a lot of people are working on that one," said Astarte. "Like the big rush to find the Alzheimer's gene."

A couple of days later, Michael and Harlan took me over to UCLA. By now everybody was accepting that I was dropping out of school. But they were happy that I was interested in something, anything. The new lab was a big room full of boxes and crates, equipment halfway unpacked. I asked to see what real chromosomes looked like. So Michael showed me slides with monkey chromosomes and cat chromosomes. I stared at the familiar pairs of bulgy little rods.

"I wish I could see Billy's," I said. "And my own...I wanna know which genes came from my Dad, and which ones from my Mom."

The adults did this long weird silence. It felt so weird that my hair stood on end. Finally Harlan cleared his throat and told me an amazing secret thing.

"Three of your dad's semen specimens are still in deep freeze," he said.

I stared at him open-mouthed. I felt like some retard Earthling in a movie, seeing the mysterious spacecraft open and the visitor from outer space walk out, like in *The Day the Earth Stood Still.*

"There were five to start with," he said. "We used two to get you."

Chills chased over me. The idea of something left from my Dad that was physical and alive was so exciting that I felt high, like I'd swallowed a hundred Ecstasies. It was like seeing light from a galaxy that had traveled gigabillions of miles, when the star had actually died by the time its photons hit your eyes.

"Are they...uh...still good?" I asked in a hoarse voice.

"Sure," said Michael. "For a hundred years yet."

"Why did you keep them? Were you guys going to do me a baby brother, or something?"

"I just never had the heart to...dispose of them," Harlan said.

Michael explained more. He said: "Dad was worried about Billy's family trying to claim the specimens later. Billy's mother was...a problem for a while. She made all kinds of threats. So she was never told about the sperm samples. Billy's were stored under Harlan's name, by Harlan and Betsy's physician. They just carried a coded marker, to distinguish them from Harlan's. After Dad moved to California, he transferred them to a cryobank here."

"Can I...uh...see them?" I asked.

Harlan hesitated. I could see that this was really personal and scary for him.

"I'll think about it," he said.

One evening, in my bedroom, the candle had burned out in front of my Dad's and Orik's pictures. I felt so depressed, I wasn't going to light a new one. Suddenly my Dad's voice talked in my mind, the way it sounded on the sound track of the Valhalla film. He said, "Even if you think Orik is dead, don't give up. He'd like being remembered."

"He's not dead!" I whispered.

I tore the house apart till I found a new candle, and lit it.

The next time I dropped in at LAYA, Sylvette explained why missing kids are hard to trace.

"Adults leave all kinds of legal footprints...paper trails. When adults use fake IDs and fake SSNs and stolen credit cards, they can't avoid using the banking system. They cash checks. They sign papers. They rent cars. You dig? Even the drug business has to use banks to launder money. Sooner or later, they screw up on their paper trail. But kids...runaways...they can make it for a while without bank accounts or credit cards. They can hide in the cash economy. Fake ID is easy to get. Even when they get arrested in some other state, juvenile records are sealed, so the skip tracers can't find them."

"I've done every shelter in town. Where else can I look for him?"

"Homeless camps...squats. Dangerous places for you. Your folks know you're doing this?" She frowned at me over her glasses.

Another caseworker put her head in the door, and said, "Dija hear what happened in court today?"

They were talking about the Rodney King trial, which was going to end soon.

"Hey, Sylvette, what's going to happen when they let the cops off?" I asked.

"Trouble," she said, stacking her files.

At night, Chino had been walking the Strip in desguise, showing Orik's pic to street people and asking if anybody had seen him. He talked to drag queens and sex workers. "This one drag queen," he said, "her eyes changed when she saw the picture." She wouldn't tell him anything, though. He was following her, when a police car pulled up, and the cops got out and started to hassle her. She argued with them, and they took her in. Chino hung back, and stayed out of it.

"Needle in a haystack," he said.

Orik's parents had plastered California with posters saying "Shawn, we love you...come home." On the Internet, when I checked into a new Website for runaways, I actually found a posting of theirs. Like Orik was going to cruise the Net while he was starving and homeless! Even making a phone call was a major deal.

The second week in April, I got to go with Michael, Chino and Harlan to this cryostorage company in Culver City. As we parked, Michael told me they stored all kinds of stuff here — spunk from champion bulls, DNA of Egyptian mummies, bodies of people who thought they could be resuscitated a thousand years from now. I got a chill — I was going to be in the same building with corpses that might go into deep space.

At the reception desk, all the ladies knew Michael, because he stored his own tissue and blood samples there. It was real space-agey, with the shiny cryotanks, and huge generators in case the power blacked out. There was this *hissss!* as an assistant popped a tank lid open. Icy smoke came rolling out, the same liquid nitrogen that slides down the rocket booster carrying the *Columbia*. The carousel full of glass tubes turned and stopped at the right one. As Michael put on gloves and pulled up the tube, I could see my Dad's faded handwriting on it. Michael knew I wanted to touch it, so he put it in my hands. Some people go crazy about getting to hold a glass that Madonna drank out of. I went crazy holding that tube with my Dad's sperm in it. My hands were shaking.

"Whoa, don't drop it," Michael laughed.

Harlan looked strange, as the smoke rolled around him. His face was a mask — he was trying not to show his feelings, but I could see how carefully he put that tube in his briefcase.

"What about the other two?" I asked.

"We'll leave them here...for now."

In Michael's lab at UCLA, we thawed the tube, and Michael dabbed some on a slide.

"Damn, look at this," he said.

Harlan took a quick look, then I almost knocked him over to get my eye to the microscope. If I had seen my 60-second variable star swimming there, I couldn't have felt more awed. I'd never seen live sperm before, just photos in textbooks for sex ed class. There were thousands of them, wiggling their little tails.

Harlan was shaking his head. His face was really sad — maybe he was remembering a lot of things.

"Would you like to see half your dad's DNA?" Michael asked me.

He put the slide onto his electron microscope, and zeroed in on the sperm's head.

I stared at the fuzzy little spiral, feeling a letdown. "I'm kind of confused about what DNA is."

"That's what molecular geneticists are figuring out...what it is. Each chromosome is a body carrying certain genes, or groups of genes, that are arranged at different loci, or locations. Like...you've helped Paul edit at the studio, right? You know how every frame in the footage is numbered, so he can hit a command on the EPIX and go right to the frames he wants to edit? Well, DNA locations are in a natural chain like that. We are just beginning to find out what's on the footage — there are billions of loci in the human genome, and we only know maybe 15,000 of them."

"What are genes made of?"

"Proteins."

"But what are proteins made of?" I asked.

"Sequences of amino acids. And these are found in orderly arrangements too. And the amino acids are made of...it's like looking inside molecules to find the atoms, and looking inside atoms to find the particles."

"Why do I only get half?"

"Because it takes two, male and female, to make a baby. Humans have 46 chromosomes...23 pairs. So each parent gives you only one set of 23, or you'd be a mutation of some kind. Even the sex chromosomes...the X and the Y, right?...they carry other traits, sex-linked traits, like male baldness. The body of each parent shuffles the 46 chromosomes, like a deck of cards...then one set of 23 gets copied off into the egg or sperm, and contributed to the new offspring. Each locus is where there is specific information about something...say, X for female or Y for male, or your eye color, or immunity..."

...Or everything I hate about myself, like curly eyelashes, I thought.

"...Just imagine this copying process going on for 200 million sperm a month in your body! There are special cells in your testicles, with a full set of 46 chromosomes, that are budding off to form tiny bodies that each have a head with 23 chromosomes in it."

Michael went to the Xerox machine, and copied a page of Science Magazine. "When your mom had herself fertilized with Billy's sperm," he said, "one of those 200 million sperm joined with one of the 300 or 400 eggs that she will release in her life. And voila...we have the beginnings of you."

Mr. Miller had never explained it so good.

Michael frowned at the Xerox copy. It had streaks across it.

"Your toner needs changing," said Harlan.

"Yeah, sometimes the human copies aren't perfect either. Two hundred million sperm a month, times billions of people a year, times the millions of years that people have been around. It's amazing how few mistakes there are. But now and then we get a booboo. An extra sex chromosome gets added, an XYY or an XXY or an XXX, so you're infertile, or you're a hermaphrodite. Or one animo acid gets left out of the chain...or it gets duplicated twice...or it gets shuffled to another address...or it's just defective. Sometimes the booboo has a lethal effect...the baby dies. If the booboo is beneficial, it may get passed down to descendants."

"So the gene that protects against HIV may be one of those."

"It's not that simple. Vince gives me blood to study. I need to find out exactly what happened with him, too. He shared needles with a guy who died of Kaposi's sarcoma. Why didn't he develop fullblown KS? KS has killed thousands of gay men...but it's been around a long time, and it used to kill mainly elderly Italian and

Jewish men. It may be caused by a different virus. I've found traces of Epstein Barr virus and HHV6 in his blood. And the brain degeneration that some guys get — is it maybe related to Alzheimer's? There are a lot of questions yet. We can't develop a vaccine till we really know what's going on here...it would be a gift to humanity."

"Cheap food and cheap medicine," said Astarte, putting books on a shelf. "Two of the big needs. The drugs are too expensive."

I was looking at the universe of wiggling little shapes again. Some of them had stopped wiggling.

"So this is really valuable, to have his DNA, huh?"

"I can't do his cell culture, because I don't have the full complement of DNA. So having these samples is...sentimentally wonderful, but scientifically only so-so. If only we had a blood sample...."

It turned out that Michael was doing a genetic study of the whole family. He had immortalized everybody's blood samples and cell cultures — as many relatives as he could persuade to cooperate. He had plunged them into the smoking breath of the Cryo God, inside that tank. It was expensive, he said — ten thousand bucks to freeze blood samples of 50 people, and more money needed for liquid nitrogen and running the tanks.

Michael was grinning at me. "Hey, kid...you wanna join our Valhalla here? Have your cell culture live forever?"

I grinned back.

"Sure," I said, holding out my hand.

He pricked my finger, got a big blob of blood, and inoculated it with lab virus that made the cells keep growing. I was half nuts with excitement. Chino was watching and said, "I've suffered like hell from malaria, because I didn't happen to inherit the immune factor for malaria."

"But genes aren't everything," said Michael. "Genes give us the visible person. But there are other things too. Environment influences everything alive. Mosquitos grow bigger in the arctic than they do at the equator. Different diet makes Asians grow taller when they move to the U.S. Chemicals affect us...babies are born smaller if their mothers smoke. And there's all the invisible things that we are...emotions, feelings, our minds, our spirits. They affect us too."

"Mr. Scientist here," Harlan teased, socking him on the shoulder, "pondering the imponderable."

"It's a dirty job, but somebody has to do it." Michael socked him back.

Michael loved socking around with his dad. I wouldn't ever be able to do that with my Dad. I felt sad, and put my eye back to the microscope, staring at those sperm on their 2-inch voyage to nowhere. It was exciting to see them, but not exactly as fun as the living Dad that I wanted to bring back from the stars.

"So what about blood type?" I asked. "That's inherited too, right?"

"You know your type?"

"It's O."

"You sure?"

"My Mom told me when the silver fulminate exploded and I bled all over and had to go for stitches. Yeah, I'm sure."

"The ABO blood group is an important marker on parentage," said Michael. "There are three main genes for clotting factors...A, B and O. A and B are co-dominant, so you can inherit one from each parent and be AB blood type. The only recessive of the three is O. To be type O, you have to get a copy of O from each parent. So...there's a test on this tomorrow! If you're Type O, what are your parents' blood types?"

"My Mom is type A," I said.

"Don't cheat now. Do the family tree, like your teacher showed you. And do the math."

I scribbled the equations. "Mom has to have O, because she gave it to me," I said. "So she's an AO."

"Correct. And your dad?"

"Billy could be...AO or BO...or OO like me."

"Right."

Harlan seemed to be thinking about something else. "Billy was type AB, I think," he said from the other side of the room.

Michael shook his head. "Dad, your memory is going. Okay, William...what about Billy's parents?"

I covered the sheet with a tree of parents and kids.

"You're doing great," Michael said. "That's how a single recessive can get passed quietly along in the genotype for many generations. *Thousands* of generations. There are genes that have been carried in the human genome for tens of thousands of years, especially the mitochondrial DNA handed down through each mother. We can count the frequencies of different genes in the populations, and get a fix on where things started."

It was like astronomy...the farther you look out into space, the farther you look back in time.

Harlan yawned. He was tired.

"Billy's old medical records are in the box," he said.

What box?

Amazing how much stuff was still left from my Dad's life. Today was the day I'd felt closest to him. Looking over at Chino, I remembered what he'd said about looking for my Dad with people who knew him. Chino felt my look, and ruffled my hair. Even though it was a parent kind of touch, a nice chill rolled through me like icy smoke.

The next week, things really started to fall apart for me. The prom was coming up. I invited a couple of girls, but they said no. They were afraid I had AIDS. I was doing the lone warrior thing now, and it was hard. I had to watch my back all the time. If school was this bad, my Dad must have lived through some fierce harassment going to the Olympics. I couldn't even imagine it. I kind of understood why gay kids kill themselves.

As for sex, forget it — except the kind you can do alone.

"I might as well be queer," I told Mom. "I get treated like I am."

Mom had finally complained to the principal, but he didn't do much. Marian complained. Even with Councilwoman Prescott charging into his office, Mr. Franco insisted that I had brought it on myself by associating with gay kids. Mom had me talk to the school counselor about my depression, but it didn't help, and I didn't trust the counselor anyway.

"If you want to transfer next year," Mom said, "you can move into town and stay at Harlan's on weekdays. You can go to Fairfax, which is a very liberal school."

I was not exactly thrilled by the idea of living at Harlan's all the time. He'd been really uptight and remote for a week anyway.

That Friday, after a really nasty day in the hallways, I came home with spit in my hair and told Mom that I wasn't going back.

Grandpa called to say he was sorry, but he understood.

"We'll sue the school. Worst comes to worst, we'll get you a tutor," he said. "You need to be on a fast track anyway."

"I don't want any lawsuit or tutor," I told him. "I want friends."

Wednesday, April 29, 1992. The jury was getting ready to hand down its decision on the cops who beat Rodney King.

That morning, Mom and I went to L.A. to check out schools. Then we dropped by Harlan's to say hi. Harlan looked upset about something. He took Mom in his office and closed the door. After a few minutes, I heard her yelling. She was going off on him. I knew that she and Harlan didn't get along in the past, but this new thing was serious. Through the closed door, I could hear her shouting about how all men are bumbling Pinheads. When she came out, Harlan was still sitting at his desk. His shoulders hung limp, and he looked grey.

Mom was storming out the door.

"Get your stuff, William," she said. "We're going home."

"Let him stay," said Harlan. "I need to tell him myself."

"Well, I hope he tears your head off," she shouted from the driveway. "William, call me when you're ready, and I'll pick you up."

She got into the dusty old Rambler and slammed the door. The tires screamed, and she was gone.

I looked at Harlan, who had the weirdest expression on his face. At first he looked down. He couldn't look at me. But finally he did. Those ancient green eyes of his — eyes that had seen dinosaurs — stared straight into mine.

"What's going on?" I asked Harlan.

Harlan had a big envelope with the address of Michael's lab on it. "Come on in and sit down," he said.

I did, with that feeling of icy smoke.

"Michael did some more work on your DNA," he said. "There's something you need to know."

— 19 —

L.A. GOES NOVA

Something in Harlan's voice made me turn to ice crystals. I felt like a numb unfeeling meteor racing through space. He put the two charts side by side and pointed. These were output on DNA tests — I knew what they looked like now, with banding and everything. Something like the spectometry analyses that they do on stars. I looked at the banding on the Billy Sive chromosomes...at the banding on mine.

Harlan's hand was holding the charts. The hand was freckly with old age spots, and it was shaking like it had a tiny earthquake in it.

"Remember our talk about blood types a couple weeks ago?" Harlan asked me.

"Yeah."

"Well, I got out Billy's medical records. They were put away in a box of old stuff, that I keep in a safe-deposit box at the bank. And I was right. Billy was type AB."

"So?"

"It means that...well, what it means is that Billy isn't your biological father. He didn't carry the allele for the O blood type."

228

I stared at him. On the evening news, when the apartment building fire happens, or the drive-by shooting of a gangbanger, or the earthquake, the TV reporter is shoving his mike in some dude's face, and the dude is shaking his head and saying, "I can't believe it happened." The mike of destiny was now in my face, and I was sure it hadn't happened.

Harlan pulled more lab sheets out of the envelope.

"For you to be type O, you have to get the O factor from both your parents, because it's a recessive. Your mom has it, but your dad has to have it too."

I pushed the charts away.

"Dad's records must be wrong," I said. Then I added, "Doctors make mistakes."

Harlan shook his head. "That was my first thought. Michael did the whole number...ran the DNA scans over and over. You remember how this works, right? A sperm has only half the father's chromosomes, but it's what he contributes to the baby, right? Michael went to the locus...you know, the number on the DNA footage?...and he found the blood type gene, and did the banding. Every single scan came up AB. We're 95 percent sure. All you need in a paternity case is 90 percent."

Harlan ran his finger across the two charts, showing me. The blood type bands looked really different.

This was annoying. Was it my Mom's Barbarian genes getting in the way, keeping my Dad's genes from expressing themselves?

"Michael told me that different sperm can carry different things," I said. "Maybe some other sperm carried the O thing."

Harlan shook his head no. "Not possible. Your dad was AB. An AB person is heterozygous for types A and B. This means that a sperm will carry the A factor, or the B factor. There isn't any O factor in there anywhere. The only way you could get that second O copy is from a different man."

"Well, who?" I jumped up.

Harlan was pulling himself together. "Don't yell at me," he said in Chino's kind of voice, when Chino was being the officer.

"Who was it?" I demanded. Suddenly the horrible old feeling of wanting to smash the whole world was there again.

He looked straight into my eyes. "The only O carrier in the picture is...me."

My eyes blurred. Every nerve in my being was fighting this information.

Finally I said, "You think *you* are my biological Dad?"

"Looks like it."

"How can you be my Dad?" Something burst inside of me. "My Mom doesn't even *like* you enough for that!"

Harlan's hand had stopped shaking.

"I'm trying to remember how the snafu could have happened. It was fifteen years ago! Hard to remember details. There were two sets of specimens, Billy's and mine. They got taken at the same time. Somebody must have mixed them up. Maybe Doc Jacobs did it... or his nurse. Or the cryobank mixed them up. Maybe I mixed them up. I went to get them when Betsy decided she was ready to start the procedure. I went into the tank and pulled the vial out myself." He threw up his hands in disgust. "Hell, maybe Billy mixed them up! It was just before the Olympic trials...we were pretty stressed about a lot of things."

"Maybe," I yelled, "they mixed it up with some other dude's."

"Maybe. But I don't think so. Michael did a DNA scan on me, and compared it to yours. You and I are a 95-percent match."

He put his own chart down in front of me, and lined it up with mine. The bandings did match.

All of a sudden, I was seeing myself from outside — another kid who was going violent, throwing those lab reports in the fire, wrecking the house, running out in the street and throwing himself off a freeway bridge. I didn't want to be that person, but somehow I couldn't pull any feelings or will power from anywhere. Instead I just stood there, turning to deadly chaotic space crystals.

"It's not fair," I said in a weird squeaky voice. "My Dad wanted a kid of his own."

"But you *are* his kid. Spiritually, emotionally, mentally. No different than it was for me. Don't you see?"

"Excuse *me*." I went in my room, and slammed the door.

Chino came in — voice through the door. The Rodney King verdict was due any minute. "They're gonna shoot and loot," he said. A crowd had gathered at the L.A. courthouse, he said. Payback time, he said. Gangbangers, blacks, Koreans, Latinos, Jews —

everybody who hated anybody. Gun stores were jammed with people, being pissed off when they found out there was a 15-day wait to buy a gun. Gay businesses along the Strip were worried about trouble, and a few bars had a shotgun behind a counter, he said, but mostly it was business as usual. Industry people were pooh-poohing the rumors, but he'd just dropped by the studio, and Paul and Darryl had put Valhalla on evacuation standby.

I had my ear to the door, spying.

"You look like hell," Chino told Harlan.

"I told William," Harlan said.

"How'd he take it?"

"Not good."

"He'll get over it."

For a while I leaned my elbows on the dresser, staring at the picture of Billy.

My ex-Dad stared back at me, with that eternal frozen grin. Other kids at school had divorced dads. All of a sudden I had been divorced from mine. Worse than divorce. That grin hid a whole universe of lies. Nothing was what it seemed. I had thought my mother was this normal neat Mom, but she turned out lezzie. Chino the war hero turned out queer. My best friend dumped on me. My girlfriend couldn't have sex. Even Auntie Marian wasn't my aunt. So what was I? Everything got sucked into this black hole, and came out different on the other side. My Mission was a joke, and I was tired of being lied to.

I blew the candle out — even though what had happened wasn't Billy's fault and now he was alone too.

Then quietly, without saying anything to anybody, I got ready to leave.

It was cool how my research had gotten me ready for this. Documents — I used white-out and xeroxing to alter my Dad's birth certificate, so his age was mine, then made a new xerox on Harlan's copy machine when he was away from his desk. I could get a fake SSN later on. Money...what I had, plus $130 from the cash drawer in the kitchen when no one was looking (they were all watching the CNN news). Then I packed — clothes that didn't call attention, my collection of documents.

Hiding the backpack under the bed, I waited for it to get dark. The dark sky was going to see me go.

News voices and CNN sounds filled the house. Mikes of destiny being held to sweaty mouths. By 4 P.M., the verdict was "not guilty". The jury had given the cops permission to beat people and be brutal. Permission to spit on me at school. Permission to shoot Billy Sive. The phone rang — my Mom calling from Malibu. She had gotten home without any problems, and wanted to know if I was all right. I wouldn't talk to her. By 5, the news said that fires were being set by rioters all over town. On La Brea, 40 blocks from us, people were looting a big camera store called Sammy's.

"Lock and load," said Chino. He pulled his gun case out of Harlan's office closet.

Harlan got out an old cowboy type pistol that he had.

I felt no chill, just numb, as Chino pulled on his shoulder harness and loaded his 9 mm. automatic. As he took his shotgun and some boxes of shells, he said he didn't think the rioting would hit West Hollywood, especially residential neighborhoods like ours. WeHo was not a gang realm. Maybe just the businesses on the Santa Monica Strip — if rioters decided to throw in some anti-fag payback.

"But," he added, "war is about surprises. So everybody stay right here. You too, William. Don't get some bright idea that you're going to see Elena and Teak, because they're right in the middle of it. Michael and Astarte are okay at UCLA. Harlan's in command. I'm going over to the studio...I'll look in on you when I can. Don't expect much from the police — they'll be overrun, and probably call in the military. The phone system will get pre-empted soon, so you won't be able to reach me. If you have to bug out, go through Beverly Hills, because they'll have private security on the streets. From there, take Beverly Glen or Sepulveda over the Hills to the 101. If the 101 is closed, just go west on Mulholland. It turns into a dirt fire-road in Topanga State Park, but the Jeep can make it through to Malibu. I'll meet you in Malibu."

He looked at me briefly. "You going to be an officer?"

"Yessir," I lied.

What was one more lie? Would Chino buy the lie? I held my breath. It seemed like he did. He had a lot on his mind, and I had been such a good boy that he trusted me.

Chino left his 4 Runner as an extra vehicle. He jumped in Paul's spare car, heading for Valhalla.

As I watched Chino drive away, I knew I would never see my

commander again. The *Memo* was a fantasy, and the fantasy was over.

Laying on my back on Paul's lawn, under the eucalyptus tree, I stared up at the sky and petted Son-of-Nefertiti, who was sitting on my chest. I remembered her snuggling between me and Ana, and felt a terrible puncture of pain that tore me open like a meteorite going at light speed. No Cat Nebula — just a cat. Through the tears, I looked up into those sunny branches, heavy with blossoms and dainty shadows. It was weird to remember that it was spring. Honeybees hummed and darted around the abandoned tents where Teak and Ana and I had slept. Life was as big as the universe, and didn't care about my little heartbreaks.

Pretty soon, Paul, Darryl, Rose and Vivian were home from the studio, and they came over. The studio was closed up, and Chino was staying there as security.

The adults all ate in front of the TV. I wasn't hungry, and choked on the burger that Vivian handed me. All TV channels had nothing but L.A. live. The whole country was watching. We were right there in the news choppers, looking down on the city. Fires were being set everywhere, black smoke churning up, choppers flying through it. The fire department was already maxed out. Rioters were storming L.A. police headquarters now. They were stopping traffic in South-Central to drag white people out of their cars. At 6:30 we actually watched the truckdriver get dragged out of his truck and beaten by some black men.

Harlan didn't say any more about blood types. Typical adult behaviour — game over, on to other stuff.

Was this a bad time to run away? It was the *perfect* time. But I was going to need food. When nobody was in the kitchen, I grabbed some granola bars and candy bars, and sneaked them into my backpack.

Vivian and Rose were arguing about politics.

"It'll be Watts all over again," Vivian said. "We'll burn down our own black asses."

"Sweet pea, it's not a black thing this time," Rose said. "It's a human thing."

Finally, Harlan went into his office and downloaded a screenplay. "Nothing I can do," he said. "Might as well not waste time."

When it got dark, I quietly went into my bedroom. My heart was thudding. That world of fire and destruction called to me — a real war, not a movie war. Los Angeles was going supernova, blowing herself up in a humonguous self-destruct mission, bright enough for the whole universe to see. A real black hole, where I could let myself be sucked into oblivion and not hurt any more. It didn't matter anyway — everything was lies. Grabbing my jacket and backpack, I undid the window screen, and crawled out into the banana trees outside. I had to move quietly, because those big leaves made a lot of rustly rattling sounds. I almost yelled as a spider web plastered itself on my face. The patio was empty and dark. Son-of-Nefertiti sat on the wall, with her eyes glowing in the dark.

Lucky that Chino wasn't there — he might have heard me.

A quick look at the sky — Leo would be crossing the meridian. But the sky was strangely bright, and no stars were visible.

I sneaked down the alley, and came out on Rosewood a couple blocks down, heading towards La Brea. I knew West L.A. pretty well by now. La Brea was dangerous — fires there. But LAYA was on La Brea too, north of Hollywood — over 50 blocks from here. Maybe I could get there, and Sylvette would do me a favor, and not call my parents.

Clifton was a little residential street north of Rosewood, not much traffic. None of the adults I knew ever drove that street so I used it to walk towards La Brea. At 9, I started worrying about cops picking me up for breaking curfew. But no cop car went by.

By the time I trudged the 40 blocks to La Brea, it was late, and I was tired. North and south on La Brea, fires everywhere! So I raced across the street, into the residential area of Hancock Park. Everybody was locked up in their houses. I crawled into somebody's hedge and spent a scary night there. The sky pulsated with the sound of choppers and police sirens. I was remembering shelter stories about homeless people being raped and set on fire. If I was going to die, it had to be quick. At one point, there were strange rustlings in the bushes, and I opened my Scout knife and got ready to fight for my life. But it was just a possum waddling by. All night, the animals were restless and on edge. Two cats had a fight next door. A rat ran up the driveway. Dogs barked everywhere. Ants bit me, and a rock dug into my back.

Suddenly I woke up with a jerk of muscles.

It was getting light, and I was sore from sleeping on the ground. My watch said 6:35. Beyond the leaves, there was no sky — just yellow-brown clouds. When I crawled out, the whole sky was dark with smoke. The sun was a spooky orange ball trying to shine through. "Hey!" somebody yelled at me from the house. I ran like crazy, around a corner, through another hedge. Then I walked north on Highland — it was safer, all houses. Nobody hassled me — I looked like somebody's kid going somewhere.

When I got to the Santa Monica strip, I eased into a crowd by a TV store, and caught more CNN news. The storeowner had turned up the volume, so we could hear the reporters talk into their mikes.

Three fire reports a minute were coming in. The police were totally outnumbered, so they were pulling back and letting things happen. Latino and black rioters were hitting Korean and Jewish businesses, just like Chino had said. Shopping centers and malls were slo-mo fireballs. Koreans were fighting from the roofs of their stores, armed with shotguns. Firemen were hit with rocks, bottles and sniper fire. Just blocks away, big coils of smoke were twisting into the sky. Chopper rotors were going *throb-throb-throb-throb*. The buses had stopped running.

Chino was right. Whatever was real, was here on Earth. Now I could really be part of it. By now everybody had probably noticed that I was gone. They were going crazy looking for me. "Goddam kid's a loose cannon," Harlan was probably saying. They'd probably called Chino at Valhalla, if they could still get through on the phone system. I hoped Chino didn't get hurt or something. If he survived Vietnam, he could survive the L.A. nova.

A tall black man looked down at me. My stomach clenched.

"Hey, vanilla boy," he said, "you be in the wrong place, wrong time."

"I'm on my way home," I said as I turned away. "Thanks."

Walking north on Highland, eating a granola bar, I stopped to hear somebody's TV through their open window. Microphone voices of destiny said that the central city was rapidly being engulfed by looting and arson. Through somebody's patio door I could see a big screen TV, and a dizzy helicopter view of endless fires. Black smoke billowing right near downtown and the Civic Center. Two thousand National Guard were coming. Police and fire departments were pouring in from other counties.

Gasoline sales were banned, and a 7 P.M. curfew was now in effect. My heart started pounding harder. Jeez, this was getting serious.

With a good telescope, somebody on Mars could probably see L.A. burning. My Mom would be going crazy.

Farther on, somebody else's TV told me that the rioting had reached East Hollywood. Big fires were now burning on Hollywood and Sunset. Fox and Warners and CAA and William Morris had closed down. Studios in Burbank were on standby to evacuate. I wondered if Valhalla would burn, and felt kind of bad. Would the looters grab Paul's EPIX? Would Chino let himself be shot to death protecting the EPIX? Hollywood, which stayed open 24 hours a day, was closed. We didn't need an action movie now — we had the real thing.

I got thirsty, and realized that all the restaurants and supermarkets and fast food places were closed. But in the middle of all the craziness, lawns were still being watered, so I drank out of somebody's sprinkler by the sidewalk. Another house owner screamed at me and I ran.

Lost among hundreds of other people who wanted to watch things happen, I watched too. I tried to use everything I'd learned from Chino about war, so people wouldn't notice me.

Along La Brea, people stood staring at the smoking pile where Sammy's Camera had been. On Curson, a car full of blacks was stopped by several white guys. They tried to turn the car over. The black guys got out and scattered the vanillas around pretty good. Just out of curiosity, I stopped at a public phone, and put in a quarter to dial the LAYA number. But the circuits were all busy, like Chino said.

My feet were really tired now. Before I went the last blocks to LAYA, I went by the fire at Frederick's of Hollywood. The looters were grabbing ladies' panties and bustiers that were thrown all over the street. From a distance, I watched cops arresting people for looting. I saw a whole parking lot full of people with handcuffs on. Some looters were breaking into a gun store on La Brea, and they were taking shotguns out of there, AK-47s, everything. And I saw somebody actually start a fire. A couple of guys pulled over by this building with a pickup, and they had some things in their arms, and put them by the building, and after they drove away, the fire just went *ha-whoosh* up the side.

Finally the LAYA building was ahead. The clock over the reception desk said 4:30. The lobby was full of scared kids who'd done like me...come in to get off the crazy streets. Sylvette was there, behind a bigger pile of files than usual. Looking harassed, she glanced up from her desk. Her phone was silent.

"We're full up, so you'll have to...oh, it's you." Her tired eyes focused on me. "Sweet Jesus, you picked a *terrible* day to look for your friend."

"Uh," I said stupidly. "I wanted to check in myself."

"Yeah, you and half the world," she said. "We filled up on the first night of the riot. Squats burning down, scared kids... Check with us tomorrow. If things let up, some of these clients might check out."

My stomach sank. "Anywhere else I could go?"

"Try Children of the Night, Covenant House... They're not far. I'd call there for you, but the phones are down. Better get somewhere before curfew 'cause they're taking people in."

Back on the street, reality kicked in. As I wandered through the smoke and chaos, trying to stay out of the way of firemen and racing armies of looters, I got real hungry, and found two bananas and a package of Oreo cookies that some looters dropped outside a supermarket. I hid behind a dumpster and gulped the food.

Then I dragged myself to Covenant House, seven blocks away. It was full. Before the phones went out, they'd heard that Children of the Night was full too. I was hungry, tired.

Suddenly it was night and I was on this deserted street all glittery with broken glass, where a little mall had pretty much burned down. I got warm near the last crackling flames. The street lights were shining, and the whole area was real bright with other fires. But nobody was around. Halfway down the mall, in front of a burned-up beauty store, a young guy was laying face down on the pavement. He was short, hair in a buzz cut like me. A dog was licking his face. Something about him seemed familiar, like I was seeing myself.

Maybe he was hurt, and I'd be the big hero and save him. So I walked over there. The dog ran away.

He wasn't me, and he was dead. The top of his head was blown off, and this red jelly was hanging out of it. The dog had been eating it. My hair bristled all over my body. Was I on the other side of some black hole that had sucked in my Dad's death? Did my Dad look like this when he'd just been killed? Suddenly my stomach seemed to wrench out through my eyeballs, and I threw up everywhere...bananas and Oreos gone sour and fiery.

But then I felt better. This was something I had to know. So I sat down beside him, and looked at him. I had seen gazillions of people die on TV and in the movies — Darryl had told me all about the special-effects firecrackers that blow holes in a stunt guy's clothes — but I never saw a real dead person before. I touched his fingers. He was stiff, but still a little warm. I thought about how maybe he'd been with his girlfriend earlier in the day. Maybe his sperm was still alive inside of her, wiggling away. Maybe he'd been one of those fighters up on the roof there with a shotgun.

Finally I wanted to see his face.

So I took his shoulder, and rolled him over. The middle part of him wasn't stiff yet, and he slumped over funny like. Of course he wasn't me, or my Dad. He was Korean, older than me. His slanty eyes were open a little, staring at me. For a minute I thought of Shuga. This was like what Chino saw. I tried to imagine I was Chino, loving this dude, and seeing him dead like that. The picture of Harlan seeing Billy dead, touching him, didn't hardly come to me — I didn't know what to do with it now. I touched the dead guy's hair, then the red jelly. It was cold and wet. A smell like fresh hamburger stuck to my fingers.

Walking back to Highland, where I felt safer, I heard somebody's TV through the window. The CNN lady was saying that scattered rioting was now happening in Pasadena, the Valley, San Francisco, Chicago. I walked along the dark street. Everybody was home — lights on, gates locked. Finally I found another safe hole, inside the hedge along the golf course on Beverly. I curled up there. The old feeling of the flowing geometry came over me, and I flowed out of my body and flew through deep space without a spacecraft. Far out there was a nebula that flickered with all the colors of the rainbow. I was a flashing star — on, off, on, off, alive, dead, alive.

I jerked awake. When I crawled out of the hedge, the sky was dark with smoke, like a volcanic explosion had happened. The leaves were sooty. Lawn sprinklers were running on the golf course, just like it was a normal day. As I washed my face, I saw that the course was deserted. Cars parked on the street were covered with ashes from the sky.

It was time to get back to LAYA.

"Nobody checked out yet," said Sylvette. "Situation still too hairy. Sorry."

Drooping, I was just walking away, when she said:

"By the way, your friend, what's his name." She hunted in the papers on his desk. "He checked in the first night. His squat burned."

"Say again?"

"Your friend Shane...Shawn. I didn't know he was here yesterday. Somebody else checked him in." She picked up a file. "He's using a different name. He came in to see me and I told him you were looking for him."

"Where is he?" I felt that icy smoke.

"He just checked out. He was too paranoid to stay. You just missed him."

"Did he say where he was going?"

"No."

Energy exploded through me. I raced out.

"By the way, he's wearing..." she yelled after me.

I ran down the hall, bumping into staff, raced through the lobby, bumped into a big black kid, nearly fell down the steps, stumbled onto the street. A few shabby kids were standing around, smoking.

"Shawn!" I yelled. They stared at me.

I ran to the corner, screaming his name. A couple of guys in the middle of a dope deal stared at me. I ran the other way, back past the LAYA entrance to the corner of La Brea and Hollywood, looking wildly in every direction. I didn't see him anywhere. I'd blown my one chance. If only I had woke up earlier!

"SHAAAAAWWWWN!"

The street was empty, except for a girl in torn sooty jeans standing by the bus bench. She was bent under a heavy backpack and wearing hoody-looking dark glasses.

I leaned against the brick wall, and cried for a minute. Then I turned around again. The girl was still looking at me. She was skinny, with scabs on her arms from old bruises. She looked like one of Teak's clubby girlfriends. Under her black beret, her short hair was dyed purple, stuck together and dirty. Her skin was coffee brown.

She wore tons of makeup, plus a nose bead and platform shoes. When she took off the dark glasses, her slanty eyes blinked between black make-up lines. She looked jittery and scared.

She stared at me. "Finder?"

I stared back. The girl turned her back on me, like she was afraid of me and wanted to cross the street. Then she looked at me again.

"It's me," she whispered in a familiar voice.

"Orik?" I said, not believing.

His face and his elf eyes were starting to appear spookily through the makeup. He was the same, but not the same, somehow. There was no feeling in me at all.

"Let's go," he said.

"How'd you get dark skin?" I interrogated him.

"Cosmetic tanner. Come on...let's get out of here," he said.

As we crossed the street, I still wasn't sure it was Orik. I kept staring at his little gold earrings, long fake eyelashes, purple lipstick and nose bead. Even purple fingernail polish and silver rings. He looked around nervously, like someone was watching from every store window.

"We can find some bushes somewhere," I said.

"Nah. Not safe. Too many bugs."

We passed the dealer, who was waiting to sell drugs to the next shelter kid. The dealer looked at us. We walked by.

"Why'd you check in?" I asked.

He scratched his crotch. "My squat burned down the first night. I lost everything but my backpack and what I had on. Sylvette gave me the last bed she had. You leave home too?"

"Long story."

At the corner, he looked around nervously. "Got any money? I'm starved. Maybe we can find something open."

"It'll be safer in West Hollywood."

"Why?"

"A guy I know, a PI, says the riot won't go there."

The buses still weren't running, so we dragged ourselves for 50 blocks, detouring around the fire areas. In WeHo, it was just like Chino had said — no rioting. The sidewalks were full of people, everybody talking about the riot. Bars and restaurants were actually open. Except for the smoky sky and soot on the cars, it felt like a party. Orik looked around nervously.

"Hello, this is the queer part of town," he said.

"And?"

"Forget it...I smell food."

We stopped at the first restaurant we found, because I didn't want to go clear to Six Gallery, where my Mom might look for me.

Inside we sat in a booth. "What'll it be, miss?" asked the waiter, looking at Orik. I bought us plates full of eggs and hash browns and toast. Orik ate fast, keeping his eyes on the windows. While I studied his hard eyes and tight face, he lit a cigarette, dragging on it like an expert, with lots of attitude.

"How come you're running away?" He offered me a smoke.

"Things got complicated." I lit up too. We didn't comment on each other's smoking — that wouldn't have been cool. Now we didn't have to worry about our parents smelling it on us.

"Your mom is a neato lady."

"My so-called father is not so neato."

"She get married again?"

The ashtray filled with butts as he listened to my thriller tale of two test tubes getting mixed up. He didn't share his own story. "That is like...*sooooo* bizarre." He sounded like Teak, and this irritated me. He lit another smoke, and scratched his crotch again. "But if this dude is your real dad, and he isn't being mean to you, why are you running away? Your mom loves you. You're crazy. I don't have a choice, but you do."

It had me off balance — my old friend so old and hard, acting like a commander, telling me what to do. Finally the restaurant made us leave so they could put other people at the table. On the street again, we stared at the orange sun, low in the smoky sky. The smoke was thinning a little. Was the War of the Worlds going to end?

"We've gotta go somewhere," he said. "I'm a vampire now — can't stay out too long. Where did you say your dad lives?"

"9022 Rosewood. That way." I pointed.

"Your mom there?"

"She probably freaked and came in town to look for me."

"Would she snitch and call my parents?"

"She *hates* your parents."

242

"Then I'm gonna stay with her."

He started toward Rosewood. I stood where I was, in shock.

"Come on, dummy," he said over his shoulder.

"I *hate* home. I'm leaving there!"

Orik turned around and waved his arms at the burning city. "Hey, Finder...find on. Maybe you'll find something out there. You can have it! It's all yours!"

He kept walking. I watched him get to the corner, feeling torn in half. When he went out of sight, I panicked and ran after him as hard as I could, almost falling down, yelling, "Wait...wait!"

"What?" He turned around again.

"It's not safe there. Your parents have a private eye who watches the house."

"Like — today too? In this mess?"

He was still walking towards Rosewood.

I thought a minute.

"There's a safe house," I said, thinking of Rose and Vivian down the street. Even if the Heasters' PI was sitting on our street video-taping Harlan's house, he probably wasn't paying any attention to the two women's house, and we could get there by the back alley.

"Are you sure it's safe?"

"Trust me."

"I don't trust anybody, bitch."

My cheeks burned. He had really changed.

"Takes one to know one," I shot back.

Our feet were tired, and I had a blister. I led us on a zigzag special-forces kind of course. In the backyard of an empty house for sale, we waited in the bushes till dark. Then we hurried down the alley to Rose and Vivian's house, and knocked on the back door. They were there, of course, and let us in. Their brown faces were tight with worry. I remembered meeting them at Matador Beach that day, and Chino asking me if I wanted to break their knees with a tire iron.

— 20 —

RETURN OF
THE VOYAGER

I told Rose and Vivian: "This is the friend of mine that, uh, ran away. I met him out there. He needs a place to crash. Is that cool?"

Rose and Vivian didn't smile or hug me, so I knew I was in serious trouble. But for the moment I was off the hook, because they were into taking care of Shawn. He had this glow of mysterious danger around him, like the commander of a manned space probe who had just returned from a voyage around the solar systems, logging near misses with comets and asteroids, almost getting sucked into Jupiter.

Orik's eyes squinted at Rose with questions. He was still nervous, and kept scratching at his sticky hair, then his crotch. Rose noticed this and dug bottles of head-lice killer and crab-killer out of the medical kit in Chino's 4 Runner.

"You aren't going to call my parents, are you?" Orik said.

"Not if you don't want us to," Vivian said.

"Please don't," Orik said as Rose threw him the medicine.

In Rose and Vivian's laundry room, Orik stripped by the washing machine. He dumped everything into it, including the backpack, while I dumped in chlorox and turned on the hot water. In the bathroom, he stood naked and rubbed the killer stuff into his head hair and body hair. He was taller than me now, skinnier but more muscle, old bruises here and there, his classifieds bigger and hairier — more impressive than mine, in fact. Even his tits looked more adult. Where the purple roots were growing out, his head hair was blindingly blond. He didn't seem to care if I looked at his body. I desperately wanted to hug him, or something. But we were back to the old he-man stuff. And he felt so alien now, and older than Harlan.

While I got him some jeans, underwear, and a T-shirt, Rose and Vivian put him in their guestroom. Orik touched the clean sheets.

"The last real bed I slept in was at Sunny Valley. At least those nazis gave us sheets."

He slid into bed, stretched, put his arms behind his head. "I...uh...lost your new address when I ran away from Sunny Valley. Couldn't remember it."

"I waited for you to show up. I looked everywhere."

"I had to keep moving. The parents kept tracking me down."

He rolled away from me, and buried his head in the clean pillow. Was he crying? I wanted to put my hand on his bare shoulder in what I hoped was a he-man kind of way. In fact, I wanted to crawl into bed with him and get him warm, even though he still might have live crabs on him. But it was not the reunion I had imagined. Then his breathing told me he'd fallen asleep.

Outside, Rose and Vivian looked at me. Suddenly I was, like, seeing them for the first time — how much they cared. I had pretty much taken them for granted They were good for money and rides. I didn't know much about them. And I had even bragged about dating Rose. How did these two black women see me?

"We had to call your mother," said Vivian.

"Yeah, I know," I said, feeling tired of it all.

Back in Harlan's house, Chino stood fixing me with his gaze, holding a coffee mug. I had prayed I would never see that look in his eyes. The coffee was vibrating from his tiredness because he hadn't slept for 48 hours. I looked around — at Harlan checking his pistol. At my Mom with her arms crossed — she and Marian had come back into town the long way. At Vince. Even Paul's cat was feeling the bad vibe...she looked up at Chino with a nervous meow.

"You disobeyed my direct order," Chino said.

"But I found Shawn."

It came out squeaky. On top of everything, I was getting the Curse of the Voice Change.

"You put our lives at risk. We were looking for you on those loco streets out there. You risked *my* life. Some guys tried to stop my vehicle and mess with me. I came as close to getting smoked as I ever did in Vietnam."

"I...I'm sorry." My face flushed with despair.

"Sorry isn't enough. Why do you want to hurt your family?"

Something felt punctured inside me. "What family?" I said.

Harlan shook his head and walked away into the kitchen.

"I don't have a family," I shouted. "It's all lies."

Chino looked at the others. "I give up." He went into the den.

"I'll go tomorrow," I yelled. "Shawn and me'll make out okay. It takes two, remember?"

"Go," said Chino from the den. "You don't have a clue what one is, let alone two. Maybe the street will teach you."

"Harlan," he called, "take the night watch. Let me sleep till 0700. Wake me if anything serious comes down." Slowly he put his gun, ammo, knife, pager and phone on the coffee table. Then he lay down on the sofa, with his clothes and shoes on, and closed his eyes.

Suddenly I was wrenchingly sorry about something or other, but I couldn't take anything back.

Everybody else was sunk in kitchen chairs, looking depressed. Harlan and my Mom didn't say anything. The emotion of three days was too much — my shoulders were shaking with tears. Then my stomach was shaking, and my eyelashes stuck to my cheeks. I threw my backpack against the hall wall. I ran against the wall a couple of times, finally fell on the floor. Weird animal noises came out of me. Wasn't anybody going to come and make it better? Surprise, surprise...none of them raced to my rescue. The old psychological trick — ignore the kid's drama, and he'll stop manipulating you. So you try worse and worse drama.

"Go to your room and do that," my mother said heartlessly.

I dragged a blanket to the patio and dozed off in the dark on Vince's old lounge chair, listening to CNN through the window.

Suddenly my muscles jumped. I had seen the dead man's head with the red jelly hanging out of it. The night had passed like a nanosecond. That spooky red sunrise light glowed on the banana leaves over my head. Another morning of the War of the Worlds, the human supernova. Paul's cat was laying on my chest, her head towering into the sky like the Cat Nebula so long ago. Over on Robertson, a siren was screaming. From inside the house I could smell coffee, and hear the CNN newscaster's voice still going strong. Over 3000 fires had been started. But the riot was losing its blast force — National Guard rolling into town now, lots of arrests, people looking for bodies in the ashes. The dead Korean was probably in the morgue now. Would his family find him? What family?

In the kitchen, everybody was having a meeting about me. I spied at the window and listened. The banana leaves around me were covered with soot from 3000 fires.

"...It's a shadow on us. It keeps getting darker, darker." My Mom's voice was breaking. "So much death. We've lost so much. After all the years of fighting, I'm afraid I'm going to lose him."

"If he was a student of mine at Prescott, I'd tell his parents he needs therapy," said Marian. "Maybe even a private clinic for a while."

Jesus, were they going to send me to a place like Sunny Valley?

"No way," my Mom said. "He does *not* need drugs and psychiatrist bullshit. What he needs is for the shadow to get lifted. The shadow isn't his fault. He didn't know what it was for a long time, but he knew it was there, and he's been fighting it all his life. I can see that now."

"The shadow isn't our fault either," Harlan barked. "Nobody in this room invited Richard Mech to kill Billy."

"The shadow is still around, and *that's* our fault...we won't let it go," Marian snapped back.

"We have to make it go away," said my Mom.

It sounded like she was pacing back and forth in the locker room when her track team was falling apart. She started yelling at them, and she sounded just like me. I definitely got the yelling gene from my Mom. But this time she was yelling at the whole Universe. "I'm a mother, I know life has to be! I don't accept losing my kid to a goddam shadow! All these dead people hanging around us...they're not haunting us. We asked them to be here. We won't let life happen. Chino...20 years of marriage to some bones in the jungle. Marian here, handcuffed to Joe's coffin. Me with my hammerlock on Marla's ghost. And Harlan, after 15 years you *still* don't let Billy go. You've..."

A sound of Harlan's fist being slammed on the table. Dishes clattered.

"You have no right to talk to me that way!" he roared.

My Mom's fist slammed. More dishes fell.

"I *do* have a right! I'm the mother of your kid that you turkeyed into life. You've tried, I know...but you're still wearing Billy around your neck like a goddam gold medal. No wonder William can't let go of a dream about a dad he thought he had! He's only following your role model!"

There was a long, long silence, and a sad meow from Son-of-Nefertiti. I could almost hear the soot sifting through the leaves around me. Then clink, clink...someone was picking up broken dishes. Finally Harlan's voice said quietly, "I used to pray to be delivered. Maybe I still haven't prayed enough. Maybe if we pray... Chino?"

Chino answered from the bedroom. "Yo."

"That place you always went when you're down?"

"Yeah."

"Maybe we should all go there."

"I always get there and never have the guts to make the right prayers." Chino's footsteps came into the kitchen.

A deep strange thrill went through me. He was talking about Point Reyes. The Launch Pad of the Spirits.

"Would you deign to pray with me, *Miz* Heden?" Harlan's voice was a little sarcastic.

"Why not? Whatever works." My Mom sounded tired. "Maybe that's what William needs to see...all of us dealing with this together. Churches don't own prayer. Everybody should pray. No wonder my kid is saying '*What family?*'"

Footsteps — several of them left the kitchen.

Harlan sighed. "This is nothing like Watts, is it? Chino, where were you when Watts happened?"

"I was 11 in 1965. My mama took me up to the rez till Watts was over. No, this isn't Watts. Watts was frustration. This is hate now. This *is* the American Vietnam. The way those fires started so fast — there's professionals out there, man...using Spec/War

248

incendiary stuff." A coffee mug clinked. "As soon as the phones are back up, I'll call and reserve a camp site at Point Reyes."

I sneaked back to Rose and Vivian's house and looked through Orik's window. Had he run away during the night? No, there was a lump in his bed.

While the city calmed down, my Mom and Harlan took Orik to some doctor, who checked him out and did a bunch of tests. They were paranoid that Orik had a disease I could get. Orik knew what was on their minds, because he said, "I thought AIDS was something that homos get. My parents really lied to me about that one." He was still worried about his parents finding him, so he stayed inside — never even went near windows. He kept his girl drag on.

I had wanted to find my best friend. Now there was this old stranger who wore Orik's face like a Halloween mask. The face had blond fur turning to an actual beard. He was shaving almost every day now — Harlan got him some new shaving stuff. Orik was fascinated by Harlan and spent time talking with him, which pissed me off. When we were alone in his room, Orik told me about his six months on the street. We lay around on the bed and talked, but we didn't get naked and it didn't feel like old times.

I was burning to know why he hadn't contacted me.

"So you ditched your mom and got away?" I asked.

"They'd had me on some heavy drugs. I was really out of it. But I was clear enough to look for a truck stop on the other side of town...I could hitch and find you. I only remember flashes. I'd blink out, blink in. Found the truck stop. I was really hungry and frozen...listened to the truckers talk, heard one going to L.A. When he went in to eat, I sat with him...asked him to pretend I was his kid. He knew I was a runaway, but he was cool."

"Jeez, he might have been a pedophile."

"What was I going to do? Call my mummy and daddy? He bought me a big steak and fries, and I rode all the way with him."

And you sucked him, or whatever, I thought. *That was his pay for helping you out.*

"I slept or blacked out most of the way. I don't remember much. He'd stop to service the truck, and call his wife, and..."

"His *wife?*"

"...And three kids. He showed me their pictures. Then he'd service the truck, and get us food, and crash next to me in the bed in the cab."

My skin was crawling, but I was going to die rather than ask him straight out if the trucker molested him.

"...When we got to L.A., he gave me fifty dollars, and dropped me at the first light off the freeway. Said Hollywood Boulevard was where kids were kicking it."

"So what happened next?"

"Oh...I ate out of trash cans for a few days, slept in Griffith Park. Learned about going to fast food places to get what they throw out. Finally some kids told me about LAYA, so I went there. Seemed like a good deal — place to eat and sleep for a month while I found a job. Shelters throw you out after a month if you don't have a job. Three weeks later, no job. Nobody wants to hire somebody my age. And I was still having blackouts...people thought I was weird. I couldn't remember my social security number. To get a fake SSN and fake ID, you have to have money. My money was gone. I didn't have clothes for job interviews. My Orange County bus pass wasn't good in L.A. The last week, the case worker called me in..."

"Sylvette, right?"

"Yeah. Sylvette was cool. I'd told her how my dad beat me, all the religious stuff, so she knew the problem. She said my parents had been in touch. They'd called every shelter in the country, I guess. I'd been stupid and given her my real name. Sylvette kind of broke the law...she told me my parents were coming. She told me to try to get into a good squat. I freaked, and left right away. I stood on the corner of Hollywood and Fuller, and it was rush hour, and billions of people going by in their nice cars, and it was...like, I knew I was all alone."

The question was screaming inside of me. Why hadn't he called me?

"I looked for you, and looked for you," I said. "Children of the Night...Covenant House...I finally went to LAYA, but you'd left."

"By then...well, I heard about different things you can do to survive. It took a couple more days, before I got fed up with eating garbage, so..."

I froze. Now it was going to come out. He was going to say something like *...So I finally walked over to the Strip, and turned two tricks in one night...got $100 both times. The second guy fed me a good* *dinner. Once you do it...once you know that you always have one last resource, which is your body, the rest is easy.*

"Some guys hook," I said.

"Hey...don't diss the working guys. When it's four days, and all you've eaten is a pizza slice out of a dumpster, you think about the bag of groceries if you're lucky to pull a trick who has a nice car."

"So you hooked."

"No way."

"You...like...let hundreds of guys pet your kitty. You hooked in *drag*. I can't believe it. Why did you do that?"

"I *didn't* work. What's with you?"

"Don't BS me. I know what goes on."

He opened the bedroom window, leaned out and lit another cigarette. Rose and Vivian had told him they'd kill him if he smoked in their house. Orik of the Sun had become a chainsmoking fiend.

"Hey," he said, "there were things that I didn't do, just because my dad believed I was bad enough to do them. I didn't hook. I didn't do drugs. But I did other things that Dad never talked about. Like, I was a total *thief,* man. I stole."

My mouth dropped open.

"I broke the 8th Commandment a gazillion times. I met this gang who were into stealing, and jumped in. The Klepto Kings...five of us. We shared the squat. We shoplifted. We grabbed purses. Now and then we got a good purse, jewelry in it, credit cards. We got stuff out of trucks that were unloading. Then we'd fence everything...except the best clothes. We were good, man."

For some reason I'd never considered this possibility.

"So what happened to the Klepto Kings?"

"Dunno. I came home the other night and the whole block was burning. The squat was gone. I don't know if they were in there, or what. All my money and the stuff I'd gotten together burned up. And my wig! I didn't hang around because there were cops and firemen everywhere. Huh-uh, I didn't work. No way was I going to get arrested for hooking, and turned over to my dad with some old man's spunk up my ass."

I was clenching my teeth, getting really worked up.

He laughed. "Jesus, you are *upset.*"

I flushed. "You're retarded."

He looked over his shoulder at me, smoke rising past his long fakey eyelashes and his earring. He looked so pretty, I could almost want to take him to the prom.

"I have some pride, *fruta*," he said. "I didn't do certain things."

So he knew some of the secret gay words. "Don't call me *fruta*. You're the *fruta*," I yelled.

I went to smack him in the face, but he gave me a real street kick in the leg, and knocked me down.

"I can't believe I missed you, you Pinhead jock," he said, and started to cry — just like a girl.

"Hey, boys," shouted Rose. "Boyzz. What the hell's going on? Chill, okay?"

Chino was impressed at how Orik had evaded the expert detective work of the police and two P.I.s, including himself. "Want to let me in on your secrets?"

Orik laughed. "I don't think William wants to find out."

"Why not?" I shrugged.

He opened a pocket in his backpack, which wasn't the old one I remembered, and took out a few bent polaroids.

Chino, Harlan and I looked at them. They showed a slender girl in extreme model poses, on the street by a club doorway. She was a club kid, somebody that Teak might kick it with. Black net tights and platform shoes made her legs look eternally long. The black velvet skirt was ripped off at mid-thigh. A nasty silver bustier squeezed her waist and pushed up her titties. Over that she wore chain belts, with silver skulls dangling. A long silver scarf was wrapped around her neck. Her face was made up like a skull — white, with fierce black holes for eyes and black lipstick. Her black hair was twisted up in all kinds of crazy braids and knots.

"My hot wig," he said. "It burned up in the fire. That's why I'm wearing the beret."

"Pretty girl," Chino said.

"She's a mess," Harlan said.

"Glamoroussss, huh?" Orik asked me.

"Extremely glam, if you're into vampires," I said. "Does she suck blood at night?"

Orik's documentation was in another zip pocket. There was a student ID, and an L.A. bus pass with the name Martha Bane. The birthdate made him just over 18. In the girl's photo, her hair was slightly combed. There were transcripts for Belmont High School. Letters from "Mother".

"Why did you do this?" I asked.

"I *lived* this way, stupid. I passed. It was a primo way to hide."

"That's disgusting...living like a girl."

"My face was on posters...on milk cartons in the supermarket," he screamed. "What was I going to do? Let myself be made and dragged back to Sunny Valley?"

But you could have called me! I wanted to yell.

"What grand mistress of illusion taught you?" Chino asked.

"A drag queen, Heliotrope. She was sooo glam. I never appreciated drag queens till I met her. She did makeup for a lot of club kids."

"I know Heli," said Chino. "I ran into her on the Strip when I was showing your picture around. I had the feeling she knew you."

"Yeah. She's in prison now. We had a wake after her sentencing. She's dead in there."

"So when you weren't stealing, you were...socially, I mean..." Chino prodded.

"Hanging out at the Temple, Arena Cafe, Silk...the Kleptos had a club clique. We had to wear some of the neat stuff we stole. I even dated sometimes, if I felt safe...if I could get a good meal at a fab restaurant without giving it up."

I was furious that he was talking about this with the adults there, so I let him have it. "Dating *guys?*"

He grinned. "Why not? I was the hottest girl in Hollywood."

"What if a guy groped you?" Harlan wanted to know.

"Had to use my karate a few times," he admitted. "One guy, I must have neutered him. He wanted to park halfway up Laurel Canyon. I kicked him in the nuts really good, and threw him out of his BMW. But I didn't want to take his car and have the cops after me. So I walked all the way back."

"But...supposing he found out his hot date was a guy?"

"Never happened. Heli taught me how to tuck."

Chino's and Harlan's faces said they knew what tucking was. I would have to find out.

"And you never got arrested," Chino said.

"Almost. Twice. We got away, though."

Chino clapped Orik on the shoulder. "Good job, kid."

Orik's shoulders slumped. "Another little problem. I can't go outside till I get some new clothes and a wig. All I have is what I was wearing."

Everybody helped to fix him up. Chino went back to his room, came back with a box of makeup and some women's clothes. I had never thought about Chino's PI work making him use a woman's disguise if he had to. All my ideas about his masculinity were now a wreck. Chino was giving Orik some jars of stuff, fake eyelashes, an impressive brunette wig with long hair that felt real.

"I don't do investigations any more," he said. "So you might as well borrow this stuff."

"You have no idea," Harlan said dryly, "how fast our mary marauder can turn into a Mexican lady. No flamer either. He even fooled me once. He looked like some kid's mother from East Los."

The ladies got into the secret too — my Mom went in her overnight bag and found new pantyhose. Vivian gave some neat jewelry. Rose gave a pair of girl jeans and a turtleneck. While everybody sat around the bedroom and watched, Orik shyly showed us how he filled two condoms with water, and put them carefully inside the one bra he owned, which was this black lacy thing that he'd looted at Frederick's yesterday.

"Heli always said, Girl, you got to *jiggle*," he explained to us. "The turtle's good — it hides my guy neck. The hands are a problem, though. Hard to hide."

He put on the platform shoes and walked around, doing what Teak would call a sashay. The bra jiggled just like Ana's did. Any straight guy would have wanted to get his hands on it. Everybody clapped. Rose and Marian helped him with the makeup and wig and eyelashes. Pretty soon, my best friend was gone, and we were looking at the girl in the polaroids.

Orik stroked the black wig, and pulled it on. "This is soooo fine. It must have cost." His tone irritated me — he sounded like Teak.

"Real human hair," said Chino.

All of a sudden I knew where Chino's ponytail went.

Orik looked at me through his eyelashes, like a girl would.

"Martha, huh," I said. I was ready to wring his neck.

"Marta, if you prefer. My hair's combed now. Wanna go out with me?"

"Sure," I said. "I'll give you a big hug and pop your titties."

To give his disguise a real-time run, we drove into Santa Monica, where there was no rioting, to a Thai restaurant that Vince knew. I was fried with embarrassment, but I went along because I wanted to see the whole world penetrate the disguise. But nobody looked twice at the girl sitting with us. She was starved and ate two plates of noodles and beef.

When we came home, the doctor called. He'd rushed the tests through. There was secret adult talk behind doors. Harlan said, "By the way, we're leaving for Point Reyes at 0700 tomorrow. So you boys pack tonight."

When I helped Orik pack, he said: "The doctor says I need shots."

"For what? I suppose you have AIDS."

"Nah, just gono, and a couple other things."

"How did you get it?"

"Will you get off my back? Maybe some girl."

"So you were with girls."

"A couple."

"As a lesbian, huh?" I couldn't believe how mean I felt.

His shoulders slumped. He leaned out the window, and lit a cigarette. "My parents believe in that nice world of theirs. Maybe that's why I did what I did...so they'd know what liars they are."

I leaned out too, and smoked with him. "Why are you telling me all your stuff? Aren't you embarrassed?"

The pretty girl stared into my eyes, smoke drifting up. "If you have a problem about anything I did, I want to hear it now."

His eyes were hard, cold. My stomach sank. He definitely wasn't the same person as before. His hardness didn't have any of the menace that Chino's did. He was just a hurt 9th grader. But I was starting to feel hard too. Nothing, nothing was what I thought it was. The polaroids lay on the bed and I looked at them.

"Who took the photos? Your girlfriend?"

"The clubowner at Silk. She let me in free. People like me brought business."

"Who were you supposed to be?" I asked.

"Mama Death," he said. "She's really beautiful. Isn't she the one you always wanted?" He held out his arms, got into a movie kind of voice. "Come to me, my precious, and I will take away your pain, and fly you to the stars...."

Next morning Chino, Orik, my Mom, Marian, Harlan and me all got in the 4 Runner. Camping gear was tied on top. Vince stayed behind with the Valhalla staff — the danger was over, and Vince said he'd handled his ghosts. Chino drove us quietly out of L.A. through the back route. We went up Benedict Canyon, over the hills into the Valley, and took the 101 north to San Francisco. Chino was still disgusted with me, and he wouldn't let me be the navigator, so Shawn got to follow the 5 freeway up the map with his finger, north toward San Francisco. At San Luis Obispo, Chino slept and Harlan took the wheel.

Orik and I each slept in our own corners, ignoring each other. Now and then, he took out his compact and checked his makeup.

I felt a dead space inside of me — not even curious now about what the Launch Pad of the Spirits would be like.

Mom took a nap with her head on Marian's chest, and Marian had her arm around my Mom. It looked pretty intimate to me. My world was falling to pieces, everybody changing before my eyes.

We hadn't taken a long trip since Mom and I went to the Sierras with the Heasters. The adults drove at Warp 7 — we only stopped for gas, burgers and leaks. On the map, the Launch Pad of the Spirits stuck out in the Pacific. I was surprised that the ancient prayer place was a national park now. Just west of the peninsula, those spirits would be hitting into the Realms of the Dead like spacecraft going beyond light speed, and from there on the equation was Einstein's formula times destiny — some kind of understanding about who we really are. I wished I understood something... anything about me.

Grandpa and a lady friend met us in Santa Rosa. They waited for us at a Taco Bell at the exit, and we had the big legal meeting about Orik. The lady looked like an old *old* movie star, with a weird hat and a big fur thing around her throat. Her amazing dark eyes stared at me from under bangs of silver hair. I wondered what Grandpa was doing dating a lady.

Grandpa (who wasn't really my grandpa now) studied Orik's makeup and wig, drinking his coffee. His eyes went sad, and suddenly I remembered Harlan saying that he had once lived with a guy who passed as a woman. They had raised Billy together. Nobody had ever found out. I wondered what Grandpa was feeling, as his sharp old eyes studied Orik.

"Good job, kid," he said. "You even jiggle."

He looked around at the rest of us. "More pro bono, huh?"

"Sorry," Harlan said.

"I know I can't pay you, but..." Orik shivered.

"Don't worry, I have more money than God," Grandpa grumbled.

Grandpa ordered tacos all around, then told Orik:

"You have three options. One...you try and terminate your parents' rights. Expensive, hard to win, stressful for you. You'd have to be declared a dependent of a juvenile court. Two...you go the emancipated teenager route. You're over 14, so you qualify. But it would mean some contact with your family again. You live independently, get a job, go to school. You'd have to support yourself, and your parents would have to agree."

"Hun-uh," said Orik. "I don't want them near me."

"Third option...L.A. County can take over your custody. They're finally paying attention to all the runaway children in town. They..."

"I'm not a child."

"I know that. But the law doesn't." Grandpa was patient.

"So what's the option?"

"The state of California has finally figured out that the worst abuse cases need sanctuary, like battered women do. Los Angeles County has an agency for this now. They take in kids from outside the county. They've been forced to, by the flood of runaways who come to town."

"How would they do it?"

"They'd petition the court on your behalf...to free you from your parents' custody. Eight kids in the agency have already done it."

Orik shut his eyes. His big long eyelashes lay on his made-up cheek. None of the options sounded great.

"Think about it," said Grandpa.

— 21 —

THE LAUNCH PAD

Late in the afternoon, we got to the water, and stopped in a wornout fishing town, by the harbor. Everything was primitive and Barbarian here — old wooden houses and stores, old fishing dredges with nets. The water was nervous with breezes, grey with a fog bank in the distance.

"This is Tomales Bay," Chino told us. "We have to cross it." He was in a hurry, worried about dark coming before we got to Point Reyes.

The six of us got in a rented Barbarian boat with an engine that ought to be in a museum. We chugged into that wall of fog. Chino had a compass on his SEAL watch, so we didn't get lost.

First look at the Launch Pad was disappointing. Sandy cliffs, not very high, came looming out of the fog. Boring little waves banged at our boat as we pulled it up on the stony beach.

Then we dragged our stuff into a tiny ravine, where a few huge trees hid from storms. Chino explained that there were several ravines along the peninsula, all created by erosion. Each one had an environmental campground — no running water, just the Boy Scout campfire with a circle of blackened stones. After somebody saw a tick, all the adults got paranoid, and made us tuck pant legs into socks. We split into three camps. Marian and my Mom put their tent under a cypress, near the fire. Harlan and Chino made a place under another cypress, while the women used flashlights to find some firewood. Orik and I picked a place that was very private, under a eucalyptus with a wind-twisty trunk. After all the drama, the two of us finally had a tent together.

It was cold and damp, almost dark. Even after Mom and Marian lit the fire, and we made sandwiches and cocoa, it didn't feel like a fun Brady Bunch camping trip. Orik and I went to sleep outside, about 20 feet apart. We didn't feel like sharing the tent, and we didn't talk at all. The shadow between us was Mama Death's shadow.

Next day, the fog burned off, and we hiked out of the ravine to explore. I was even more disappointed. It was like visiting Cape Canaveral and being disappointed. The myth came crashing down like a rocket that misfired.

The peninsula wasn't even spectacularly beautiful like one of those places on "Discovery," like Tahiti or Iceland or something. I don't know why I thought the Launch Pad was some kind of fantastic moonscape with millions of rockets standing around, waiting for spirits to get into them and close the hatch doors. Reality was, it was flat and grassy and weedy, and stretched west and north for several miles. A few other hikers wandered around. As we walked along the trail, I was in a bad mood, trying to imagine Indians walking a thousand miles to die in this stupid place. Here and there, by the trail, was a metal trash can, and I felt like dropping my life in one. We passed some elk who had big juicy ticks hanging all over them.

Out on the fatal end, we sat on a boring cliff with our faces into the wind, and stared at the Pacific. The beach was narrow and rocky, a surfer's nightmare, with waves breaking on a lot of plastic garbage that was washed up. There was a lighthouse down below. On the horizon, an oil tanker was going by.

Orik sat by Harlan on a rock about 30 feet away, his wig blowing in the wind.

"Now what?" I asked everybody.

That night, the adults did their prayer thing. They sat around the Boy Scout fire. Orik and I sat there too, because it was the only action around, so maybe something neat and scary would finally happen. Everybody was in a funky space, watching the flames. My Mom was feeding the fire, trying to be the Warrior Priestess, like on the night of the eclipse a million years ago when I was a little kid. She sat crosslegged, her back straight, trying hard to be strong and wise. The fire burned quiet, like it was listening to her.

"Okay," said my Mom. "This is *not* some creepy little seance. We don't need to call our spirits in. They're here...they've been here for years, even though we haven't seen them. We just want to handle things with them. Just clean clear communication. Even if our spirits don't hear us, the Deity hears us. It'll be healing for us to get some things off our chests. Got that?"

She sounded like she was talking to her girls' track team at Orange.

The fire popped. Orik jumped.

"Supposing a spirit comes?" he whispered.

"If it's your spirit," said my Mom briskly, "go for it."

I sat edged back from the adults, bracing myself for the adult secrets that were now going to get puked up. They all had their little packages of guilt and tears, their souvenirs that they were going to burn in the fire. The whole idea was boring. I didn't have anything to tell the fire anyway. My Mission to the Cat Nebula was over. The years of remembering Billy and trying to reach him didn't matter now, and he was the only spirit I had. So who cared? Orik backed away from the fire too, nervous about all the drama.

So my Mom cleared her throat and started talking to Billy. At first she sounded fakey, but after a minute she got into it, to the point where it seemed like the fire was listening harder. For some reason I started to imagine Billy coming near the fire to listen.

"...Stop feeling bad about how things didn't turn out the way we planned..."

Tears ran down her face. She held the snapshot of her and Billy on the bike. "...I want you with us in the present as a guardian angel or something, but not as the past..."

She tossed the photo in the flames.

The whole circle of adult eyes watched it burn.

Why didn't I toss my secret box in the fire? It was right there, in my backpack, six feet away. Why not burn the whole backpack?

Harlan didn't say much, when he talked to Billy, and a few people whose names I didn't know. The pictures he put in the fire were in an envelope. I wondered if he thought of burning the other two semen specimens. What was he going to do with them? Marian talked to somebody named Bobby, and Joe, and a baby she lost, and burned her wedding picture. As Orik and I got more uncomfortable, it seemed like the fire got brighter with a roaring sound in it, that made masses of sparks swirl up at the stars.

By now, I could imagine a thousand shadows around us — lonely shadows who hadn't quite jumped off yet, living on that land for a thousand years. I could feel them. They were hanging around us because nobody had made a fire for spirits in a long time, maybe since the whites conquered America.

Then Chino leaned over to his backpack, and took out a little wooden box, carved with dragons. It was his own secret box — full of photos, military patches, pieces of paper. He actually handed the pictures around, and we all looked at the ancient history, young SEALs in headrags sitting around after an op, kids not much older than me and Orik, drinking beer and holding up the severed heads of dead VC. Right away I recognized Shuga, in field dress, standing under a tree. As he talked quietly to Shuga, I felt a huge rush of chills all over my body, like somebody rolled me in frozen cactus. It felt like this dead man's powerful presence had moved close to the fire, right behind me, actually. My back was cold.

"...With you, I felt things that were missing. Not just passion and love. I mean tenderness...respect...trust. My destiny. After I lost you, I let your memory become something that almost killed me. But it also gave me a family...a chance to care for children the way I wasn't cared for. If I pull the trigger again, I'll do it to protect my children..."

One by one, he was putting his photos in the fire. Photos that some historian would pay pounds of rare metals to get. The one of Shuga, he held tenderly for a minute before he spun it into the flames.

Suddenly the whole thing was too extreme for me. I didn't belong here anyway.

"Well, here goes *nothing*," I yelled, and threw a handful of dirt in the fire. "Excuse me *you*, Billy Spirit. Don't come around, 'cause I am over you."

Then I ran off into the dark.

My eyes were so used to the fire that I stumbled over tree roots. Thousands of shadows saw me coming, and followed me in a mass.

Harlan got up to follow me.

"Let him go," I heard my Mom say. "Give him his space."

Up the ravine, on top, I felt like going somewhere, having my own private drama with the spirits. Cold and clean, out over the edge. For a minute I stood there, looking up at the dark sky. Never had the sky seemed so totally mine as it did at that moment. I had never seen the sky so dark, with stars standing out so bright, their colors so rich, like jewels, and clouds in the Milky Way so smoky with their millions of stars. The dark sky was my mother, father, boyfriend, girlfriend, everything I could love. I had always belonged to it, and it had always belonged to me. The turning of the sky was so familiar, that I knew exactly what I would see. Lyra was just making its right ascension in the east. It was a summer sky now, with the Summer Triangle there, and its heartbreaking view to the center of the galaxy. *We love you,* the stars seemed to be saying. *We are your real family. We're waiting for you. When will you come?* The default was death. I knew that now.

Footsteps ran behind me. It was Orik, his wig lifting as he ran. "Where are you going?"

I kept walking.

"I'm coming too," he said.

"Don't bother," I said, not looking at him.

He stopped, looking hurt.

All alone, I went across the big open, following the stars west.

Even in the dark it was easy to follow the trail through the grass, heading west, west. Bushes and rocks had shadows in the starlight. I felt better, like the day I ran away into the riot. Destiny, Chino had said. He'd been alone when he met his destiny. Everyone at the fire was all alone when it hit. The big adult lie about family and love, when all the time you are really alone. Ahead of me, a big meteor fell slow, slow, slow, slooooowwww...leaving a glowing green scratch in the atmosphere, exploding into fireballs over the western horizon. It was a signal from the stars. They were showing me where to go.

Finally I could hear the faint roar of the surf.

At the point, I sat there for a long time, shivering, collar turned up, arms wrapped around my knees. Wind was ruffling my hair. In the dark, everything was bigger, more mysterious and beautiful. The lighthouse, like a variable star, lit up the pebble beach, with ugly jumbles of sharp rocks and star shadows under them. I could almost see faces in the rocks and waves. The tide was up, and big waves came misting and gnarling and jumbling in, higher, higher, over the rocks, breathing their cold wet breath on me. The breath of the spirits was so cold and wet, that I shivered and smoked a last cigarette to calm down.

It had to be easy to go down there, to let the next big wave take me away into the default. Nobody would know for sure if I did it. It'd be my last secret. They could believe I went for a walk in the dark, and slipped on the rocks. The Coast Guard would find my short little body in a couple of days, with a couple more inches battered off it. I could see my Mom and Marian and Vince crying, even Harlan doing a tear or two, and Chino silent and gloomy. And Orik...who knew what he would do? Who cared? Anything was better than all this pain. What was it really like out there beyond the default? Just...dark? Just...nothing? Was I just imagining what I felt around me? Were there really other worlds to get born into? For real, not just in the sci-fi movies?

Another falling meteor went ripping down the sky, like an answer to my thoughts. I shivered, holding myself.

Suddenly a shape with a star shadow moved in the dark near me. I jumped with fright. A huge light went off in my brain. A spirit! I was about to run for my life when it turned into Orik, his wig blowing in the wind. The lighthouse beam lit him.

"Gotcha," he said.

"Eat shit and die."

"Ooooh. Potty mouth."

I didn't answer.

"Thought I was a ghost, huh," he said.

I glared at him.

"I *am* a spirit, stupid," he said. "What's with you?"

"Why didn't you call me?" I burst out. "We would have come and got you! You would have been safe! You had my number! Why didn't you come?"

"Why? Because I couldn't remember the number."

"I told you to memorize it," I yelled.

"I did. But I couldn't remember it. The drugs, I guess. My brains got real fuzzy."

Was this true? It didn't matter now anyway.

Turning my back on him, I threw away my cigarette and stripped down to my Jockeys.

"What are you doing?" he asked. "It's dangerous."

Just wearing my shoes, I walked down onto the beach, pebbles slippery. Then I took off my shoes. Something alive squinched under my feet. Orik tore off his wig and stripped to his own Jockeys, the ones I gave him. His bra came off, the condom titties falling out. He ran after me, slipping on rocks and seaweed.

"Don't," he called.

"Hey, *fruta*...why should you care?" A huge gulp of emotion came up, like a dark hot wave.

Orik was shivering all over. "If you go, I'm coming with you," he barked in my ear.

"You swore you'd come, and you didn't."

"I couldn't."

"Whatever," I said, trying to sound cool. I was shivering too. My knees were quivering like they did when I thought about sex.

"That's the deal we made," he said.

"I didn't forget. But you did."

"I didn't forget. I'm here, aren't I? This way they'll *never* find me."

He held out his hand to me.

After a minute, I took hold of his fingers. They were cold and clammy, but his grip was strong. Our eyes met.

"Cool," I said, biting my lips.

We didn't take off our underwear. There was no point in a last quick look at each other's naked classifieds, which had gone tiny and scared anyway. Then we took a deep breath and waded out. He caught my wrist, and I held his. The black water was terrifyingly cold and powerful, shocking the breath half out of us. It would be nice if the Coast Guard found us laying dead across each other. That's the way a screenwriter would do the scene. The two best friends, faithful unto death. What a payoff! Except our bodies would probably get dumped on the beach five miles apart.

Rumbling icy waves tore the gravel from under our feet. We were sinking and stumbling. I forged ahead. I wanted it to be fast and over.

A huge wave hit me, and Orik's wrist slipped out of my fingers. Then I was being swept, swirled, tumbled and shredded in total terror. I was alone! He was gone! Water stung my nostrils. My body knew it was going to die, and it fought to stay alive. A rock hit my hip, tearing me. Far away I heard Orik yell. My mouth was vomiting bubbles all by itself. I absolutely had to breathe, and sucked in water. Now I was going to choke slowly, horribly.

Instead a calm warmth began to fill me like a golden light. My body relaxed. I was pissing happily, letting go. I was crossing the default. I felt sleepy. Dizzy lights lit the water churning me. I was tumbling slowly, over and over, round and round, going down into a black wormhole in the deep. The hole was long and slender, like tornado tubes I'd seen on TV news, except I was going through it. Memories whirled around me...birthday parties, toys, games, tools, ideas, urges, dangers. Ahead was a opening. Beyond it, a hot blue-white star was rising, or setting...I couldn't tell which. It was pulsating, throbbing like a heart. A hot wind from the star filled the tunnel.

Someone was standing there, dark against the star.

I recognized him right away. He looked like he'd been waiting a while. I moved closer to him...somehow it didn't feel like I was walking. He was looking at me, thumbs hooked in the waist of his running shorts. His singlet riffled against his body in the star-wind. The oldie athletic shoes, blue ones, said TIGER on the sides. His dirty-blonde curls blew in the solar wind. He had a funny little tattoo on one shoulder — a girl. I finally got a good look at his eyelashes. They were long.

I felt embarrassed. I'd dissed him, and told him not to be here.

Billy moved closer. He didn't walk, just moved. I felt so close to him. He was so real — pores and freckles in his skin, little glints on his hair. He looked strong and healthy and fit, like he'd been training hard, the way I'd seen him in old photographs. His hair looked clean, like that solar wind had blow-dried it. I tried to say something, but it seemed like I didn't have a throat to talk with. He just looked at me with love and care in his eyes. Was it okay to go to him? Was Ana's dad around somewhere? And Shuga? And where was Orik? He said he'd be right there with me.

Billy was saying something. Somehow I felt his words in my mind, like strange colored hieroglyphics of future civilizations being hologrammed into me...like that magic wisdom I'd always been looking for. He knew I'd be making a decision, he said. The decision was up to me. If I went with him, out of the tunnel and into that blue star rising, there was no going back.

If you do this, it isn't bad or good — it is what you decide. But your future will be different.

What future? I screamed holograms to him.

Billy's holograms hit me hard, neon blue and purple, edged in xyzium. *You asked for a father, and life gave you one. Are you going to throw him away? You asked to be a commander — you have the chance to command yourself. Are you going to throw it away? If you do, next time will be different.*

Orik was definitely not there. Through the long tunnel came a horrifying hologram of crying. Somewhere he was crying and yelling at me. Suddenly the piss-off went away, and I was filled with peace and quiet.

Adults talked about peace a lot...it never was anything that I wanted much. But now I felt it. I was the blue star rising. I was the light. I was the love that Billy felt for me. Billy had been waiting there who knows how long to help me decide. The peace lasted for hours, maybe, before Orik's screams started pulling at me. "Fiiiinder! Noooo...." The holograms thudded into me like shockwaves. Colors of Orik's voice whirled around me. He was running after me down the street. He stumbled and fell. I turned my head, losing sight of Billy for a nanosecond, and looked back through the wormhole.

Suddenly I was over a beach in the dark. I was a solitary navigational fix of watching. Down there, a body was laying on its back. It was scratched and flattened, looking like a dead jellyfish. The body was mine. Orik was kneeling over it, pumping its chest, giving it mouth to mouth like you see on TV. He was screaming like a maniac. "I *order* you to live, man! You better live or I'll kill you!"

As he pounded on my chest like a lunatic, I could see a scrape on his back and it was bleeding into his crack. Not far away, the black wig lay on the beach, looking like a dead cat.

Choking up salt water, I lay on the sand gurgling, gagging. I stared into his face, into a bleary black sky. Stars swam over me. Finally I tried to sit up. He was sobbing, holding my head against his chest the way I did Chino's that day in the cemetery. I had lost my underpants in the water.

"I'm sorry — I couldn't do it," he sobbed.

After a while we struggled off the beach and groped around for our clothes in the dark. We hadn't planned to wear them again, so we hadn't noticed where they dropped. Athletic shoes glowed white in the beacon flashes. Orik pulled on his wig, but he couldn't find his socks. I was shivering as I finally dragged my jacket on. Our cigarettes were actually dry in our pockets. We shivered and shivered, and smoked to calm down.

"You owe me one," he croaked.

With our clothes damp and itchy with sand, we stumbled slowly back across the dark open. We were freezing. It took a long time, because our legs were shaking and we were pretty sore. A marine layer moved in, and the sky was now blank. More ghostly shapes drifted in front of us. *Gotcha*, the elk seemed to say, as they stared at us. Then, in the distance, we saw flashlights coming. Voices.

"Williaaaam...

"Shaaawwwwwnnn..."

In a few minutes, they were in front of us — my Mom, Chino and Harlan. They looked pissed and scared. Their flashlights blinded us. Harlan looked like he almost had a heart attack from worry. I could see how devastated he was.

"How'd you find us?" I felt stupid.

Chino said, "Tracks in the dew."

They marched us back to camp like prisoners. We were basically strip-searched and our combat injuries exposed, with deep embarrassment. Out came the first-aid kit, stinging alcohol, antibiotic smeary stuff. In the firelight Orik and I glanced at each other. We looked like war refugees on the news. I felt like I was seeing them all too clearly.

"I won't comment on how stupid it was to go off in the dark here," Harlan said quietly. "We just want to know how you got in trouble."

Orik and I didn't say anything. Chino got sarcastic. "You boys going to tell us the big secret?"

Still shivering, I shook my head no. Explain what happened after I went under? I would rather die than snitch on myself.

My Mom threw up her hands. "You see? All these months, some progress, and…boom! we're back to Square A. Nothing works with him."

"We're amateurs. All these years," Marian cut in, "he should have been in professional therapy."

Always the therapy with Marian.

"No," Harlan said. "That's like blaming him for something that wasn't his fault."

While they argued like we weren't there, Orik and I struggled into dry clothes. They made breakfast, pancakes and bacon and everything, and everybody stuffed themselves but me. The bacon tasted strange. I could have been dead by now, eating starlight in the Realms of the Dead.

My Mom said to me, "We know you're hiding something. When you're ready to come clean, don't come to me. And don't run to Chino. You go to Harlan. It's time for you to deal with him."

A couple of hours later, we were crossing Tomales Bay again. Chino and Harlan taught my Mom how to operate the boat, and all three of them sat in the stern while she drove, with her hair blowing in the wind. Orik and I sat in the prow, spray dashing over us, watching the mainland come near. The bay was so incredibly beautiful — xyzium blue under a clear sky, fishing boats everywhere. The colors hurt my eyes. Everybody else felt different, lighter. The boat actually rode higher in the water. I was the only one who still felt heavy. I couldn't stop shivering, and puked over the side of the boat.

Behind us, the Launch Pad of the Spirits was sinking into the sea forever, like Atlantis going down in ancient history, and its spirit finally going to the stars to be a galaxy new as the baby I'd been.

— 22 —

THE ANCIENT SAGE

When we got to the mainland, I was burning up, aching all over. My throat was sore.

"Flu," Marian said.

Probably I had swallowed some water pollution. They made Orik ride in the other car so he wouldn't catch my bug. I curled up in the back seat under two unzipped sleeping bags, and slid into a blur of gas stations, voices, freeway signs, swallowing aspirin. My mind kept fighting to think about what happened while I was drowning. I had dreamed in the water. No, an experience, not a dream. Billy being there was real, more real than all my Mom and Harlan's stories...as real as Orik's yells. I heard them when I was unconscious, or whatever.

Everything was cutty. Sleeping, waking up. Door shut, curtains almost shut, a sliver of palm leaves moving up and down the sky. Blue sky — smoke gone. Harlan's face over me. Too sick to fight him. Phone ringing down the hall, in the office. The house quiet. His hand with pills in it, then a glass of juice. His hands again, with a box of Kleenex. A wet cloth on my face. Sliver of sky now hot sunset purple. Where was Orik? Scared somewhere, running away again? His parents paying that PI to look again. His parents finding him, dragging him off.

I opened my eyes.

The curtains were open, waving in the wind. The sky was blue like it had never known clouds, ever. Hot clear, like a star had cleared it with star wind. It was the most incredible color — a churning boiling blue, like melted stars. I stared at it. My mind was clear, an extreme clear. Everything had hard edges, like a knife, and glowed with a fierce spirit inside. I felt very different, very changed. I didn't ache.

Harlan was sitting on the edge of the bed, patient, quiet.

So here I was. My voyage had finally brought me to Yoda's hut, and I was face to face with the old Sage whose words of wisdom were the last thing on Earth I wanted to hear. I felt like I was seeing him for the first time, really clearly, like that xyzium-blue sky. Harlan was fifty something...he didn't have a long white beard, or flowing cloak — just a five o'clock shadow and the terry dragon robe that he sometimes wore over his sweater and chino pants to keep warm, because his circulation wasn't so good any more. The blue square of the open window, and his worry, was reflected in his eyes.

"Where's Shawn?" I mumbled.

"Safe in Malibu with the LaFonts. He's staying in Ana's bedroom."

"So Mom dumped me on you," I croaked.

"My turn to be nurse," he said, straightening the bed covers.

Mom had always fixed up the bed when I was sick. A funny little pain went through my heart.

"Feel like taking a shower? Here, wear this...it's warm."

Too weak to fight him, I put on the dragon robe and wobbled through a wash. In the steamy mirror, a pale grundgy teen alien stared at me. His hair and eyelashes were growing wild, like weeds. How long had he been sick?

"Hungry?" Harlan asked. He was wearing a different sweater now. "You like toast? Hot milk?"

How many days since Point Reyes, when I ate last?

At the kitchen table, I sat drooping. The old dog came and lay by my feet. While the milk heated, Harlan put a towel over my head, rubbing my wet hair drier. A bowl landed in front of me like a lunar module, with buttered toast swimming in steaming milk and sugar.

"An old healing remedy...my mother's," he said. "Before she turned on me."

I could smell his after-shave in the robe. Dragons of his care coiled around me, tighter, tighter. I fought them off, choking. Suddenly I was flashing back to Point Reyes, to waking up on the beach and finding myself terrifyingly alive. The toast tasted of fierce colors, so alive in my mouth that it almost squirmed. The dragons were alive, fiery nebulas of human destiny caught in space, exploding around me. Tears welled. I was remembering the beach, Orik holding my head. The memory cut like broken glass.

"You're a better cook than my Mom," I whispered.

Vince came through, with his briefcase. He had been bicycling, leaning against the wind. He looked healthier than usual. He really was getting well.

"Hiya, babe," he said, ruffling my hair. "Welcome back." He went out.

Later, clouds came in. Outside, rain whispered in the banana leaves, mist glooming down right over trees and chimneys along Rosewood. I curled on the sofa with a quilt, wrapped in warm dragons, watching the TV news and remembering that L.A. had just gone through a stellar catastrophe. Police processing the thousands of arrests. People digging in smoky ruins. All of it happening thousands of light-years away.

While I watched, Harlan built a fire in the fireplace, to make the room warmer. Suddenly my mind went from jump-cut to still...I was seeing him really clearly again, as he kneeled there fussing with paper and matches — like I'd twiddled the focus on my new telescope and found the pulsating 60-second star. It was sharp in every detail for the first time. He got down on one knee with a grunt, because his hip hurt him. His hair was the color of Chino's guns — shiny metal-grey — and never seemed to get thinner or greyer, just more like metal. No matter what anybody else in WeHo was wearing, Harlan always wore those retro-looking chino pants.

"So...you and Shawn decided to depart this life together," he said, almost to the fire.

"Something like that."

"And?"

"Shawn chickened out, and dragged me out of the water."

"He did CPR on you?" Harlan lit the fire with a match.

"Whatever he did, it worked."

The fire was eating up through the wood — nice neat supermarket wood, not the wild snags on Point Reyes. I saw fire clearly for the first time. Flames were clean, like orange water flowing upwards.

"Well, where do you go from here?" Harlan asked over his shoulder.

"I don't know."

"There's the knee-jerk thing of therapy and counseling," he said as he put on another piece of wood. "I don't necessarily believe in it."

"Counseling sucks."

"Maybe if you can talk this out with us, and be honest with us about what's been going on with you, we won't have to go that route."

Hot tears ate up my eyes. I cried for what seemed like hours, burying my face in the dragon sleeve because I was so embarrassed at losing control. Was I having a total breakdown or something? Were they going to stick me in a clinic like the one Shawn got put in? Outside the house, rain stopped, mist lifted. Then sky darkened, and rain closed in again. Wind whizzed by — palm leaves jounced. Rain hit the windows. Harlan put more wood on the fire, patient, quiet. Magically, from nowhere, he had Kleenex. I blew my nose.

"Talk to me," he said.

I drew a deep breath. "Billy was there."

"What do you mean?"

Little by little Harlan got the story out of me. My mind was still fighting with the question of exactly what I had seen, how scientific my observations were while I was drowning, and if it was just my imagination. His face changed as he listened. He sat staring at the fire for a long time.

Finally he said, "Your mom says you've had this death wish since you were little. Accidents...being reckless... It's about wanting to be with your dad, isn't it?"

Words burst out of me.

"It wasn't fair that he got killed! I wanted to do things with him, like other kids do with their dads. Shoot hoops. Go fishing, for chrissake. I mean...Shawn's dad went off on Mom about how I had this *abnormal* childhood. But it was people like Jerry that took my Dad away from me!"

The flames were licking up with hungry energy.

"You don't have to kill yourself to get to your dad," Harlan said quietly.

Now I was fighting him like crazy again, turning into the Pinhead geek who always ruined things. "Billy was what I had...I saw him in my dreams...even if I'm not his kid..."

"You *are* his kid," Harlan said.

"I don't feel like anybody's kid," I sobbed.

"He wanted you to be born as much as I did," Harlan went on. "There's more to this parent business than genes, boy."

Did he believe me? Did he? Down the hall, the phone was ringing in his office, and he let the answering service pick it up. Finally he said: "Some people have a fancy name for it."

"For what?" I croaked.

"Near death experience."

My whole body went prickly with excitement.

"Usually people see loved ones who died...partners, friends," he went on.

"Did you ever see anything like that?"

He shook his head. "I'm not the type. Vision always came hard for me."

So he did believe me. Words tried to rush. I choked on them.

"Maybe Billy was there to encourage you to go back and live your life," Harlan said. "Ever think of that?"

I stared out the window. Maybe he was right. But I still fought it.

Next door, Paul and Darryl's house was dark — the studio was running late again. Chino's window was dark — he was in Sacramento with Marian. The storm was really hitting now — rain slashing outside the windows, palmetto leaves thrashing.

"So you've decided to stick around?" Harlan asked.

"Why not?"

He smiled a little. "Could be interesting. And you've got your friend back."

Still too nervous to talk about that, I stared at the fire. It was nothing like the magnetic crazed fire on Point Reyes, but it calmed me down — though I needed a cigarette in the worst way.

"Shawn's really scared," I whispered. "He still hasn't decided. I'm afraid he'll run away again."

"Can I talk to you man to man?" he wanted to know.

"I'm a man." I glared at him. Why wasn't this obvious?

"You're 14...an old 14. You're getting to be an adult. But are you a real man?"

Adults had their fuzzy logic. "Try me." I smiled a superior smile.

"Once upon a time, I had a friend like yours. It was a different time...so different that you can't imagine it. The country was screwed down tight. People weren't open about sex, even straight married sex. So I had feelings for him like you do for Shawn. But...we both denied them. It had some terrible consequences. Long story. So there's no way I'd step between you and Shawn. He's a good kid. But there are dangers here, that I see. So I'll make a deal with you."

"What?"

"The two of you moved heaven and earth to find each other. We know you'll run away again if we interfere. So we won't. Your mother and I have talked, and we agree. Okay?"

"What's the rest of the deal?" I said in a smothered voice.

"Be responsible. A real man is responsible for his own life. He has his own rules for making himself responsible, and he lives by them, even if those rules put him at war with the world. A real woman lives the same way, I might add. Like your mom. Maybe I should say a real human. So don't make the excuse that you're just a kid. That's bullshit. In other countries, people your age are running political movements, leading guerrilla armies..."

"Did you always live by your rules?" I shot back.

His eyes were fierce, clear, so alive. Or was it how I saw colors now?

"I don't have a perfect record," he said. "But I've been careful enough. That's why I'm still around. The question is, how responsible will *you* be?"

"How do you know what the best rules are?"

"Living through things gives you something to measure by. It's like a yardstick. You find out if your rules are long enough."

"You mean...we always have to go through it?"

"Yes, we do."

"Can't we just watch a video or something? Who decides we have to go through this torture?"

"What some people call a mistake, or a sin, is a chance to learn what works. Little kids learn about hot stoves by touching them. Life doesn't protect us from the hot stoves. It's one of the mysteries that I think about as a writer — that people become great only after they make some huge mistake that shows them something new. And the people who go through life pissing and moaning about their mistakes, they push away their learning. So they never amount to much."

Was this the ancient Wisdom? Harlan definitely had ancient arthritis going, the way he limped. But was he worth listening to?

He bent over to pat his old dog, and kept talking.

"Look at Chino and the things he did in Vietnam, and how they drive him now. Your mom, and Vince, and the pain they put themselves through, and how they changed. Hell, look at me. I made some colossal mistakes. So I can't stop you from touching the hot stove. I can only tell you how hot it is. But will you listen?"

Suddenly my eyes snapped open. I'd fallen asleep on the sofa. The fire had died, and the VCR clock said it was after midnight. Through the door of his little office, Harlan sat in the silver light from his Mac screen. The movies don't tell you that the old sorcerer is a workaholic, so he can't leave his spells alone. I felt good, seeing him there at his work, being creative and making money too. He and my Mom both...they knew how to earn money and take care of themselves and their families.

Harlan heard me yawn, and turned. On the wall, were the photos of me. Suddenly it was so clear to me — how much he had wanted me to be in his life.

"Off to bed," he said over his shoulder.

A little boy part of me was there. "Hey, uh...Harlan?"

"What?"

"Nah. You'd be shocked."

"Hard to shock me."

"Tuck me in?"

He laughed, and helped me wobble down the hall.

The little bedroom glowed with warm light. While he yanked down the covers, I crawled in with the dragons on, and slid down deliciously under the quilt. Outside, rain roared in the palms and banana trees. Lightning flashed, making me feel safe and hidden. He sat on the edge of the bed, and brushed a hank of hair off my forehead.

The touch made me shiver all over. He smelled of that kind of after-shave that old guys use.

"I suppose you want a bedtime story too," he said to me.

I grinned and pulled the quilt up to my chin.

"*Cat in the Hat? The Lorax?*" he asked.

"Mom said you used to call me Falcon."

"When you were little."

"Why did you call me that?"

"I always loved birds. They seem so free...I knew I wasn't free. Birds can get up high and see everything in perspective. I started seeing people as different birds — their personalities, their dreams for themselves. Your mom, for instance. She's a goddam hummingbird. Little and feisty as hell. Billy —" He laughed. "Billy was a roadrunner. He could clown, and make you laugh. Then he could kill a rattlesnake with one peck, and swallow it whole."

His face lit up as he talked. "And Vince...I always saw him as a snowy egret...long legs, gorgeous feathers...."

I had to smile, cradled in the magic of his words. "What about Shawn?"

Harlan cocked his head. "A gull, maybe. He rides every wind easy, like he rode the street."

"Chino?"

"Oh, he's a cormorant. Ever watch a cormorant fishing? Ducks through the waves, never wipes out —"

Yeah, that was Chino.

"So one time Harry and Chino took me to visit this Green Beret friend of theirs. He'd killed so many people, he didn't want to be around humans anymore. He had a master falconer's license, and lived all alone up in the Adirondacks, with his birds. When we got there, he had just live-trapped a young arctic peregrine...the most beautiful animal I ever saw. Snow white. Ernie, that was the guy's name, was teaching the bird to fly from his glove. When you fly a falcon, you actually set him free. No collar, no leash..."

Harlan held his wrist up. I could see the bird sitting there on the leather glove, wings tucked, straight and proud.

"And when you throw the falcon in the air, he goes off and hunts. He dive-bombs his dinner...POW! Grabs a pigeon right out of the air. But he always comes back...of his own free will."

The old man's wrist moved in the air. I could see the bird

launch into the sky, and hunt...then zoom back to the glove.

"Whoa," I said. "Do falconers keep the birds till they die?"

"Oh no. They release them after a couple of years. Especially now that falcons are endangered."

"So when I was little..."

"...You reminded me of that white peregrine, the way you dive-bombed anything you wanted. From the minute you started crawling. Your blocks. Your toy trucks. You dive-bombed astronomy. Now it's Shawn...the way you went after finding him. Jesus, you even dive-bombed death itself."

I lay there glowing at this wonderful Barbarian chronicle out of my past. Was this a metaphor? I remembered the word. A metaphor for all the things he wasn't going to say about his heartbreak? About how he wished for years that my Mom would agree to live near him, so he could help raise me. How he made do with my photos. But he never forced himself on me. Maybe he even prayed...that someday he'd look up, and see his lost falcon flying back to him. He and my Mom and Chino and Vince, even Marian, had been flying me, letting me learn to hunt and learn to fly home.

A tear was running down my face, into my hair.

He smiled a little, and shook his head.

"I'm proud of you, you know that? You have the gift to go out there and see things that most people don't ever see."

Suddenly I wanted his love. I sat up and threw my arms around him. My spirit dived into my father, my own Darth Vader, and took hold of his powerful and mysterious and terrifying spirit. His spirit glowed around me like a hot golden light, coiling into me like a dragon on fire. He wrapped his arms around me too, and held me against his chest, very hard. He held me and rocked me for a long time. I was feeling what his boyfriends had felt — his strong arms, his smell, his deep slow breathing.

I talked into his neck, his hair.

"Could you and my Mom...get along better? Like, could the three of us do things together, sometimes?"

His body shook with a deep sob. So I rocked him a little, too. Here I was again, comforting a weeping adult.

He could hardly talk. "I'd like that. Talk to her about it."

"I want to come here more."

"You come and go whenever you want."

"Can Shawn...uh...be here too? Like, sleep over sometimes?"

"We have to do what's safe for him. But...if it's the right thing...."

Lightning lit up the room — the furniture, scattered clothes, Billy's picture. The candle hadn't burned since before Point Reyes. It didn't matter now.

"I *am* very pissed at you about one thing," I said into his neck. "What?"

"You didn't give me the gene for being tall."

Harlan laughed. He gently tweaked my nose.

"I gave you my beard genes, though," he said. "You can start shaving more often, you know."

"How else do I look like you?"

"Your hair, your nose..."

He took hold of my weedy chin and rubbed it. "Sleep well, son."

"You too, Dad."

His limping footsteps went away down the hall, up the stairs. Vince might be waiting, standing naked in the lamplight, taking off his watch. They'd slide into each other's arms, and feel good hugging and pressing together. I liked thinking about it. Did straight kids feel good about their straight parents being together? Did they like hearing the neat sounds at night, from down the hall? Did they feel safer knowing their parents loved each other instead of beating each other up and trying to kill each other, like on the evening news?

A new thought glowed awake. Was Chino the one who mixed up the semen samples? Was it an accident? Did he do it on purpose? Did he decide that it was better for Harlan to be the father, than a guy who was dead? Chino had wanted kids too. He was even there when I was born. Did he think of me as his kid? Was that why he held himself back from me? How big was my family, anyway? Where were the ends of this mystery? It didn't seem to have any end, like the light curve through the universe.

Feeling so happy was a spooky feeling. How long would it last?

Next day Harlan started talking about the Box. Vince came down the ladder from the crawl space with a long brown box, the kind where my Mom always stored old tax stuff. He put it on the living room floor. The word "Montréal" was written on the side. Harlan went abruptly out of the room. We could hear him slide open the patio door, and go outside. From somewhere in the area, the sound of a helicopter came louder through the opened door.

Vince sighed and sank into the sofa by me. "Go on," he said. "Open it."

The clean smell of cedar hit my nose. My Dad had put little blocks of cedar in the box, to keep bugs out and try to keep everything clean. Inside was all this primitive archive stuff — old and yellow and brittle, like the Dead Sea Scrolls or something. Newspaper clippings. An old *Time* with Harlan and Billy's face on the front. The typing of a book my Dad had written called *The Front Runner*. An envelope spilled photos from Montréal, taken by some news-agency guy from the stands. Autopsy photos from the Montréal morgue. Billy's head with dark and matted hair, forehead blown away. Underneath was the most important stuff: clothes. A suede jacket with a voguey-looking New York label, very wrinkled. Billy's track shoes and track shorts. A pair of broken glasses. A singlet with the Olympic rings and faded stains on it. My hair stood on end. They were the exact same ones that I saw when I was drowning.

Vince sat silent, not touching any of the things. In the bottom, there was an old stop watch and another pair of old track shoes, black Tigers, the same size as my Dad's feet.

Rich kids inherit trust funds and houses in Bel Aire. Straight kids get family albums. What I got, was this.

Billy's jacket was long for me, but the shoulders fit. The watch fit nice on my wrist.

"This stuff is mine now?" I asked.

"It's yours," Harlan said, coming back in. His eyes were red.

I humped the box to my room, and shut the door. With the candle burning, I sat up half the night, reading the *Time* article, looking through the clippings. I gloated over how famous Billy was, how he had half the country in a heart attack because he was gay and wanted a gold medal. I flipped through Harlan's book, and learned surprising things, like how my Dad hooked for a while, when he was broke and living in New York. I wasn't going to diss him about it, though.

There was one picture of my Dad that got my attention. On the back he had pencilled "Working out in Washington Square, 1969." He was young then, really goodlooking, but his eyes were sad, like he already had a lot on his mind. His body wasn't shaved smooth, like gay guys do today. He had shiny black curls on his chest and in his armpits and crotch. He stood with one foot on a park bench, tying those black Tigers. Something about the bulge in his shorts made me feel his pain and loneliness, a closeness with his sex. By then, he was out and his first two children had been taken away from him. He still wanted desperately to have a family, a kid that he could raise and be honest with. Years later he and Billy decided to have kids together. I could see him in the doctor's office, jacking off, catching his hot sperm in a cold glass jar. The sperm that was half of my genes had grown in his body, lashing its little tail toward its destiny. Most sperm got spat right into a woman's body, but this one had to make a long lonely voyage, like the Galileo space probe was doing — as long as the voyage I wanted to make to the Cat Nebula, before it found the distant galaxy of my mother's body.

I had always known that I came back from the stars to pick my Mom. But Harlan had reached out to the stars to pick me.

I feel asleep in the pile of photographs, curled up in Billy's jacket, with one track shoe in my hand.

A few days later, Chino came home. It was neat to see how happy he was when he got home — how much the other men cared about him and missed him. I would have to knock myself out to get back on his good side. So I confessed everything about Point Reyes.

Chino studied me as I sat there by the fire in the dragon robe. He looked different — eyes clearer. He listened, head bent, nodding now and then. He didn't seem surprised when I told him about the drowning experience.

"Did you tell your dad about the *Memo* dream?" he asked.

"Not yet. Too many other things to tell him. But I will."

"So you knew all along, huh," he said.

"What do you mean?"

"Like I told you...some people know things in dreams. If Billy was your dad, you would have seen his face in the dream. You had a photo...you knew what he looked like. But you didn't have a picture of Harlan. So the man in the dream had a helmet over his face. Understand?"

These days my skin was always going goosebumps, but I never got used to it. This time I actually shuddered with the goosebump feeling. He was right. Now I understood the dream for the first time.

"And 23...that's the chromosome count, isn't it?" I said.

"Maybe." Chino had a faraway look in his eyes.

"What about the 60-second variable star? What was that all about?"

The moment I said it, my eyes went to Harlan's old stopwatch that I was wearing. It had 60 seconds on it. Was this it?

"Chino, did you ever think about...uh...suicide?"

"Quite a few times," he said. "SEALS had a high suicide rate. We got wired as tight as astronauts...except astronauts don't have to go shoot and loot. Gay SEALS have a hard time. I'm probably the rare survivor."

He smiled a little. "Not to change the subject, but I've...arranged for reports of runaway Shawn sightings in Las Vegas. My final op as a PI guy. I believe that his parents aren't watching this sector very carefully right now."

As I got better, the men finally talked about boyfriends a little with me. One night Harlan and Vince made the best hamburgers I ever ate, with avocado from Rose and Vivian's backyard tree. I felt good enough to eat them, and we talked while we were doing dishes, which was a weird but casual way to get into this freaky subject. The funny thing was, they were actually kind of shy about discussing it. But they somehow knew that Shawn and I had fooled around since we were little. Was I getting the Dad Talk About Sex, after seeing other people do it on TV all my life?

"Hey," I said, "we never did anything radical."

"What's radical, to you?" my Dad asked.

"The, uh, wild thing seems pretty radical to me."

"Scares you, huh?" Vince asked.

"Kind of." A long menu of questions scrolled down my mind. "Isn't it kind of...uh...like being a woman? I mean, why would a real guy do that?"

Harlan laughed. "Real men love to submit. I found that out when I joined the Marines. Some of the stuff I saw going on...and I wasn't ready to try it either."

We were clattering around the kitchen. Harlan was scrubbing the broiler. I was putting stuff in the dishwasher.

Vince put away the leftover avocado. "Yeah, I'm a real man, all right."

My face was burning. "Shawn's dad said it's filthy."

"Then heterosexual sex must be filthy too. Straight men use their penises to urinate, then stick them into women. But straight people don't seem to have a problem with that." Vince was reorganizing the refrigerator. An old head of lettuce arced into the trash.

"But guys get ruptured, and stuff..."

Harlan's eyes squinted with wizard laughter, as he put soap in the dishwasher. "Ever wonder how Jerry got so well-informed?"

"Yeah..." I grinned.

"Women get ruptured when they have children. When you were born, your mom tore like hell. I heard her screaming...it shocked the hell out of me. And a woman who has a dozen children — her womb can actually prolapse. So...does this make childbirth unnatural?"

I wondered how Harlan got so well-informed. My Mom must have hammered it into him.

"So if we can make a suggestion..." Vince said.

"Sure."

"Making love is like making a hamburger...lots of ways to do it, and they're all wonderful. The important thing is the feelings."

Harlan was wiping the counters. I had the feeling that he was a little less comfortable discussing this subject with me than Vince was, even though Chino and Vince had hinted that my Dad was the ultimate Sage of wisdom about gay sex. Vince hinted about photographs that Dad burned at Point Reyes...nude photos from his hooker days. He had taken them out of the Box. Maybe he didn't want me to see them.

Harlan's voice had gotten a little hoarse.

"You like apple pie?" he asked.

Later, full of food, we sat staring at the fire. I was tired now, sitting on the floor, leaning against the sofa right by their legs, and stretching my feet toward the fire. I leaned against Harlan's leg, like his old dog Jess was doing on the other side. It felt good, and I finally asked my Dad the ultimate question.

"Did you...uh...did you ever like sex with women?"

"Yeah, I halfway enjoyed it now and then. But it was always foreign to me." His hand stroked the dog's head.

"Mom always said you hated women and stuff."

Vince snorted. "Hate, no. Attitude, yes."

Harlan didn't think this was funny. "And people go through their changes. I've seen gay men and lesbians who swore that they weren't attracted to the opposite sex at all...and all of a sudden they meet an opposite that they can't resist."

"I was bi for a long time...then I lost interest," Vince added.

"And we've both seen men who were straight, but they had one intense overwhelming thing for one guy. Who can explain it?"

"So maybe I'm bi?"

"How did you feel about girls?" Vince asked.

"Some girls are geeks. Some girls are very cool."

My cheeks burned again. Teenagers were supposedly out there having all kinds of sex. It was supposed to be a national moral problem. How come I wasn't getting any?

"But...it's different with girls," I said.

"How so?" Harlan wanted to know.

"Women have these *little* lips."

Both men laughed.

"Now that you've decided to stay on Earth with us, you've got time to figure out who you are," my Dad said. "That's what life is...time. But I want you to understand something."

"What?"

"My parents tried to force me to live up to their expectations. I will never force you to live up to mine."

I had never been so sick in my life. People came to see me. Mom and Marian came, looking relaxed and happy. I wondered if they were an item now. Teak and Elena came, with stories of going through social withdrawal during the riot, because they couldn't club. Chino came with news that he hadn't noticed the Heasters' PI around for a while.

And Orik came in his girl drag. The LaFonts felt bad about what happened to him, so they were helping him out. They wanted to get back in good with the rest of the family again. The wall between me and Orik had melted. He lay on top of my covers, and put his head on the pillows beside mine, and somehow our fingers twined together. The sky didn't fall, and Jesus didn't come down from the clouds looking pissed because I was holding hands with another boy.

"Hey, girlfriend, you're...uh...really kind of gorgeous," I said.

"Oh yeah?" He grinned.

"You rescued me for real," I said, staring into his eyes.

"Lots of ways to rescue," he said, staring back.

"Yeah."

"If my parents find out, my Dad is capable of anything...*anything*. I'm their property. They are gonna want me back, no matter what. And they talked about..." His eyes were lasering into mine with a look that I'd always wanted to see there.

"Talked about...what?"

"About getting *you* away from your mom. Like having somebody else in your family go to court for your custody. My parents think your mom is possessed by the devil."

I felt a chill go over me.

"They'll have a hard time finding my Mom's parents," I said. "Her dad's dead. Her mom's family moved back to Lebanon. My Mom's dad worked with some oil company."

"What about Harlan's parents?"

"His mom is still around, I guess. She tried to get Michael away from Harlan. But she couldn't do anything legally, because Michael was adult."

"Does she know Harlan is your dad?"

"Probably not."

"If she finds out, she might try to get you."

"Grandpa told you what *you* could do," I said.

"It's all pretty scary. I could lose either way..."

"Have you decided what you're gonna do?"

"Yeah," he said. "But before I do it, I want to have a special time with you."

Our fingers tightened together. I touched his hair. It seemed like it lifted all by itself without any wind. We were nervous about anybody walking in on us, so all we did was hold hands.

"Where?" I whispered, going all sweaty and horny.

He put his face very close to mine, fluttered his fake eyelashes against my cheek, and said, "Disneyland."

— 23 —

FIRST TIME

Before Orik took Grandpa's advice and did his legal thing, he had one last weekend of freedom. Harlan let us have the house to ourselves, and he and Vince stayed next door at Paul and Darryl's. They kept an eye on the house though.

We planned a magic weekend together. Early on Saturday morning, with the sun ascending over an Orange County that wasn't a sector of some fantasy universe, just Earth and everyday, Chino drove us down to Disneyland. We spent the whole day there, with Chino keeping us in sight. We were a guy and his girl, getting to be kids one last time. Our backpacks were light — a change of clothes in case we got wet on the water rides. Chino bought us Mickey T-shirts, and we pulled them right on.

Orik's titties jiggled nicely underneath Mickey.

All day long, we were totally hyper, running through the trees and caves on Tom Sawyer's Island. Shawn's wig-hair lifted as he ran with me. We wore Chino out. All the extreme rides that we could cram into a day — Splash Mountain, Big Thunder, Indiana Jones, Star Tours, Space Mountain, holding up our arms as we went down the big drops, so we could be with the experience, laughing at Chino who went through the rides two seats behind us, no smile, no arms. When we did Splash Mountain, and our log boat went down the waterfall, with everybody screaming their heads off, Orik pulled up his Mickey shirt and flashed his Fredericks of Hollywood bra and his size 38 jiggles at the hidden camera that takes souvenir pictures for tourists. But when we checked out the picture display, his photo wasn't there.

"Some Disney employee censored it," Chino said.

As we whirled through the space rides, falling through galaxies, meteorites whizzing around us, screaming our heads off, the thought flashed through my mind that this might be the closest I would ever get to deep space.

All day long, we held hands. We were the two romantic teenagers. A few old dudes and old ladies looked at us. We must have made them want to be young and hot again. One of Orik's hooters popped during Indiana Jones, and he had water down his shirt. He bent over against me, so nobody could see, and stuffed that side of his bra with toilet paper, which he carried in his backpack for emergencies.

That night we caught our breath at two tables in the Blue Bayou. Chino had made the reservations. The restaurant was indoors, but they tricked you into thinking you were outside under the night sky with people going by in boats, starting into the Pirates of the Caribbean ride, and fireflies glowing among the trees — I had never seen a real firefly. Quieter now, we ordered big hamburgers and lots of fries. Now and then we giggled. Orik whispered something about how the waiters all thought we were going to get married after high school, have six kids and live happily ever after. Before the hamburgers came, Orik suddenly pulled a card out of his backpack. It was a big one, with lots of roses on it, wet from Splash Mountain.

He wrote something in it, then handed it to me. It said: "I will never forget this day. Your best friend forever...love, Shawn."

I got a lump in my throat.

"Why Shawn?" I said.

"We're men now. We should use adult names."

I swallowed hard, reading the card a second time. What was I going to say back? *I don't remember when I didn't love you. That day at the lake was definitely not the beginning of the movie. I loved you in basketball...when you were getting your measles shot. I loved you in*

Blockbuster Video and math class. I knew I loved you when your dad was beating you, and when I didn't know where you were. I even loved you when we were gaybashing that poor little fruta at the mall. But I loved you most of all out there somewhere near the Cat Nebula.

We had a slammin' dinner, and a long talk about our dads...what it means to have fathers, and not have them, and the straight father thing, and the gay dad thing. Chino had his dinner alone two tables away, watching everybody. By the time we watched the Electrical Parade, it was late and we were getting tired, sitting on the curb waiting for an hour, with my "girlfriend's" head on my shoulder. Finally all the fantastically lighted fairies and animals went by, but I didn't notice them much, because Orik's back was burning under my hand. Finally it was after midnight, and we slept against each other in the back of Chino's vehicle, holding hands and secretly feeling each other a little, while he drove us back to L.A.

He dropped us at Harlan's door.

We hugged him, and he watched while we let ourselves in and locked the door.

The minute the door was shut, Shawn and I gave each other the look. Our hearts were thumping and our knees were shivering. Then slowly we got into each other's arms. It was scary...we knew we weren't going to stop this time. With hair getting in each other's eyes, and Mickey smashed between our chests, we wrapped ourselves around each other. Our smells blended. We leaned against the hall wall, pulling up T-shirts. My hand got in his bra, and popped the other condom. We giggled like crazy and I played with his boy breast, and the nipple loved my touching, big and hard as Ana's.

My bedroom looked really lived-in now. The lamp lit all the pictures on my bureau, casting wild shadows on the walls. All the people I loved — my Mom, Harlan, Billy, Chino, Vince, Ana, Teak (whose whereabouts weren't known at the moment), the Valhalla clique, and of course a big framed one of my Mom and Marian together. The candle was out — I didn't need it any more. Outside, a mockingbird was singing, kept awake by the street lights. Billy was close to us, making his golden glow in the room, as Shawn turned back into a boy before my very eyes. I helped Shawn take off his wig. With his head in the pillow, he looked in my eyes as I lay against him. My fingers shook as I peeled off his eyelashes. Cream got most of his makeup off okay.

His fingers were shaking as he touched my eyelashes. "They're more beautiful than God's," he whispered.

"Girlie eyes."

"Guys should have beautiful eyes. Don't cut your eyelashes."

"Oh yeah?"

"Can you let yourself have beautiful eyes?"

He took my head by the ears, and started kissing my eyes. He kissed my chest and called me baby. I caught up with the fading light of two boys kissing in a dark corner of a club, open mouths together, tongues sliding, thighs between thighs. I kissed his hair, his neck. He had scars on his arms and back — I kissed them. As he kissed my belly button, I pulled the tape off the tuck between his thighs, and that was how I learned about tuck's. He said ouch because it tweaked his hair. We managed the whole thing without taking our mouths off each other — warm breath against each other's bodies, words said into each other's skin and sweat. It was important to show our feelings while we were doing it, because that is the real forbidden thing — the kissing and saying I love you...not just having sex, which we'd already been doing for years, except we couldn't call it that. All the sermons and laws and parent attitude hadn't stopped us. We had won. We groaned with frustration, wanting the kiss to be more total than our bodies could manage. I wanted our spirits to kiss their invisible DNA together for 20 billion years of the universe, if that was possible. Kissing and touching was so enough that we didn't want to do the wild thing, not yet anyway. So the condom fell on the floor, and we did everything else but.

I woke up with a jump. Was he gone? He was gone for sure. No. He was there, on one elbow by me, lighting a cigarette. The night had gone, though, and it was light outside the windows. Even on Earth, there were gravity curves in time. The clock said 6:35 A.M.

I yawned and stretched. "Shawn and John. It even rhymes."

He lay half across me, and I helped him smoke the cigarette. His messed-up hair had been caressed so much that it looked polished. He ran his tongue along my eyelids, then down my cheek and back into my mouth for another long smoky kiss.

He said, "I wanted to kiss you so much, that day at the lake. I wanted to kiss you all over."

"You never told your dad what we did, huh."

"No. He tried to make me tell. The therapists tried. But I never told."

"Did you ever kiss anybody else?"

"Nuh-uh. Do you believe me?"

"Not even Donnala?" My fingers were running through his hair. I fluffed it up so it looked like wind was lifting it.

He laughed. "I tried with girls. Like you did. Not the same, though." He voice changed, and his body suddenly tensed. "A few things did happen. But not this."

A few things?

"Like what?" I asked.

His voice shook. "Things. I couldn't stop them."

"People, like, did things to you?"

"Something like that. A couple of times."

Like rape? He was trying to tell me something so horribly secret, that he couldn't. Suddenly tears were running down his face. "But I never worked, okay?"

"Hey, it's okay. I believe you." I was stroking his cheeks, trying to wipe the bad thing away. He had shaved close yesterday morning, but golden hairs were sticking out of his chin again.

"I never gave up the important things. You got my virgin. The rest of the important stuff, nobody wanted it. Like kissing, giving love...nobody wanted it. Weird, huh?"

"You don't have to tell me. I kind of knew."

"Promise you won't do this with any other guy, okay?"

"I swear. How about you?"

"I swear." He leaned off the bed to his backpack, and got out one of those black snap-boxes that you keep jewelry in. Inside were two gold rings, with tiny diamonds all the way around, set in stars.

"You stole them?" I asked.

"We did a truck in back of a jewelry store. These were in my cut. I kept these for us because of the stars. Friendship rings, okay?"

"Sure." Now I knew he'd really wanted to find me.

He put one on my finger. "Put the other one on me."

I did. We looked at each other. I grinned because this was so cool. Every Barbarian chronicle has to have a ring as part of the story.

"It's funny," he said.

"What?"

"We did exactly what the Rev. Dwight said kids should do...we waited for the right person."

Finally we wore each other out, and woke up at noon. Other than eating a huge breakfast and watching most of one movie, we spent the rest of Sunday showing love in every weird way we could think of — on the bed, on the floor, on the sofa, in the shower. Even out on the patio, naked and squirting each other with the hose because it was more fun to clean up that way. Paul's cat found us on the lounge, drying off, and wanted to cuddle with us. The wall was high enough that the neighbors couldn't see anything.

"Are you having fun yet?" I asked him.

After we quieted down, we lay on the lounge in each other's arms, soaking up the sunshine, and I had a nosy question.

"Hey, what did the doctor do to you that time? After the lake."

"Don't ask."

"I want to know."

He sighed. "Some strange doctor, not the one my folks always went to. I had no idea what was up till I was on the table. They told me it was a physical for military school. He even strapped me down. Then my parents," he said violently, "had him put some instrument up my butt, and test me."

"Nasty! For what?"

"To see if your spunk was there."

"Jesus!"

"It hurt like crazy. I was...like...screaming and everything. So my dad put his hand over my mouth. And..."

"He was there?"

"Oh yeah. Nothing that anybody did to me later was that bad."

On Monday morning, while I threw our sheets in the washing machine, Shawn got his backpack together. Harlan and Vince came over and cooked us a big he-man breakfast, and didn't ask us any questions. Then without any drama, Shawn squeezed my arm and went out the back way. He was being so brave that it broke my heart, because it was going to be a long journey...longer than going to the other side of the Universe, longer than being cryophased, so he wouldn't die of old age on the way..."boldly going where no man has gone before," like in *Star Trek*.

I stood in the door and watched him getting smaller and smaller as he walked down the alley.

All alone, like Clint Eastwood riding into the bad guys' town, he was taking the bus across town to the office of Los Angeles County Adolescent Social Services on Wilshire. He was going to give LACAS his real name. He was going to tell them he was gay, and running from abusive parents.

When the county told the Heasters that they had Shawn, his parents freaked.

But now there was nothing they could get the police or the private investigators to do. If they kidnapped him, they'd be in major trouble with the state of California. The agency gave him to a case-worker, and put him with ten other runaway kids in the Mary Byrne Children's Home. Grandpa told me the county had six homes for minors who wanted out from their families. Most of them were straight kids who had drug or suicide problems, or they were being molested or beaten at home. The Mary Byrne kids were lesbian or gay or bisexual. Some, including two of the girls, were poz. One girl wanted a sex change operation so she could be a guy. Some had been in trouble with the law, and were on probation. Some had been in psycho wards. In the past, Grandpa said, minors didn't have anywhere to run to if they had trouble at home. Now, in the whole United States, there was this one agency that had beds for 400 kids.

Shawn called a straight lawyer — Grandpa showed him the number in the Yellow Pages. The law firm did pro bono stuff for kids. With his case worker and the lawyer present, Shawn told his parents that he wanted them to give up custody.

I wish I'd seen it...a scene like no movie ever made.

At first the Heasters were freaked. Then they were insulted and furious. They made a dozen trips up to L.A. and tried to talk to Shawn alone...tried all the Jesus moves on him. Like...he wasn't really gay. It was just a phase. It was the Devil's fault. He'd die of AIDS. Yada yada yada. Marilyn cried and cried, and Shawn said later that his mom might come around some day. But Jerry had destroyed every bit of Shawn's trust. So Shawn wouldn't even talk to them, except when his case worker and lawyer was there. The case worker found out about two beatings that sent him to the Costa Mesa emergency room. She matched the hospital records with the scars. She could see how afraid he was. Finally, when his parents just wouldn't leave him alone, Shawn got up the courage to throw the real stuff at them. That he'd had boyfriends...that he'd lived as a drag queen. He threw the club photos in their faces.

"If I die of AIDS, or whatever, that's my business. My life belongs to me!" he yelled.

When Jerry heard this, it was over. He wasn't going to wear rubber gloves for any son of his. He could hardly wait to sign the piece of paper. The county was evil too, because it took care of queer kids, instead of punishing them and making them go straight. Marilyn cried, but Jerry screamed at her, so she signed.

I never expected Jerry to give up so easy.

"It's right in the Bible," Harlan explained to me. "If thine eye offend thee, pluck it out."

"You mean...like...actually pull out your own eye?" I felt sick.

Shawn also went to court to change his last name. He took the name Shawn Sun, and that's what went on his ID. He kept his mouth shut, and the county and the Heasters didn't find out that he had been in touch with us. But the Heasters wrote my Mom a long threatening letter, saying it was all her fault that they'd lost their son. They were going to find some relative of ours who would have legal standing to sue for my custody, and haul me out of that pit of sodomite hell where she'd let me fall. They told us that they'd get to their Assemblyman, and have LACAS closed down because the county wasn't doing anything to stop kids from being homosexuals. The state of California was condoning and fostering homosexuals. This was how they saw it. Jerry had joined some organization of men called Promise Keepers, and he was talking big about stopping immorality in the whole country.

Grandpa put that letter in his Shawn file.

"Good thing they don't know who my real Dad is," I told Grandpa.

"Let's hope the Heasters don't find out. If they locate Harlan's mother and her son Kevin," Grandpa growled, "they would be only too happy to help out."

The county was very controlling. They had a million rules, like no sex in the house, no drugs, no smoking, 6 P.M. curfew. No smoking was the worst. Shawn had to get a job, so he worked as an usher at El Capitan theater. The paycheck went to the county, who took out his room and board, put the rest in his bank account, and wouldn't let him touch it. He had a hard time getting five bucks.

The county said he had to go to school. So they enrolled him at EAGLES. The school was for gay drop-outs, in a few rooms donated by the Metropolitan Community Church, with two gay teachers, some paper and pencils and one old computer all paid for by the L.A. school district. Most of the EAGLES students were desperados like Shawn. Some were local kids who'd dropped out of their home schools because they were tired of being spit on and slammed into lockers. Some were runaways who came to L.A. and lived independently. A few were working boys. They lived with friends, or in squats, and came to school in their nice clothes, after their last trick of the night.

A few were on probation. A few were county kids like Shawn.

County kids could go into foster care. They tried putting Shawn in a foster home. But he made sure he didn't get along with the foster parents, so they sent him back. Once or twice a week, between his job and the county curfew, Shawn took the secret bus ride over to West Hollywood to be with us.

"I don't need a foster home — I have you," he told my Mom the next time he saw her.

He cried on her shoulder. My Mom patted his head like she did me when I bawled on her shoulder.

"Why did my mother have to change?" he wanted to know. "Why didn't she stay the way she was?"

At home, inside the closed-up plastic on my table, the mirror disaster still lay waiting in the diamond dust.

— 24 —

HAPPY ENDINGS

My Dad says that a story is supposed to end in 120 minutes. The special effects guys blow up the building, the heroes escape at the last minute, they kiss, and it's over. Even though Luke's father dies, he and Obi-Wan Kenobi and Yoda come back from the spirit world because they care a lot about Luke. So *Star Wars VI* has a happy ending.

Real life is not like the movies, I guess. So I put my *Star Wars* collection in Harlan and Vince's video library, and left it there.

My Dad was working on a new book, which was about everything that happened after Billy was killed. I asked him why he messed around with stone-age stuff like books, when there is TV and the Internet. He said that secrets told in books will always be important. You don't need upgraded software to get into a book. You can take a book on a 10,000-year voyage into deep space, and it will still work when you crawl out of the cryotank. So when the Big War comes, and technology goes away, like the movies say it will, the exchange rate will be one book for a package of seeds or a pile of rare metals, Dad says. Maybe even somebody's life for a book, if it's a good one.

My Dad is so smart. That's a neat angle that I never saw in any movie about the space-age future.

At first, Harlan wanted the whole world to look at me and say, "That's Harlan's boy." But Chino thought it was a bad idea to announce anything. Dad and Chino actually had a fight about it. Dad was yelling about why the hell should we hide. "If any of the goddam Browns ever show up and want custody, we'd duke it out in court," he yelled. Chino yelled back that it was stupid to put such sensitive information in the public record, and his voice gave me shivers. My Mom was still operating off the old paranoia that drove her into years of isolation. She was yelling that Chino was right. So Harlan was outvoted, and everybody decided to wait till I was 18.

What matters is the love, not the piece of paper.

On September 7, I was 15, and it was my first *real* family birthday. Marian had the party at her house because she had a bigger yard. Smoke drifted away from the barbecue, past the students in one end of the yard, and the adults in the other, and me shuttling back and forth in a cool new T-shirt and slacks that I had dragged myself to The Gap to get. Shawn couldn't come, because he had gotten caught smoking, and the county made him stay on campus. I felt really hurt that he didn't think enough of me to stay out of trouble and get to my party.

Teak came out with his new boyfriend Emilio. They both were pretty tweaked. Teak's butt was only six inches wide now, and he looked like one of Madonna's voguey boy dancers in a jacket and satin shirt and the tallest platform shoes he could walk on. He was a hardcore partier now. He'd had his own birthday a week earlier, and swore that he'd left a message on my machine inviting me.

"Everybody got sooooo drunk and trekkin' and noisy that the place threw us out," he told me.

I pulled myself together. No retard boyfriend was going to spoil *my* birthday.

At the apple tree, Mom and Harlan and Vince and Chino and Paul and Darryl and Michael were hanging out together. All of them were in black tie and tux, even my Mom. Suddenly they started laughing about something. Vince made a comment, and my Mom made a little scream, then they all laughed harder. Harlan went to grab my Mom's hand. She was too fast for him and pulled it away. Suddenly I felt good about how happy they looked. My Mom's hair was cut extra short with the first grey in it, and she actually looked pretty cool. Vince looked amazingly healthy, with a red rose in his lapel. Dad had had his 57th birthday in August. Chino was 42 now. Mom was 35. Grandpa was 60 something. Marian was 40 something.

My family. Shawn's family too. If Shawn wasn't here for this, it was his problem.

I was shivering with pride, introducing my Mom and my real live Dad to my friends.

"Delila, this is Harlan...this is Chino...this is my Mom. Joel, meet Harlan...my grandpa..."

Dad gave me one of those he-man cards that said "Happy Birthday, Son." The picture showed a dad and his kid fishing together. Inside was a checkbook for a bank account, with $500 in it. And a key ring with no key on it.

"Every deposit you make, I'll match it," he said. "When you're 16, get yourself a car."

Dad's arms felt so good — my nerves always went nova when his DNA was close to me. My face burrowed into his white shirt front and breathed his smell of unglamorous but reassuring after-shave. Then I actually got to hug Chino. He smelled clean, like a tree. My Mom smelled like wild flowers. The pile of presents, and a chocolate cake with my name on it (which Paul and Darryl and Rose and Vivian had baked with their dainty hands) was almost too much for me, because of the love in it.

I bawled like a baby when everybody sang "Happy Birthday."

Grandpa arrived with that lady friend, Francesca Bellini, and introduced her to everybody. Even a dumb jock like me could see that Frances was a very glamorous lady. Teak stared at her with flaming envy, and hissed in my ear, "Oooo girl, she looks like Madonna, only *old*. She's soooo vogue. And skinny to die for." Francesca wore an oldie movie star kind of black suit. Her silver hair was boy-cut, under a black hat that looked like a flying saucer, with lots of feathers on it. She had a nice humming voice that wasn't scratchy, like old people's voices usually are.

I really liked Frances, but I still couldn't figure out why Grandpa was interested in her, till Grandpa said, "Frances is an important person in your family tree. After my wife left me, Frances and I raised Billy together. We broke up for a while, and then a few months ago..."

Frances smiled. "For all purposes, that makes me your grandmother, darling." She shook my hand. She was actually wearing black gloves. Her perfume was around me in the air, like an invisible nebula.

Teak kept staring at her. Finally he just blurted at Frances, "Gawwd, you're the first old drag queen I've ever seen. I mean, you don't see really *old* drag queens around. Oops...I didn't mean to insult you..."

"I know what you meant. Yes, I *am* aging gracefully, aren't I?" Frances gave him a big wink.

I dragged Teak to the other side of the yard, and hissed, "That is not a drag queen, you invalid. That is a woman."

"That is the ultimate *loca*, my man."

"Excuse *me!* My grandma is not a drag queen. F you. You wanna punch in the face?"

We didn't finish the argument, because just then I heard Eileen's voice behind me. She and Glenn had showed up, with weird smiles, standing close together. "Happy birthday surprise!" they said, then stepped apart.

Behind them was Ana.

I forgot all about Grandma Francesca. My girl buddy had magicked herself into a beautiful woman. No makeup or special effects were necessary. She was 15 now, but she vibed like the kind of older woman in the movies who has affairs with boys and teaches them major stuff about sex and love. She towered over me, wearing a long dress and no jewelry. Her amazing hair was loose all over her shoulders. She looked like a white satin meteor. But she was skinnier than ever, and her eyes had dark circles.

Being a guy who was raised by goddesses, I recovered my cool.

"Is this the Ana who calls me on the phone?" I said.

"Payton got down on its knees and begged us not to inflict her on them for another term," Eileen said.

Ana and I stood under the apple tree. She hugged me, and I could feel her 20-year-old breasts melt my shirt lapels.

After Marian caught Teak looking for liquor, and chewed him out, he and Emilio left. They were going back into town, to the midnight drag show at Arena.

My family was nervous about Shawn and me being together. I could feel them having dramas about where Shawn had been and whether I was doing safer sex or getting infected with something. But they didn't try to separate us.

Michael and I were getting used to being half-brothers. Michael told us more about other AIDS-related diseases that are being studied, like CFS. People don't like to talk about CFS, especially the religious Pinheads. You can get it like the flu, he said. So they can't do big sermons about it, or use it to pass laws that put people in jail. He kept talking about the questions that weren't answered.

It didn't matter much, because Shawn and I know that we won't live very long. The big war is coming, and we'll be two of the young leaders. Chino says there is going to be a political movement in the high schools, like the '60s movement with college students that Vince told me about. It'll start with affirmative action and gay rights, and other groups will join up. Maybe after we do walk-outs from schools, and paralyze the country like the fires did to L.A., people will see the youth power and have some respect.

I hope we go fast, because I don't want us to suffer. One time Chino talked to me about having to shoot a wounded SEAL buddy in the head, because he was too hurt to move and the enemy was coming. This time I'll be the one to rescue for real — I'll do Shawn, and then do myself.

School had to be handled. I checked out EAGLES so I could be with Shawn every day. EAGLES was on Santa Monica Boulevard, in an old storefront. But it was too noisy for me, too many dysfunctional kids, too much drama. I couldn't have studied there. Mom wanted me to enroll at Flintridge Prep for their magnet science program. But I decided on Fairfax so I could be with Elena and her girlfriend Shayla. Fairfax was cool...nobody bothered the gay kids much, and nobody bothered me.

Fairfax had the first Project 10, which is a counseling program started by Mrs. Uribe, one of the teachers. Elena and Shayla were helping Mrs. Uribe to run the program, so kids who were gay or whatever, or suicidal about their questions, would have someone to talk to. Sometimes I hung with the gay crowd. Sometimes I went my own way. Sometimes it was hard to say what I was. Some gay students were just as mean and cliquey as the straight students.

"Actually I'm straight," I'd insist.

They'd boo and hiss.

"Yeah, straight to bed with Shawn," said Elena.

Elena had quit clubbing. She was still the tiniest *macha* in town, but nobody slammed her into lockers any more. In fact, the skins and jocks moved to the other side of the sidewalk when they saw her coming. She stomped around in a black leather jacket and combat boots, with a stunner in her backpack and a blue rose tattooed on the back of her neck. Her head was shaved and she wrote wild gothic poetry. Shayla's mom had thrown Shayla out, so the two girls moved in with Elena's mom.

Elena was now best friends with a black guy, Charles Beaumont, who was 17 and drew fantastic stuff and wanted to be a Disney animator. When I wasn't with Shawn, Charles and I hung out together. Charles was part Jamaican, with amazing hazel eyes. He was out to his parents, and they didn't have a big problem with it. After he graduated, they were sending him to CalArts Northridge. I got to visit the Beaumonts' house in South Central, though I didn't ride the bus there, because that was still a dangerous sector of the Universe for a vanilla kid. Charles and I would spend half the night talking. He was the most together gay kid I knew. He said he was still a virgin, and he was going to wait for the right guy. He actually told me this.

"Your family *lets* you be with your boyfriend?" he asked.

"Yeah. They're not permissive, though. They expect a lot from us," I said. "We don't get away with shit."

I was getting a bad case of potty mouth.

Teak showed up again. Emilio had moved out and left him with a $600 phone bill. Teak didn't like Fairfax, so Nancy enrolled him at EAGLES. She moved into West L.A. so Teak could live with her and not have the long bus ride to school. But he only went to EAGLES one day a week, and was tweaked when he got there, and had fights with the teachers because he spent too much time in the boys' bathroom putting on his makeup. Away from school, all he did was club and rave and hang out at After Hours. We all worried about him using crystal. I didn't know if Teak was full of disease now, and he didn't say. I still tried to be his buddy, and talk to him about his life.

"Save the drama for yo mama," he said.

After school I met Shawn. We'd walk home and spend an hour together in the empty house. Then he'd go flying out the door to catch the bus and make the 6 o'clock county curfew. Once in a while he and I ditched classes and spent the morning around the city, and then he had to go to work. Shawn had a new friend in his house...a runaway named Shadow who said he was 16. Shadow had been in a few psycho wards, and his file said he tried to kill himself 21 times. He had used so many aliases, and so many sets of ID, that the county didn't know who he really was.

Shawn talked about Shadow a lot, which bothered me.

I was getting more responsible...working for Marian, learning about politics. Astronomy and the astronaut thing were on hold. The 10-inch mirror was back in its box, with the scratch on it. Genetics was on hold, too. But I still wanted to change the world. Maybe I'd help Michael discover what was really happening with disease, so people wouldn't be lied to. Politics were interesting too, just like Chino said. Right now I wasn't sure what I wanted to do.

Meanwhile there was "quality dad time" with Harlan. He took me on a trip East. We went to places where he'd been with Billy. We didn't go to Montréal, though. My Dad wasn't up for it. But we went to New York and Fire Island and Philadelphia. We looked across a housing development in Westchester County, and Harlan said it was a forest once, and he'd scattered Billy's ashes there. Like Dad said, there was something called time, and he helped me start to feel it passing.

We even went fishing together. One weekend Valhalla chartered a fishing boat and went out past Catalina. I didn't know how much my Dad loved the sea till I saw him grinning and wet with spray and driving the boat. He taught my Mom how to fish better, and she caught a bigger tuna than he did.

Another day, Dad said it was time for some "closure." He and I went out alone in a smaller boat that he rented at the Santa Monica pier. It was a beautiful day, and we sat in the boat for a long time, surging up and down on the waves, with our hair blowing in the wind — his metal-colored hair and my grown-out curls. His dark glasses were staring at the horizon.

"I used to daydream about this," he said quietly. "The three of us on the water off Fire Island — just a lazy day, fishing poles..."

"You, me and Billy?" I asked.

He was opening his briefcase, and pulled out the two last glass tubes from the cryobank. They were thawed already. Something in the way he leaned over and put them in the water, so gently, gave me this powerful feeling of how much he still loved Billy.

"It didn't seem right to put them in the fire," he said with a little smile as they sank out of sight.

We sat there for a long time, my Dad and I, just feeling time. That was when I finally told him about the dream.

Dad's mother was still living in Buffalo. Sometimes it was scary to wonder if the custody war would happen. We kept watching for the Heasters to show up. Were they still watching us? Our Costa Mesa house was still on the market, and Chino did one last surveillance from there. He told us the trash said that the Heasters were bankrupt from paying the PI — so he didn't think they were going to sue us. They hadn't reported my Mom to Children's Services for being a lesbian and "recruiting" me. But Mom was paranoid, so she kept our passports handy. She and I would get on a plane and bolt the country, she said...maybe to Denmark or the Netherlands.

From the night he put his Vietnam photos in the fire, Chino was different. I had this feeling that his stepdad had molested him when he was a kid. No wonder he went so cold when I flirted with him. More than ever I would pick him for the commander of my school ship *Memo* — except there would never be a *Memo* now.

Dad told me more about what Chino did in Vietnam. That war became important to me because it was a great Earth war, and some veterans who'd been there were homeless now, eating out of dumpsters along with kids that I knew. I couldn't understand why the United States killed so many young guys in such a stupid war. But I felt proud to know that Chino had rescued so many American and

Vietnamese POWs. One day I asked Chino if my Dad had sent him on a mission to turn me.

"I wasn't so sure I could turn a *loco* kid," he said.

By October 1, Marian was campaigning like crazy. She wanted the Latino vote, and spoke at different immigrant organizations. Mexicans liked her, because here was one Anglo who knew that L.A. would be half Spanish-speaking in a few years.

At first she got lost among the big names — the Perots and Clintons and Barbara Boxers. But one night I sat with Mom in the front row, and listened to Marian talk to a church packed full of black people. She told them she had a dream too, that the Republican Party would wake up about human rights. Suddenly I felt like I was seeing her for the first time, standing there in her grey suit, with her hair battened down for combat, and suddenly I felt way proud of her. In November, Marian surprised everybody who said a Republican couldn't win in Malibu. In January, while D.C. was doing Clinton's inauguration, my aunt quietly went to Sacramento to start her first session in the Assembly.

Marian told me that she was really concerned about bills that the religious Pinheads were starting to bring to state legislatures. People like Jerry wanted to close all the legal doors that let their kids get away from their control. They wanted the right to beat their kids. They wanted longer sentences for status offenses. They wanted fooling around to be a serious crime for young minors. They wanted it illegal to harbor a runaway. And they wanted it to be a felony for gay men and lesbians to have children. I was impressed — Marian was pissed, and she was going to fight for kids. I actually started liking her.

Mom and Marian hadn't said anything publically, and they each had their own bedroom, but I still wondered if they were an item.

After everything Shawn and I went through to find each other, it was weird when things changed.

Shawn had his own world now, the system, and his life was different from mine. One day, Shawn didn't meet me on the corner when he said he would. I went crazy for 24 hours, calling his house and leaving messages with whatever kid answered the phone. I found out he'd been with Shadow...just hanging around town, he said. He insisted he wasn't having sex with Shadow. The more I bothered him about it, the more he defended his right to have some friends of his own.

"Don't be possessive. Give Shawn some space," my Mom warned me.

But I was pissed, so I decided to spend more weekends in Malibu, to be with Ana. Malibu guys were hot for her all over again. But I was still her best boyfriend, she said. Glenn and Eileen had expanded the restaurant in Malibu, and were getting the money crowd now. Eileen's health was better. I wondered if Eileen had an immune gene too. Maybe that was why she lived so long, like Vince did.

Ana had really missed me in New York.

One day we were snuggling, and I asked her, "You ever think about having kids?"

"Oh, I love kids."

"But how are you going to have kids if you don't...?"

"I'll probably die an old maid."

"Have artificial insemination, like my Mom."

"Yeah...really. Maybe after college, and putting the Green Party in control of Congress, and stuff."

"I'm serious. If you ever want a kid, I'm your man. Nobody has a more positive attitude about family than me. We'll do the turkey baster thing."

"Are you serious?"

"Would you like to have a kid with me?"

"I'd love that," she said right away. "We'd be good parents."

"Mnnn." I cuddled against her.

"Not yet, though," she said.

"Don't worry, I'm not going to do anything."

"Anyway," she said, "I wouldn't get pregnant now because I don't have periods. It's because...because I work out a lot, and I..."

"You don't eat."

She stared into my eyes.

"If my Princess doesn't eat, she's going to die," I said.

The pupils of her eyes got big and black. She stared at me for what my Dad would call a beat. Then she whispered, "I don't want to die."

Teak was back. He and Nancy moved to Malibu again. This way, he'd be several light-years from the club scene and the wilder kids at EAGLES.

He threw his arms around me and said, "I am soooo over it."

"I missed you, you big *queena*."

We lay around on our beds and talked, and it was like old times, except I wouldn't tell him my heartbreak about Shawn. He told me his adventures — how he ODed twice and woke up in the emergency room. It scared him so bad that he was trying to stay off drugs now. He planned to switch to Fairfax, study hard and really graduate. We made plans to upgrade his computer. He looked good, but I heard him barfing after he ate. He said he had a nervous stomach now, but I figured out that he had lost all that weight by making himself do like Ana did.

We agreed that we'd try to stop smoking.

Marian put Teak in charge of her mailing list at her office. When he went into town, he hung out with Elena and Shayla and a few other recovering clubbers. This was how he met Charles and fell madly in love. But Charles was in love with his art.

I never did find out when Teak had his first time. It was one of those secrets that got buried in the backyard of the Universe, in a black hole that only a kid would know how to find.

One Friday afternoon just before Christmas, Mom and I had the first son-mom talk in a while. We were going to Malibu, west on the 10 freeway, in the rush-hour traffic. I was worn out from all the drama with Shawn, but I could tell that Mom had something on her mind. "Goddess, where does the time go?" she said. "Another year, and you'll have a car. Another year after that, and you can enlist."

She looked at me. "If you still want to."

Why do adults always think that time flies? Don't they know that days never end — especially when things go wrong?

"I'm not sure what I want to do," I said.

"Have you definitely broken up with Shawn?"

"Don't mention that heartless creep to me."

I looked down at the star ring. Was I going to take it off?

We stopped at the pier, to eat lunch at Alice's. Mom had the mahi-mahi and I had the hamburger. It was a warm day, so we opened the window and let the breeze blow over our table. Out there was the ocean where I almost met Billy for real. It was laying there under the deep blue shadow of a marine layer. Three years had passed since I had the *Memo* dream — three turns of the star year. So far, I had found everything I was looking for, and then lost some of it again. Did I have everything, or was there more?

The wind tugged at my hair...my curls were growing back in.

"Mom, why do things hurt so much?"

She shrugged and said, "Maybe we have to hurt so we'll appreciate when we get healed." She pulled out an envelope of snapshots. "I didn't have the heart to burn these. And you never got to see them."

I looked through them, while the waiter took away our plates and brought Mom her cappuccino. One snapshot showed a little boy with long black curls. He was with two women and two guys, looking at a lot of wild geese on a lake. The women had their arms around each other, and the guys had their arms around each other.

"The guys are Chino and my Dad?"

"That was the last time I saw them, before I broke contact."

Something weird whirred in me, at the way the two men stood, like they'd been together. I wasn't jealous...just uneasy and curious. There was still so much that I didn't know about my family. For a minute a picture flashed in my mind, of my Dad making love to Chino, with that huge tenderness he had. My stomach was quivering.

"Were my Dad and Chino ever...close?"

She shrugged. "With gay men, who knows what counts as close?"

"Who's the pretty lady?"

"That's Marla," she said, keeping her voice steady. "She loved you so much. She could get you to do things that I couldn't. I always had to arm-wrestle you."

"I don't remember her."

"Not surprising, with all the ugliness around. And you were only three. Maybe that was why you couldn't remember dreams. You didn't want to remember all the drama about Billy."

"You're not going to burn them, are you?"

"Do you want them?"

"Yeah, I do. For the family box. She's family, huh? I want all the family in the box. Everybody dead and everybody alive, all together."

"Oh baby." My Mom broke down and cried, right there in the restaurant...not sobbing or anything, just silent crying...cried and cried for Marla and for time. A tear ran down my cheek. I felt like two galaxies were colliding inside me, tearing through each other. Our two hands held each other, with the sea breeze blowing over us.

"Oh baby, I love you so much," she whispered.

"I love you too, Mom. You're the best," I croaked.

After lunch we hung out on the pier, watching people fish for sand sharks. Mom blew her nose. We had our arms around each other, like we were on a date. She wrinkled her nose and sniffed me.

"I *hope* you stop smoking," she said.

"I'm working on it." I changed the subject. "So...are you and Marian an item?" I asked.

"I guess you could call it that."

"What do you mean?"

"It's...evolving. Like it always was."

"I really thought she was your aunt."

"Sometimes a thing is right under your nose, and you don't see it. When I was a student at Prescott, I gravitated to her right away. At first she felt like an older sister. All these years she's been there for me...and I wasn't always there for her."

I frowned, watching a guy reeling in a poor little sand shark about 18 inches long. It flipped and twisted, bending his pole.

"So when did you and she know?"

My Mom shrugged.

"Oh, there was never a moment when we got hit by lightning," she said. "There's LUGs and LAMs. For some women..."

"LUGs?" I said.

"Lesbian Until Graduation..."

"That's definitely not Elena!"

"...and Lesbian After Menopause. Sometimes loving women doesn't kick in till later. Michael talks about some genes that don't kick in till people are 30, or 40. Really makes you wonder if there are sexual orientation genes like that..."

"But not a lesbian like you. She's...bi, right? I mean, she was married all those years, and had kids...she loved Joe."

Mom shrugged again. "Yeah, this orientation thing...the way it really works is still a profound mystery to me. It's kind of variable, like those stars you were always talking about."

"So are you really in love with her?"

"Yes, I do love her," said my Mom softly.

"What happens if she gets outed in Sacramento?"

"We deal with it, that's all. Marian won't be the first bisexual woman to hold public office."

I thought about the virus of hurt and jealousy that was eating at me. How would I know about myself if I didn't try sex with girls? Or would Ana and I happen because we liked being together, and not because each of us needed to prove something?

"There's a lot of things I don't know about my family," I said. "Like Grandma being a drag queen. I mean...is she?"

The fisherman unhooked the sand shark, and left it laying on the pier. He walked away to the parking lot. Our eyes stayed on the shark. Its gills were struggling to breathe air instead of water.

"Honey," she said. "Frances isn't a drag queen now. She's a post-operative transgendered person."

"Huh?"

"She had all the operations. Grandpa helped her pay for it after they got to be friends again."

Mom was grinning at my shocked expression, as I was trying to take in the idea of surgery on a person's military secrets. She gave my waist a girl buddy kind of squeeze.

"Nobody," she said, "ever knows everything about their family. A family is a whole universe. Nobody knows everything in the universe."

"I always wanted a grandma."

"Well, you've got one now."

The poor shark was drying out. It was moving its tail, trying to swim. The edge of the pier was a foot away. It would never get there.

"Some people are such bastards," said my Mom.

Because she was a warrioress of the Great Shoe Goddess Nike, she walked over there, picked up the shark by the tail and dropped it over the edge. It hit the water swimming, into the next wave.

We walked back to the car. The old Rambler, where I'd had the *Memo* dream, was gone — Marian had made Mom get rid of it. Sitting in our parking space was a shiny grey Lexus. No more underpaid Barbarian teacher. My mom had a good job in politics now. She walked with a bounce in her step.

Looking at the new car, I really saw, for the first time, that I had truly accomplished my Mission. I should get a medal. Victory was mine. Other missions would come, and I could handle them — I hoped.

As Mom clicked off the car-alarm and opened the door, she said, "Harlan's meeting us in Malibu, so we can all get our heads together and plan some holiday stuff."

"Cool," I said.

"A real family holiday, huh?"

"Hey...I'll even help you guys bake some cookies, or something."

My mom laughed a neat laugh...almost like a girl giggle.

As I opened the Lexus' passenger door, the sun sparkled on the stars on my ring. It seemed like the dark sky had coiled around my finger. I knew then that I didn't have to take the ring off.

That was when I also knew that the 10-inch mirror was going to get polished that weekend. I had a whole block of time, and I would burn through it — 40 hours nonstop if I had to. I wasn't sure where things would go from there. But it was important to finish the telescope, because it was part of the Mission. No matter what happened between me and Shawn, or me and Ana, the mirror was about something more — something mysterious and magical that was reflecting to me from Life. Maybe Life isn't totally about loving other people. Maybe it is also about loving myself — about being married to my destiny.

Maybe that's what Wisdom is...knowing what new star to hunt, no matter where I have to voyage inside myself to find it.

About This Book

Like most books today, *Billy's Boy* is the child of desktop print technology and electronic wizardry. Since my books become collectibles for some people, this hardcover volume is designed with beauty and durability in mind.

I admit to having the most antiquated computer on the Wildcat team. *Billy's Boy* was written on my PowerBook 170, fondly known as T-Rex, because it is a dinosaur — purchased the first month that these landmark laptops came on the market, and my constant companion on book tours. I decline to go running after the latest notebook with the latest bells and whistles.

The book was designed on the Macintosh 6200 of Barbara Brown Desktop Publishing, using Aldus Pagemaker 6.0. Fonts: Caslon for the dust jacket, Jansen for the text. Both were chosen for their clean functional look, which seemed appropriate for a student who is into science. Wildcat co-founder Tyler St. Mark clinched the choice by remarking that Jansen made him think of *Boy's Life*.

Jacket art and halftone illustrations were created by artist Jay Fraley, on a Macintosh 8500. He used the Photoshop program to manipulate photographs of a boy's telescope and cap. Since the rest of the production team are scattered around California — Jay in Laguna Beach, Barbara in La Crescenta, Tyler and I and proofreader Alan Taylor in Los Angeles, proofreader Kim Krause in Santa Cruz — we ping-ponged fonts and gifs and corrections on the Internet, thus avoiding travel and UPS costs.

Review copies were printed by Country Press in Middleboro, MA. Color separations and 1200 dpi laser copy of the text went to the Banta Book Group plant in Wisconsin. We never send disks to a printer because there are too many surprises in the way different computers read fonts — even in the age of wizardry.

— *PNW*

COMING SOON FROM WILDCAT PRESS

Girl Grassroots
Autobiography of Patricia Nell Warren

Our next major new title. Revealing glimpses into the life, loves and writings of a landmark author who has always been unconventional, contrary, and willing to push new frontiers.
ISBN 1-889135-03-8, hardcover, nonfiction $24.95

El Atleta
By Patricia Nell Warren

Long-awaited Spanish edition of *The Front Runner*, offered in a passionate translation by Latino poet Luis Bauz. This marks the eighth language in which *The Front Runner* has appeared. Edited by bestselling Spanish author Raul Thomas and Mexican poet Raul Zamora.
ISBN 0-9641099-2-1, trade paperback, fiction................................... $12.95

One Is the Sun
By Patricia Nell Warren

First published in 1991 by Ballantine, the true story of a great woman chief who lived in southwest Montana in the mid-1800s. Resonates with real-life action, spiritual truth and powerful women characters, from Earth Thunder herself to her Arrow Girls. Illustrated by the author.
ISBN 1-889135-02-X, trade paperback, fiction $18.95

Saga of an American Ranch
Anthology of Patricia Nell Warren writings

Roundup of magazine articles about the Grant-Kohrs Ranch in Montana, where Warren grew up — today a popular national historic site. Warren reveals a different side of her persona as she writes with love and insight about animals, grass, weather, tribes, pioneers, cowboys and cowgirls.
ISBN 1-889135-01-1, trade paperback, nonfiction $15.95

The Gay Messiah
By Tyler St. Mark

This first novel by the popular short-story writer chronicles the fantastic events surrounding a charismatic young bartender cast as an AIDS spokesman, who walks among the condemned and dying — and works miracles.
ISBN 0-9641099-9-9, trade paperback, fiction................................... $21.95